STANDPOINT

A GRIPPING THRILLER FULL OF SUSPENSE

DEREK THOMPSON

Published 2015 by Joffe Books, London.

www.joffebooks.com

©Derek Thompson

This book is a work of fiction. Names, characters, businesses, organizations, places and events are either the product of the author's imagination or are used fictitiously. Any resemblance to actual persons, living or dead, events or locales is entirely coincidental. The spelling used is British English except where fidelity to the author's rendering of accent or dialect supersedes this.

Derek Thompson asserts his moral right to be identified as the author of this work.

All rights reserved. No part of this publication may be reproduced, stored in retrieval system, copied in any form or by any means, electronic, mechanical, photocopying, recording or otherwise transmitted without written permission from the publisher. You must not circulate this book in any format.

ISBN-13: 978-1511628235

Chapter 1

Thomas Bladen focused his binoculars on a block of shipping containers far below the lookout. As a prolonged ferry blast carried across the port like a cry of mourning, he surveyed the slate sky, tracking a gull as it veered across and crapped on a Bentley. He smiled for the first time that day: welcome to Harwich. If he hadn't been so far away — and on surveillance — he'd have thrown the bird some bread for a second run.

The laptop bleeped — another image stored. He bent towards it amid the stench of damp and decay of the near-derelict room. His colleague, Karl McNeill, lightly tapped a window and made a customary grunt of approval. Thomas ignored him.

"Hey Tommo, check out the red-head; eleven o'clock — by the blue sports. I'd do some deep cover work there, right enough. I'd even forego the overtime!"

Thomas glanced over and grimaced. Prat. After putting the binoculars down carefully, he attended to his camera, readjusting it six inches to the right. Then he squeezed the button and watched as another square of panoramic mosaic gradually uploaded to the screen.

"I don't know why you bother with that old bollocks, Tommo. Overkill if you ask me, and the job's not even on yet."

"I like to be thorough," he held a finger up to keep Karl at bay. And I don't like to be disturbed.

"Hardly worth it though, for a Customs' promo, unless you're after impressing the boss?"

Thomas paused and moved the camera again. Here it comes.

"But then, weren't you and Christine co-workers and playmates before she became boss?"

"That was a long time ago." He stared at the sequence of images before homing in on the sports car. "She's married," he announced with satisfaction.

"Who? Christine Gerrard?"

"No, your dream date in the blue sports. I see a wedding ring."

"I wasn't looking at her fingers."

The room fell silent again; Thomas preferred it that way. Magnify the row, scroll right and . . . Something snagged his attention; he stopped on square 34, captivated by a lone figure leaning out of a four-by-four, with high-powered lenses.

"Karl, how many spotter teams are on today?"

"Jeez, pay attention. Customs are on the ground, Crossley's lot are on the far side and then there's us two, in the penthouse."

"'Course, yeah." He tried to ignore square 34 and fell back into the rhythm of the job, while Karl rustled a newspaper and muttered something about tits.

"Tommo, didya ever think, when you signed up with the SSU, that you'd one day rise to the third storey of a genuine shit-hole?"

He smiled without turning round. "Well, I had my hopes . . ." Adjusting the magnification, he took a clear shot of the four-by-four's number plate. As he worked, his fingers tingled, or else he imagined they did. Whoever the stranger was, he didn't appear on the duty roster, and Thomas was a man who didn't like surprises. He photographed what he could, collecting details — an expensive shirt, an ornate wedding band and a designer watch. One thing was clear — this gate crasher wasn't short of a few quid.

The walkie-talkie crackled into life; mystery man would have to wait. "This is Control; we have a green light. Repeat; we have a green light."

Suddenly professional, Karl called in their readiness. Thomas had seen that metamorphosis many times now and it still fascinated him.

"Thing is," Karl mumbled, leaning towards his eyepiece, "if they gave us rifles instead of cameras, we could sort out the bloody smugglers ourselves."

"Thank you Rambo; maybe that's the reason they don't arm us?"

At the next ferry horn, Thomas checked the time and turned to catch Karl's big performance, watching as he scrunched his face up, cartoon style.

"Thar she blows!"

The ferry slowly manoeuvred into port and they watched from their vantage point, primed like racing dogs in their traps. Thomas tried to concentrate, but that tingling feeling kept pulling him back to the lone spotter — still there and focused in the same direction.

The slow tally of vehicles and pedestrians snaked out into a warm Essex afternoon; a dark blue Customs van inched forward to greet the traffic. After three cars passed, the van doors slid back and four uniformed officers fanned out. The lone spotter tensed up; Thomas could see his binoculars twitch to attention.

A white Transit was diverted to one side. The driver brandished paperwork, but it made no difference. A Customs Officer took his keys and unlocked the back doors.

"Got ya, you bastard!" Karl hissed triumphantly.

The Customs team removed several boxes and the Transit's suspension lifted. Thomas focused in on the driver. He'd be making his excuses now, trying to bullshit his way through by talking about a party or a restaurant or stocking up for Christmas — in June. But he looked more nervous than he ought to be.

"Nicked!" Karl growled with relish, and popped open a celebratory can.

Thomas laughed. Typical Karl: enthusiasm of a Labrador and the loyalty of a Premier League footballer on the make. Last assignment, he'd been Benefits Fraud team, through and through. Now it was HM Customs, providing fly-on-the-wall footage for in-house use. Karl seemed to love it all, but as far as Thomas was concerned, the Surveillance Support Unit was just a cheap labour source for any government department in need.

Other vehicles slowed, as if to enjoy the spectacle. One, a red Astra estate, held back the queue for a few seconds, prompting a chorus of car horns. Thomas rattled off a couple of shots then switched over to binoculars, picking up his walkie-talkie.

"Control, from Team 3; the red Astra exiting — worth investigating? Over."

"Control, from Team 2 — suggest we ignore that," Ann Crossley over-ruled him. "It's just a family. The driver must have porn stashed under his seat!"

Thomas wasn't convinced, but he knew when to hold his tongue and kept the Astra in sight. As it jolted forward, a rear window lowered a few centimetres. It drew level with the Transit, and a short piece of pipe poked out. On instinct, Thomas panned left, framing the Transit driver's face; the man looked like he'd seen a ghost. It was over in seconds. Even after the driver slumped to the ground and the red car had dissolved into the traffic, no one else seemed to react. But it had burned into Thomas's brain, in slow-mo. He tasted the fear and helplessness, and swallowed it down.

The walkie-talkie blared into life. "A passenger's collapsed. Ambulance required immediately."

Something clicked at the back of Thomas's mind. Square 34! He shifted the camera along; there was only one empty car space — the four-by-four was gone, but the ferry was still unloading. He darted from square to square, tracking along the car lanes until he found it. He clicked frantically, no time to focus, hoping he'd get something useful.

Karl jammed an earpiece to his face and embarked on a running commentary. "Jesus, they think the poor bastard's been shot. He's still breathing; not much blood loss — can't have been much of a weapon."

Thomas shuddered. Karl made it all sound matter of fact but then, he reasoned, for someone with Karl's military background, it probably was. "So," Thomas felt the sweat trickle down the sides of his face, "when do you start your new job as a Samaritan?"

Soon, the view was choked with blue lights and sirens, as an ambulance and the police put in an appearance. Thomas watched through the window, without magnification; he no longer felt like taking a ringside seat.

"What about that, Tommo?" Karl spluttered gleefully. "I can't work out where there's a clear line of sight — unless it was at close quarters — like maybe a zip-gun? Hey, it could have been your family from the red estate! Crossley's going to look pretty stupid at debrief. What a shot though, if it was, I mean — moving vehicle and all; even I couldn't have done that, in my day."

"Your compassion's overwhelming."

"Still," Karl pondered aloud, "it's not much of a hit if he's still alive."

Unless that was the intention? Thomas recalled the haunted look on the driver's face. "Well, anyway, it's not our problem," Karl picked up the walkie-talkie and called for authority to stand down. "Right Tommo, are you coming for a late lunch before we head back? This will be the worst promotional content ever made. What's the betting it all gets mysteriously lost in the editing process?"

And even as Karl said it, Thomas decided that some of his own footage, especially the four-by-four, wouldn't make it into the report. Rule number one: Don't get involved. Rule number two: If you have to get involved, get involved alone.

"You coming?" Karl insisted.

"Nah, you go ahead. I'll be here a little longer."

"Suit yourself. I'll see you back at base."

Or, as they both knew better, The Railway Tavern in Liverpool Street.

* * *

Thomas sat perfectly still for a couple of minutes and breathed in the silence. Out the window, he could see things returning to normal down there.

He took new shots of the area around square 34 and lined up the rows above and below. Half an hour later, Photoshop had smoothed out any inconsistencies. It was like Spot the Difference for idiots, with the four-by-four missing. And only the new version would be available for public viewing. As soon as he'd finished, he pulled out his mobile and hit the redial button.

"Miranda Wright," she sang.

"Hi, it's Thomas."

"What can I do for you, my darling?"

He savoured her voice like a warm cognac. "I'm after something," he said, opening a file on his laptop.

She gave a filthy laugh and he drew the phone in closer.

"I need a number plate checked . . ."

"Well, it'll cost you — dinner tonight."

"Done; and listen, make sure this is kept anonymous." He read the letters out phonetically, emphasising each number, the remnants of his Yorkshire tones lost in cool precision.

"Eight o'clock it is then — you can pick me up at work."

"Thanks, Miranda."

"Don't thank me till you see where we're eating. And dress up for a change!"

Chapter 2

Karl performed a slow handclap as Thomas shouldered the door to the office, a bag in each hand.

"You took your time — I waited a good hour for you."

"I'm sure you managed to prop up the bar without me," Thomas said, "I had to do something with my laptop."

Karl grinned. "Maybe it's all those weekend wedding shoots, clogging your hard-drive."

Thomas nodded wearily and eased past him to his desk — Karl, on another fishing expedition. "What time does the boss want us in?"

"Five o'clock, amigo."

He sighed; it was still weird sometimes, thinking of Christine as the boss. Cutting it fine though — Miranda would go spare if he was late again.

"Fancy a pint later, Tommo? The rest of the gang are going, but they never stay long . . ."

"Sorry," he cut him off. "I have plans."

Karl baulked. "Normal people don't have plans. They eat, date, drink themselves stupid; but you have plans. Do you know, it's been a year since we started working together and I still don't know you."

Thomas nodded, half-listening. Something was bugging him, besides Karl's attempts at camaraderie. Real tip of the tongue stuff. He'd seen something familiar today — only he didn't know quite what it was. "We'll do it sometime soon, Karl; Scout's honour."

"That's more like it!" Karl sounded almost convinced.

Thomas unpacked his laptop, loaded the report template and made a start.

* * *

At 5 pm prompt the office door at the far end of the open-plan room swung open. Karl waited at a respectful distance, while Thomas set his screensaver password then led the way. Karl followed closely behind, muttering paranoid in a pretend cough.

The rest of the team were already in Christine's office — they had been there for nearly half an hour. Thomas shared a who-knew glance with Karl. Then he nodded to Christine with the briefest of smiles, taking in the sight of her. She looked every inch the professional. And two years on, he could still recall every one of the inches beneath that tailored suit.

Christine broke eye contact and cleared her throat. "I'll make this brief. As you know, we've lacked a permanent Senior Officer for months now. I'm delighted to tell you that Bob Peterson will be our new SIO from next week."

Thomas felt her words like a fist to the guts. This would be the same Bob Peterson who had taken Christine under his wing — coincidentally, a short while before the big break-up. And Bob had most likely helped himself to a whole lot more besides.

It took a moment or two to realise that Christine was still talking. "—Bob's a good man; I served under him about eighteen months ago."

He narrowed his eyes. That was a new way of putting it. He cleared his throat; Karl's eyebrows nearly scraped the ceiling.

Christine blushed, but stuck to the script. "Bob wants to do individual reviews as soon as poss, to get to know you all. Right; I gather we had some drama at Harwich today — Karl?"

Karl gave a concise account, leaving out the redhead and the lager.

Christine made notes as she listened, avoiding Thomas's glances. "Okay everyone, thanks for your time. Karl, Thomas — reports by ten, tomorrow. And thanks to everyone else for completing them today. That's all."

Thomas blew a breath from one side of his mouth. Creeps. Trust the brown-noses to get their reports in early. Strange though that no one had mentioned the red Astra. He dismissed the thought and focused on the way the strip-light glistened off Christine's lipstick, sensing the moisture gather on his own lips. Funny, it wasn't like him to play happy memories in the workplace. Christine opened her mouth to speak again, but he was through the door before she'd got a word out; nothing like paperwork to take the sting out of bad news.

Karl sidled over to his desk. "Sure you won't join us now?" There was an edge to the voice as if he was really saying: 'I see your pain and I want us to understand each other better.'

Thomas considered. Maybe. More likely, it was a case of: 'Please don't leave me with these tossers.' Either way, Thomas sat and watched them go. He had nothing against Karl personally; he actually liked the bloke. They were different to the others in their Surveillance Support Unit team; everyone else around them had a degree and a career-path, using the SSU as a way of picking up contacts and experience. Karl had transferred in from the Army — glory days that he never tired of talking about. Which was still a step up from Thomas's own route — via a humble Civil Service desk job and a love of photography.

Christine Gerrard's door yawned open. He swivelled round and the neon glare stretched across the carpet. "I had a feeling you'd still be here."

He leaned forward, lacing his fingers together tightly. "Just making the most of the quiet." He hated lies, his own most of all. But if he'd said, 'Still taking in the good news,' it would have meant a round of questions and answers. And he didn't have the stomach today.

She leant against the doorframe, stroking the carpet with her shoe. Every second swing, her leg escaped from the pleats of her skirt, which only served to remind him of everything Bob Peterson had cost him. Christine tilted her head to one side, as if to read his thoughts. "Listen. We're okay, aren't we, about Bob Peterson? I had no say in it."

"Sure, why not?" He yielded the words with some difficulty. She nodded and retreated into her office, closing the door. He slammed the laptop lid shut; maybe he'd ring Karl some time about that drink.

Chapter 3

Thomas glanced at his watch as he got out of the car; just made it. Caliban's — in garish green lettering — reflected in his windscreen. Inside, Miranda was draped against the bar; she looked edible. "I like a man who comes on time." Her laughter, even at his expense, thawed his edginess in an instant. She took pity on him. "Care to guess where we're going, then?" Sheryl, the manager, stopped fiddling with glasses and waited for his response.

He never fared well in front of an audience. "Not fussed."

"My, how you sweep a girl off her feet. Last of the great romantics." The women cackled like a hen party at a strip-show, and Miranda peeled herself away from the bar. "Come along then; you drive and I'll navigate."

Twenty minutes later, they were at a restaurant in Shoreditch, surrounded by marketing execs and multimedia entrepreneurs. "What do you think, then?" Miranda whispered. "The chef here wants out and I'm looking to bring proper food to Caliban's."

He nodded, took another slice of the tuna and followed it down with a mouthful of wine. "It's good."

She pivoted forward and passed a folded piece of paper across, like a love note. "So, here's my side of the bargain."

He cupped a hand over hers, palming note and hand.

"And there was me thinking you were only after my body." She leaned back, her cleavage tilting away, out of range. "Hey Thomas, remember that first meal we had together, in Leeds?" She squeezed his hand then retreated to her glass. "You were really trying to impress, that night; you 'ad the strongest curry on the menu and all that Yorkshire bitter. It was a classic — they told us to leave when you got too pissed, and then you stood up and said every true Yorkshireman could hold his drink. But you still chucked up on the way home!"

It was a familiar script. He knew his lines as well as his cues. "You wore your purple skirt and those bangles we bought at that wholesale place. And tons of pink eyeshadow. Everyone stared when you spoke because you sounded like a Londoner off the telly."

"Oh yeah? Well, what about when you started making up Cockney rhyming slang then puked over your denim jacket?"

He grinned, recalling their apples and blurrgh. "Wonder what happened to that jacket? They're back in fashion now."

"You gave it to me, after I made you dry-clean it. I've still got it somewhere . . ." she sighed, and he downed some wine to avoid looking at her. "Anyway, open your present."

He unfolded the paper and read it slowly. Bollocks. His knife clattered to the plate and the missing synapse fired up in his brain. It was that distinctive wedding band; and now he knew exactly where he'd seen it before. Even so, he read the paper again, in the vain hope that he was mistaken. Fat chance.

"Problem?"

"Yeah, you could say that," he bit at a nail. The mystery four-by-four was registered to a Robert Peterson in

Southampton. "Miranda, you remember me talking about Christine Gerrard . . ."

Her face soured. "Wonder Woman, you mean."

He yielded a weary smile; Miranda remembered everything. Wonder Woman, because, when it came to Christine and Bob Peterson, he'd always wondered.

"What's the trouble?"

That was unexpected — a touch of genuine concern. "Dunno. May be nothing. But the vehicle you got checked for me belongs to that bloke Christine used to work for." Now was his chance to say more or say nothing; he settled for nothing.

She studied him for a good half minute. "Look Thomas, I can't pretend I'm her biggest fan, after all you told me, but you know you can always speak to Mum and Dad if she's in serious bother."

He loved the way she liked him to know that he was still considered family, even though the two of them were no longer together. "Well, let's leave it for now." He took another sip of wine, imagining that snidey bastard Peterson tangling with Miranda's family. What a clash of cultures that would be: Oxbridge player versus the East End's finest.

"Hey," she lifted her glass and the colour of the wine reflected in her eyes, "let's go dancing!"

"Can't; I have to work later."

"Civil servants don't work nights."

"This one does."

"Oh, go on, Thomas; it's been ages since we went anywhere."

He didn't mention that it was hardly surprising, since she'd been seeing some second-rate footballer for the last couple of months.

She made puppy eyes at him and wriggled in her seat.

"Alright," he relented. "As long as I'm in bed by one-thirty."

"If I didn't know you better, Mr Bladen, I'd swear that was a come-on."

One of these days, Miranda, these games of ours are going to hurt someone.

Chapter 4

Beep beep beep. He forced his eyes open, took a second to focus then flailed in the direction of the alarm. He rolled over slowly and surveyed the empty side of the bed. Ah, Miranda. He stretched under the duvet and adjusted the bulge in his boxers. How was it, he wondered, that two people could have such a complicated . . . he searched for the word. Relationship?

In the kitchen, he picked up her coffee cup from the night before and studied the lipstick print. She might have stayed, if he'd asked, he told himself as he placed it carefully in the sink. Only he hadn't asked.

By eight-thirty he was in the office, looking and feeling as if he'd pulled an all-nighter. He slumped at his desk and typed up the notes, closing his eyes now and again to recall the details. It still didn't make sense. He opened another document, copied out a few separate sentences and saved the file for Karl — the lazy bastard. He was in the middle of a tricky combo, yawning and trying to rub some life back into his face, when the main door opened.

Ann Crossley nodded curtly and took up her seat on the other side of the room, without a word. How cheery.

But then, what more could he expect from another Foreign Office wannabe?

An email pinged in from Karl, entitled: 'Help!' It read: Hung over, please cover for me. Should be in by 9.30, but if not, ring me. Thanks. It was sent at 2 am. Even Karl's emails were late.

* * *

'Doctors,' Christine Gerrard had once told Thomas, back when they'd shared a bed as well as office space, 'doctors assert that coffee on an empty stomach is bad for both the digestion and the liver.'

They don't know shit, thought Thomas, as he waited impatiently while the vending machine spat out a chemical cappuccino, the perfect concoction to kick-start his working day. A chocolate bar helped, too; it saved on sugar in the coffee for a start.

Right. Time to do some thinking. He took the spoils back to his desk and unlocked his drawer to get a writing pad. He drew three overlapping circles — like a maths problem — and labelled them Docks, Christine and Bob. Then he stared at the page for a few minutes before adding in squiggles and notes.

So what did he know? First off, it would be a cruel twist of fate if Bob Peterson had just happened to put in an appearance at the docks that day. Unless . . . unless he was sussing everyone out, ahead of his appointment? Now there was a thought. Maybe Christine knew, and they both wanted to crosscheck the reports with Bob's own observations? He bit into the Twix.

It was a reasonable assumption, but full of holes. It had been a routine assignment — they weren't even front of house — so why would Peterson bother? He boxed in Bob's name and started shading, inking him out of existence.

Maybe Bob Peterson's snooping around Harwich was some kind of payback for the fateful day Thomas had made his surprise visit to Christine's executive development weekend. Who mentors someone in a country hotel, for Christ's sake? His breath caught in his throat at the memory and he laid the pen down, spreading his fingers wide. It had all been a misunderstanding, surely? So why had he wanted to lay Peterson out — and still wanted to now?

Crossley was mumbling on the phone. She met his eyes and bent her head. "We're back today, sir; same positions. My team are on their way there now." She paused and covered the phone. "Where's Karl?" she hissed.

"He had some personal business to sort out." That was weak. He fired an email off to Karl: Get your report done and get your arse in here; we're going back over to the docks.

And where was the lovely Ms Gerrard? No sign of her. Nine-fifteen and all's definitely not well. Ping. Karl had responded:

Ha ha. Report's already done and attached. Please print without changes then meet me onsite; and pick up some painkillers on the way. You're a pal!

Thomas opened the attachment, reviewed, edited and corrected Karl's speed typing then added the extra sentences. After printing both reports, he sealed them in an envelope and slid it under Christine's door.

* * *

Karl's sallow face lit up as Thomas rattled the plastic container. "Thanks Tommo, you're a life saver. I got you the usual — sausage and egg on white, no ketchup. " They exchanged gifts solemnly, like a battlefield Christmas. "Listen Tommy, sorry for taking the piss about Christine. Honest to god, if I'd known that Bob Peterson was coming in to run the show . . ."

Thomas accepted the half-apology with a shrug; it was his own fault really, for confiding in best buddy Karl that one time. He devoured the sandwich and tried to put all thoughts of yesterday behind him.

"Anyway," Karl's voice lifted a little, "I met this wee lass in the pub last night and for a while I thought I was in love . . ."

Thomas set up his camera slowly, making Karl wait for the cue to conclude his shaggy pub story. "Go on then, how long for?"

"About three pints."

Introducing . . . Karl the stand-up. Thomas could almost hear the boom cha in his head.

After the previous day's drama, it felt good to get back into routine. Vehicles came and went without incident; order was restored. Customs were more visible today, making it easier to get decent shots. By lunchtime, the Customs team they were following had unearthed four rampant alcoholics, three pornographers and a couple of illegal immigrants — a good morning's work by anyone's standards.

Karl nipped out for a comfort break, leaving Thomas alone with the soothing sound of the gulls. He made the most of the time, reviewing the day's mosaic, happily without Bob Peterson.

The mobile rang, the same default ringtone as the day he'd bought it.

"Hey you; it's me, Miranda. Well, say something then."

"Hello?"

"Very droll. Look, you will be at Mum and Dad's on Sunday? You did promise and they haven't seen you in weeks . . ."

"If I promised then I'll be there."

"Great. You can collect me from Caliban's at one-thirty."

"Your wish is my command."

"Careful or I'll hold you to that, and then where would we be?"

Thomas grinned to himself. "In trouble."

"See you, babe." Miranda hung up.

He was still staring into the past when Karl returned with fresh rations.

* * *

By late afternoon, Karl had recovered sufficiently to regale Thomas with another instalment of Army Adventures. This time it was peacekeeping in Kosovo. Early on, Thomas had learned two things about Karl. Firstly, that he enjoyed talking about his time in the Forces — a lot — and secondly, that he didn't like his monologues interrupted.

Karl spoke with gruff fondness about his regimental comrades, but his anecdotes tended to lack specifics such as places and names. Thomas had pieced together that Karl left the Army suddenly, and his transfer into the SSU had been down to some string-pulling. Strangely, Karl's trips down memory lane never ventured anywhere near the point, two years ago, when he'd actually joined the Surveillance Support Unit.

There wasn't much for their Customs team to do between ferries, so that left plenty of downtime for conversation. Thomas knew just which buttons to push, and soon Karl was waxing lyrical about Black Mountain and an Irish adolescence spent avoiding The Troubles and chasing anything in a skirt.

Thomas met him halfway, offering up childhood summers in the Dales and on the Yorkshire Moors. "So why did you come down to London then, if Yorkshire was so idyllic?"

This, Thomas knew, was Karl's way of saying, 'So what were you running away from?' He didn't miss a beat. "Nothing to keep me there. And I'd met this London lass."

Karl cheered. "Hooray! Thomas Bladen isn't a virgin after all."

He flipped Karl the finger and continued. "My uncle ran a local newspaper in Leeds, and they needed a cub photographer and general dogsbody. I wasn't getting on at home and I'd been taking pictures since I was a boy . . ."

"Sounds like a match made in low-wage heaven. So, what about the girl?" Karl edged forward a little in his chair.

"This girl, right, she wanted to be a model. And my uncle, well, he always had an eye on the next chance; so he sets himself up as an agent. Nothing suspect, mind."

He paused; did he really want to go into all this now? But Karl was waiting, like a toddler gazing at an open packet of biscuits. "Okay, she was about my age and didn't know her way around, so my uncle suggested I look after her. Then we got together, left for London, and moved in with her folks . . . the end!"

"That's not much of a story!"

No. It wasn't. Not when you missed out that it had been Thomas's idea to look out for Miranda, and with good reason. Or the part where his uncle's friend wanted her to do topless poses and wasn't keen on taking no for an answer. Or the finale where Thomas lamped him, broke the guy's nose and got the sack.

Karl pushed for more. "So you got to London, delivered the princess to the grateful king and queen, and all lived happily ever after?"

"Yeah, for a few years anyway."

"Come on, Tommy; and then what?"

"And then all good things came to an abrupt and frosty end."

"Sure, that's a sad story. Methinks you left all the best bits out." Karl laughed deeply, and Thomas found himself joining in, even though he didn't get the joke. "Still, at least you've got your old pal Karl to tell your troubles to."

"We must be grateful for small Murphys."

Karl took a bow. "Listen Tommy, if you're at a loose end over the weekend, you're welcome to come by and share a few cans."

"Not this weekend — I've got a wedding shoot booked."

"Really?" Karl's brows almost knitted together.

"Uh-huh." Better to lie than admit he was having Sunday dinner with his ex-girlfriend's family.

Ann Crossley's voice broke through on the radio. "Team two to team three. We've been asked for a Friday round-off with our Customs colleagues, as soon as this next ferry is unloaded. Refreshments will be provided!"

Karl sat to attention, nodding furiously. "You up for it, Tommy Boy?"

He shrugged.

"Okey dokey, Ms Crossley," Karl responded, giving Thomas a thumbs-up. "We'll join you as soon as we've packed our toys away." Another ferry horn blared out. "So, it's drinks at the captain's table, eh? And maybe we can find out about yesterday's gun-crime statistic."

"Karl, can you do me a favour and not ask? I think it's best if we leave it."

"That's all very well, but my report sang our praises and scored us a few points against the rest of Ms Crossley's groovy gang."

"No it didn't — I changed it."

Karl raised his chin. "Now why would you do a thing like that?"

Thomas sighed and scratched at his neck. "You know how Crossley is. After all, we were the ones to pick out that suspect car — not that it's proven," he backtracked. "So it's less complicated if we leave it out and stay 'on message.'" He made finger speech marks, the way Crossley did when she was running a brief.

"Well, well, you've got it all figured out. Right oh, mum's the word."

Yeah, thought Thomas, but for how long? "Look, tell you what, why don't I give you a ring on Saturday and sort out a get together?"

Karl nodded and glanced out the window. "Here they come, last of the high-rollers!" He yawned and tracked the first vehicles off the ramp. "Now, that's an expensive-looking van. What do you think Tommo — see that great big silver thing with the logo and details on the side? It's a classic double bluff; it's so in your face it couldn't be bent — what do you reckon?"

Thomas stopped taking photos of the Customs team and panned right. He almost dropped the camera when 'WRIGHTS — the Wright Way to Do Business' glared into view. Oh Jesus: Miranda's brothers' van.

"How about we buzz the team on the ground to give them a tug? A tenner says the van has been back through here in the last three weeks.

Thomas rested his camera in his lap and squeezed his hands together to stop them trembling. "I wouldn't bother." True, in a dishonest sort of way.

"But come on — the Amsterdam ferry!"

"Nah, we could be wasting everyone's time. No one wants to be stuck here, filling out unnecessary paperwork on a Friday. Let's leave it to Customs — it's their call."

Karl tilted his head, tick-tock fashion, weighing it up. "Fair enough."

Thomas felt the sweat clinging to the small of his back. He picked up binoculars and flicked around the Customs officers to see if anyone seemed interested in the silver van. Then he swept along the lane of traffic for a suitable decoy. "Control, from team three," he kept his voice calm and controlled, "there's a blue sports car, six vehicles down the line. It may be nothing, but it looks like one in the car park that went out yesterday." He could feel Karl scrutinising him and turned slowly, matching him in a staring contest.

Karl reached for his walkie-talkie. "Driver was a redhead; large wedding band and a humming bird pendant." He watched Thomas's face the way a cat looks at a baby bird.

Thomas went back to his binoculars, hardly breathing until the silver van was clear. The static burst from the walkie-talkies made him flinch. "Control to teams two and three; we're doing a check on the blue sports car, over."

Karl clicked off. "I'm not sure what just happened there, Tommo," he set his own walkie-talkie down carefully. "But I'll tell you this for nothing, as a professional courtesy: it's a fool who underestimates me."

"Never have, never will," Thomas replied, smiling until his face hurt.

Chapter 5

Thomas burst awake like a swimmer breaking the surface, gasping for air. He lay there panting. Jesus. Never again. That was the worst thing about drinking too much: it always brought on the nightmares.

First, he'd had one of his classics — finding Christine and Bob Peterson together at the country hotel. Only, in the dream, he confronted them instead of letting Christine shoo him on his way. Now, he pushed past her and landed one on Peterson from the off and didn't stop until Peterson was a bloody pulp. Usually he'd wake up then with his fists clenched, but this time it tipped over.

Back in the house in Yorkshire; he and Patricia, kids again, huddled under the blanket as he read his Beano annuals aloud by torchlight to drown out their father's rage downstairs. The jagged tension, building in degrees to an explosion of crockery or a door slam, followed by the muffled silence of their mother's submission. Then the slow, heavy footfalls up the stairs until their father reached the very top step, the one nearest his bedroom. They always held their breath together beneath the blanket, listening. And just when he felt he couldn't hold it any longer, the scene exploded into thousands of tiny mosaic pieces.

He snatched at the clock: eight thirty. It was Saturday, a day of leisure, and he was a little disappointed. The previous night gradually revealed itself in a blurred montage of images. Karl had been drunk too — he had an almost medical susceptibility to alcohol. In a parallel universe he'd have been a good, cheap date.

Memory stirred. What time had they arranged to meet today? And wasn't there something about bringing his passport? He shook his head to loosen the memories, and pain signals rebounded from all corners of his brain.

He was drifting through the supermarket with the rest of the drones at ten o'clock when a text came in from Karl: Good craic last night. Don't forget driving licence & passport. 3 pm Holloway Rd tube.

He filled his trolley with whatever came to hand and added in chocolates, flowers and a quality bottle of wine for Sunday. Couldn't very well turn up at the Wrights' place empty-handed. As he pulled away, he checked the rear mirror and did the thing he always did, driving a full circuit around the car park, just to make sure no one was waiting for him. So far, no one had been.

On the way home, he pondered Bob Peterson again. Say Bob had been checking on the teams. Why that Thursday, particularly? The high-street gridlock soured Thomas's thoughts as he waited at temporary lights. Maybe Peterson wasn't there for them at all; maybe he was watching the ferry? But he was there well before the ferry arrived. Two things out of the ordinary had happened that week — the shooting on the Thursday and then Miranda's brothers coming through on the Friday. The lights changed to green and he put his foot down. And what the bloody hell did Karl need to see his personal ID for today?

Karl was already waiting outside the underground station when Thomas arrived, at five to three. He looked in fine shape, untarnished by the previous night's excesses. Lucky bastard.

"Great to see you Tommo; you won't regret this — got your documents?" Karl seemed really chuffed that he'd turned up, as if that were ever in doubt — pub promises being the social equivalent of signing in triplicate.

Thomas tapped his coat emphatically and followed Karl to his car. He watched as Karl checked casually around the vehicle. Old habits died hard.

Inside, the Ford Fiesta smelled overpoweringly of oranges.

"Hop in," Karl said cheerily, flinging an old newspaper on to the backseat.

"Did you murder Mr Del Monte and stash the body in here?"

Karl nodded and smirked.

"Oh, right. Yeah, 'scuse the aroma — I spilt a two-litre carton last week. It's dried out fine but . . . anyway, I quite like it."

Before Thomas could comment, Karl thrust in a CD of the Undertones, cued up a track and then did a murderous accompaniment to 'Perfect Cousin.' Karl would have made a perfect cousin himself — if only he'd taken a vow of silence. He waited until Karl had slaughtered the song to the very end.

"Okay I give up. Why the ID?"

"You'll see," Karl winked.

Top of the list of things that Thomas hated was surprises; second was more surprises. And the smell of oranges was now a possible contender for third place. He stared out the window as the streets of Camden flickered past, his mind rushing through the possibilities: white slave trade, booze cruise to Calais . . .

Karl tapped the wheel in time to the music, more or less, attempting to harmonise with the singers in places a lesser man would fear to tread. After a twisting series of back-roads, the car came out into a nondescript industrial estate. Karl parked and switched off the engine. "I thought it was high time we got to know each other properly, now that we're acquainted professionally. And where better than at a club where we can unwind and be ourselves?"

Thomas nodded dumbly. Drinking club? Strip club? Poker club?

Karl got out and stood in front of the car, swinging his keys.

"Come on, then. Are you gonna sit there all day?"

Seeing the look of glee on Karl's face, he took his time. Karl showed his driving licence to the security camera then had him do the same. He pressed his hand against the reinforced steel door as Karl held it open. This underworld was clearly members only.

They went inside and Karl smiled at him briefly, as if he had passed some test of brotherhood. They crossed the lobby and walked up to a desk surrounded by reinforced glass. Karl took out his two forms of ID and pushed them through the drop chute. A woman retrieved them and kept them below eye level. When they were returned, with nary a smile, Thomas followed suit. This time she requested £40 for a visitor's pass, which she informed him did not include the cost of equipment.

Thomas glanced at Karl and handed over two twenties. Thanks a lot. And he was still none the wiser. It could be an S & M club for all he knew.

"Right, Tommo," Karl slapped him on the back, "Welcome to the club!"

An electronic buzzer hummed and clicked, releasing a door at the end of a short corridor. On the other side, to the left and right, there were rows of doors. Thomas breathed deep; the air tasted subtly of smoke and machine oil. He keyed up his other senses and became aware of a muffled thud thud in rhythmic succession all around him.

Karl twisted the handle on a side door and pushed. A woman stood with her back to them, legs slightly braced. If their presence distracted her in any way she didn't show it, as she emptied her weapon into the target with calm precision. Thomas nodded to himself. So that was it — a Gun Club.

She placed the pistol on the counter, removed her ear-defenders and turned around. Thomas could see that all her actions were exact and measured. She smiled their way and Karl shifted his weight side to side, like a dog waiting for treats.

"Glock, I presume?" he asked.

Thomas figured that was for his benefit.

"You know me so well!" she leaned forward and tapped Karl's shoulder. He reddened.

"Teresa, this is Thomas — my pal from work."

Thomas flinched; he never mentioned the 'w' word.

Teresa eased past Karl and checked a small screen on the wall behind him.

"I'm done here. The bay's free for another hour. I'm off to the bigger equipment," she made it sound like a gym. "Maybe catch you gentlemen later, in the bar?"

Thomas got the door. Teresa picked up her Glock 9 mm, removed the magazine and checked the weapon. She seemed to take her time about it, and Karl didn't seem to mind.

Thomas waited until Teresa had gone.

"Glock?"

"The choice of champions! Standard law enforcement issue, 9 mm; seventeen in a clip," Karl sounded like a survivalist train-spotter. "Now, wait here while I go get us some equipment and practice material."

Left alone, Thomas looked at the end of the bay. Terrorist targets glared back at him. An options menu on a small wall screen told him there were fourteen pistol bays — one was closed and one designated private — clearly, a busy day today. The bigger equipment, as Teresa had politely put it, was another eight bays' worth of fire-powering fun. He was about to venture into sub-menus when Karl returned with two cases.

"Right then. Before we start, a few ground rules."

"Who uses this place?" Thomas cut in.

"Mostly armed forces and police, that sort of thing — current and former."

"And all this is legal?"

Karl raised an eyebrow.

"I'd hardly bring you otherwise, now would I?"

"And Teresa; is she . . ."

"Now, now," Karl waved a finger. "The first rule of gunfight club is that nobody asks what anyone does. Members expect confidentiality. You of all people can appreciate that."

Karl ran through the essentials: only one person at the yellow line; no talking while using the equipment; loading, operating and emptying; the stance; breathing and squeezing; ear-defenders on unless everyone's hands were empty. It was a regular Handguns for Dummies.

Karl had a Buddhist-like calm, if you could forget about the firearm. Stripped of banter and bravado, he was a man in his element, comfortably loosing off rounds in tight formations until the magazine was spent. He put his weapon down and shifted the headgear.

"Now, you; and remember to allow for the kickback."

Thomas stood at the line and felt the cool weight of a Browning in his hands. The ear-defenders cocooned him, sealing him in with his thoughts. He gripped the handle tightly and watched the tiny, almost undetectable tremor of the barrel. The paper circles awaited him, and he leaned forward slightly, breathing into his stomach as he crushed his finger against the trigger in a single, fluid movement. Then he waited, statue-like, as the dulled whine of the bullet echoed in his head. After three more shots, he stopped and put the gun down. He was, even by his own estimation, shit.

Karl clearly thought that laughter didn't count as speech.

"It's fine — for a beginner and all. Let's try something a little more provocative."

At the flick of a button, terrorists swivelled towards them in a ragged line. Karl took the stand and quickly got into his stride. Head and heart, just like in the movies.

"Now you."

Thomas stepped up and something clicked in his psyche. When he looked into the anonymous, printed faces, his mind went slipstream. He saw teachers, the Neanderthals at school, Bob Peterson and his own father. And now, when he pulled the trigger, he was rewriting history, redressing the balance of power in his head.

He finished the salvo and placed the gun down, touching it gently like a talisman. The targets bore the conviction of his thoughts; every one a body shot.

"That was much better, Tommo. I think we've found your brand!" Karl applauded. "Better than many I've seen, picking up a gun for the first time."

"Thanks," he acknowledged, justly pleased, except it wasn't the first time.

* * *

The bar was actually a café, which was a relief. Guns and alcohol hadn't sounded like a good mix. Karl pointed him to a couple of comfy chairs and went off for coffees. Teresa waved from across the room, keeping her distance. Thomas glanced from table to table at the crowd — singles, couples and groups, and presumably every one of them proficient with a gun. He didn't feel reassured.

Karl seemed different somehow, since the shooting practice. But then, Thomas reasoned, thirty-six rounds from an automatic pistol would do that. "Right then Tommo, what's on your mind?" Karl blundered up and slapped a tray on the table.

"What . . . what do you mean?"

It was a well-practised stalling technique; if in doubt, act distracted. He reached for a cup carefully, but Karl didn't look impressed.

"Come on, Thomas, cards on the table. I've brought you into my confidence, shown you part of my secret world . . ." Karl grinned and eased back in his chair, ". . . How about returning the favour?"

Thomas peeled his back away from the vinyl upholstery. Every breath seemed to spread the dampness.

"I'm not sure what you're on about. You've obviously invited me here for a reason — if it's to join your private army, on today's performance, you'd best put me down as a driver," he searched Karl's face for a punchline. "Beyond that, I'm clueless."

Karl smacked his lips. "You can play that innocent abroad line as long as you like, but I don't buy it. Something happened yesterday — I'm not sure what."

Thomas felt himself blushing. Stupid bastard. He tilted his head towards the coffee. Yeah, that'd work, hiding in the coffee steam.

"Anyway," Karl continued, sipping at his cup, "I'm pretty sure you're clean, so I guess that puts us on a level footing, whoever you represent."

It sounded like a cue.

"Sorry, you've lost me — who I represent?"

"Come on now, Tommo, enough with the games. Why else would you be in the Surveillance Support Unit?"

"How d'you mean?" Thomas leaned forward, leading with his jaw. "It's just a job, that's all; forget the mission statement and the badge — we're the hired help. All right, I grant you most of 'em are more ambitious, but not me or you, right?"

He stopped short; Karl was staring at him intently, still as marble.

". . . And I s'pose it's also a proving ground for the likes of Ann Crossley and Christine Gerrard, on their way up the greasy pole?"

He'd run out of things to say and opened his palms flat. If there were any aces in this conversation, he didn't have them. No one spoke for a good minute, before Thomas braved the silence.

"You were expecting more?"

Karl toyed with the sugar sachets.

"Shit. You really *don't* know, do you?"

"Not yet . . ." Thomas narrowed his eyes.

Karl slumped back in his chair and gazed at his hands.

"God, Tommo; what a pickle of bollocks. Let's take a step back. You've been in the SSU for . . ."

"Two years," he filled in the blank even though Karl already knew it.

"Okay, well it's a little bit longer than that for me, and I started in West London. Some time ago, I was asked to participate in a *covert review* of the SSU, from the ground. There were concerns about information going astray . . . And before you ask, I don't know what — and even if I did know, I wouldn't tell you."

"So how are you involved in all this?"

"Not at all, officially. I'm just a pair of eyes and ears, as you've probably figured out. But I thought, after that van yesterday, that you were definitely . . . you know . . . representing some other party as well."

"I just felt they were innocent."

"*They*? You have a good memory," Karl blinked slowly.

Thomas swallowed hard; he could feel the heat at his armpits. They finished their coffee in uncomfortable silence.

"Look," Karl said eventually, "I messed up, okay; I read the signs wrong. You don't socialise, you doctored my report; you convinced me to let someone go through at the docks — Christ, you may even have picked out a gunman. It all added up to you being in the SSU for more than a mortgage and a pension."

"Like you, you mean?" Thomas was still adjusting to the idea that Karl had another life going on.

Karl soon tired of being stared at.

"Let's not let this screw up a perfectly good working relationship, eh Tommo? What do you say?"

"Deal," Thomas stretched out his hand. "As long as you introduce me to Teresa when I bring the drinks back."

As Thomas stood in line, watching as Teresa ambled over to their table, he had a revelation. Right up there with gravity, the faked moon-landing pictures and real men not liking opera. He rushed the coffees back then excused himself to the gents. He locked the cubicle door behind him, sat on the toilet lid and took deep, slow breaths. His pulse pounded in his ears. This was something he hadn't felt in a long time: fear. He speed-dialled Miranda's mobile and stared at the graffiti on the inside of the door. Even at a gun club, there was apparently someone willing to do the nasty with strangers for ten pounds. Some helpful soul had even added pencil drawings.

She picked up first ring.

"Miranda Wright — at your service!"

"Hi, it's me. Listen, I'm going to ask you a question; it may seem a bit odd."

"Are you okay, Thomas?"

She must have sensed the concern in his voice; she'd cut straight through the usual double-entendres.

"I need to know if an Irish guy has been at Caliban's recently, asking questions. About five-foot eight; short, reddish-brown hair. Check with Sheryl and *be* discreet."

"I'll ring you back."

"No," he insisted, "just text me."

"Okay. I'll come over later tonight. You don't sound good."

"Fine."

Back at the table, Karl was in full flow.

"All Ulster men are romantics — it's the Celtic blood; poetry is in our veins."

Thomas took his seat; the hammering in his chest had slowed a little.

"I thought that was Guinness?"

Karl's eyes lit up at the prospect of a joust.

"Whereas, your Yorkshireman . . . he has no finesse. It's all whippets and coal."

Teresa turned towards Thomas. He pulled it together and went for broke:

> "Because of the light of the moon,
> Silver is found on the moor;
> And because of the light of the sun,
> There is gold on the walls of the poor.
>
> Because of the light of the stars,
> Planets are found in the stream;
> And because of the light of your eyes
> There is love in the depths of my dream."

"Well, well," Karl mimed applause. "Is this a hidden side to you, Tommo?"

Thomas smiled; more like a poetry book from a Leeds charity shop. One he'd bought, back in the day, to impress Miranda. Even now he could recall one or two, word perfect. The poet Francis Carlin would have been pleased, had he not been dead for a hundred years.

The three of them found an easy rhythm of conversation, where nothing much was said, but everyone seemed to gel. Teresa continued to play one off against the other. Thomas saw early on that he was on to a loser; where Teresa was concerned, Karl was smoother than a vaselined billiard ball.

As he watched Karl in action, it was hard to believe that his buddy was anything more. As if the previous conversation had never taken place. Then the text came in from Miranda. One word: *yes*.

Chapter 6

Miranda's car was already at the end of his street. At first he felt relieved and then reality started to dawn. The charade he'd kept up for the last couple of years was about to come apart at the seams. He slowed, weighed down by the conclusion that he was as big a liar as Karl.

She waved from the car as he approached. God knows how long she's been waiting. Probably turned up, got no answer at the door, saw the car and decided to stay put, bless her.

The car window slid down.

"About time; shift your arse — this takeaway will be stone cold!"

It was all he could do to stop himself from kissing her.

She followed him inside and he heard the clank of the wine bottle in her coat pocket. With the oven on and the meal reheating, Miranda sprawled out on the sofa, leaving a deliberate space. He opted for the armchair and perched forward, cupping a loose fist.

"Are you gonna tell me what's up, then?"

He rubbed a knuckle on his chin. This was it: the end of life as he knew it. "You know how I never talk about work? Well, it's time to break that rule."

Miranda reached for her wine. Maybe she was trying to inoculate herself against bad news. He copied her, on the off chance that it might work.

"What . . . what do you think I do for a living, Miranda?"

She frowned.

"We agreed that I'd never ask, just like you never ask about Mum and Dad's business. You told me that you take photos and that's good enough for me. I dunno, stuff like accident investigations, crime scenes, maybe? One time you also mentioned delivering packages . . ." she looked up, studying his face. ". . . And you said that it was all government work."

Which he translated as: 'Is it really government work?' He took a gulp of wine and felt the heat rise to his face. Let's try a different approach.

"Remember a couple of years back, when your dad was being fitted up by that dodgy copper."

"Course I do. Your pictures saved his bacon. What's that got to do with your work?"

Sod it, shit or bust.

"That's sort of what I do for a living, some of the time. You know, photographs, where people don't know about it."

Miranda sat upright.

"What? Like some sort of spy?"

Nervous laughter followed, as if she wanted to be wrong about this.

"Not exactly," he looked away. "I do surveillance — pictures, film, audio."

The buzzer went off in the kitchen. Miranda got up. For a moment or two, he wondered if she'd be coming back.

"Look Miranda," he called out to the kitchen, "I owe you an explanation."

The only reply was the clattering of the oven door. Miranda returned with a tray full of tins. She spooned out the food and put his plate down beside hers.

"Is it dangerous, then?"

He'd seen her like this before, calm and controlled — on the outside. He shook his head and tried his best light-hearted smile — the sort people use at funerals when they've got nothing useful to say.

* * *

He started at the beginning — a straightforward Civil Service job, at State House in High Holborn. That much she already knew, but he sketched in some of the detail. The Patent Office was on floors three to fifteen, with the Royal Navy occupying ground to two. He mentioned the Russian gift shop across the street that everyone thought was a front for a spy-ring. Ironic now, all things considered.

He glided over the backdrop to that time, when he and Miranda had separated, and the trench warfare that led up to it — no sense in raking up the past again. After the split, his lowly desk job had kept him going, somewhere to while away the day until he could photograph the underbelly of the city. Even lunchtimes had been spent taking pictures — in nearby Bloomsbury, or the odd panoramic shot from the thirteenth floor of State House. Hiding from life, like every other pen pusher who thinks — or hopes — that they're destined for something better. And his personal pipe dream, back then, had been that the right portfolio could get him on to a national newspaper.

There had been one particular man in the building who shared his fondness for unorthodox hours — an inhabitant of the fifteenth floor, where mere mortals weren't allowed.

Comments in the lift about his choice of camera — the one he brought to work religiously, as if to say 'fuck you' to lifer colleagues — led to an invitation to photograph the skyline from the top deck, and the chance to show his wares to someone who shared his passion. That was how he'd met Sir Peter Carroll, founder and patriarch of the Surveillance Support Unit, although Thomas didn't know that at the time.

A few weeks later, an opportunity arose for some weekend overtime as a stand-in cameraman. And, he freely admitted, a little bit of intrigue and interest in a Miranda-less existence. Wind forward two or three months and he was called up to the fifteenth floor for a formal interview with Sir Peter and two lackeys, under the watchful eye of a painting of Churchill.

He ended his monologue, swerving past any mention of the assignments themselves. Miranda's eyes looked capable of swallowing him, as if she were physically seeing him in a new light. She drained her glass and set it down carefully on the table.

"Mum and Dad aren't gonna like this."

He nodded rhythmically; she was right. John and Diane Wright took a dim view of the establishment, and here he was, coming out of the secrecy closet. And when all was said and done, they were still family to him.

An uneasy silence hung over them. Miranda finished her meal with the same fixed expression, as if she wanted to slap him, hard. He couldn't really blame her.

"So why tell me now?" she paused and folded her arms. "And how long has this been going on?"

He put his cutlery down; his appetite had died.

"A year or so."

"Bollocks!" she glared at him, "I don't believe you."

"Well, maybe eighteen months, give or take."

She was still glowering.

"Look, it's no big deal — I just work in the background."

"Right, so what's the story with the Irish geezer you were asking about?"

He blew out a long breath; crunch time again.

"I think someone might be checking up on me."

She started laughing; he hadn't expected that.

"Serves you bloody right — one of your lot is he? Or MI-27!"

She turned away and a part of him died inside. Instinctively, he reached out and touched her arm. Her face changed. Scorn gave way to concern; that made him feel worse.

"Why don't you tell me about it — I'll go stick the kettle on."

"I was at Harwich yesterday and I saw your brothers' van coming off the ferry from Amsterdam. It was definitely Sam and Terry. I kept Customs off their back."

"No point me asking what you were doing there?"

"My job. Look Miranda, I'm trying to help. The place is crawling with Customs and Excise at the moment. Whatever the boys are doing, they can't do it there."

She opened her mouth to speak, but Thomas headed her off at the pass. "I don't care what they're up to. I just wouldn't want any trouble for them."

She nodded, as if he'd just flashed the family loyalty card at her. "And the Irish geezer?"

"Like I said, he could be investigating me."

"Could be?" she sounded exasperated. "For what — is he interested in the family?"

"Honestly? I don't know."

"Well, you better bloody well find out."

"Okay," he conceded. "But will you help me warn the boys off, tomorrow?"

She picked up the remote control and flicked through television channels. If she'd been a cat, her tail would have been twitching. She settled on a made-for-TV film of no interest to either of them. He stole glances at her as she sat there, avoiding eye contact. Surely he could trust her of all people?

Out of desperation, he snorted like a horse and she stifled a smile; she always liked that. He nestled into her side of the sofa and felt her leg against his. Her handbag started buzzing.

"Mobile," she said, deadpan.

Still not out of the woods yet then.

"Hi Sheryl, how's business — many punters in?" There was a long pause. Miranda's eyes narrowed. "Oh, really. Alone?" she looked daggers at Thomas. "Keep him there . . . no, if he looks like he's gonna leave, chat him up and spike his drink. I'm on my way." She snapped the phone shut. "Your Irishman is at the club right now. Get your coat."

The car grumbled menacingly; Miranda held the wheel like it was a lifebelt.

"Either you sort this today, or I will."

It wasn't a request; it wasn't even a threat. But he could feel the walls going up around her.

"When we get there I'll take the side door — you go in and speak to him."

He knew what else was coming.

"Miranda, don't call your brothers."

They stopped at the lights, opposite a billboard for a building society. An old advertising slogan popped into his head: because life's complicated enough.

* * *

Miranda parked. He touched her shoulder lightly, but she shrugged it off.

"You better deal with this, Thomas."

He pushed the swing door: high noon, in uptown London. There were maybe a dozen punters in the room and Karl was sitting in full view of the bar, reading a copy of Private Eye. He seemed engrossed in his magazine, chuckling away, giving every indication that he was enjoying himself enormously.

Miranda appeared behind the bar and Sheryl sidled over to her, flattening her New Yorker tones to a whisper.

"He's been drinking a pint of shandy for ages."

"Shandy?"

"Yeah, when he ordered it, he said that's what real men drink these days!"

Karl laughed aloud suddenly as if he were listening to every word.

Miranda opened her mobile, selected a number carefully and held the phone up as if she was trying to get a signal. Thomas read her, loud and clear. Resolve this now or the Brothers Grimm would turn up, like working class cavalry. He couldn't blame her. Nothing was more precious to the family than Miranda. He held on to that thought and tried to walk tall to the bar, clocking the cover of Private Eye — Tony Blair grinning like The Joker.

He ordered a drink — Southern Comfort and lemonade — which Miranda made sure he paid for. Glass in hand, he drew up a chair and faced Tony Blair. Karl didn't stir.

"What are you doing here, Karl?"

"Can't a man enjoy a nice quiet drink and a read of his comic?"

"Cut the bullshit, I'm not in the mood."

The magazine lowered like a drawbridge.

"I've been asked to tell you, as a friend: the conversation we had earlier today — it never happened. It's off limits — comprendez?"

Thomas knew now how an ant felt under the magnifying glass. His friend was threatening him. For a second or two, he thought about smacking him one. But Karl was becoming a more unknown quantity every minute.

"Then this place is off limits too. Understand?"

Karl smiled a conciliatory smile.

"Agreed. I take it that the staff are out of bounds as well?"

No laughs today. They sipped their drinks in unison. Thomas felt the tension reach out across his shoulders. He held his position; hard, unyielding and still close enough to lamp Karl if the need arose.

"One more thing Karl — there better not be any bugs here."

Karl reached into his pocket and Thomas flinched; they both saw it. Karl pulled out a small plastic case, and slid it across the table.

"As a show of good faith. On Monday, we reset the clocks and it's business as usual. Deal?"

"Deal," Thomas lifted the lid for an instant, clocked the electronic device then closed it carefully.

Karl drained his drink and rolled up his magazine.

"Well Tommo, I must be off. It's been grand. See you at the office," Karl picked up his glass and took it over to the bar.

Sheryl started towards him but he carried on walking.

"Nice meeting you . . . Miranda, isn't it?"

Thomas remained at the table, with his back to the bar, until Karl had gone. The door was still moving when Miranda sat down to join him.

"He won't come here again."

"Thanks," she said quietly, staring at the table.

His face softened and he rolled back his shoulders, like a boxer winding down after a successful bout.

"And Thomas," she was close enough to kiss him, close enough that he could smell her body's scent below the perfume; "Don't bring your work into my life again."

The blood drained from his groin in an instant. He palmed the plastic box into his pocket, locking eyes with her all the while.

"I think I'd like to sweep this place for bugs, as a precaution. It'll be Monday before I can get the equipment."

She nodded; maybe she was adapting more quickly than he'd expected. Leaps and bounds. Yesterday she only knew he was a photographer; today he was Spiderman.

She snatched his glass away as she got up from the table.

"You know your way home."

He swore under his breath and thrust his hands into his jacket, crushing his hand against the box until his fingers were numb.

* * *

Ten-thirty at night, the doorbell rang. He paused the film — a black and white comedy more than sixty years old. He was still smiling as he checked the silhouette through the glass.

Miranda didn't move; she kept that model profile thing going on, knowing its effect on him. He managed to open the door without ripping the handle off. "We never got to dessert," she said, slinking past him, with an overnight bag over one shoulder and a carton of vanilla Haagen-Dazs in her hand.

Chapter 7

Thomas blinked, in the Sunday morning half-light. All around him was the faint, unmistakable scent of ice cream. He pulled a spoon from under his shoulder and stretched his arm out, contacting Miranda's leg. Oh yeah.

She stirred, looked up at him like the cat that had got the ice cream and rewarded him with a delicious smile.

"Well, we haven't done that in a while."

She crossed her thigh over his and shifted closer — but not too close — honouring their unspoken rule: whatever happens today is only for today. And now it was tomorrow. He shaped a hand around her breast, but she held it to one side: down boy.

"Let's just sleep a while."

He closed his eyes and tried to think of something other than sex. Karl came to mind first, and he wondered what a therapist would make of that? Where did he stand with Karl now — could they really reset the clocks? He twitched and Miranda playfully slapped him to lie still. And what was Bob Peterson really doing on the scene?

Miranda groaned in protest.

"Look, if you really can't sleep," she flicked his erection and paused, opening her eyes wide to see his reaction, "Milk and one sugar, thanks."

He disentangled himself and reluctantly left the bed, glancing down at his misplaced enthusiasm. Not today, by the sound of things. The kettle took its time so he waited in the kitchen, taking the pistol stance and handling a lethal fork while doing replays in his head. Something else he hadn't told her about.

Miranda was feigning sleep when he returned to the bedroom, breathing a little too heavily — always a giveaway. He plonked the tea down and started gathering up clothes from around the floor. Along the way he lifted the ice-cream lid and flung it into a bin.

"Aren't you coming back in again?" she pouted, drawing back the sheet like the world's best show and tell.

He didn't need a map and directions.

* * *

Miranda's mobile alarm sounded at ten-thirty.

"Get up you lazy bastard — I've got things to do. I need to stop by the club."

It was funny, the way that Miranda sometimes avoided calling it Caliban's, even though she'd named the club herself. All part of her dumbed down, East-End girl made good façade. She had done well for herself though, opening Caliban's a little more than a year ago; purchased largely with her own money from a lucrative modelling contract in Bermuda, plus a contribution from Mum and Dad — which Thomas always read as: other people's money.

She always smiled when she saw her photograph on the living room wall; it was a spontaneous walking shot, from the streets of Leeds, taken with an old 110. True, it had dated, but somehow that just added to its eighties charm. Sometimes he'd move the photo around, just to try and throw her off guard, but it was always on one wall or another. Christine Gerrard, in her time, had hated that picture; another reason to treasure it.

Miranda stood before the picture gallery, head cocked to one side and a thin smile upon her lips.

"If you follow me down to the club, I can drop you back there after dinner." The subtext: you're going home alone tonight.

On the drive over, whenever they paused at traffic lights, he could see Miranda glancing back at him. Once or twice she gave a sly wave in the rear mirror, but her face was distant. Another clock reset, it seemed.

He parked at Caliban's and followed Miranda to the back office. Sheryl was her usual indispensable self — coffee ready and waiting as they entered. He sometimes liked to think that she was the daughter of an American crime family, with the Wrights as part of an underworld exchange programme. But he never asked; everyone needed secrets.

Miranda settled at her desk and pored over the accounts. He left her to it and went into the pool room across the way. Sheryl followed him.

"Fancy a quick game?" she racked up the balls and bent forward enticingly.

He mustered an eggshell smile.

"Sure, why not."

And it was a quick game. Sheryl played to win; she meant business. Small wonder that Miranda had appointed her as manager of Caliban's. Best of three became best of seven and still the balls were sinking faster than his self-esteem. Part way through game six, 4-1 in Sheryl's favour, Miranda appeared at the door. Sheryl looked over and they shared a glance. With that, she killed the remaining stripes with clinical precision and then iced the black.

"He's all yours," she called across to Miranda.

"Thanks for keeping him entertained," she winked, heading for the door.

As Thomas passed by Sheryl, she touched him lightly on the shoulder; "She tells me everything, you know."

He hoped she was joking.

Outside, he transferred the chocs, wine and flowers to Miranda's Mini Cooper. She took one look at the bouquet and shook her head.

"They're past their best — we'll pick up something better on the way."

Fair enough. He liked to make a good impression with Mum and Dad, especially today when he'd be delivering an avalanche of bad news.

* * *

The Wrights' house screamed working class with money, from the expensively paved drive to the retro coach lamp at the door. They'd dispensed with the wrought iron gates a couple of years back, after a police raid took them off the hinges. Miranda's brothers — Terry and Sam — had already arrived, their BMW and Peugeot parked side by side; they shared a large house out towards Canning Town.

Miranda pulled out her key — all three children still had keys — for a while, Thomas had one too, but he'd turned his in when Miranda had left for sunnier climes. Dire Straits' 'Brothers in Arms' was playing through the hallway like mood music. Thomas almost waited at the door until 'Money for Nothing' kicked in — a family anthem if ever there was one.

Diane, mother to the clan, waved and disappeared into the kitchen. Miranda peeled off to the living room to meet with the rest of them, but Thomas carried the spoils to Diane. Even in profile, she was a fine-looking woman and her genes had generously found their way to Miranda. Diane turned and smiled. "Sit your arse down and pour us both a glass of wine."

Bliss. No pretensions, just honest to goodness real people.

"How's things, Thomas?" she glanced up as she basted the chicken, and winked. She'd left off the rest of the sentence, which would have run: 'How's things, Thomas, with you and my daughter?'

"Not bad," he blushed and Diane smiled again. He knew both she and John still held out a fragile hope that Miranda and he would one day get their act together. As John had succinctly put it, "Stop fucking about and settle down." One Christmas, John had got so royally pissed that he'd declared: "I sometimes wish I had another daughter, so you could start again from scratch."

Thomas survived his gentle interrogation and sauntered on through to the others. John and the boys gave a cheer at his arrival. Miranda kept her distance. "How's business, Thomas?" John asked casually, just as always.

Miranda looked daggers at Thomas. Yeah, John would get an answer and a half today. She retreated into the kitchen, morphing from successful businesswoman to mummy's helper in the blink of an eye. They weren't a throwback family, just traditional. Presents under the tree and Queen's speech at Christmas; cemetery visits on Boxing Day and sovereign rings for the boys' twenty-firsts.

John picked up a remote control and the wall slid back, revealing a TV screen that almost qualified as a cinema. Highlights from the last West Ham game flooded the room. Thomas watched with mild interest. He'd been to a few games with the boys over the years, but it didn't really light his candle. For a while he'd even tried following the York City club, out of loyalty to his home region. But deep down he still believed football was for people who didn't have the balls for rugby.

Sam had once had a trial for West Ham youth team, straight out of school. Somehow this still entitled him to offer comment on every pass and volley. Terry, not to be outdone, punctuated every unsuccessful manoeuvre with 'bollocks' or 'that was shit,' the two brothers relishing their double act. John looked on proudly at his sons and

Thomas, if he could have, he'd have taken a hundred photographs from all angles to capture the feeling forever. The boys looked up to him, the parents thought the world of him and Miranda — well, he didn't even have words for what they had between them.

At the table, with John carving, Thomas made an extra effort to join in with the banter. For a while he could forget his painful duty and just enjoy the company; that and Miranda rubbing her foot up against him under the table. But by the time the dessert bowls were passed around — no vanilla ice cream, thankfully — he had a sinking feeling.

"So," he broke the easy chatter. "I've, er, got a bit of a problem." The clan all shifted in a little and he cleared his throat. "I was at Harwich last week — I saw the van come back from Amsterdam."

John Wright shot a surprised look to his sons. Thomas carried on. "The thing is, well, it's not a good place to do business right now."

The boys hadn't said a word. John was first to speak. "How d'ya mean, Thomas?" John's voice had a quiet authority. Or maybe it just seemed that way because Thomas had never seen him in a rage.

Miranda shifted her foot away and sat up a little straighter. "Thomas was working there, Dad, taking pictures."

John nodded, eyes narrowing. Terry piped up. "No sweat, we didn't get stopped or anything."

Miranda cut in. "No, and that was thanks to Thomas."

He gaped at her, open-mouthed — so much for trusting and sharing.

She clocked his face and turned beetroot, whispering to herself: "Bollocks!"

"That'll do, thank you," Diane stopped eating.

John sat back in his chair, scratching his chin as he looked over at Thomas. "Do you want to talk about it?"

Thomas nodded; at least he'd been given a choice. "I was on a film assignment for Customs & Excise — a training film." So far so good, successfully tiptoeing the line between truth and bullshit. "Someone with me wanted the van checked, but I persuaded him not to bother."

He felt Miranda squeeze his hand under the table; he couldn't tell if the clamminess was his or hers. John took a sip of his beer — somehow he'd never made the conversion to wine. "And when was this exactly?"

Thomas looked along the table to Sam and Terry. "On Friday."

John leaned forward. "I told you two to leave it well alone — how many trips has it been now?"

"Five, Dad," Sam said.

A stranger might have itched to know what they were carrying. Thomas, he was just happy that they'd got through without incident.

"Well, thanks, Thomas. Do we owe this Customs geezer anything?"

He shook his head quickly.

John looked straight at him, like a dog deciding whether or not to attack. "So what's the problem, then?"

Thomas twisted his paper napkin. "There's this bloke at work — another photographer — only . . . only he might have taken an interest in my private life."

"Do you want me to sort it out for you?" Sort him out, more likely.

"No, it's taken care of now," he looked to Miranda for encouragement. "But I'd be a lot more comfortable if you'd let me check your house over for . . . electronic devices."

"You mean like the Old Bill might use?" John's face twitched.

Thomas swallowed. "Well, it's probably nothing; I'd just like to be sure."

"It's alright, Dad," Miranda pitched in, "he's doing the club for me as well."

Diane stepped into the fray. "Hold on, let me get this right, Thomas. Someone's been checking up on you and you think they might have planted stuff here, in our home? What kind of business are you involved in?"

"Mum, give him a chance. It's just a precaution."

But Diane was having none of it; it wasn't hard to see who Miranda took after. "No, let's have it all out in the open. You involved in drugs or something?"

The Wright family creed: no drugs or prostitution or porn. Some might say that wouldn't leave a lot to profit from, but they'd be very wrong.

"Alright," Thomas tapped the table, "here it is. About a year ago I changed jobs — still Civil Service but I became a specialist photographer." He stressed the word so that hopefully it would say things that he wouldn't have to. Diane recoiled like he'd just punched her.

"Well, you never bloody said! Did you know about this, Miranda?"

"No Mum," Miranda admitted in a quiet voice, "I only found out yesterday."

Thank you, Judas.

"Hold up," John raised a fork. "If we're gonna talk about this, let's get comfortable." Like a sofa would make it all easier.

John mainly listened and didn't ask too many questions. Everyone else picked at Thomas like he was the day's special.

"So let me get this straight," Terry laughed. "You've been leading this secret life for over a year and you never told us!"

He shrugged, like a desperate plea for clemency.

"Hey, give the boy a chance," John calmed the mob. "Never mind what he kept from us, for a minute; he still did the boys a favour and we're in his debt."

"Just let me sweep the house for . . ."

"Intrusions," Miranda chipped in helpfully.

"Well," John concluded, "that's about it. Miranda, why don't you and your mother make us all some tea."

Oh bollocks, Thomas thought; here comes the real discussion. John waited less than five seconds after the kitchen door closed. "I don't like deceivers, Thomas, but I respect loyalty. The main thing is that you still looked out for Sam and Terry. I appreciate that. All I want to say is this . . ."

Thomas braced himself. John and the boys leaned in as one.

"How much do you think we could charge to check out other people's places for these intrusions? I know plenty of people who would be interested in that sort of service."

"Hey Dad, I could get some cards printed."

Thomas looked over at Sam. God help him, he was serious.

* * *

Miranda seemed unseasonably chirpy on the drive back to Caliban's; a marked difference from Thomas who felt like he'd lost a tenner and found a black eye. "Cheer up, babe, it'll be fine."

He rubbed a thumb against his forehead in disbelief. "Your dad wants to offer a counter-intelligence service to the criminal fraternity, your brother wants to get me business cards and your mum probably hates me now."

"Nah, I talked with her while you four were playing The Godfather. She knows it wasn't personal, what with you not telling any of us."

Seconds out, round two. "Look Miranda, it's the Official Secrets Act not a bloody Cluedo game."

"So, do you like your job, then?"

Now there was a question he'd never been asked. Not even Christine Gerrard had drawn that one out of the hat, come appraisal time. "Most of it, yeah. But I don't like the idea of being at the other end of the lens."

Miranda squeezed his thigh. "You used to pose for me though!"

In the club's car park, she turned off the engine. He wanted to say something meaningful; he been thinking about it all through the drive over. The best he could offer was: "Look, I'm sorry."

She kissed him matter-of-factly on the cheek and that hurt more than anything else. And she'd know it. Nothing pained him as much as Miranda drawing away again.

He trudged towards his car and consoled himself. Not a bad weekend, all things considered. He'd played with guns, had some great sex, shared a family meal and admitted to the people he cared about most in the world that he'd been lying to them for months. Oh yeah, and found out that his best mate at work had been spying on him. Roll on Monday.

Chapter 8

He got into the office early and flicked the main lights on. At the far end of the room, Christine's sanctuary was ablaze like an electric fly-killer. Ann Crossley's chair had a bag hung over the back of it so someone had already started playing brown-noses with the boss. But then, today was the big day when Bob Peterson joined the gang. In all the weekend's excitement he'd almost forgotten that piece of joy.

At 8.15, the impossible happened; Karl had somehow twisted the space-time continuum and arrived before most of the rabble. As soon as he was in the door, he marched over to the vending machines. Good to see that military training hadn't gone to waste. Then he appeared at Thomas's desk with coffees and two Twixes. "I, er, think I may have been a bit over-dramatic. All quits now?" Karl put the goods down and extended his hand. Thomas reciprocated, grabbing the payoff before Karl changed his mind.

Karl had clearly been at a different 'prioritise your work' seminar. First on his agenda was clearing out the spam emails from the web filter, with occasional commentary. "Jaysus, you'd think they could at least spell sperm? Fancy writing it with a 'u'!"

"Why do you bother reading them?"

"I don't read all of them — I just find some of titles intriguing. Lookie here Tommo; what do you reckon? Genuine herbal Viagra from Naples!"

Christine's door opened and the sound of chatter and laughter floated out. Thomas and Karl exchanged a customary glance of contempt. Ann Crossley strode out, with all the confidence that a Cambridge education could buy, even if it had diluted her native Cardiff accent along the way.

"Good morning, gentlemen!" she crooned and returned to her desk.

"Ann, have you lost a few pounds by any chance?" Karl asked.

She glanced over herself admiringly. "Well, yes, as it happens."

Karl daggered in with lightning speed. "Because I found a fiver on the carpet."

"Karl," she scowled, "you can be a real prick sometimes."

"That's because sometimes only a real prick will do!"

She huffed and fired up her laptop.

"Why do you do it, Karl?" Thomas shook his head. Karl just flashed a grin. Out of the corner of his eye, Thomas saw a figure filling up Christine's doorway. The elusive Mr Peterson was surveying all that he owned. Thomas snapped a Twix finger in his teeth and stared at the screen, waiting for the inevitable call to visit the grown-ups. He managed a good five minutes of stoic activity under Bob Peterson's gaze, including Karl's emails declaring that Bob Peterson must be a busy man if he had time to engage in a one-way staring contest.

At eight thirty a mobile alarm went off; Bob Peterson cleared his throat. "Thomas, could you pop in please?" The poor sod was obviously a slave to the clock.

He drained the last of his coffee and picked up a notepad and pen. He imagined, for an instant, that Bob Peterson had been one of the targets he had fired bullets into. It helped put a smile on his face.

He sat down and tried not to react as Christine closed the door and sat closer to Bob than he would have liked.

"Thomas, glad to have you on the team."

He noted the lack of a pronoun — a good way to spot liars and sociopaths. Even so, he made the supreme sacrifice and shook Bob's hand.

"I've arranged to see everyone over the next couple of days, but I really wanted an opportunity for the three of us to, er, clear up any lasting misunderstandings."

"Do you mean the one about me not knowing you two were carrying on together before Christine and I split up?"

Bob and Christine exchanged an 'I told you so' glance; Christine folded her hands earnestly. "Thomas, we've been through this. Bob's interest in me was purely professional — when will you get that into your thick . . ." she paused and Thomas touched his tongue to his lip. The next words used to be: working class. But patronising the lower ranks would never do in front of her boss.

"—Head?" Thomas offered, generously. He had to be smart, smarter than Peterson, anyway. He glanced at Bob's hand — same ring as he wore at Harwich. As clear as the blow-up he'd printed at home. He swallowed his pride and did what needed to be done. "Look, can we start again? My stuff with Christine is all in the past, but your arrival stirred things up a bit for me."

"Sure, sure!" Peterson beamed as if he'd just successfully hidden a pair of Christine's knickers in his back pocket. "I've checked through your record, Thomas, and it's exemplary. I'm sure we can work together — I'd hate to have to lose you from the team."

Thomas made no attempt to hide his shock. He looked straight at Christine, who seemed similarly surprised. "I'll wait to hear from you, then."

"Absolutely," Peterson opened the door, as if he was making a point. "Don't go too far; I want the whole team in at 9.30."

Thomas returned to his desk with a face like thunder. Christ, he'd really made a mess of that; nearly played his hand too soon. He went over to Karl. "Fancy a walk? I need some air."

"Be right with you Tommo, just closing down. Don't forget to lock your laptop."

Something else he hadn't done properly.

* * *

Karl ushered him to a café five minutes away. They both ordered a full breakfast. "I take it that your tête à tête wasn't all you hoped for?"

"I made a complete dick of myself," he shook his head slowly. "I accused him of sleeping with Christine before we'd officially split."

"Don't be expecting a good appraisal then!"

Two preposterously large mugs of tea arrived. Karl waited until the waitress had turned her back then made pretend swimming strokes over his tea.

Thomas just sighed; he'd lost his sense of humour.

"You know, Tommo, I loved and lost this girl, once. We were both stationed in Germany and we got together quickly. It was all brilliant and then I had to go back to Blighty on some urgent family business."

Thomas stopped drinking tea and paid closer attention.

"Anyway, she bumps into this officer on base, while I'm gone — turned out that she'd had a bit of a thing with him, over in Cyprus." Karl rotated his finger to show the passing of time. "So I get back to barracks and there's another fish in my kettle, so to speak."

Thomas had already decided that Karl made these phrases up. "How long were you away, Karl?"

"Long enough, evidently. I wasn't very mature about it all. And unfortunately for me he was a nastier fighter," Karl lifted his sweatshirt to reveal a series of white scars.

Thomas gasped.

"Listen now, I was no angel either. We wrecked the bar, apparently. I was certainly pretty wrecked at the time!" He winked then calmly took a sip of tea before he continued. "Anyway, not to be outdone, I tried a different tack and sent some photos of them together to his wife. Did I mention he had a wife?"

Thomas remembered that Bob Peterson was married, too. "And?"

"His wife divorced him. And later on, so I heard, the 'Officer and Bastard' married my lovely Jennifer." Once he'd stopped talking, the waitress returned; Karl's face lit up like a beacon. "Beatrice, you're a sight for sore eyes. Your husband is a very lucky man!" He was rewarded with a demure smile and the all-day breakfast — so named because it could take a slow eater all day to finish it.

Further conversation was parked as they made their way through a meal fit for a king — a king who enjoyed mushrooms, eggs, tomatoes, sausages, bacon, toast and beans.

Thomas clapped his hands appreciatively. "That hit the spot."

"You can always rely on your uncle Karl to make things better! Come on now or we'll miss the party."

* * *

The team filed into Christine's office, all clutching pen and paper. Karl had brought along his Homer Simpson pad and novelty snake pen.

Bob Peterson introduced himself and shook everyone's hand warmly. It was the usual 'we're in this together' speech, with a potted history of where he'd been working before and the assurance that he wasn't going to bring in change for change's sake — which always meant the exact opposite.

Christine chipped in here and there, as if they were a double-act already, and managed to not look in Thomas's direction. At one point Peterson made a joke about Sir Peter Carroll and asked Thomas not to repeat it the next time he saw the 'old man upstairs,' a blunt reference to Thomas having been interviewed by Sir Peter himself. Thomas swallowed his pride and smiled on cue.

Later, Ann Crossley asked about an accelerated development programme and Peterson agreed to look into it. Thomas managed not to mention that Christine herself had done something similar. So far, so good.

Karl wondered aloud what had made Peterson come to their branch of the SSU. Peterson laughed it off without committing himself. Thomas had been listening through a haze of indifference, but now he saw an opening. "So Bob," he adopted a matey tone, "how was the move up from Southampton?"

"A nightmare — still a work in progress!" Peterson grinned. "Most of our things are still in storage — I was working in Southampton right up to Saturday night. We're still waiting to exchange on the house so I guess I'll be commuting, unless one of you has a spare floor?"

Laughter all round. Thomas laughed too, at Peterson's audacity — the lying bastard. Gotcha! Christine's face was a study in marble. Then an alarm bell went off in his head. What if she and Peterson were engaged in their own little re-enactment society?

Later, Thomas sat at his desk, deep in thought. He had what he wanted — Peterson's denial, even though the photo proved he'd been at Harwich — but he didn't know what to do with it. 'Bang to rights' as Sam or Terry would put it. He smiled at himself. How ingrained the Londonisms had become after years of living there. Even his accent was more East End than Yorkshire, these days. On those rare occasions when he contacted his own family, the first thing they usually said was that he gone 'all southern.'

Karl had stayed on for a few minutes — probably a prelude to his assessment. Thomas watched as he walked out of Christine's office, holding up the Simpson's pad as a face. Karl, his only ally — someone he still didn't know if he could trust.

"How did it go, then?"

Karl took a deep breath. "Fantastic, Tommo. They're thinking of putting me up for the George Cross."

"You're a funny man, Karl McNeill."

"That's just what Bob Peterson said — now are you sure you weren't listening at the door?"

Thomas held up a hand, Honest Injun style. His mobile bleeped; a text from Miranda: Thanks for a lovely weekend. M. x. He blushed and switched off the phone, remembering to pick up a sweeping kit from Stores, for Caliban's and the family home.

Chapter 9

Karl drove out to the docks with Thomas riding shotgun. He didn't say much to Karl; he was too busy thinking.

Peterson didn't need to lie; he could have mentioned being at Harwich, now that he'd met the team. He could have explained it as an informal assessment before taking charge. But no; something smelt fishy and Peterson was a week-old prawn.

By the time they arrived at their hidey-hole, overlooking the action, Monday weather had really kicked in — a drab, half-hearted downpour that set the mood. They sat, munching on sandwiches and peering through binoculars like schoolboy birdwatchers. Matter of fact, Thomas could identify the different gulls — Herring, Common and both types of Black Headed Gulls; not that he thought Karl would be interested.

Karl soon declared he was bored of scoping for women and went back to Private Eye. Thomas took to staring out at the sky, or what was left of it, as rain sprayed the windows in rhythmic bursts. It was, to quote Karl: "Shiter than a field of slurry." Clearly, the man had the soul of a great poet.

After a further hour of struggling together with the cryptic crossword and generally wasting taxpayers' money, the walkie-talkie spluttered into life. "Control to all units; we're calling it a day. Come down and get some close-ups."

* * *

The Customs teams went about their work, with little regard for the Floaters — a moniker the SSU had never managed to shake. The filming was supposed to be impromptu sequences, but as every good photographer knew, off-the-cuff material needed a lot of preparation. A dry lens, no reflections or glare, no inadvertent staring into the camera; it took time to stage that level of spontaneity.

Karl did the bare minimum and homed in on the youngest and prettiest Customs Officer. He swaggered about, displaying the subtlety of a Great Dane with a hard-on. Thomas drifted along behind him to witness the charm offensive at close quarters.

"Ah me, I do so love a girl in uniform!"

The woman turned, saw Karl's beaming face and lifted her shoulders. "You must be the Floater everyone's been warning me about." Before Karl could answer, she flashed a smile. "So how do you want me?"

Karl did his thing, manufacturing life-like shots under cover from the rain. Thomas was regulated to bag man, moving equipment while the maestro was in full flow.

"By the way, whatever happened to the shooting victim?"

Thomas jerked to attention behind Karl; very slick, right in the middle of a sequence — classic misdirection.

"Funny you should ask." Little Miss Flirtatious turned and made a Marilyn Monroe pout for the camera. "The way I heard it, he was whisked off to a private hospital somewhere."

Karl moved from behind the camera and looked directly at Thomas, just for an instant — a regular Holmes and Watson moment. "Hey," Karl knelt down near her to change his data card, "I wonder where all the booze in his van went?"

Karl's supermodel looked over to Ann Crossley. "She supervised it."

"Well then," Karl chortled, "We'll be alright for the Christmas Party! Okay sweetheart, I'm all done here — I just need to get the steam off my lens."

She gave him a little wave and went off to join the others, glancing back a couple of times on her way.

"You know, the camera really loves her."

"Looked like it wasn't the only one." Thomas folded his arms.

"Come on now, Tommy. I was working my subject, like any good photographer."

Thomas squatted beside him while Karl put his trusty Nikon to bed. Thomas eyed it suspiciously. He preferred a Canon; but they'd had that debate many times over.

"You look pensive, Tommo — what's eating you?"

"I don't do let's pretend very well, Karl. And you heard what she said . . ."

"Just keep to your boundaries and let me do my job."

Thomas stalled him, arm outstretched. "But what exactly is your job?"

Karl walked around him. "Don't go there, Tommo; don't go there."

* * *

17.45 on the dot, as requested. Christine's door was already open. Thomas knocked politely on the frame; start as you mean to go on.

"Thomas!" Peterson cried delightedly, as if they were at a class reunion. "Come in, have a seat."

On the desk was a fan-spread of reports, all bearing Thomas's name.

"I understand you and Karl McNeill were on duty when the firearms incident took place at Harwich?" Before

Thomas could reply, Peterson added, "But there's nothing in your report."

It was a pawn-to-king-four gambit — obvious, but effective. Thomas responded in kind. "I keep my reports factual and we were concentrating on the Customs Officers." Facts. A light went on in his head. If he had any snaps of the red car heading up the exit lane, he'd probably have the registration number too.

"And these?" Peterson pawed at one of the mosaic shots. "What are these about?"

Thomas shrugged it off. "Just background detail. I like to set up early and get a feel for the location."

Peterson stalled for a second and Thomas caught it. "Christine tells me that you have real potential."

She shifted forward in her chair. "Bob and I have discussed this, and we think you're ready for development. It means additional training in Staffordshire and it could open doors for you in the future."

Thomas wore his best fake smile. Christine continued, "We'll need a decision by the end of the week — there's an opening next Monday."

Peterson was staring intently at the mosaic photograph from the day of the shooting. Thomas kept his eyes firmly on Christine, which was no great hardship, and leaned back a little to keep Peterson in his peripheral vision. No doubt about it though, she was looking really good today.

"One thing I would like to ask you," Peterson slapped the photograph down. Thomas jolted awake. "What's your opinion of Karl McNeill?"

"He's very good at what he does; seems to read people well," Thomas played it safe and stayed vague.

"But what about personally? I gather you two socialise from time to time."

Thomas concocted a cross between a laugh and a cough, each as fake as the other. "Well, we have the odd drink, now and again — I met him last weekend, as it happens. I get the impression there's more to Karl than meets the eye. But I s'pose we all have our little secrets."

Christine became a study in scarlet and Peterson dropped his pen, which rolled off the desk; they both froze. Bingo, right on the money.

Thomas decided to push his luck. "If you don't mind, I need to be away soon; I have a date I cannot break." Yeah, looking for bugging devices in Dagenham, followed by a takeaway curry for six.

"Oh." Christine looked surprised. Not disappointed, he noted; just surprised.

"That's fine." Peterson extended a wet-fish handshake. "Thanks for your time and your candour. Let Christine know about the training."

* * *

Miranda always said that men couldn't multitask, but Thomas found that London traffic always afforded him time to think. So a burst water main at Burdett Road was practically a gift. By the time he'd ploughed through to take a left at Bow Common Lane, he'd found one thought that he just couldn't shake. And it wasn't a good one.

Peterson would have scheduled an arrival time at Harwich that day and known precisely where he'd parked; probably the vehicles around him too. He was a pro after all. Then Thomas had given him — bloody given him, mind — a mosaic showing the whole panorama without Peterson's four-by-four in it. As good as saying: 'I know you were there and I'm keeping it to myself at the moment.' Stupid, really stupid.

And now, suddenly, he was trainee executive material when earlier in the day he'd been facing the heave-ho from the team. Peterson had him snookered; not accepting the training meant showing his hand and accepting would put him at arm's length.

Desperate times and all that; he swung the car into the first available space and fetched out his mobile. "Hey,

Karl. Listen, any chance of a chat at the club, some time soon? Wednesday? Nice one; see you tomorrow."

The Wrights left him to go about his work. All except Sam, who followed him around like a lost sheep: nothing new there. When Thomas had first brought Miranda back to London, Sam had only been about thirteen. Talk about hero worship. Thomas had rescued Miranda from the clutches of doom. Or more precisely, from the paws of Butch Steddings — modelling agent and all-round scumbag. Even now, Thomas and Miranda still used the word Butch as code for something dodgy.

By 21.30 Thomas had his feet up and John Wright was handing him a beer. All clear, no trace of Karl's handiwork on the premises. And sadly, no sign of Miranda either. If she were playing hard to get she'd put in a cup-winning performance tonight. No reason to expect her at Caliban's on Tuesday night either, for his next debugging booking. The only bit of good news that night was that no one had mentioned the business potential of Thomas's new career.

By the time he got back to the flat in Walthamstow, it was close to midnight. The answering machine light was flashing insistently. He put the electronics case down in the hall, set the two door locks and hit the magic button.

"Hello Thomas, it's your mother. Just ringing to see how you are and when we can expect a visit. Your sister and the kids send their love and so do me and your dad." No names just titles — nice.

The next message was Miranda. "Hi, sorry I won't be there tonight or at the club. Sheryl knows the score."

He dithered for a second then stabbed the delete button. "Of course she does," he seethed in the dark, "you tell her everything."

Chapter 10

Karl held the heavy metal door open as Thomas stepped through. It felt as if that door was shielding him from the outside world. Once the formalities were dispensed with, Karl led him to a bay and went off to procure the equipment.

He leaned against the wall and gazed out at the targets, seduced by the stillness. A perfect backdrop to the maelstrom of his own thoughts.

Karl soon returned with two Browning 9mm pistols. "You won't find any answers staring down there!"

So there were answers to be had? He opened the case and, under Karl's supervision, primed the weapon and took the stand. He closed his eyes for a moment and let the roar in his ears carry him. The barrel wavered. Sweat massed at his brow and his armpits felt sticky, as if the growing web of deceit and half-truths was oozing out of him.

He sighed, took aim and squeezed the trigger. Somehow he'd expected the first shot to settle him, but it had the opposite effect. The barrel shuddered — no chance. He flipped the safety catch and put the gun down.

Karl stepped up beside him and put a hand on his shoulder. "It's all about being able to close in, to focus on one thing. No distractions or prevarications. Because if it came to it, that's what the other guy would do." Karl nudged him aside and drained the magazine without breaking a sweat. "Now, try again."

Thomas lined the target up. His stomach contorted and he fought against it, making himself breathe steadily to counter the nausea. It all came back to him then, the first time he'd held a gun.

* * *

1984. Maybe not the dystopia Orwell had predicted, but in Yorkshire, a police state nonetheless. Night after night, woken up by the sirens; the procession of policemen, like the invading Roman army they were learning about at school. At first it was exciting; they played at Blake's 7, from off the telly, space rebels against an evil, galactic federation. Or else they tried to get close to the horses.

But the screw quickly tightened and then it wasn't fun at all. When coalmining collapsed, so did the world they all knew. There were arguments at friends' houses and rows at home; relentless shouting and door slamming. School became a refuge from home.

Every day his dad swore vengeance on 'that heartless tyrant bitch, Margaret Thatcher.' It was the first time he'd seen his father so full of hatred. In some ways, childhood fell away. The older kids talked about a revolution. They hadn't covered that in class, so it didn't all make sense.

And then there was that day, playing around in the greenhouse. That's when he found it, wrapped up in newspaper and hidden in an old rucksack: a real gun. Next day his dad came home unexpectedly, caught him red-handed. He really went off on one; raged at him, threatened him — his own son — to keep his mouth shut about the pistol and to never go in the greenhouse again.

Thomas had been so frightened that he'd pissed himself, right in front of his dad. Even now, just thinking about it, his face burned.

* * *

He swallowed hard and heard the echoes of his own laboured breathing. How long had he been standing there? Just pull the fucking trigger. One, two, three, four in rapid succession, gunning down his shame and the past. As if that was ever really possible. "Done," he called aloud. As he stepped back, he saw Karl leaning casually against the wall, watching him. "Peterson and Christine asked what I thought of you, yesterday. I told them you were dependable."

Karl nodded and packed away the pistols, game over. Thomas waited for him in the corridor. Maybe it had been a mistake coming here this time. The strangled whistling of a familiar tune made Thomas turn — 'I Shot the Sheriff' — Karl of course, the stupid bastard. "Come on amigo, something closer to home," Karl passed him a larger case.

Thomas balanced the rifle comfortably, nestling it against his shoulder. The weapon smelt different, and the realisation amused him. He wriggled his face closer in to the sight and inhaled then released. The crosshairs barely moved as he levelled up and fired. He felt the recoil in his shoulder and shrugged a little, preparing for the next one. Now he saw the hole, placed close to the inner ring. Five shots followed, each within an inch of the original.

"Very good. Amazing what a little time and preparation can accomplish. Now, step aside and let me show you what a professional can do!" Karl was still a much better shot. He made short work of the remainder of his ammunition and lowered the rifle with a sigh. "The bar, I think."

* * *

"Drink up Tommo — nothing worse than cold coffee."

He swayed the cup mid-air. "Peterson wants to send me on some special training next week. I reckon he wants me out of the way."

"I'm not surprised. Remember that wee Customs lass I was doing so well with?"

Thomas arched an obligatory eyebrow.

"She's been reassigned — she told me when I rang her last night; did I mention I picked up her number before we left? Anyway, it looks like someone's having a bit of a clear out."

"Well, I'm staying put."

Karl gave him the kind of look that he used to give his sister Pat when she still believed in the Tooth Fairy. "Think so? A quid says they split up our dream team within a fortnight."

They both did mock spits and shook hands on the bet. Thomas toyed with the rim of his cup. "When I was a kid, I used to pray at night for Jesus to end the Miners' Strike and save their jobs," he sucked in one cheek. "Yeah, stupid, I know. But I was ten. It was the last time I ever thought about relying on anyone else."

"Hey though," Karl brightened, "just imagine if he'd ever achieved it. We'd have got him over to the six counties on the next ferry out!"

"Look, I owe you an apology, Karl, for thinking you were prepared to . . . you know . . ."

"Fix up your drinking hole? Understandable, under the circumstances."

Karl wiped his face with a napkin. "Listen, I know you feel you're in the middle of everything, but — and don't take this the wrong way — stick to what you're good at and leave well alone."

Thomas pondered that for a second. The problem was, he was already involved.

* * *

He didn't sit down to eat until after 10 pm; a cheese omelette with bacon bits in it and bread that was only good for toasting. He cleared away methodically and switched on the immersion heater. Now or never time. He drummed on the desk while the laptop fired up and didn't linger on the default image: Rievaulx Abbey, beset by lightning. Sifting through the unused images folders, he found what he was looking for — two pictures of the red car at the port. Not his best work by any means — slightly blurred, though enough detail across the two frames to put together a complete registration number.

He dialled Miranda, without thinking of the time, and asked another favour.

"That depends. If it's for your job, the answer's no." She sounded distracted, probably by all that background music.

"Are you in a club?"

"What?"

He was pretty sure she'd heard him and wasn't that a man's voice close by? "Are you with someone?"

For a few seconds there was silence then he heard a familiar tone. "I've got to go, Thomas. Just text me whatever you need. Bye."

The room went cold. He sat for a while, staring into space, taking it all in. Sleep was off the menu now — a familiar part of the pattern. He washed up and sent Miranda the text. Then he grabbed his car keys and an SLR camera, promising himself that he wouldn't end up outside Christine's flat again.

To begin with, he just drove around, looking for a prospect. The radio was tuned to some late-show, where the emotionally stunted could unburden their souls. And in between the confessionals, a talk-jock served up a hearty stream of platitudes.

'That must have been awful for you. Do you have a message for any listeners in a similar position?'

"Yeah," Thomas spoke directly at the radio, "get a life." Like he had a life? He flipped the station to something more melodic and cruised the City of London to the tunes of the eighties; happily cocooned until The Human League struck up with Don't You Want Me? Ouch; too close to home.

Thoughts crept into his brain, or out of it. Was Christine still single — had he imagined some sort of buzz between her and Peterson? He smiled, taking his own bait: only one way to find out. No harm in taking a drive by her flat later. Driving past without stopping didn't really count. He glanced down at the camera, mute beside him on the passenger seat, like his conscience.

At Archway he pulled over and took the tripod from the boot. He found a suitable position, set the camera up and started timing the traffic. After twenty vehicles, he opted for a timing of seven seconds. He waited, enjoying that delicious sense of anticipation. Despite all the technological progress, at heart it was magic — that's what it was. A moment in time, in all its shame and glory, captured forever.

He was reverently packing everything into the boot when he heard talking. He cocked a fist and moved to the blind side of the car, crouching to get a better look. It was a woman, stumbling along the street towards him, having a conversation with herself. From the look of her, she was maybe seventeen; seventeen going on twenty-five. And she'd had a skinful.

"Alright mate?" she grinned as he stood up. "'Ave you got the time please?" She was too drunk to be scared of approaching a stranger at night. But that was okay because he was scared enough for both of them.

"It's late — you should be at home."

She started laughing and teetered about like a Jenga conclusion. "I missed my lift and I'm too skint for a taxi. I got college tomorrow . . ."

Hook, line and sinker. "Alright," he conceded, feeling he'd been played like a cheap violin. "Do you need a lift somewhere?"

"Nice one," she gave him a wavering thumbs-up. "Ever heard of Battersea?"

He nodded wearily. No good deed goes unpunished. In the end, he crossed the river, found the nearest cab office and left her there with a tenner. Better that than explaining to an irate family that he was just a Good Samaritan, and nearly twice her age.

By the time he was safely over the Thames, he'd given up on Christine's and opted for home. As he parked up, he noticed the small handbag in the passenger door. Brilliant — something else to be sorted out. He opened it carefully, as if it was a steel-sprung trap. There was a passport-sized picture of two schoolgirls; all grinning smiles and too much lipstick. Also inside were a college card and timetable, a door key, a nightclub matchbook, two tampons and a packet of condoms — one missing. Clearly, a woman for all seasons. He noted the college address; another good deed for tomorrow then, before work.

Chapter 11

Thomas got waylaid by traffic on the way to Battersea Technology College. He left the bag in a padded envelope at reception, with a note suggesting she be more careful in future.

In the office, Karl was already sifting his junk mail for gold. "Tommo, come and see this. Why would any man want to increase his sperm by 500%? Hey, unless he was a donor and paid by volume!" Ann Crossley looked over without saying anything. Karl called Thomas to one side. "When are you telling Christine that you won't require the key to the executive wash room?"

"No time like the present," he glanced at her door. "May as well get it over with."

"Don't be too long — I'll get the coffees in," Karl stood up and wandered towards Ann Crossley. "Can you imagine a man with five times the sperm? Where would he keep it all?"

Christine was on the phone. She saw Thomas approach and waved him in. "Okay Bob, leave it with me and thanks again for your time." She put the phone down and did her best to bury a smile. She used to do that with him, when they were exchanging glances at work, back in the day.

"I thought I'd tell you right away that I won't be taking up the training offer."

Christine frowned. "I think you're being very short-sighted. Bob went through your files very carefully — and despite your macho display — he was impressed by what he saw."

I'll bet he was. Thomas pushed his tongue against his lower front teeth to make a poker face.

"You're making a mistake, you know."

And there was something about the way she said it that made him pause and sit down. The best defence might not be attack, but it was better than no defence at all. "I was in your part of the world last night — I nearly popped round."

Christine did a good impression of a rabbit caught in headlights. "I was busy," she snapped, "and you shouldn't assume I have no life of my own."

It all sounded a bit Jane Austen from where he was sitting, but he got the message loud and clear: stay away. Which only made him more determined.

* * *

At Harwich, in the afternoon, Crossley radioed in; she sounded smug. "Thomas, Christine wants you to ring immediately. You're to report to Sir Peter Carroll, first thing tomorrow morning. Top priority."

Thomas relayed the news. Karl sucked a tooth. If he'd played his cards any closer to his chest, he'd have worn them as a tattoo. "Well now, Tommy Boy; looks like I just won a pound. Another two says Crossley knows more than she's saying. Has Sir Peter ever asked for you by name before?"

"Now and again. I've done the odd pick-up, up north. Maybe he thinks southerners get a nosebleed if they venture further than Watford."

"Yeah," Karl stared ahead, "or maybe you've pissed somebody off?"

It was the first time Thomas had visited Main Building in Whitehall. He'd seen Sir Peter in a few buildings since State House in High Holborn. It was as if the old man couldn't settle. And every time, including at Whitehall, Sir Peter kept his distance from the various offices of the SSU.

The security guard eyed Thomas up and down. In most governmental buildings, Thomas knew, security had been contracted out to agency staff — the engines of bureaucracy made safe on minimum wages. Main Building was not one of those places. Glancing left to right, he counted five people in the reception area who stood or sat ramrod straight and took their duties very seriously; no skiving with the television on here. Most, if not all, would be armed.

"Thomas Bladen?"

He nodded and held up his ID. Despite the twenty or so years since the SSU had existed, there was still a hard core of resentment and mistrust from the real security and armed services. Chummy here, sneering back through the reinforced glass, was clearly not a member of the SSU fan club.

"Hand please." Fingerprint checks had already been introduced, last time he'd attended Sir Peter. And even though he had nothing to hide — nothing that would show on a hand scan, anyway — he still twitched a little as the scanner went about its business.

An escort appeared, to take him up to the top floor. No conversation in the lift, not even a gripe at the weather. And above them the cameras silently filmed every nuance; despite working in surveillance, Thomas could never get used to that.

The lift rose to the top floor, which made him smile; some things never changed. A grey carpet extended before him, complemented by grey walls and a series of identical navy blue doors. The only way to tell them part was by the acronyms — ATFA, SA2A and NORAD Liaison. This was need-to-know taken to extremes. They rounded a corridor, he and the silent wonder, along the dog-leg, past FRD, CIA — surely not — and then finally a door labelled SSU. The escort knocked curtly then opened the door for him. "I'll be back to collect you."

100% pure charm.

Sir Peter Carroll was sat behind his desk in a navy blazer and tie; he had a look of the Cheshire Cat about him. "Thomas, good to see you!" he stood and extended his hand, but that was as much as he moved. Behind him, the familiar portrait of Sir Winston Churchill adorned the wall, with a great cigar in his mouth and a paperweight of a spitfire by his hand. *There's no place like home.*

Thomas had seen that painting maybe a dozen times, most of them at State House when he'd been showing off his photographic prowess. "How can I help you, sir?" He knew the old man would like that.

"Thomas!" Sir Peter elongated the name in mock disapproval. "Will you join me in a whisky?"

He nodded, happy to accommodate his benefactor. They sat for a minute or two, savouring their drinks. Thomas had never been sure how far the informality thing stretched; it had all been pretty loose before he'd joined the SSU but he'd never pushed it since he joined the payroll.

"I'd like you to collect a package for me; from Leeds."

A Yorkshire pick-up. Coincidence? Thomas didn't subscribe to them. "Where do you want it delivered?"

"To me, here in Whitehall — Highly Classified."

He nodded; if Sir Peter were studying his face for a response he'd find none.

"You'll leave for York from St Pancras station, Friday morning. I thought you'd appreciate the chance to spend time with your family up there."

Terrific. Must remember to book the street parade.

"Retrieve the item from an office in Leeds on Monday morning. Then straight back here — understand?" Sir

Peter lifted an A5 brown envelope from an in-tray and picked up a telephone to summon the escort. "So . . . what do you make of Bob Peterson?"

"Don't know much about him," he played dumb. "I gather he's been working out of Southampton." Give or take the odd bit of moonlighting.

Sir Peter laced his fingers together, like a judge about to pass sentence. "Not really your sort, eh, Thomas?"

Thomas shrugged and stuck with his glass.

"I'm sorry you turned down the training — Bob was very keen."

Blimey; good news certainly travels fast.

"It's sensible to get Bob on side," Sir Peter leaned across his desk. "Winning a war is easy — that just takes superior forces. But winning the peace . . . ah, that takes superior intelligence. Do you follow?"

"I think so, sir." It all added up to a cryptic pitch for be nice to Bob. Three raps on the door brought the conversation to an end.

"Monday," Sir Peter said as the guard closed the door behind him.

Outside, Thomas felt for the envelope; he knew better than to open it on the street. Even though, on past experience, it would only contain travel times, an address and a named contact. It was still before eleven. He rang Christine to check what she wanted him to do next; back to base it was then. On the way over he called Karl.

"Ah, the happy wanderer! How did it go?"

"Fine thanks. Listen, turns out I'll be away this weekend — when do you fancy meeting at the club?"

"Well now, let me check my packed social calendar . . ." Karl paused for about three seconds. "Yep, this week's good — pick a day."

"How about tonight? — I know it's short notice . . ."

Karl backtracked like a Lamborghini slammed into reverse. "The thing is, Tommo, there's this senorita."

"It wouldn't be Teresa by any chance, would it?"

"A gentleman never tells. Why don't we make it Thursday night?"

"Done."

* * *

The office seemed deserted when Thomas arrived. The team would still be at Harwich. And Peterson, with any luck he'd be under a bus.

"Hi there," Christine poked her head out of her door, "fancy a bite to eat?"

He blinked a couple of times; did a comedic search behind him.

"Come on, you must be hungry?"

"Sure, why not — I've just got to make a call."

"Great! I'll power down and get my bag."

It had been a long time since they'd strolled along the Thames together. The water shimmered in the sunlight; slow lazy bow waves brushing the banks as the tourists motored up and down. Given the choice he would have lingered awhile to watch how the shadow lines sliced across the concrete. But it was Christine's gig so he kept quiet and played follow my leader.

He remembered the bistro, a spit away from the Tate Modern. It had been the site of that first try-out lunch with Mummy and Daddy. No surprise then that Christine made small talk about her parents; people who wouldn't make space in a lifeboat for him if the ship went down in flames — in shark-infested waters.

"Anyway, enough about me; how are your family, Thomas?"

The coincidence bell rang so loud in his head he could hardly hear himself think. He muddled through with a mixture of old news and half-truths, grateful when Christine claimed them a table.

"Here, this is good. A great view of the North Bank."

They agreed to share a bottle of wine — her treat. He quickly got into the rhythm of their non-date. There was nothing at risk here since not only had she no interest in him romantically, he still had Bob Peterson marked down as her bedtime companion. On those terms, he could afford to relax and enjoy himself.

"I really do wish you'd think about the training, Thomas," she had a certain way of saying his name that could still set his teeth on edge. The tone dragged him back in time, just before the ice age had set in. He avoided a skirmish by drawing on the healing power of wine. "I know Bob's appointment was a shock . . . but that shouldn't stand in the way of your future. Hmm?"

He smiled. As the early afternoon sunshine picked out her auburn highlights, it was easy to recall what he'd first seen in her, two years before. By dessert he'd noticed her legs again. Best stop now, Thomas, before your tongue runs away with you. Christine, oblivious to his gaze — or used to it — was enthusing about her parents' stables, where she still kept a horse.

He replayed the first time he'd met her mother, when she'd inquired pointedly: "Do you ride at all?" And the killer line he'd never delivered: Only your daughter. Cue canned laughter. Not for nothing had Mrs Gerrard later described him as coarse, behind his back of course. Guilty as charged.

His mobile went off. He made that stock face that all people do, suggesting they're irritated by a call even when they're secretly delighted.

"Hi babe. I've hit a problem with that number. Sorry about last night . . ."

He cut across her. "Sorry, you've caught me at a bad time. Can I ring you later? Great — speak to you then." Touché Miranda. He switched the phone off, pre-empting an abusive text.

Christine ran a fingertip around her wine glass. "Girlfriend trouble?" she lifted her head square to his.

He leaned out of the sun. "There is no girlfriend. How about you?" He said it casually and glanced to one side to give her space to respond.

"Me? No, no girlfriend either. My lesbian phase ended at boarding school." She kicked him playfully under the table, tapping her handmade Italian shoes against his brogues. "This is fun, isn't it? We should do this more often; we are friends after all."

He adjusted his crotch under the tablecloth and then raised a glass. They clinked a toast, friends forever. Or for the time being, anyway.

* * *

He didn't ring Miranda back until the evening. Either she couldn't or wouldn't pick up, so it was at least an hour before she returned the call. Another hour, in which he cooked or worked or went to the toilet, with the mobile at his side.

"Hey babe, how's it going?"

He kept it low key. "Yeah, fine; sorry about this afternoon, I was involved in a work thing."

"No problem," she managed to make it sound just the opposite. "That number you gave me doesn't exist. Hello? Are you still there?"

"Yeah, I'm here, Miranda."

"I'll read it back to you in case I got it wrong."

He checked on his computer as she spoke. "No, that's the one. Not to worry." Except that now, he was really starting to worry.

"Listen, fancy coming over for Sunday lunch? Just me this time!"

"I can't. I'm off to see the folks."

"Blimey, hell's finally frozen over! How long you away for?"

"A long weekend." There was a pause. He squeezed the phone closer, to hear her breathing.

"Well, if you fancy some company up there . . ."

If you only knew. "The thing is, it's also a work trip."
"Oh."

That was a conversation killer. She said to get in touch if he needed anything and left him to it. On the lounge wall, a seventeen-year-old Miranda gazed back from a hazy St Paul's Street, Leeds, in the summer of 1994. The warmth of her smile lit up the frame. He closed his eyes and tried to pour himself into that photograph. No such luck.

He didn't ring his family until Thursday morning; no point building the visit up if he could play it down. His mother started planning an itinerary while they were still talking. And she said that his father would be pleased to see him; she made it sound like a solicitor's appointment.

Of course, he'd stay with them — they wouldn't dream of him booking somewhere. He made a note to cancel the hotel in York. She closed the call with 'give our love to Miranda,' even though the break-up was years ago.

* * *

Karl was uncharacteristically quiet, had been all day. It was as if someone had super-glued his personality shut. Thomas had tried several approaches without success. Still, today was Thursday, so at least they would be able to talk on neutral ground.

Funny, the way Karl never questioned why he kept going back to the gun club; he'd never really asked himself that either. It felt safe, in a way. Not like being around Miranda and her family, but a different kind of sanctuary. Or maybe it was just Karl. He understood the pressures of the job and the demands it made. You became guarded, even to those closest to you.

"Are we still on for tonight, Karl?"

His oppo looked up from his eyepiece and gave a thumbs-up. "Roger that!" It still sounded like a watered-down version of Karl. "Got your jim-jams packed for tomorrow, Tommo?" It was the first time he'd mentioned the pick-up job.

"Uh-huh."

"Well, be careful, okay?"

"Karl, I'm touched, I didn't know you cared."

"Listen, laughing boy, just keep your wits about you."

Strange times indeed.

By the evening, Karl's introspection pills had worn off. They practiced with a Browning and a Glock, and then Karl nipped out for a .44 Magnum. Thomas felt completely intimidated by the sight of the thing — like that time he and Miranda rented a porn film. Still, he rose to the bait and made a complete arse of himself, to Karl's evident joy.

"Are you sure now you're not related to Clint Eastwood?"

More like Clyde the monkey. Later, Karl was his usual chatty self; firearms seemed to give him a new lease of life. By the second pastry, conversation had turned to the marital status — or otherwise — of their colleagues.

Karl was in the chair. "Crossley — not a chance; either plays for the other side or she's saving herself."

"What is it with you and her, Karl?"

"Let's just say we had professional differences in the past. And despite her best efforts, I'm still here. We've buried the hatchet and all, but I doubt we'll ever be pen-pals."

Okay, crunch time. Thomas took a slip of paper out of his pocket. "I know I was supposed to mind my own business, but I did some checking on our mystery red car and the number plate's a fake."

Karl lowered his plate. "I can't say I'm not impressed. Even so . . ."

"Come on Karl, this is all wrong," Thomas raised his fingers to count off the points. "First someone gets shot and they take him to a private hospital. Ann Crossley removes the vehicle and the woman who told us about it gets transferred. Then the car I thought was suspect turns out to have false plates."

Karl gazed at the ceiling as if seeking inspiration. "I'll tell you what, Tommo, seeing as how we're trusting each other. I'll make you a deal. I'm gonna write something down and put it in an envelope. Don't open it until we get together again on Tuesday. If I'm right, I'll let you in — I mean it. But if what's written down is totally wide of the mark, will you agree to let all this go?"

Like that was ever gonna happen. "You're on; I do love a magic show."

"Me? I'm Ulster's answer to David Copperfield, so I am. Now, sit yourself here while I find some stationery."

Thomas relaxed a little; he was starting to feel like he belonged. Teresa came over; it was easy to imagine her in a uniform. He was still lost in the 'regulation skirt' when she coughed, bringing him back to reality.

"Where's Action Man?"

"Action Man — brilliant!"

"Because he tries all the equipment here."

Nought out of ten for deduction.

"So, are you thinking about becoming a member?"

Now there was a thought. Might also be his best chance of finding out about Karl. He shrugged.

"I'm sure someone could vouch for you."

"Is that how it works, then?"

She smiled enigmatically; too keen. He noticed a cluster ring on her right hand; could have been an old engagement ring. She flexed her hand then massaged her neck self-consciously. "Coffee?"

He shook his head. If he had any more coffee today he'd be able to walk to Leeds.

"Well, well, this all looks very cosy!" Karl had tiptoed across, doubtless using his Action Man skills.

"I'm trying to find out your little secrets."

"That shouldn't take long — simple man that I am."

Yeah, right.

"Here you go, Tommo. Remember, not to be opened until Tuesday."

The envelope had a daub of wax on the back; blue wax, like a birthday candle. He held out the envelope, wax side up. "Just making sure."

* * *

Back at the flat, he packed a bag and threw in an AGFA Isomatic 110. Because sometimes he just liked to take snaps. Round about midnight, he put down The Adventures of Sherlock Holmes and cut the light.

He always thought that if his father was called upon at the Day of Judgement, it was the one thing he could say in his defence: that he had introduced his son to the great works of Conan Doyle. Tonight he'd made a point of re-reading The Red-Headed League, a classic study in misdirection. And come to think of it, Karl had reddish hair too.

He lay on the bed, pondering the incongruities. 'Oh, give over, Thomas; it's just a story,' he could hear his mother chuckling. Even as a child, he had always had 'a head full of questions.' He got undressed and eased into the cool sheets, wondering if Miranda were sleeping alone tonight. Or Christine, come to that.

In the early hours of the morning, a car alarm went off. He dragged himself to the window to check. Unlikely it would be his own car, since: a) the only reason anyone would break into it would be to fit a better stereo out of sympathy and b) he never put the alarm on.

A few doors along, a yellow Ford Escort was revving up for all it was worth, the throaty rumble making the window tremble against his hand. A young woman was stood at the kerbside, arms folded. He caught the gist of it straight away; Sharon didn't love Kevin anymore, but Kevin wanted to prove his love by pissing off her parents and all their neighbours.

He flicked the curtain behind him to get a better view. An RS2000, with four round headlights — four of them! How did a toe-rag like Kevin afford a car like that? Probably wasn't even insured, never mind the bloody tax.

Tax — of course! He shrugged away the curtain and let it fall back into place. Thank you, Kevin. The wall-clock showed it was nearly two. He didn't bother putting the light on; hopefully this wouldn't take long.

He fired up his personal laptop — where he kept copies of all his photographs. Stuff for work, recent shots that had never made it into his official reports, even a set of wedding photos for Miranda's cousin. All filed, in an orderly system. It only took a minute or so to navigate the folders and subfolders — red car, four pictures. Two of those were partials of the front, at an angle. He magnified the appropriate sections, and positioned them side by side onscreen. Together, they formed a Rosetta stone, a complete registration that differed from the number plate.

He basked in the blue-green glow of the laptop, staring at the pictures; he was getting good at this. Unlocking a drawer, he lifted out a surfboard key-ring — a Bermuda present from Miranda. He pulled the thing apart, inserted the memory stick device and uploaded the crucial files. Now he'd sleep like a charm — mystery solved.

As he crawled back to bed, checking that the alarm was still set for seven, he wondered if Kevin was back in Sharon's good books now. He hoped so; as far as Thomas was concerned, he'd earned it.

* * *

By seven forty-five, he was out of the flat and walking up Hoe Street — that still made Karl laugh — for Walthamstow Central Underground. The walkway was littered with rubbish bags, discarded cardboard and old newspapers. He fell in step with the rest of the ants, swerved around the offer of a free newspaper and disappeared into the maze of platforms and walkways, unaware that someone else had fallen into step with him.

He surfaced at Kings Cross and headed straight to the ticket office at St Pancras. In the queue, he picked up a text from Miranda: Have a good trip. Mx.

And although he'd memorised Monday's reporting instructions, he still pressed his hand lightly against his jacket. He could feel Karl's magic envelope there too. The train was called early so he made the most of it, grabbing a copy of Private Eye on the way — just to see what Karl found so amusing.

Once Thomas had passed safely through the barrier, the person trailing him made a call. Sir Peter Carroll liked to be kept informed.

Chapter 12

Thomas left the train at Leeds, for a one-man nostalgia tour. It was a routine that he'd never deviated from over the years. Starting off with the Indian restaurant on Merrion Street where he'd taken Miranda for their first meal together. The place was closed; he pressed his face against the tinted glass. The décor had changed again. It was classier now; looked like there was a bigger fish tank too. He preferred it before.

Next stop Hyde Terrace, the bed-sit — sneaking in with Miranda after hours because the landlady on the premises ran a respectable property. Except when her gentleman friend came over on Wednesdays and Saturdays. Good old Christian hypocrisy — a little piece of home. He wondered if she still owned the place and if she'd recognise him as one of the teenage lovers she'd threatened to call the police on; probably not. He settled for a slow walk past.

He had a love-hate relationship with Leeds. It marked the transition between Pickering and London. Leeds was where life had begun to take shape. Being away from home, that first job with photography, meeting Miranda; the good things. But Leeds had also felt soulless; and all that grief with Miranda and Butch Steddings was like a bitter echo of school life. Yep, nothing like revisiting teenage angst for working up an appetite. He'd never tell him, but cafés without Karl just weren't the same, so a pub lunch was the order of the day. Caliban's aside, he wasn't a huge fan of pubs. But the Angel Inn scraped through on atmosphere alone. Thanks to Private Eye and a problem with the sandwiches, he lasted a full forty-five minutes.

And finally, on to the main event: the Art Gallery, along The Headrow. Portraits fascinated him; the way they captured something of the inner person and revealed it forever. He'd tried to paint Miranda once — it was rubbish, of course. But the actual process, the way he'd been able to study her for hours and to see how the light changed her features — well, it was almost a religious experience. She hadn't taken the piss either, not even when he'd said he wanted to be a professional photographer one day.

He checked his watch — time to go — and skirted around a gaggle of college girls outside, slowly smoking themselves to death. He made the station in plenty of time, unlike the delayed Scarborough train.

* * *

At York, he saw his mother standing by the car, as he exited, looking out for him. She waved enthusiastically and he reciprocated with a slow hand. If he'd been any more non-committal he could have doubled as a stunt pope. His father remained in the driving seat, hands on the wheel.

After the obligatory greetings they joined the Friday traffic, slipping across the Lendal Bridge and along the A64 before it clogged up for the evening.

"How's sis?"

"Now, Pat'll be coming over later," his mother changed the subject without drawing breath. "She said to say that Gordon sends his apologies. He's been working long hours and doesn't think he'd be at his best."

Thomas studied the veins on the back of his hand. "How are they getting along these days?"

His father let out a deep sigh, but his mother kept to the script. "He moved out for a few days last month — said he needed a bit of room to himself. He's under a lot of pressure, you know." She said it earnestly, as if to convince all three of them.

Yeah, right. The only pressure Gordon was likely to feel was in his elbows, when he was on top of some tart in Whitby. "Why didn't anyone tell me Pat was having difficulties?"

Thomas's father half-turned. "Because you're never around — not for this family, anyway."

And there it was: gloves off, round one.

"Come on James, let's not start."

Father and son stared at each other through the mirror. No one spoke again.

* * *

It was hard to get too worked up about seeing the house, which had been his second childhood home, and he'd left in his teens. But it still held ghosts. He rolled his eyes at the memory of that final-straw row with his dad, over 'drinking and backchat.' Maybe one drinker was all the house could bear.

As soon as they got inside, his mother rushed straight into the kitchen to put the kettle on. It was like he'd never been away. Tea, the great panacea for fractured families, now with added digestives.

Thomas and his father sat in the parlour glancing in the general vicinity of each other. Stalemate. Thomas knew his father would crack first; a childish power play, but one he excelled at. All it took was time, and he could wait.

"So, 'ow's life in London?" his father relented.

"It's okay." Hardly the response of the year, but anything too enthusiastic or dismissive would invite further discussion. And we wouldn't want to use up all that sparkling banter on the first day, now would we?

After tea, his father tried again. Rugby — Malton & Norton's season compared with York then football — Leeds United getting robbed again in the final minutes. Thomas didn't bother to remind him that he'd lost interest in sport years ago, not counting the odd West Ham game.

Everything had settled by the time Pat's key rattled in the door. "It's only me." It sounded like she'd brought the little ones as well.

Thomas tried to recall when he'd last seen them and reached into his pocket for some guilt money.

"There he is!" Pat pushed the door to, beaming as if she'd just won the lottery. He eased out of the chair and opened his arms. She squeezed against him, the way a limpet fights against the tide. "It's really good to see you," she whispered, sniffing back tears.

Gordon. That little shit. One of these days he'd get through to him, using Gordon's head for Morse code.

The kids kept their distance at first, hardly surprising as he rarely saw them. All it took was a few words of encouragement from Pat and a few silly noises from him. Pound coins helped as well.

"I thought we could all have tea together," Pat suggested. "Me and Thomas could walk down to the chippie."

He nodded, seduced by the thought of getting out of the house. Fish & chips — a feast for the prodigal son.

"Here," his father held out some notes, "If you eat at my table, you're my guests."

And that about summed it up for Thomas; he was a guest. As soon as they shut the door behind them, leaving the kids hammering on the old piano, Thomas blew out a breath like an over-inflated balloon.

Pat laughed and grabbed his arm, winching him in close. "I have missed you though. You should come up more often."

"So I hear."

She looked away and pulled him towards the gate, still arm in arm. There had always been an easy peace between them, despite their differences. Pat had moved four streets away, settled down and continued the family line. Whereas Thomas, he'd abandoned them all, changed his accent and become a stranger. Pat never questioned that — she understood his reasons.

She waited until they were stuck in the queue outside the fish & chip shop. "How's Miranda?"

"Still single," he paused, reading between the lines. "As am I."

She shook her head faintly, as if she didn't believe any of it; sisters — too clever by half.

He waited until she'd paid for everything and stopped her at the door. "I'll pay for this lot. Give Dad his change, no need for him to know. I'm sure Mam can use a little extra."

She gave him a playful punch and he doubled up in mock agony. "You always were a silly beggar! Come on, I'm famished."

* * *

It was a typical family scene, three generations eating together; adults with plates on knees, but children up at the table; a bottle of ketchup passed around and hot, sweet tea to wash it all down. Except, for Thomas, it was as alien now as that terrible weekend he'd shared with Christine Gerrard and her parents. It wasn't that Pickering was smaller — no, it grew bigger with each infrequent visit. But the house, rooms and inhabitants alike — they all seemed narrower.

He walked Pat and the children home afterwards, doing a stint as Uncle Piggy-back. He didn't go inside though, not if Gordon might be around. It was Pat's life after all, and lamping someone rarely solved anything. As he wandered back the long way home, a police car blared in the distance. He smiled broadly for the first time that day; he'd make time to see Ajit before Monday.

Ajit was the only school friend he'd bothered to stay in touch with. They had two things in common: a love of photography and a secret they'd never discussed.

No one cared much when Ajit joined the class in 1988, except the throwbacks — and every school had them. It was racism all right, but with a twist. It wasn't the fact that Ajit was Asian, just that he'd come from Lancashire. Or so they said. School life was a proving ground for every would-be alpha-male fuckwit. Thomas had experienced a little of that himself when they moved to Pickering, after Maggie Thatcher broke the miners in two. But any son of a miner was hailed as a hero, even though all he'd done was stand in the street in York, collecting money for them.

Day after day, Thomas had watched Ajit run the gauntlet; watched as the gang formed into a leader and four lieutenants. Thomas knew it wasn't his fight. He and Ajit were both members of Photography Club and shared a few laughs, but that was about it. Still, wrong is wrong, when all's said and done.

Originally, he'd only meant to scare off the main bully, give him a bit of a thump to show him what it felt like. That was how it started, anyway. But it developed a life of its own. He followed the ringleader, and trailed the group to where they smoked and drank cider after school. He bided his time, did nothing while the shoving and the tripping up and the sly punches on the arm continued; just stood and watched. He and Ajit even fell out over it. 'Some friend you are!' Ajit had snapped. Some friend indeed.

On that final, momentous night, he'd gone out fully prepared: black jacket, gloves and balaclava. That Friday, he'd waited in the shadows; even pissed in a bottle to avoid leaving evidence, and chucked it over the wall into the fields. Over an hour, sitting there in the dark, watching.

And the more he waited, the stronger he felt. Like he was invincible.

The lad had ambled right past, half-cut on cider. He'd crept up behind with the speed of a cat, swiped him across the head and kneed him in the back, almost climbing on top of him with the momentum. Then, as the boy went down screaming, Thomas scrambled over him and legged it.

The screaming followed him as he'd crossed the road; not that it troubled him any. He scuttled into the first alleyway, pulled off the balaclava and folded it carefully into his pocket. He heard a front door slam and somebody call out in panic, but he kept on walking; he walked tall. A few streets on and he heard sirens; ambulance or police, could have been both. It didn't matter; for the first time in his life, he'd seen justice.

When he came home, his mother was watching television. His dad was still down the pub — nothing new there. "Cup of tea?" he said it in a quiet voice and his mother obediently scuttled to the kitchen, leaving whatever she'd been watching.

He opened the stove door and carefully placed the balaclava inside, as if it were a funeral pyre. Then he knelt and watched as they burned, feeling the heat against his face. When his mother returned, the smouldering embers were still visible on top of the coal. She didn't ask; mothers never do.

He'd stayed up later than usual even though he was tired. Pat was over at a friend's; she tended to do that on Fridays. She was a smarter girl back then. His father came back after closing time, reeking of beer and resentment.

Things escalated quickly, and this time Thomas stood between his parents, blocking his dad's approach as he swayed around the room — big mistake. The slap caught him unawares and knocked him to the floor. He sat there in a daze, unable to hear what was being said for the roar in his ears. His mother was a statue, no help there.

He remembered getting up and readying his fist. Even though he'd likely get a good belting afterwards, this time he was going down fighting. But his mother intervened, grabbing him roughly by the shoulders to move him to one side. Children hitting their parents back, that was crossing the line.

"Go to bed, James," she'd seethed and his dad had meekly complied.

Thomas had watched with a mixture of amazement and contempt.

"You shouldn't interfere," she'd scolded, as she checked his face for injury.

"Someone should."

"You watch your tongue. He's still your father when all's said and done." Then she sat down to watch the television, as if nothing had happened. "He doesn't mean it, you know," she'd said later without looking at him. "It's just, sometimes . . . the drink brings it out o'him. His dad were the same."

Thomas didn't reply. He rubbed his cheek until the side of his face was sore. Hopefully he'd have a bruise there next day; either way, he'd never forget.

Saturday's local paper ran a front page about a violent attack that had left a boy in hospital. Suspected skull fracture, facial abrasions; cracked ribs. Not quite what Thomas had bargained for, but he wouldn't lose any sleep. On the Monday, a policeman came to school assembly to talk about personal safety.

No one messed Ajit about any more. Nothing proven of course, and the rest of the bullies were hardly likely to speak to the police. On the Wednesday, Ajit didn't come to Photography Club after school. And on the Thursday he caught up with Thomas, alone.

"Look Thomas, don't take this the wrong way, right, but I can't hang around you for a while. My parents want me home straight after school, what with the attack." Then Ajit lowered his voice. "Listen, right, I don't know if it were you or it weren't you. I don't want to know. I'm grateful — he got what was coming to him. But that's an end to it. That's all I'm saying."

Three weeks later, Ajit returned to Photography Club; the pack leader never came back to school. Rumour was that the family had moved away, fearing a vendetta.

The breeze stirred and he touched the side of his face. It was turning cooler. Odd really that he'd ended up working for the government and Ajit had become a police officer — something for a psychologist to chew over.

* * *

Saturday was market day and his mother was in her element, showing off her visiting son to every shopkeeper she knew. Then tea and a bap at the new Victorian tearooms — a contradiction that only he found amusing. He sacrificed Saturday afternoon on the altar of television, sat there with his father watching every sport known to man.

It all unravelled after dinner — he should have seen it coming. Leeds had dropped points for no good reason and he'd made the mistake of bringing in a bottle of whisky as a peace offering. By the time he'd got back from seeing Pat and the kids — with Gordon still playing the invisible husband — the bottle was half-empty; or half-full, if you happened to be an optimist. Either way, it didn't take long for old resentments to surface, on both sides.

"What right do you have to judge me, eh? You swan about up here when you feel like it, like some great conquering hero. And you look at us like we're the shit off your shoe. You know your trouble, eh? You're a bloody snob. Ever since the day you met that London tart and you abandoned us."

Twelve years had added weight to the grudge. It was all calculated, of course, in the expectation that Thomas would stand no criticism of Miranda or her family. So he withdrew into himself, waiting for his father to implode.

Silence had always been his weapon of choice and he'd honed it like a sabre.

His father crossed no-man's land to deliver another volley. "When we stood shoulder to shoulder . . ."

Thomas winced. Here we go again . . .

". . . Shoulder to shoulder as they closed pit after pit — the working man were at war. Months we stood together, while that daughter of the antichrist laid this country to waste. Neighbours — begging for 'andouts, looking in supermarket skips for food."

Tears of bitterness rained down; he wiped them away with a fist. The other hand stayed tightly on the glass. "And when I heard you'd got a job wi' 'The Government,' the very people all working-class folk had been at war with, I were bloody ashamed."

There it was: the cold truth.

"You've betrayed your own class, Thomas; turned your back on your roots. I mean, who are you? Who the bloody hell are you?"

Thomas looked to his mother, sat quietly, staring at the carpet. He wondered if she felt the same way. He headed for bed. It wasn't even nine o'clock, but he was exhausted. The whisky had been manipulative; he knew that. But you have to know where the bleeding comes from before you can cauterise it.

He read for a while, too agitated to sleep. Once Sherlock Holmes had resolved The Eligible Bachelor, he sent two texts. One to Miranda, which read: Can I come home now? And tried to tell himself he was joking. And one to Ajit, to try and arrange a meet-up. Then he turned out the light and sank into a dreamless sleep.

* * *

He woke early on Sunday to the sound of sparrows scrapping on the roof outside. His eyes felt tight against his skin; he'd been crying in his sleep — hadn't done that for some time. He rubbed his face as if he could disguise the evidence.

Tiptoeing around the house reminded him of stolen weekends on the moors. A note left on the table — back on Sunday — and two days of absolute freedom. Ajit's dad would drive them over; sometimes there'd be three or four of them, the car jammed to the gills.

Time check: seven thirty. He crept out quietly. It was a fair distance but he didn't mind the walk; the exercise was good for him, it made him feel grounded.

Ajit was late finishing his shift. Thomas waited in the foyer, sipping machine coffee. The notice board was a library of misery: rabies, terrorism, drug abuse, domestic violence — he read that one twice — and HIV. He figured if you read all that for too long, you'd never want to leave the police station.

The desk sergeant picked up a telephone, nodded to whatever he was hearing and cleared his throat. "Ajit will be out in a bit. You the one from London?"

Thomas smiled grimly, primed for the put-down.

"It's a bit different up 'ere — more sense of community, like. I dare say you've noticed that."

He didn't bother mentioning he was a Yorkshireman by birth; his accent would have made it sound like a mockery. Sense of community? Easy words.

The secure door buzzed and clicked — just like the gun club. Then Ajit sprang the door wide with one large hand. He had a smile to match. "Thomas, my man!"

They did a round of macho handshakes and shoulder slaps, until the sergeant asked them if they wanted to be alone together.

"How long you up here for?"

"Heading back tomorrow."

Ajit led him out to the car. "You could have stayed with me and Geena."

"What? And miss playing Happy Families?" He turned abruptly and saw a brown car waiting at the junction.

There was no traffic at all. "Could you call it in for me?" He felt the blood draining from his face.

"What's got into you, Thomas? Are you in some sort of trouble?"

"Can you just call in a PNC check — as a favour to me?"

Ajit reached for the radio. Thomas had already pulled out a small pair of binoculars and started reciting the number plate. Ajit stared, open-mouthed. "Bird watching," he explained.

The check back came quickly. "'s all right, Thomas, it's one of ours! Out of town CID. I wonder what they're doing, coming over the borders!" Ajit peered at Thomas closely, as if he could see past his defences. "Right then, 'ave you got time for a walk in the wilds? 'Cause by the look of it, the town don't agree with you."

Thomas brightened. "Aye, that'd be great. Mind if I drive — it makes a change from London."

"You never did take to being a passenger."

Too true.

* * *

Ajit filled the passenger seat; he looked as if he'd been poured into the car. It was a different story at school, but a growth spurt at the end of his teens had provided a Sunday rugby side with a formidable prop forward. Now, when he laughed, the whole car seemed to shake. Although, Thomas thought, that could just be the suspension.

Thomas began to relax in his friend's company. When he'd decided to leave Leeds and go with Miranda to the brighter lights of London, Ajit had been the first person he'd told. It was the kind of easy friendship moulded by years, that doesn't require regular phone calls; where a missed birthday or a late Christmas or Diwali card is no big deal. Now, driving out across the North York Moors, they were like teenagers again.

"Did tha hear about the Hasselblad on sale at auction, down in London?" Ajit was as excited about the camera as a virgin on a first date.

"Hear about it, I went to view it at Sotheby's!"

"Yer jammy bastard!" The car rocked again.

They parked up on Ferndale moor and raced up the ridge like children. Thomas was light on his feet, but Ajit powered past him like a steam engine. From the ridge, the land swept out towards Rudland Rigg. Thomas half wished he'd brought a kite.

"So, come on then, London boy, what sort o' bother are you in?" Ajit made a playful jab at Thomas, which he fended off with a slap.

"You know I work in the Civil Service . . ."

"Aye. Patents or summat?"

"Well, I transferred; I'm a photographer now."

"You lucky beggar. Is it leaflets and that, or something more exciting?"

Thomas took a long breath. "Outdoor work, mainly."

"Nice — buildings or forestry?"

So much for the 'trail of breadcrumbs' approach. "Mainly people; the sort who don't know they're being watched."

"By heck, Thomas Bladen, you're a dark horse."

Thomas caught the way that Ajit's face froze for an instant; maybe he was remembering a time that he'd rather have forgotten.

"Are you allowed to tell me who you work for, then?"

He blew a dandelion head and watched as the spores drifted at the mercy of the breeze. "SSU — Surveillance Support Unit."

"Blimey, who'd a' thought it; one of them coverts. I won't say owt, obviously." Ajit gave a wink the size of Catterick. "Still durn't explain your bit of bother though."

Thomas pushed the binoculars to his face and said nothing.

Ajit seemed to take the hint. "Give us a go, then," he swung wide towards Rosedale Abbey. "Buzzards are out — Geena and I come up here regularly."

"I thought the suspension was a bit worn out."

"Give over!" Ajit gave him a shove and continued tracking the buzzards. "You know I'd help you, Thomas, as much as I can of course," his voice warbled with concern.

Thomas smiled for about a second. Even now Ajit believed in the letter of the law; he admired that in a way. "Thanks Aj; I'll let you know if I need you."

They stood side by side for a long time, gazing out across the rich moorland; neither one spoke. Then Thomas sighed and the spell was broken. He wanted to tell Ajit that it was good to be back, despite everything, but there was no need.

"Right then, me little Cockney Sparra, let's get you back to the bosom of your family."

"And you back to Geena's."

"I'll bet that sort of wit goes down a storm in London."

"I have to ration the tickets to keep the crowds down."

Ajit contorted himself into the driver's seat. "Don't give up your day job."

No chance of that now, not when it's getting so interesting.

* * *

Ajit declined the offer to come in and say hello to the folks, but he asked after Pat and wished her well. Back in the mists of time, he had gone out with her for a short while. After Thomas had left for Leeds, of course.

"Is that you, Thomas?" his mother cooed. She knew perfectly well it was; she'd been standing at the curtains when the car pulled up. "Door's on the latch. Come in, kettle's already on."

He grinned; one day, scientists would research the psychic ability of mothers to know when to make tea. "Is he up yet?"

"Well . . . your father's not feeling too great. He's asked if you'd like to go over Fylingdale this afternoon . . ." she waited, hands apart in nervous tension, clapping them together triumphantly at the answer she'd hoped for.

Afternoon. Wow; must be a hell of a hangover this time.

"He doesn't mean it, Thomas, you know that. You're his only son when all's said and done and he just wishes you were back here; we all do. Oh, I know too much has happened for you to want that — you've got your own life now — I'm not stupid. But it doesn't stop us wishing."

Thomas slid an arm around her waist. "You're a very wise woman."

She looked him up and down. "Wise enough to know not to bring a bottle of whisky into the house. He can't 'andle his drink — never could, lets all the demons out. I think you did it on purpose," she gave him a mock slap on the arm. "Come on, sit yourself down — I'll make your favourite breakfast. I've got in smoked bacon and eggs."

His father didn't surface until after one, announced by a groan; he couldn't tell if it was the door or his dad. James nodded carefully, acknowledging them both in one sorry movement. On the table was a steaming mug of tea and a paracetamol. He lowered himself to the chair as if it was a hot bath and took his medication. "I'll be right as rain in a bit." He looked as if he'd slept in the rain.

Thomas put the newspaper down and enjoyed the spectacle of his dad trying to tackle some toast. It might have been his imagination, but his mother seemed to have made it extra crunchy.

* * *

Eventually, they made it out to Fylingdale; Thomas ended up doing the driving, as his father didn't feel up to it. He pulled in by the side of the road so that the wind buffeted the windows and gently rocked the car. When he was a kid, Thomas had been told that this was the Weatherman helping him to sleep.

Despite the wind, Thomas left his jacket open, enjoying it against his skin. He closed his eyes, lost to the elements and swallowed by the moors. And his first thought — the only one that came to mind — was wishing Miranda could feel this now, beside him.

His father tapped his arm. "Remember that old bunker we found on't moor? They've opened it up to the public — I'll show you."

'We found.' Close enough; Thomas and Ajit had uncovered the hatch in a thicket, running around like crazed puppies. His father had shouted, 'give it a rest or go play somewhere else.' And so they had. Ah, hangover weekends, such a staple of childhood memories.

At first they thought they'd discovered a secret tunnel into Fylingdales airbase — Fylingdales, USA, as some locals called it. He remembered Ajit and him writing a letter to the base commander about doing a school project on it. Then a nice man from the USAF came to Photography Club with a wings patch for each of them and a donation to the school. It turned out that the bunker didn't go anywhere; it was an isolated installation built as a test.

Seventeen years or so later, the sealed door had been exchanged for a lockable one and the Cold War relic was now a freebie tourist attraction. They managed a five-minute tour, grabbed a leaflet and set off across the moorland. Thomas didn't say much afterwards, but he noticed his dad wincing with the exertion of the walk. He stopped and waited, made like he had cramp.

"Yer taken any good photographs lately, Thomas?"

He smiled, knowing that good automatically excluded talk of London skylines. "Aye. I went to Wales for shots of the red kite. I'll send you prints if you like."

"Yeah, do that. Wales in't so far from London, is it?"

A subtle way of reminding him that Pickering was about the same distance. He conceded defeat by changing the subject. "We'll need to make tracks soon or dinner'll be burnt to a crisp."

They both laughed. As if Thomas's mother would ever let that happen. Growing up, Thomas often wondered what she'd seen in his father, although he'd been a muscular man in his younger days, when he worked the pit. At times like this though, when his dad laughed, then he understood.

He slowly shook his head. Fathers and sons; they made the hundred years war look like a skirmish. On the way to the car they passed a family making their way up the slope, the boy screaming with laughter as his dad raced on with the boy squarely on his shoulders. Thomas had to look away.

Chapter 13

The family had given him a good send-off, Sunday night. A light tea and then a round of happy — i.e. highly edited — memories; photo albums all present and correct. Pat brought the kids; Gordon even put in an appearance later on, to take the children home. Dad was off the drink for the night; he only usually drank on Fridays and Saturdays. Maybe that was why Thomas had always hated Fridays.

Ajit came over first thing Monday morning, like the cavalry. Destination: Leeds. Geena waited in the car and Ajit stood at the gate, as if he were guarding Thomas's only means of escape.

His dad raised a hand in greeting from the front door. "By heck, Ajit, you'll be needing a bigger police car soon."

Thomas eased past his folks and called his goodbyes. His father had a love-hate relationship with Ajit. Loved the man, but hated what he'd become — another rant for another Friday night.

"Have a safe journey, son, and don't forget about sending those photographs."

Son — blimey, one for the diary.

Geena moved to the back seat, but not before she had swarmed over Thomas. "Come 'ere, you big lump."

He glanced at Ajit. Compared to him, he wasn't even a lumpette.

"So," Geena piped up as soon as the car pulled away. "'Ave you told him, then?" Ajit said nothing. "Three months gone!" she cried, "You're gonna be an uncle, Thomas!" She ran a hand where the bulge would appear.

Thomas didn't ask why he was only finding out now; secrecy seemed to be catching. "Crikey, what did your dad say, Ajit? Has he fixed a date for you, then?"

Ajit flexed his lips and launched into a parody of Mr Singh senior. "Ajit, now see here, I'm an 'onourable man with an 'onourable son . . ."

Thomas stared hard at his friend. "You 'aven't told him yet either, have you, you great pudding?"

"Men — you're bloody useless," Geena laughed even as she said it. "Leave it to the women — I've already told your mam."

"What?" Ajit instinctively turned round to her.

"Eyes on the road, you big lump," Geena pushed out her hand.

Thomas had a flash of inspiration. "A month or two from now, you'll both be great lumps!"

Geena leaned in, between the front seats. "Yeah and it wouldn't hurt you to do a bit o' settling down."

Ajit looked daggers at her. She made a 'What have I said?' face and fell silent. Thomas reached for the radio to drown out his thoughts.

* * *

At Leeds station, he separated out a rucksack and stowed the rest of his stuff in a locker. He'd completed a walk past on the Friday so he knew where the office was — a typically drab MoD building. The security process was less sophisticated than Whitehall, but no less formal. After an ID check and sign-in, he was shown to a side room. Away from family and friends, old ideas returned to haunt him. Like how he'd got the gig for a Yorkshire pick-up at all. Perhaps this was Peterson's revenge? If so then Sir Peter Carroll was in on the gag. Anyway, he was here now.

Just about the time he'd started counting ceiling tiles, a woman entered the room — mid-thirties, not big on words. Her epaulettes identified her rank as a captain — good to know he'd learned something from Karl. He found himself unconsciously closing his legs and straightening his posture. She might have been in Leeds, but her accent was pure South East England, as if the two of them were on an exchange programme. "This way if you please, Mr Bladen."

He followed her down three flights of concrete steps. His breath hung in the air; the basement was big on atmosphere, but small on heating. And the blast-proof doorframe only served to remind him of the Fylingdale bunker. The Captain produced a swipe card and approached the keypad. He instinctively turned away until he heard the last of the bleeps.

She levered the door mechanism and swung it, beckoning him in without speaking. Inside the room were two safes, a table bench like something out of a school science lab and a couple of chairs. It all looked like a full-sized logic problem. While he took a seat, the good captain produced two keys, which she held up one at a time, as if she was performing a trick. He almost clapped. She inserted a key into the safe on the left, in precise movements. The mechanism gave way with a clunk then she pulled back the reinforced door and started unloading the contents.

It was money, a lot of money. Holy shit. The packets of currency piled up on the table.

"That's fifty-three thousand pounds."

No it wasn't. He pressed his palms together, as if to stem the sweat. Jesus. He focused on the mound of sealed packets. That indefinable itch was kicking in. "Can you count them, please?"

She did as he asked, counting the fifty-seven packages out, just as he had the first time. Next thing he did was glance around the room for CCTV. What the hell was going on? She seemed genuinely perplexed, but that cut no ice with him.

"Check again."

"The requisition order states that fifty-three thousand pounds are to be couriered and that all contents are to be cleared from the safe." She waved the paperwork in the air — it could have been in Greek for all he cared. On the shelf behind her was a single DSB — document security bag. He stood back and watched while she bagged the goods like an upper-class bank-robber. Then he noticed the split in the bag. He took a deep breath and tried to ignore the adrenaline racing in his veins.

"I can't take it like that. Don't bother sealing it — I'll need a new DSB."

Her head flicked up. "It's the only one we've got here. I'd have to go all the way upstairs. You have your rucksack in any case."

She pronounced it rook-sack, as if it were an exotic object. And she clearly wasn't used to being given orders by civilians. Tough. He didn't waste words. "I'm not taking that package in that DSB. So either you get a new bag or you can stick it back in the safe."

"But you'll miss your train."

He did a double take. Miss my train? Two years he'd been fetching and carrying for the SSU. No one at the collection point was supposed to know the courier's travel arrangements. It shouldn't have been possible.

She broke eye contact. "Very well," she blushed scarlet, "Wait here."

"I'll wait outside, thanks. And best lock the door with what's in here."

She wavered then thought better of it, ushering him out quickly. Once the door was reset, she rushed upstairs two steps at a time. He pressed himself against the wall, felt the cold surface hard against his skin. He touched Karl's envelope through his jacket and wondered if this was all some kind of sick joke. Maybe that was it; someone would be out soon to admit to the wind-up.

A minute or so on and he started to wonder if they'd abandoned him down there. Think Thomas, think. He could always leave — just walk away and call it in as a no-show. But that frisson of fear was also exciting; it was like the feeling he'd had that first time at the gun club. As if there was a bigger picture. And knowing that, he had questions that needed answers. Like since when did the SSU act as bagmen for currency? And if they'd always been, since when did they start sealing confidential packages in front of the courier?

The Captain clattered back down the stairs — she looked as pale as he felt. She handed him the DSB then remembered that she had to unlock the door again. His going off message like that must have thrown her completely — not part of the plan, whatever the plan was. His paperwork was duly signed and countersigned then she bundled him out of the building. What had really burned the stew was his insistence on keeping the ripped DSB as evidence. If looks could kill, she would have been a soldier. Then again . . .

Outside, in the street, he pulled the rucksack in tight over his shoulder and sprinted for the first taxi he saw. He directed the cab to the Art Gallery and stood at the roadside until he was sure it had gone. A large coffee helped to stave off the shock. He threaded through the crowds and took his place in the taxi queue.

* * *

At the station, he retrieved his bag and had another coffee. All in all, he'd done well. Neither DSB was sealed — a simple sleight of hand distraction before both bags went into his rucksack — or was that rook-sack? He laughed into his coffee. A profitable retirement as a stage magician; Karl could be his assistant. Karl, in a non-speaking role — now that would be magic.

The London train was late, leaving him too much time for introspection; the coffee wearing off didn't help his mood either. Ajit and Geena — shit, they were starting to behave like adults. Okay, Ajit had always been responsible. But, a baby! And Pat looked all set to become a one-parent family in the not too distant future. Mum and Dad were the same of course, like that was supposed to be a comfort. And to top it all, he had just played Secret Squirrel and walked off with fifty-seven grand — with four of that unaccounted for. Watson, we have a problem.

The tannoy finally delivered an indifferent apology and announced that the train was in. He quickstepped up to first class and tried not to look smug as the poor bastards in standard walked further down the platform. He found his reserved seat and quickly abandoned it for another, which had no seat behind him. A few rows away a student — by the looks of him — settled in and upped the volume on his earpieces. Thomas counted to twelve and stared out the window, eager to be free of Leeds; he didn't relax until they were on the move.

A few minutes out of the station, as if answering a scratchy mating call, the train manager appeared and made a beeline for Grunge Boy, checked his ticket and pointed him towards cattle class. Thomas couldn't help but smile; nice try kid.

As Grunge Boy approached, he mouthed something that looked like wanker. Thomas gently angled out the tip of his boot. Grunge Boy was too busy flipping Thomas the finger and went down like a sack of shit.

He grinned; the bloke looked a lot grungier, face down. Then he noticed how straight the back of his hair was and a wave of panic swept over him. For a moment, he considered checking him for ID, but he calmed himself and laughed it off. "Are you alright, mate?" He figured

Grunge Boy must be okay if he was well enough to keep swearing.

Thomas smelled her perfume before he saw the woman — something a little more upmarket than he was used to. She asked without words if the seat opposite was taken. He did the polite thing, shook his head and scanned the rest of the carriage for options. Sod it, he was settled now and the journey was less than three hours — he could grin and bear it. It was an attractive perfume after all, on an attractive woman.

"Ooh look — matching rucksacks!" she lifted hers up from the floor to show him. He patted his own rucksack on the seat beside him and tried to quell the warning bells in his head. Any fishier and he'd be in Whitby harbour.

He had to admit it; first class really was first class. True, it was more of a finger bowl than a mug's worth, but the coffee was good and strong — and free. He glanced up at the woman opposite, now deep into her copy of Feng Shui Gardening. Hardly reading matter for spies. He sighed, remembering the game that he and Miranda used to play in Leeds — the name game. Pick any stranger and give them a name based on an arbitrary feature or characteristic, usually the first thing you notice. The advanced version involved picking occupations and back-stories.

Chelsea Girl — as in the flower show — looked over from her magazine and made a half-smile. Maybe this was how spies went on the pull. Maybe he was thinking about everything a tad too much. He hid himself in The Return of Sherlock Holmes and left her to it. He loved the way that everything in the stories had a purpose — no excess fat. If only real life were that reasonable.

When the remainder of Moriarty's gang were safely under lock and key, Thomas put the book down to rest his eyes. He couldn't shake the high strangeness of the morning. Had he done the right thing in taking charge, back in Leeds? Perhaps it really was some sort of test?

More likely Sir Peter Carroll got his kicks from moving pieces around a board, playing Churchill in his war room.

Thomas had always felt, deep down, that the old man had a soft spot for him, what with being a civilian and everything. Once, back in State House, Sir Peter had waited patiently while Thomas had spent fifteen minutes setting up a skyline shot at sunset. Not a word spoken until the magic moment was captured. Come to think of it, he'd given Sir Peter a print of that.

Right; time to get busy. He launched from his seat, stepping carefully over Chelsea Girl's stylish feet as he headed for the toilets, rucksack in hand. He did wonder if he'd be mistaken for a pornographer in need of a quick fix, but needs must.

Even in first class, there was someone incapable of flushing the toilet, or keeping their first class piss off the seat. He slammed the lid down and pulled a pair of gloves from his jacket. Best not to put fingerprints on the money while he was transferring it back to the old, torn DSB. Yep, all fifty-seven thousand, still there. It weighed less than he'd expected, not that he was in the habit of ferrying huge amounts of cash around.

Someone tried the lock from outside. He didn't bother responding; he had other things to think about. He'd keep the unsealed DSB and add it to the bugging device that Karl had given him in Caliban's; he was fast building a trophy spy kit. He checked the rucksack was secure, flushed the toilet and opened the door, only remembering to take off his gloves halfway down the carriage.

By London, he and Chelsea Girl had totted up less than five minutes of conversation — a personal best in stonewalling. He let her exit the train first and gave her a couple of minutes' head start.

* * *

Sir Peter was very specific about the delivery time — which left a conundrum. How do you kill a few hours with fifty-seven grand to look after? Simple really — you take it to the movies. Leicester Square was a 'phantasmagoria of cinematic entertainment' — he'd read that once on a tourism leaflet. He picked a foreign film with subtitles. Miranda had made him sit through a dozen foreign films when she'd returned from Bermuda. But once he'd seen Rififi, he was hooked.

Sadly, this wasn't even Rififi's second cousin. After two and a half hours, the tortured Breton artist had left her diplomat husband and set sail for Tangiers with her daughter and a cat called Filou — like the pastry. At least, that's what he thought had happened; he'd tuned out for a while, absorbed by the soundtrack of his thoughts, trying to make sense of a very difficult day.

He arrived at Main Building with twenty minutes to spare. He'd decided to check in early, then kick his heels in the foyer, maybe count some tiles. He approached the reception desk, relieved to have finally made it.

"I have a personal delivery for Sir Peter Carroll." He passed his ID through the slot.

The woman on the other side of the glass looked him up and down. Nothing like a hearty welcome, and neither was this. A colleague beside her picked up a telephone and a round of military whispers ensued. It was a quick game. "Sir Peter Carroll is no longer in the building."

He took out his orders and studied them again; there was no mistake. "Can you check to make sure?"

Again, the look that told him he was about as welcome as Karl on Ann Crossley's honeymoon. He put the bag down and massaged the sweat into the back of his neck. "Is there any way of reaching Sir Peter?"

"Sir Peter," she stressed, as if to reclaim the name from the lips of an infidel, ". . . is unavailable." There was a long pause. "Is there someone else I can call for you?"

"Forget it," he narrowed his eyes, "I'll come back tomorrow."

Outside, the screech of London traffic brought him to his senses. He checked his watch; still time to make it back up to Leeds, but the building would likely be closed. Why hadn't he rung ahead when he'd first got to London? Easy answer: because he'd never had to before.

His mobile held five numbers now: Miranda, her parents, her brothers' place, Karl and the Pickering homestead. And by his own reckoning that was probably two numbers too many. His thumb hovered over the choice of speed-dials. No contest, under the circumstances.

John Wright picked up immediately. "Yorkshire Tourist Board." Funny man — he must have clocked the caller. "Alright, Thomas, how was your time away?"

"Good, thanks; not long back. Listen, all right to pop over tonight?"

"You're always welcome! Bring some money — we'll play some cards."

Bring some money; that had to be the understatement of the decade. "Nice one, John," he fought to control the shake in his voice. "I'll train it up and grab a cab at the station."

"Don't be daft. Ring from the train and one of the boys'll meet you."

"Thanks mate." He began to breathe easy again. The boys would be there too. The Wrights' home was the safest place he knew. And there was always the chance that Miranda would put in an appearance, especially if he texted her.

Back at his flat, he decanted dirty clothes, picking up clean ones and his personal laptop. He was in the middle of deciding whether to take along a camera when the phone rang. Fantastic, Miranda must have got his message.

"Hello?" Silence. The kind of metallic silence where you think you can hear whirls and echoes, but really there's a cavernous emptiness. He waited, a minute or more, his heart pounding as he strained to pick up clues —

breathing, background noise, anything. He put the phone down and straightaway drew the curtains. Easy, Thomas. Probably just a wrong number, some old dear, as deaf as a post, who'd misdialled.

The phone started up again, its tinny, synthetic sound reverberating through the flat. He crept to the window — nothing in sight either direction. The phone was still ringing relentlessly: number withheld. Now he was really freaked. Whoever it was, he'd answered before so they knew someone was in. Stupid — he might as well have hung a banner outside: 'cash available to good home.'

The racket from the phone died; the silence afterwards was deafening. He tiptoed to the front door and double-bolted it. There was only one choice — he could either stay there with a bagful of money or make a break for it.

He grabbed his rucksack and bag — no time to change now — and went to the back door. He pressed his face tightly against the frosted glass and waited. There was no sense of any movement out there. The door opened with a creaking click; he never oiled it on purpose. He locked up and took the metal steps two at a time, down to the excuse of a garden. His eyes scanned the debris — bingo, just what the doctor ordered. He grabbed a piece of wood that had been dumped there and weighed it — good enough to do some damage.

The gate swung back and bounced a little against the back post. Another pause, listening out into the open space, breath held, straining for clues. At the point where he needed to breathe again he stepped into the back alley, club in hand. Fear was turning to a simmering rage. He slammed the gate shut and took practice swings with the stick. But all that lay before him was a few old dustbins, half a motorcycle and the usual mixture of newspapers, discarded milk bottles and dog shit.

He trod warily, the stick primed by his side. Nothing stirred except his own overwrought imagination. At the end of the alleyway he dropped the stick and broke into a gallop. Call it instinct, call it paranoia; call it what the fuck you like, he had to get away from there. As he closed on Walthamstow Central a bus drew by and he was so hyped up that he got on — and stayed on — just to give himself some time to uncoil. He sat downstairs near the exit and rode the bus all the way to Leyton Underground instead.

He didn't phone the Wrights until he was climbing the stairs at Barking. Terry, the elder son, was there in minutes. How Terry could afford a BMW remained a mystery to him; the Wrights' business dealings were as unfathomable as the Atlantic, and probably as treacherous. Two poor sods waiting for taxis looked on with envy as Thomas opened the car door; he couldn't blame them. Silver and chrome bodywork, sixteen valves, two hundred Nm of torque, and all the other specs that had meant nothing whatsoever to Thomas when Terry described them in loving detail. But it looked the business.

He climbed inside, squeezed his bag behind him and kept the rucksack on his knees — he felt like a first day pupil holding his satchel.

Terry talked as fast as he drove. "So this American geezer rings up and offers me a '67 Corvette — imagine that!

At that moment, all Thomas could imagine was his last coffee churning in his stomach. Terry interrupted the anecdote for some toe-curling cornering. "And I said to him: I'll give you fifteen grand, subject to sight, and he says . . ."

Look at the road; look at the road.

"American geezer, he says to me: 'Son, you got yourself a deal.' Stupid yank got the year wrong. Turns out it's a '78, but I reckon there's enough parts in the wreck to turn a profit."

"Wreck?"

"Yeah — totalled. Dad's gonna come with me to check it out, then we'll strip it down at the yard. I know this, erm

— whatcha call it — installation artist. Poncey modern stuff — great body though."

"What, the Corvette?"

"No, some mate of Sheryl's; comes into Caliban's now and again."

Thomas nodded carefully; his head was spinning.

"Yeah, she uses the car parts in her sculptures. I wish she'd use my parts."

Hand off crotch; both hands on the wheel!

The BMW arrived at Chez Hideaway with a final flourish of brakes that set Thomas's teeth on edge. Diane, matriarch of the Wright clan, was waiting at the door. Terry fetched Thomas's bag from the car.

"Thomas, come inside love — you're as white as a sheet."

And no bloody wonder after Steve McQueen's performance. He went in to the living room and looked for Miranda; it was too much to hope for, but that hadn't stopped him hoping. John met him with a beer in his hand. "John, could I 'ave a private word?"

"No problem. Come through — pizzas are on their way."

He followed John to a side wing of the house, rucksack in hand.

"We can talk here in my office — I work from home some of the time now." The room was as silent as a Mafioso on trial.

Thomas glanced around the room in surprise. It was spotless, orderly, not what he'd expected. No dodgy shipment receipts, no unpaid bills from the Revenue and no rolls of twenties — like he could talk, today.

"Take a pew. Now, what can I do for you?"

No easy way to do this. Thomas pulled open the rucksack and the ripped DSB to afford John a generous view.

"Fuckin' 'ell, Tom — this is s'posed to be a friendly game."

They laughed together. And as Thomas leaned back he saw three frames up on the wall. In the centre was a classic photograph of the whole family. He remembered the occasion well; Miranda had made him go shopping with her. Not that watching Miranda try on a succession of figure-hugging dresses could ever be described as a burden. He'd been the photographer, plumping for a 90mm lens on a 35mm camera.

To the left of that was a framed newspaper clipping: LOCAL BUSINESSMAN EXONERATED IN POLICE INVESTIGATION. Thomas turned away quickly before the blush took hold. That had been the closest he'd come to owning up about his day job, around a year ago. His back twinged just thinking about it. Two hours in situ, waiting for a copper so bent he could have doubled as a corkscrew. Waiting in shitty weather and poor lighting so he could capture the moment when Bent Cop tried to collect a pay-off, to avert a watertight but spurious case.

Yeah, lots of risk on that one, especially from the work side. Still, he'd achieved a natty set of black and whites — he preferred them for detail in crap lighting — and a half-decent sound recording, good enough for the police anyway. John, his brief and some senior officers all received an anonymous set of photos. Only the police received the sound recording.

He sensed John watching him, but his curiosity was in overdrive. The third frame really surprised him. Circa 1990: Meet the Parents, East London style. It must have been one of their first nights out after he and Miranda had come down from Leeds. The composition was too wide and contrived although it had a sort of naïve charm; it looked like a snapshot in time, a moment of stillness that couldn't last. Thomas and Miranda, front and centre, sharing a shy clasp at the very bottom of the picture. Diane and John resting hands on their shoulders. A tight-group foursome that still evoked a sense of belonging. Jesus. He'd be reaching for a hankie soon.

"I keep 'em up there to remind me what's important." John smiled and clapped him on the shoulder. "So if you're in some sort of bother, you only have to ask."

Thomas kneaded his forehead. How do you follow that? With the truth — most of it anyway — starting with the pick-up in Leeds, down to the silent phone calls in the flat. John listened, perfectly still, as if several grand in a rucksack was nothing new.

"Well, you know you can stay here, as long as you want. Terry or Sam can drop round the flat tomorrow and pick up some of your gear."

A nice idea, but not a solution. "Nah, I'll be fine once I get rid of the money." On cue, they both looked back into the bag.

"I s'pose it is real?"

Thanks, John; something else to obsess about.

John leaned back against his chair. "Okay, here's what I think. Stash the money in my safe for tonight and we'll consider the subject closed. You sleep on it and make sure you take some photos, as evidence."

Sound advice. When the deed was done, John let out a belch that would rival anything the Harwich ferry claxons could produce. "Better out than in. Right then," he clapped his hands together. "Let's go play some cards. I feel lucky!"

Everyone in the family knew that Diane was the cards maestro. Popular rumour — and the couple encouraged speculation — was that John and Diane had first met at a casino. One version ran that Diane was a croupier and John the hapless punter. Another, that John had played dumb to win her over — unlucky in cards and all that. The romantic in Thomas was happy to believe either.

He followed John into the living room. Lounges were something other people had — in smaller houses.

"Where's the bloody pizza — I'm starving. Thomas, do the honours will you; drinks and glasses in the usual place," John waved him past. The doorbell rang. "About time!" John roared over the chaos of chairs, crockery and glasses all moving simultaneously.

Diane looked over for an instant. "Thomas, be a dear and see to the door."

He passed four beer bottles over to Sam, mid-waltz, and headed for the door, wallet at the ready.

Miranda was stood before him, laden with pizzas. "Special delivery."

He stood at the door, doing the algebra in his head: sight + sore eyes = Miranda.

She deposited the pizza boxes on the hall table. "Mum said to come over; she was worried about you."

Must remember to up the size of Diane's Christmas present this year. He slipped his arms around her waist and pulled her close, breathing her in like oxygen. He was about to speak when she closed her mouth over his. She tasted of ripe cherries and vanilla again. He closed his eyes and lost himself in her scent, her touch, her sanctuary.

"Put him down, sis; some of us need food."

He felt her hand leave his back, probably to flip the finger at Sam. And then the heat of her smile against his face. He was safe, cocooned from the world in the bosom of the family: Miranda's family.

Chapter 14

The two strangers hunched down into their car seats a little more tightly to drive out the cold. The younger man rubbed his hands together, like a character straight out of Dickens.

"Can't you put the heater on, just for a little while?"

"Nikolai," the older man said in a disparaging tone, betraying the slightest trace of Mother Russia, "To be too comfortable would dull your senses. Have some more coffee if you wish."

"It's Nicholas — you know that," he scowled at the thermos flask by his feet, but didn't dare voice his displeasure openly.

The older man tutted and pressed the button for the dashboard clock. Within the next two hours, four identical snatch burglaries would take place across North London — starting now. "It is time," he opened his mouth wide to pronounce the name, "Ni—cho—las," ending with a malevolent hiss. "Take this and remember, he will be alone and unarmed."

The younger man made an audible gulp. He reached for the gun and held it flat in the palm of his hand, as if weighing the outcome of the enterprise.

"Only shoot if you have to, but try not to kill him. Such things attract the wrong kind of attention."

Nicholas put on a balaclava and slid out of the car, pistol thrust into his pocket. He padded across the street, a door-ram enforcer hanging at his side, scanning left and right like a night-time road safety ad. He mounted the steps in two stretches and paused at the door, listening for a television or a radio. It was unlikely that the owner would be awake at this hour; that gave him the element of surprise.

A prior visit to a similar property, a few streets away, had given him the dimensions of the flat and the distance to be covered inside. He let go of the gun and it sagged in his coat, spoiling the well-tailored lines. He swallowed hard, took a couple of steadying breaths then swung back the enforcer with both hands, penduluming into the door with an almighty crash.

The older man heard the sound and smiled in the semi-darkness. Two minutes at most. He hummed a little tune and flexed his gloved fingers like a concert pianist, calmly screwing in the silencer on the barrel. He released the car door and stepped outside in the chill of the early morning, resolved and unconcerned — no loose ends. A sound at the rear of the car caught his attention and as he turned, the handle of an automatic pistol smashed against his skull.

A finger pointed at the figure slumped on the pavement and then to the back of the car. The man on the ground yielded a low moan, which drew no one's sympathy. A canvas bag was placed on his head, hangman-style, and the body searched. The weapon was extracted and the body placed in the car boot. The leader directed his two colleagues with more hand gestures, and then crept across the street. He checked the safety on his pistol was off and nudged the door gently; the splinters of wood whined in protest. He stepped inside, keying his senses to the slightest sound or movement.

Nicholas was still in the living room, getting his bearings. He moved towards what should have been Thomas's bedroom and cocked his head, listening for breathing. The door was only pulled to, which gave him an extra second and a greater advantage. He grinned in the dark; his first field assignment was going like clockwork. Surprise, domination and victory — he heard the words in his head like a school motto. He flexed his shoulders to psych himself up even more, lifted the gun and rushed the door.

"Right!" he felt by the wall for the light switch. "Give me all your money — now!" The bed was empty; sheets neatly tucked in at the corners. "Shit!" he gasped aloud.

Before he could get out another word, a 9mm Browning pistol pressed tightly against his temple. "Don't even fucking think about it," Karl McNeill snarled into his ear.

Nicholas dropped his pistol as if it were molten lead. Karl slammed a knuckle ring into his face, smashing him to the floor. Then he knelt on his arms, ripping off the balaclava. Nicholas was barely conscious, which left little reason for the punches that followed. But Karl delivered them anyway.

"Karl, that's enough," a woman's hand pressed into his shoulder.

He eased himself up and turned to the man beside her. "Get him out of here and I want this damage cleared up pronto — call a team in." And even though he knew now that Thomas wasn't at the flat, he padded the rooms searching for him until Teresa ordered the stand-down. His hand smarted where the ring had cut into his own knuckle and the pulses of pain danced with the adrenaline tremor that ran through his body like a fever. "Where are you, Tommy Boy?"

Chapter 15

John Wright was already sorting out breakfast at six thirty in the morning, whistling a Beatles tune like John Lennon could never have imagined. Thomas walked into the kitchen and raised a nanosecond grin at the idea of John and Karl forming their own covers group — touring prisons to punish the inmates.

"Morning Thomas, what can I get you?"

It was a longstanding morning ritual. Diane liked a lie-in until seven-ish so John took her in the customary tea and toast. Thomas used to have a similar arrangement with Miranda, only his service was a little more personal. No Miranda today though — she'd left around eleven the previous night. Thomas conjured up the memory of her at the front door, like a child recalling their favourite Christmas.

"Tea and some toast would be great, thanks John."

"Are you sure about going into work today?"

He shrugged. What else could he do? The best thing would be to ring Christine, explain that he'd be late on-site and head over to Whitehall again to get it over with. He nodded at the thought — must ring Karl as well. That magic envelope had been burning a hole in his brain since he woke up; at least one mystery would be settled today.

Sam bounded into the kitchen while Thomas was still crunching toast. "No Miranda?" The youngest of the Wrights was as matter-of-fact about the whole Thomas-Miranda thing as the rest of the family. Ten years of will-they-won't-they had worn their expectations down to a smooth, frictionless finish.

"Nah, she went home last night." Thomas crunched his toast.

"Oh," Sam sounded disappointed for him. That made two of them.

* * *

When Sam dropped Thomas off at Barking station before eight, Thomas had the semblance of a plan. He'd make his calls and squat at Whitehall. Sir Peter would turn up eventually and, if he didn't, Thomas would wait it out. Maybe it wasn't very professional, but then nor was leaving someone holding a stack of money.

On the way down to the platform, he checked the mobile. Pat had sent a text thanking him for coming up — a technological first for her. And there was one voicemail alert. The call had come through in the small hours. Maybe Sir Peter was apologising? Unlikely, as he didn't have his personal number; at least, Thomas hadn't given it to him.

Standing on the stairway he jammed the phone against his ear, oblivious to the lava flow of people around him.

"Thomas, this is Karl — where the hell are you? Is everything all right? Ring me — it doesn't matter what time. Ring me immediately."

Thomas didn't waste any time.

"Tommo, thank God! Are you okay? Can you talk? Are you alone?" It was like a podcast of Question Time.

"I'm fine. I can talk for a sec — I'm about to get on a train. "

"Great, how long will it take you to get to St James's Park?"

"Fifty minutes, tops."

"Okay, I'll see you there. We've had a bit of a situation. And I'm afraid I've had to change your locks."

Karl rang off; Thomas stumbled down the steps in a daze. Change the locks? Why would someone need to get into his desk? The penny had dropped by the time he got down to the platform.

* * *

Karl was waiting by the ticket barriers, moving rhythmically from foot to foot. Thomas raised a hand and Karl dashed forward. "Am I glad to see you!"

"What's been going on, Karl?" Thomas stood, ignoring buffeting and abuse as people tried to move past or through him.

"Not here; let's walk," Karl escorted him out to the park. "We'll take a stroll to Marlborough Gate. They do great coffee and I'm buying."

He watched as Karl checked around them while they walked. It made a change for someone else to be twitchy. "All clues gratefully received."

"Oh right, I was forgetting. Tell you what, why don't you open that envelope I gave you."

Thomas passed the envelope over for Karl to examine. No reason, other than to see if Karl would check it, which he did. Karl handed it back and looked suitably pleased. Inside was a single page with four sentences, in Karl's own fair scrawl, which read:

1. FIRST THEY'LL TRY TO BRIBE YOU.

2. THEN THEY'LL LEAVE YOU WITH THE MONEY.

3. THEN THEY'LL ROB YOU.

4. NOW YOU'VE LOST THEIR MONEY, THEY OWN YOU.

Thomas read the note three times; he could see Karl scrutinising him out of the corner of his eye.

"So, Tommo," Karl sounded nervous; "Marks out of ten as a clairvoyant?"

He swallowed hard and folded the paper back into the envelope. "Spot on — for the first two."

Karl nodded and went off for the coffees. Thomas slumped on a bench and gazed out at the park, the sports bag containing the rucksack crushed between his legs. How the bloody hell could Karl have known what would happen? Two explanations came to mind. Either he was involved in this whole mind-game or he'd experienced something similar.

Karl returned, passing him a steaming cup. "It's Javanese, apparently. And lookie here," he rattled a paper bag, "muffins."

Thomas reached into the bag and squinted at Karl. "Can we cut to the chase? Am I in or not?"

Karl picked at a muffin and sent a piece arcing over to a waiting pigeon. "Rules first, Tommo. I will tell you as much as I can, but there has to be . . ."

Thomas didn't feel like accepting anyone else's rules today. "It happened to you as well, didn't it?" Okay, it was a bluff, but a reasonably deduced one.

"Uh-huh." Karl swigged back his coffee. "I was offered two grand, by way of an unaccountable surplus. You?"

"Four."

"Well, I suppose that's inflation for you!"

"And what did you do, Karl?"

"I took it — too right I did!"

Thomas choked on his coffee.

"Calm yourself, Tommo. I took it as evidence. All safely under lock and key somewhere. I wasn't smart enough to stay away for the night like you evidently were." Karl peered at him like he was a science exhibit. "No, but I rang ahead and had some old army pals let themselves in with a spare key. So when two thugs turned up to rob me of the readies, I had my own welcoming committee. Next day I turned up to the rendezvous with the cash, minus my £2k cut of course."

"And what happened to the two guys who came a-calling?"

Karl sipped at his coffee more slowly and stared into the distance. "You're better off not knowing."

Thomas felt dizzy, as if the park was closing in on him. He took a mouthful of sweet, doughy muffin and squeezed it down. "What happens now?"

"Well," Karl reached into his pocket then held a closed hand over Thomas's, "firstly, these are yours." He dropped three keys into Thomas's waiting palm. "Remember items two and three on my list? You had your own visitors last night and they weren't bringing you chocolates and flowers. Don't worry, the new door's top quality and nothing's been taken so there's no real harm done."

Are you taking the piss? "Except someone knows where I live."

Karl sighed. "Time to grow up, Tommy Boy. You wanted in — it goes with the territory. You can't expect to wander around in the dark without stepping in some shit."

"Thanks for that," he whistled into his coffee. "I'd better complete my delivery — I'll see you over at Harwich. We'll talk about this again."

"Indeed we will."

He binned the coffee carton and got up to go. The bag seemed heavier now, and so did life.

Karl called after him. "Cheer up, Tommo, you're in good company." His voice dropped a tone. "And listen, we don't discuss this on the job; we can't be sure it's safe there."

Thomas nodded and trudged off towards Whitehall, jingling his new door keys on their leprechaun key ring. His brain was in meltdown so he started small, one step at a time. First, he'd see what Sir Peter had to say about the money. Then he'd consider telling Karl about the tax disc on the red car. And then he'd reveal Bob Peterson's appearance at Harwich on the day of the shooting. It had all the makings of another fun-packed day.

He crossed back over the lake and followed the path to the gate. A police officer crossing the park stopped in her tracks and watched him as he moved about with his large sports bag. Mindful of the small matter of fifty-seven thousand pounds on his shoulder, he approached her, flashed his ID card and spun a line about looking for Main Building and being lost.

Outside the park, he noticed a sign for the Cabinet War Rooms and Churchill Museum. Ironic to think of Sir Peter Carroll's office, close by, with that painting behind his desk. Maybe he'd moved there for the souvenirs.

* * *

The same security staff faced Thomas as he entered the building; on a whim he saluted and they returned the compliment. They were more attentive now. All branches of the armed forces, potentially, supplied personnel for the SSU. But, like one of Karl's secret squirrel rules, people rarely volunteered where they'd come from. It used to drive him mad, but today, facing Whitehall's answer to the Spanish Inquisition, it suited him fine.

Soon he was in a lift with a different silent wonder as escort. His eyes drifted towards the escort's holstered weapon. The guard followed his gaze and tapped the holster confidently. Thomas decided to chance his luck.

"Browning — thirteen rounds," he paused for half a second; "Plus one in the chamber."

The guard smiled and relaxed. The soldier stood at ease. And all thanks to a quick round of Name That Gun.

"You were here yesterday, Mr Bladen?"

"Call me Thomas. Yeah, Sir Peter got called to a meeting; he asked me to come back today. I got some right stick about it at the office — I don't suppose anyone could tell me what his meeting was about so I can cover my arse?"

Soldier Boy smiled and shook his head. Thomas had thought it unlikely the guard would hand over a guest list, but it was worth a try. "If it helps any, Thomas, I know that Sir Peter left Main Building around eight pm. I escorted his chauffeur upstairs to collect some papers."

Thomas faked a smile to avoid sneering.

The escort knocked at the door and ushered Thomas inside. Sir Peter was up and out of his chair before Thomas had reached halfway across the plush carpet. "Thomas, my dear boy," Sir Peter grabbed his hand and shook it keenly. "I must apologise for yesterday. Simply unavoidable. Come take a seat."

Thomas sat down and waited. If in doubt, play it straight.

"So, how was your trip?"

"Fine, sir. Everything went to plan."

Sir Peter seemed to rise up from his chair a little. Thomas pressed his tongue against his lower teeth, rendering his face expressionless. He reached down to his bag and opened the zip, squeezing the handle to stop himself from shaking.

Sir Peter was very still, like a bloated cobra.

"Actually, there was one problem . . ." he kept his head bent forward. Nice and steady, Thomas, don't blow this. He lifted out the torn DSB from his rucksack in one fluid movement and thudded it down on the desk.

Sir Peter's mouth lowered about a foot. Thomas fancied that even Churchill behind him looked perturbed. "The DSB they provided me with was torn. I made them count the money out in front of me." That part at least was true.

Sir Peter stared at the sealed, torn DSB — the solid blocks of currency poking out like expensive building blocks in a substandard toy bag.

Thomas lifted his face level. "I'd prefer you check the contents, sir, if you don't mind." Chew on that, Winston.

Sir Peter broke the seal on the DSB and methodically stacked the currency on his desk. He counted the pile out loud, ending on 'fifty-seven.' "Yes, most impressive — I'd like you to accept a token of my appreciation."

The top two slabs were separated and slid halfway across the mahogany. Thomas had already considered the possibility of a second buy-off and decided what to do about it. "I really couldn't, sir — I was just doing my job."

Sir Peter sighed through his nose, as if he were deflating. Still a cobra, but not quite so bloated "Surely there must be a camera that you've had your eye on?" The old man wore an encouraging smile, like a disguise; his hand rested on the £2000, poised to push it forward.

Thomas didn't need a rethink; two grand could buy a whole lot of camera, it was true. But the two grand would also be buying him. And anyway, it would be suspicious to accept £2000 now when he'd turned down £4000 back in Leeds.

"I wouldn't feel right, sir. Besides," pause for big smile and grand finish, "there's no need."

Sir Peter returned the £2k to the pile and patted it affectionately. "Well done, Thomas, you've passed. It's a little test I have for when people show particular promise. I always knew my confidence in you wasn't misplaced."

He glanced over to the window, but there was no sign of a curly tail.

Chapter 16

He left Whitehall with a mixture of feelings. For all his bravado, he was really no further forward. There was too much going on. It was like playing several games of chess simultaneously — and losing them all.

Christine Gerrard had surprised him when he'd telephoned in, offering to drive him over to Harwich as soon as he was free. She'd gone on site for jobs in the past, but the timing was suspect to say the least.

Her Mercedes looked conspicuous by the underground station. He reached for the car door and breathed in a heady mixture of French perfume and the sound of Grieg. She smiled at him, but kept her sunglasses on.

He caught his perplexed look reflected in her face: Grieg. He wasn't big on classical music; it just wasn't something that floated his boat. But he'd always had a soft spot for Grieg; well, maybe not soft exactly. Grieg had been the musical accompaniment to a backwoods romp with Christine in this very car. He brushed the leather seat for an instant, lost in the memory of flesh against hide.

She drove off before his seatbelt was on and he waited for his underwear to settle before he spoke. "Thanks for the lift." Hardly repartee of the decade. Funny thing about

Christine; it took him time to thaw around her. Partly the whole 'my boss is my ex' thing and partly because they both knew he'd been an absolute dickhead when they'd split up. It was as if she held a silent moral victory over him.

Eventually Christine removed her glasses; she looked tired.

"Everything alright, Chrissie?"

She shrugged. "Let's talk about something else."

He steered the conversation to safer waters, encouraging talk about her parents, their fancy horses and their fancy house. Then he listened as she recited the genealogy of their prize nags, with bloodlines going back a hundred years. It was the only topic where Christine ever really seemed to come alive, and by Harwich he felt he knew every horse personally.

A text from Miranda came through as they neared the port; she'd got him the new details for the red car's owner, based on the tax disc. He shut the mobile off afterwards.

"Secret admirer?" Christine looked piqued.

He mustered a hangdog expression. "No, more's the pity. Unless Karl counts?" He pressed his hand into the upholstery.

"I had it professionally cleaned," she shot him down in flames.

Yeah, but for whose benefit?

She parked the Merc at Harwich and they sat for a while, windows down, saying nothing. Christine seemed on the brink of speaking a couple of times, but somehow never crossed the line. He watched the gulls at play and wondered what would have happened if he hadn't been so attentive that first day. He knew the answer already — everything would still have happened, just without him knowing.

"Did you turn down the training because of me, Thomas?"

What? "No," he yawned and stretched in the seat. "It's just not my style."

She crinkled her nose. "Surely you don't want to do this your whole life?"

He felt the smile rise across his face. "It'll do for now. Time I was getting back to work." He led and she followed, which almost made him nostalgic. The stairwell harboured old packing material and a fire extinguisher that had seen better days. Good for Christine to see where they'd ended up. They climbed the stairs and he found himself whistling Grieg. As they rounded the last corner she gave him a quick jab in the back and he stopped.

"Ah, so you've brought my boy home!" Karl set down the remains of a baguette.

Thomas braced himself for her reaction to the mess, but she wrong-footed him and went over to Karl. "Thomas has been given additional clearance . . ."

Since when?

". . . He'll be accompanying you on the next out-of-hours pick-up. See that he's briefed when the time comes."

"Will do," Karl's tone bordered on reverential.

She touched Thomas on the shoulder as she left. "And Karl, clean this place up; it looks like a pigsty."

"Ma'am," Karl replied.

They both played statues until Christine's footsteps faded from earshot.

"What the hell was that about?" Thomas almost tripped on the words.

"It's called playing the game, Tommo."

* * *

"Is it a pint for you, Tommy Boy?" Karl hadn't come to life until the evening.

"Uh-huh." His brain ached with the effort of thinking; competing thoughts echoed back and forth.

Karl returned with beer and crisps. Karl loved crisps; maybe it was his Irish genes — Thomas had been afraid to suggest. "Right then," Karl ripped open two crisp bags and spread them on the table, "now we can talk!"

Best start off with an easy one. "So, is Christine in the know?"

Karl crammed a handful of cheese and onion into his mouth and filled the gaps with beer. He sat for a moment, a look of contentment on his face. Then he chewed thoughtfully and swallowed. "Is she bollocks! But she thinks she is, which has its uses. Of course, you'll know about her family — rather well connected. Confidentially," he snatched another clutch of crisps, "I think she finds the idea of all the cloak-and-dagger stuff a bit of a turn-on."

Thomas hurriedly dived into his drink.

"But never forget, Tommo, there is a dagger. My advice? Tell Christine nothing; she'll follow orders. Whereas we, amigo, we're the cloak within a cloak."

Now seemed like a good time to share the red car's true registration, seeing as how they were amigos and all.

"I'll look into it," Karl promised.

"No need; I've got the details here," he passed over a beer mat with small, neat handwriting on it.

"My, my, private sleuthing — how very enterprising. How about we check it out this weekend — if you're free?"

Thomas smiled; Karl was very good at this. In only a few words, Karl had acknowledged that he had his own sources, decided the next step and sniffed around his weekend plans. "Fine by me, Karl." He put down his pint. "Now, tell me more about who ruined my door and how you managed to stay one step ahead of all this."

Karl bowed at the table. "You see, you're a bit of an odd fish, Mr Bladen. You're not ex-forces, but you're secretive and wonderfully unambitious. As you'll recall, I originally had you down as a mole for another outfit. Like as not, other people think the same. So when Ms Crossley said you were wanted by the big cheese, and you said you'd got a free ticket up north, I put two and two together. I'm guessing there was a ripped DSB waiting for you?"

Thomas raised a glass to him, recalling the comedy of errors in Leeds.

"It's standard MO from what I can tell. Not sure how Sir Peter slots into all this. Anyhow, the difference in my case was that Crossley found out I'd taken the £2000 — I still don't know how."

"And my visitors?"

"Well, they weren't selling The Watchtower. The newbie was sent in and the seasoned pro was waiting outside, across the street." Karl's voice dropped away as if he were considering how to continue the sentence.

"How did you . . .?"

"Let's just say I try to prepare for all eventualities. I won't kid you, Tommo, they meant business; they had guns."

Thomas touched his hand to his mouth then felt stupid about it.

Karl raised an index finger. "Of course, they don't have them anymore — I have them safely in my box, with the others!" He winked and took another gulp from his glass. "If you'd feel more comfortable I can let you have a piece of equipment for home."

Thomas blinked twice very slowly, as if that would somehow refocus the picture. But it was already becoming horribly clear.

Chapter 17

Thomas flicked another page of the novel and glanced out the windscreen; there was still nothing to see. Just an ordinary street — typical Saturday morning tedium. Every breath drew in the stench of orange combined with petrol. But at least he was past the gagging stage. Karl had his feet on the dashboard and a tabloid open across his legs with a bag of crisps in his lap — quite the multitasker.

Thomas shut his paperback. "So why are we staking this house out?"

Karl interrupted the pen moustache he was lovingly adding to a topless model. "It goes like this," he held up a loose fist in preparation.

Thomas mentally rehearsed a suitably impressed face.

"Thinking this through logically, all we know about the car is two things. One," Karl's index finger shot up like a nose-picker, "the red car probably held the shooter at Harwich. And two," his middle finger rose up to join it, "Ann Crossley had the victim's van taken away — now why would she do a thing like that?"

Thomas shrugged; it sounded like Karl had it all figured out anyway.

"Before we go in with our size nines, we need to know a little bit about the car and its owner. So we require a plausible reason to go knocking on their door."

Thomas nodded. "Seems reasonable."

Karl shifted his crisps and folded the newspaper. "But you know what seems unreasonable, Tommo? Why wouldn't you report the number plate to your superiors? And check this — surely the false number plate will eventually flag up somewhere on CCTV and be checked?"

Thomas felt his mouth drying out, like a lazy dog in the heat. "Then why exactly are we here now, Karl?"

"We," Karl stared at him intently, "are a team within a team. Which means what we're doing today doesn't get back to Christine — strictly off the record. And you, my mystery man, need to tell me what I'm missing. Because I know there's something."

Thomas pushed back into the passenger seat, increasing the scent of oranges. "Right . . ." he drew out the word to epic proportions, making it sound like three separate words, "time to come clean. Remember on the day of the shooting, when I asked you how many spotter teams were on?"

"Aye, so I do."

"Well, I saw someone with field binoculars, down in the car park. He was watching the ferry; and as soon as the shooting went off, he scarpered, pronto."

"Interesting," Karl tried to refold his newspaper, gave up and then scrunched it behind him to the back seat. He went back into stare mode.

"I managed to take pictures of the car number-plate and the driver. But there's a complication."

Karl opened one hand flat as if demanding the pay-off.

"The watcher was Bob Peterson, no question." The inside of the car reverberated with sighs.

"Well, you're obviously in the right job; you're a one-man secret service, so you are."

"Wait; you haven't heard the complication. I doctored the watcher out of my mosaic photo for my report — before I was certain who it was. I wanted to check it out on the quiet. Christine wouldn't have known any different but..."

Karl grinned and waved a hand up like a zealous schoolboy. "But Bob Peterson must have shat a brick when he heard that you took mosaic shots. Especially when he saw the mosaic from that morning and found he wasn't in it!"

"Yeah, you could say that."

When Karl set it all out before him, he didn't feel quite so impressive.

"So, what then? Uncle Bob tries some damage limitation? Offers you executive training, but you don't bite. Then you get sent to Leeds for the Cashback Challenge."

He considered that. "I wasn't sent by Bob though; Sir Peter Carroll... so it must follow that Bob Peterson spoke to the old man."

"Hang on, Tommy; if Ann Crossley was on the ground with a spotter team, then why does Uncle Bob need to be there at all?"

Thomas opened his mouth to speak, but Karl silenced him with two more raised fingers. "Because, Dr Watson, either something different was due to go down that day or the shooting was planned and Peterson was supposed to report back afterwards."

Thomas ran a thumbnail between his teeth. "Dr Watson?"

"Come on, Tommo, give me some credit. I've seen a battered copy of Sherlock Holmes poking out of your coat on at least two occasions — I'm no stranger to the great man myself, I might add. It should be recommended reading for the spy about town."

Thomas felt a chill. "And is that what you are, Karl — a spy?"

"Now, you know as well as I do that the Surveillance Support Unit merely assists the work of government agencies, including the security services." Karl raised an eyebrow. It's been documented in Prime Minister's Question Time."

Round and round in circles. Thomas was fast acquiring the mother of all headaches. "So now what?"

"Now, we give the good people at number 129 a wake-up and shake-up call. If you'll excuse me . . ." Karl rescued his mobile from a collection of old car park tickets and chocolate wrappers. Then he pulled out a photocopy of a car magazine classifieds page, with one ad circled and several others crossed out. Thomas gave it the once over; he'd never heard of the title. Karl looked extra pleased with himself. "All my own handiwork — see, I can use computers too! This was my back-up plan; and as sod all has happened in the last hour and a half, we might as well go with that."

"I don't get it."

"Watch and learn, Tommy Boy. Read me the phone number off the ad, will you? If no one answers, we'll have to pay the house a visit." Karl dialled and his voice morphed into leafy Sussex. "Ah yes, hello, I'm ringing about the hatchback — is it still available?" He nodded to Thomas at the reply. "Really? Are you sure — I have the ad here in front of me. Well, that is very strange. What a pity; I was planning to pay cash."

Thomas watched the lines furrow on Karl's face like a well-ploughed field. It seemed all might not be going to plan.

"Yes, I was in South London anyway. Erm, well, that . . . er . . . might be interesting. I certainly appreciate the offer. Well, naturally, what the tax man doesn't know!" Karl faked a laugh that would have been at home in Uckfield. Let's say, what, ten thirty? I'll just get a pen. One moment . . ."

Karl held a hand loosely above the mouthpiece and looked away, out the window. ". . . Jessica, Daddy's on the telephone. Go and join Mummy by the till." He lifted his hand free. "Sorry about that. Right, fire away."

Thomas winced — poor choice of words. He watched Karl cradle the mobile under his neck and jot down the address he already knew, on a space near the fake ad.

"That's lovely. Ten thirty it is then. Oh, yes of course: it's . . . Bob Jefferson." Karl went to drop the mobile back into its nest then thought better of it and dialled a number from memory. "It's Karl. I need some money — a couple of grand should suffice. Okay, make it three; and a smart jumper, and a pair of driving gloves. Looks like I'm buying the car. No, I understand. Yes, he's here with me now."

Thomas blanched.

"I'll be at the café on Jerome Street — call me when you're ready. Quick as you can, please." Karl cut the call. "Well, Mr Bladen, seems like you're my lucky charm — that's a turn up for the books. You'll have to drive this back yourself." He beamed like a cherub who'd just won a card game. "Café time — and the apprentice spy always pays."

Thomas watched as Karl tucked into his all-in-one breakfast with gusto. It looked like three breakfasts, all in one. Not that the portion size seemed to slow Karl any. Thomas, on the other hand, was finding that a conscience wreaked havoc on his appetite so he played safe with a large mug of tea and a meagre two eggs on toast. He jabbed at the eggs so that they bled yellow and swept the plate with toast, sluicing the yellow into ketchup. "What about the family with the car?"

Karl managed to cram sausage, bacon and beans into his mouth, and still talk. "The car may give us something useful, but the family is our best lead, so we'll keep a watchful eye."

Thomas set his mug down. "That's not what I meant."

Karl's mobile rang, breaking the deadlock. He checked the number, didn't pick up. "That's me away — I'll not be long. Don't let them take my plate."

Thomas was speed-dialling Miranda before the glass door had finished rattling. He gazed past a window sticker featuring a dancing sandwich, out to a grey Saturday morning. "It's Thomas. Listen, what are you up to this weekend?"

Miranda ran through her schedule at Caliban's, running on into a visit to the gym and a DVD at home. He didn't interrupt; he was happy just to hear some normality. "I might have a date Sunday evening, but we can meet during the day if you like?"

Ouch. He rubbed a thumb across his chest, as if testing a wound. Served him right for making assumptions. "Right, yeah," he smarted. "Tomorrow daytime it is, then." He felt his face tightening. No one spoke for a good ten seconds.

"You're such a dick. Of course I'm free — unless I get a decent offer today at Caliban's?"

He blew a breath down the phone: stand-down from DEFCON 3. His jaw unwound into a smile. "So I'll maybe see you later — or tomorrow." They both laughed at how crap he still was at all this. He felt like a fish that's hooked and reeled, thrown back after a few panicky gasps, but unable to resist the lure again.

"Goodbye, Thomas!"

He parked his breakfast and acted as Lord Protector when the waitress made a play for Karl's leftovers. Could you even call yourself a waitress turned out in headphones and ripped jeans that showed your underwear?

The café door pinged; in walked Karl nouveau — V-neck sweater and driving gloves. "Ta da!"

Thomas gawped, couldn't help it. "What are you supposed to be?"

Tonight," Karl slid back on to his vinyl chair, "I'm going to be . . ."

Thomas didn't give him the satisfaction. "So," he reached for his second mug of tea, "did you get the other thing?"

"All safely on board," Karl reassured him, squeezing his jacket pocket as he folded it by his feet. "Anyways, let's saddle up. I want to put them on the back foot when I'm there, so you ring me on the mobile — family emergency — in say, six minutes." Karl winked and Thomas narrowed his eyes as he sipped his tea. Karl looked affronted; his fork stalled above his plate. "What?"

The tea didn't help Thomas's mood. "You're very good at this."

Karl swooped down a fork, scraping the plate. "This," Karl whispered like a gas leak, "from the man who takes secret photos and does his own background checks on Bob Peterson. You're pretty good yourself," he took a bite, ". . . for an amateur."

Thomas raised his mug: touché. He left Karl to his washing-machine impression and went to find the gents. The waitress lip-read his request and flicked her finger towards a door with a hazard sign on it. Number one for customer service. He nodded his thanks and tried not to stare at her t-shirt, emblazoned with: 'Don't even think about it.'

Karl walked up to the house, glancing at the red estate in the drive, which he noted had been cleaned. A pity, but the forensics team were on standby so there was always hope. He rang the doorbell and straightened his jacket, making sure his sweater was proudly on display. If you could be proud of a golfer's reject.

He heard a brief exchange on the other side of the glass, aware he was a good fifteen minutes ahead of schedule. Then silence, and the door opened about a foot wide. "Bob Jefferson, we spoke on the phone — I managed to get away sooner. Jessica's being difficult so my wife dropped me off a little early. I hope that's okay?"

The woman smiled faintly. She looked tired. "Here's the ad I mentioned," he showed her the photocopy and waited while she studied it, right down to the shopping list he'd added at the bottom in blue felt tip.

She passed it back and nodded. "Won't you come in?" He clocked the accent — not a native South Londoner. Probably an incomer, the sort who called Streatham St Reatham or described Balham as 'just off the Kings Road.'

* * *

A man came down the stairs. It had to be a man, judging by the heavy footfalls. "Hello."

Karl's trained ear registered the slight twang on the second syllable.

The woman tensed, turning to her husband. He led from there. "We are keen for a quick sale. You mentioned cash on the phone? Let me show you the car and we can discuss the price."

Brief and to the point. The wife — she had the ring on — picked up her child and opened the door again. Karl played for time and went into a long spiel about his niece looking for a car to drive across France with friends from Uni. And how the friend with the car had dropped out and they were looking for a hatchback, but a car like this was really far more practical. He loved this part, getting into character, spinning a yarn and seeing where it took him, always with one eye on the bigger picture.

He let the seller see that he knew nothing about cars, asked a nonsense question about transverse engines and checked whether it took diesel or lead-free. The seller warmed to him, or his ignorance — same thing really. It was a classic con: let the victim think they're conning you; it rarely failed.

Karl's mobile chimed in, with a TV ring-tone so awful that he almost cringed himself. He made the obligatory embarrassed face. "Yes, hello darling; I'm looking at it now — you know I think Beatrice would love it. No, we're still discussing the details. I won't be long. Can't you just keep Jessica settled? Well, I can just join you at home, can't I — if she's really that bad."

He faked a huge sigh. "Right. Yes, I understand. Just give her sips of water. I'll be as quick as I can. No, no, you stay there — I'll drive over." He paused, as if suddenly aware of his mistake. "I'll, er, make my own way back." He switched off his mobile and did his best impression of the word 'agitated.'

The husband laid a hand on his shoulder. "Children are a constant worry because they are our precious jewels." He then started the car up and let Karl try out the driving seat.

Karl managed to shave £50 off the asking price and insisted they shook hands on the deal. All very proper — minus the receipt — and in record time.

They stood at the window and watched him back down the drive. He paused to wave and wondered, just out of devilment, how long they would wait there. By the look on their faces as he glanced up for the final wave they'd have waited forever, just to see him gone. He drove to the corner and flashed his lights for Thomas to follow him in his own car; mission accomplished.

* * *

Thomas had nurtured a faint hope that Karl would guide him to some secret bat-cave lair, but it was short-lived. After a twenty-minute drive through Saturday traffic, Karl led him instead to a supermarket car park. Tucked away in a far corner, a woman was waiting by a silver Ford. Karl parked a few spaces away and Thomas followed suit.

"Tommo, you remember Teresa."

She smiled, as if she knew something about him that he hadn't disclosed. He resolved to quiz Karl, some other time, about what that might be.

"Good work Karl. Nice to see you again, Thomas."

And that was that. Karl handed over a package — Thomas figured it was the remainder of the money, plus the gloves and the jumper. Then they got into Karl's car and left the scene. In the wing mirror he saw someone else get out of the Ford and walk around the red estate. Karl glanced towards him, not the slightest bit interested.

"Not our problem, Tommo; our part is done."

"No point my asking who Teresa works for, I suppose?"

"None at all!" Karl chuckled, and Thomas wondered if Karl even knew himself.

Chapter 18

Thomas pressed the intercom button and stared up at the CCTV camera. He hated being this side of the lens, always had. Too many childhood memories of his dad telling him to 'stand up straight' and 'at least try to look like you're enjoying yourself.' It was probably why he'd got into photography in the first place — to regain a degree of control.

"Why, Mr Bladen, what a pleasant surprise!" Sheryl's nasal tones smacked of a cheesy New York cop series.

He turned his face from the camera and listened hard for the steps down the back staircase. The fire door released and Sheryl stood before him, leaning against the doorframe, pop video style. She looked him up and down. "Great to see you, Thomas."

He rolled his shoulders self-consciously. Was she attractive? Absolutely. To use a Karl-ism: she could probably wake the dead in their trousers. And boy did she know it. She probably had an exclusion order from the mortuary. And the clincher, for ten points — was he interested? Not for a second.

Maybe that's why she played so easy to get. It didn't help that his defence was to close down. That seemed to make her try even harder to get a reaction. He liked to think that Miranda put her up to it — for sport — but he worried, deep down, that it was just Sheryl. Male customers loved it of course. A little piece of authentic Brooklyn right before their eyes; and Sheryl was the little piece.

He thought about the morning's activities as he followed her upstairs, mainly to distract himself from her backside; the sucking and popping of Sheryl's trademark chewing gum punctuated their journey up to the office. She had once told him that she chewed gum to keep her mouth moist and supple. He'd never felt the same way about spearmint again.

* * *

Miranda was busy looking at colour swatches. "Hey, you're a man. What do you think of this?" She held up a colour card with a thumb across it.

"It looks like lilac."

"What an insightful eye for detail. I can see why you're drawn to the camera. Fancy a coffee?"

Sheryl took her cue and slinked past him, timing a bubble pop by his face.

"I don't know why you get so uptight around Sheryl; she likes you."

"Maybe that's what I'm uptight about."

"Lighten up, Thomas, and don't flatter yourself; it's just her way. I can see you find her attractive so what's the big deal? Blimey, if I was a man, I'd fancy her."

"I never said I fancied her."

Out the corner of his eye he could see Sheryl's jeans straining as she walked away.

"Anyway, what have you been up to today?" She was still staring down at the mass of colour charts and strips of material. But Thomas had played this game before.

"Oh, nothing much. I, er, went to help someone buy a car."

"Really? Terry and Sam could have got you a good deal. Anyone I know?"

He paused for maybe a couple of seconds; a couple of seconds too long. "Just someone from work."

Miranda didn't turn, but her back arched forward just that little bit more. Then she slapped a hand on the desk and Thomas felt the three-minute warning go off.

"Why don't you just ask, Miranda?"

"Because I'm not sure I'd like the answer."

Sheryl returned and placed the coffee mugs beside Miranda. "Um, I hope this isn't a bad time." Sarcasm dripped off every syllable.

Thomas could almost feel the heat from Miranda's glare. Maybe that was why he was sweating. Miranda looked up at Sheryl, completely unfazed. "Just a few issues with trust."

"Miranda!" Sheryl raised her eyebrows and tut-tutted dramatically. "You can't trust men, honey — you know that."

Thomas looked daggers at her as she left the arena. But she just winked at him again and mouthed: 'she loves you really.' At least, that's what it looked like. It could have been 'she loves you rarely.'

"Jesus, Thomas, why did you have to take that bloody job?"

He moved behind her, gazing at the back of her neck; that smooth, lightly tanned neck that he loved to run his lips over. He laid a finger on her skin and traced a river, enjoying the familiar tingle that ran up and down his spine and settled in his groin. Miranda shrugged free.

"Knock it off; I'm not in the mood. I'm serious. Why would you want to go and do a job like that — and hide it from me?"

Tread carefully, he told himself; don't answer too quickly. This is an exam level question — and it's pass or fail, with no retakes.

"Do I need to remind you? I took the Civil Service job so we could work near each other. And not long after that you decided to call it quits."

They reached for their coffees and he noticed that her mug read 'The Boss' while his was 'The Hired Hand.' Nice one, Sheryl.

"Be honest, Thomas; neither of us was happy with the way things were."

He drew back, cradling his mug. "I was happy."

She gave it a second's consideration. "Bullshit. You just couldn't stand the thought of me being with anyone else." When she said it like that, it sounded like a bad thing. "And let's not forget we'd split up at least once before then."

Ah yes, the infamous drought of '97 to '98. "So that's why you went to Bermuda — for a whole year?"

She didn't flinch, didn't even break her stride. "I needed breathing space — we both did. The only difference is, you used yours to get off with Christine at work."

'Get off with' wasn't the term she normally used. But hey, Sheryl was only next door, like as not listening to every word. Not that he cared too much what Sheryl thought.

He resisted comment. Resisted mentioning that Miranda had hardly taken a vow of chastity over in Bermuda — or when she returned. Time to tone things down a bit. "Why are we having this conversation?"

"Because you're shutting me out, Thomas. Mum was in a real flap about you, that night at the house — I know you talked to Dad about something. You used to confide in me. Well, I thought you did — before I discovered your secret life." She put her face right in front of his.

Jesus; Sheryl must be lapping this up.

"And remember how we first got together? I trusted you. I told you about that scumbag, Butch Steddings;

about the way he was coming on to me to do his dodgy photos."

"I know," he felt his knuckles itching, partly from outrage and the lingering memory of lamping Butch. The haunted look in her eyes brought him back with a bump. He put a hand to her cheek. "But this is different, Miranda."

"No it's not. You're frightened, Thomas. I know you. Is it that Irish bloke?"

"No," he took a breath, tried it again more confidently. No, it's not Karl."

"Well what then?"

It could have been the reflection of the strip light, making her eyes glisten like that. He pressed his hand against her face, felt the warm flesh against his fingertips and wished she could understand by osmosis.

"I'm not gonna leave this alone, Thomas. And don't think I give a shit what Sheryl hears. So either you tell me now or we are going to have a major falling out." She sighed, and leaned a little against his hand. "If you can't be honest with me, then I've got no room for you in my life — it's your call."

There was steel behind those blue eyes. He picked up the reference straight away. When she'd returned from Bermuda, he'd told her about Christine. Then Miranda had got involved with some city trader, probably just to piss him off — which it had. Worse, the stockbroker believed in spreading his options. As soon as Miranda found out, she'd dropped him like a lead weight. Once Thomas had showed her evidence of a wife.

He felt ashamed that it had come to this. Miranda was probably bluffing — she'd come around in a few days or a week or so. But . . . but he'd have to tell her sometime. He took another deep breath. "Two blokes turned my flat over while I was at your parents' place. They were hardcore — after some money they thought I had. They smashed my door and they came tooled up."

Miranda paled. "Is this to do with Karl?"

"Not like that! Karl took care of it; he was looking out for me."

Miranda brushed his hand away. "Maybe I should speak to Karl, then."

"No, don't do that." Too quick, too edgy; he knew she'd pick up on it.

"So what do I do, then, Tom?" She never called him Tom, not since Leeds and Butch Steddings.

"Just be yourself. The same loveable pain in the arse you always are."

"Flattery'll get you nowhere."

He didn't believe that.

She put her arms around him. He leaned in and squeezed her back towards him, as if he could dissolve her flesh into his.

"Well you better not make any more enemies, Thomas Bladen. Because if anyone messes with you, they'll answer to me."

He didn't doubt that for a second.

He finished his coffee and pretended to be interested in her colour schemes. Then he made his excuses and headed for home, alone — probably for the best. He picked up a Chinese on the way, and a carton of milk — company for the old one seeking asylum in his fridge. He wondered if Karl had similar relationship problems? Was there even anyone special in his life? Special — Karl would piss himself at that.

The TV had little to offer so he dived back into the pile of DVDs towering on the floor. Something edifying and life-affirming — Shaun of the Dead, the perfect accompaniment to prawn chow mein and special fried rice. Miranda had long since educated him on the perils of factory-farmed chicken, but he figured it would be pretty hard to do much to a prawn other than catch and eat it.

It was a great film; he'd seen it before at the cinema with Miranda. But the joy of DVDs — for him, anyway —

was the extra features. How it was done, deleted scenes, notes on cinematography and special effects. Sometimes all that was better than the actual film.

Some time after ten, he gave up the ghost and turned off the DVD. The TV channel kicked back into life at way past a reasonable volume. He dropped it down a few notches on the level and did a double take. Sir Peter Carroll was on screen — large as twenty-two-inch life — pontificating about some political debacle.

It was too good a chance to pass up on. He reached over and dialled Karl.

"Hello?"

"Karl, it's Thomas. Quick, turn on the TV — our beloved leader's doing a turn."

"I know; I'm watching it already. How sad is that!" There was a pause. "Is everything okay, Tommo? Only you've rung me on your landline — you've never done that before. Are you going all touchy-feely on me?"

He took a breath, remembering he was number withheld on all his calls. They watched Sir Peter run rings around the other guests on the late night current affairs programme. Even the presenter was no match for the double-talk, counter-pointing and justifications. It was like seeing Freddie the Fox perform a gig at the henhouse.

Karl, who followed politics more closely — i.e. more than almost no interest whatsoever — offered his own comments and managed to predict a couple of Sir Peter's responses.

Thomas had only caught the tail end of the programme and after fifteen minutes, Karl was humming the national anthem tunelessly as the studio lights dimmed.

"So, Tommo, what's on your mind?"

"I dunno, Karl. These last weeks; I'm starting to lose the plot."

"Now that I don't believe for a second! What's really bothering you?"

"How do you cope with it, Karl?" he eased his shoes off and flexed his feet. "All the secrecy and the pretence and the—"

"Lies," Karl chipped in. "That's would be the word you're looking for. It's the price you pay for knowing. And once you know, things are never the same again."

"For a second there, you almost went into The Matrix."

"Aye, it's not a bad analogy. Only it's debatable whether we're the dudes in black vinyl, or Agent Smith. Listen, do you fancy getting together tomorrow — I'll meet you at midday, same tube station."

"Yeah, that's sounds good. Thanks mate."

"No problem. By the way, I'm glad you rang actually. Don't make plans for next weekend — we're working. I'll tell you all about it when I see you."

"What?" he sat bolt upright on the settee. "No, tell me now."

"I don't think so; phones have ears. Good night, Thomas."

* * *

Sir Peter Carroll's Daimler glided away from Television Centre. The roar of the traffic seemed to echo the applause of the studio audience. Even his opponents had congratulated him on his mastery of the subtleties of the situation.

He swirled his whisky glass and let the aroma pervade his senses. Outside, the streetlights and car lights prismed against the tinted windows. He checked his watch and smiled.

As soon as he reached for the phone, his chauffeur raised the glass screen. Sir Peter waited until the screen sealed him off before he dialled the first number, even though Trevor had been with him for years.

"Ah, good evening. I wish to get a message to Yorgi. Ask him to ring me tomorrow on the office number. He'll know who it is."

The woman sounded fearful at the mention of Yorgi's name. In the background he heard a man's voice — it could have been Yorgi, but he doubted it. No matter, he had no interest in Yorgi's personal life. He closed the call and settled his glass. Then, phone still in hand, he lifted an address book from his blazer pocket: 'P' for Peterson.

"Robert? Oh, yes, if you would, thank you. Ah, Robert, it's Sir Peter. You did? Why, thank you! Now, Robert, I'm ringing for an update on the Harwich consignment. Yes, I saw that you'd put Crossley on to it. Good, definitely a step in the right direction. I think we'll be ready to move soon, now that we've got the full team on board. Long time coming — indeed! Have Crossley get an update, first thing Monday. Capital! Now, what's the latest on the poor driver?" He scrawled down some notes and put an asterisk against Ann Crossley's name.

"Right. Send Crossley to my office Monday morning — she can update me there." He ended the call and tucked the address book back in his blazer. He signalled to Trevor that the screen could be lowered. Then, he dialled home.

"Yes, hello darling. Really? It was good of you to watch. No, don't wait up; you know how these things work. The PM likes us seniors to take every opportunity to make friends with the media. I'll be back late — I'll use the spare room. Night, night." He stared out at the blurred lights of London and his smile reflected back in the glass like a malign crescent. "Trevor, I think I'll drop in to The Victory Club."

The chauffeur nodded; Sir Peter enjoyed the deferential bob of his head. It was the little touches that made Trevor such a treasure. Their eyes met in the mirror. "Very good, Sir Peter."

He reached for his whisky and smiled again. If tonight's girl at The Victory was anything like the last one Yorgi had provided, it would be.

Chapter 19

"You've got to be able to trust your instincts, Tommo," Karl swivelled left and right at the first click of the target turning face on. "Do you want a go — it's not so different from taking high-speed photos. Okay, maybe with nine mills instead of a data-card. But the principle's the same."

There's a comfort. All those years that Thomas thought he'd been honing his camera skills he'd actually been secretly training to be Super Shooter. The idea played in his head like a disturbing version of The Karate Kid: wax on, wax off, and reload.

Karl laid his pistol down. "So, I'll save you the trouble of avoiding the topic of next weekend. We're away to Suffolk for a pick-up."

"And is this for our side or their side, or doesn't it matter?"

"See, Tommo, I told you that you'd get the hang of it eventually!" Karl grinned like an idiot. "But seeing as you've asked, this is a special request from our beloved leader."

"Dress code: casual?" Thomas straightened an imaginary tie.

"Dress code: damp-proof — we'll get kitted out from Stores on the Friday, before we leave work. You're going to be the water baby."

They spent less than an hour on the range. As Karl reminded him, time flies when you're firing guns. Afterwards in the café, Thomas scanned the horizon for Teresa. Someone as organised as Karl would be sure to have arranged a meeting.

"Relax, Tommo. She'll be here presently."

He picked at the pastry crumbs on his plate. So they were doing Sir Peter's private dirty work — and look where that got him last time.

Teresa made a play of waving as she came over, but she looked agitated. "Things have moved forward unexpectedly."

Even Karl seemed a little put out.

"There was a disturbance at the target house last night. A neighbour called the police and an ambulance out, to a domestic. It seems Yorgi went ballistic — if you'll forgive the phrase — when he came back and found the car was missing."

Thomas felt like raising a hand, to remind them he was still there. "Who's Yorgi?"

Karl and Teresa gave him the kind of look that made him wish he wasn't. "Our likely Harwich shooter," Teresa explained, glancing at Karl.

"He has a name," Thomas said slowly, reciting his thought aloud.

"And a reputation to go with it," Teresa replied.

Thomas kept quiet now while the grown-ups talked, picking up the odd snippet, here and there. Yorgi was evidently a big shot — again with the puns — and Teresa's report suggested he had left the country after the incident.

He felt his mind start to drift — funny how things bobbed to the surface when you weren't concentrating. Now that he thought about it, he'd never seen any photographs from the year Miranda spent in Bermuda.

Well, okay, a few 'here I am at the beach' pics, but no proper work photos of any kind. His mood soured; he tried to tune back into the conversation, just to escape himself.

"So what do you think, Thomas? Could you speak to them?" Teresa had lowered her voice.

"I'm sorry?"

Teresa and Karl both eased forward towards him. Teresa was still in the big chair. "With Yorgi away, this is our best chance to make contact with the brother again and offer him a lifeline — think you're up to it?"

Thomas could feel their eyes on him like sunlamps and sensed his face smouldering. "I can try." Jesus, he wasn't even convincing himself.

"Top man!" Karl patted him on the shoulder. "Right, come on then, Tommo; no time like the present."

Teresa sat in the back of Karl's car. The scent of oranges was starting to fade; now it was more Earl Grey tea than breathable vitamin C.

"So what do I say, exactly? I mean, what am I allowed to tell them?" It was the third time of asking — different ways, but the same question. Karl looked ready to pop a vein.

"For fuck's sake, Tommo! We've been through this. They let a gunman use their car as a sniper's post. And we've got the car now. There's not a lot to say."

Maybe Karl was right to be pissed off. When Thomas heard himself, he sounded like an amateur — well, he was an amateur.

Teresa played peacemaker. "All we're trying to do is offer them protection — if they want it. Let them know that there's help available. But don't spook them."

Karl hardly looked at Thomas for the rest of the journey. It reminded him of Ajit, back at school, when he'd been accusing Thomas of something, but wouldn't come right out and say it.

As they parked up, Teresa handed Thomas a scrap of paper. "Tell them they can ring here at any time, if they need us."

He nodded and gripped the note tightly, casting a last, quizzical look at Karl as he opened the car door.

* * *

Teresa waited until Thomas was at least five cars away. "What's the problem, Karl?"

"I can't put my finger on it. I mean, I trust him right enough. I'd stake my life on him not working for anyone else, but . . . well, there's something about him. I don't think we ever get to see the real Thomas Bladen, and that worries me. When it comes down to it, we don't know his capabilities."

"You'd not recommend recruiting him, then?"

"No, not yet. He's more useful to us as an outsider."

"How much have you told him?"

"The usual — only as much as we need him to know."

107, 108, 109 . . . Thomas counted on, just like he used to do when he was a child. Useless figures that kept his mind occupied; stopped him from too much thinking. His sister Pat used to tease him about it.

"You'd spend your whole life counting, given half a chance!"

But that process of measuring and timing; that's what had kept him sane when Dad went into his rages or when Mam had disappeared into the kitchen to dry her tears or to get the swelling on her face to go down. Numbers.

115, 116. He could see the house looming ahead. Surely Teresa could have told him exactly what to say, how to couch it all? He felt his stomach turning over. If he didn't get himself together his first words would be: 'Can I use your toilet?' A fine spy he'd make! He laughed at himself and squeezed the little piece of paper ever more tightly.

His legs dragged as he walked up the short drive, the sweat congealing against his skin. He remembered the time he'd first brought Miranda back to his digs in Leeds. How they'd both been too nervous to discuss how far they wanted to go. And how he'd ached for her. It wasn't just the rush of hormones and Thunderbird wine, but a need to connect with her, to anchor her to him so that she'd never leave Leeds, or him. Yeah, nice one, Thomas. Now he was at the front door with a gut ache and a hard-on. Brilliant.

He pressed the bell, realising that he'd missed a chance to copy Teresa's magic phone number for himself. He heard voices approaching — a man and a woman — and hoped to God that was sweat running down the back of his legs.

The door slowly opened. "Can I help you?" she said, even though her voice suggested the opposite. It was the same ice blonde that Karl had described. Refined, with a hint of yummy mummy — to use Karl's apt description.

"Can I come in? It's about Yorgi, sort of."

She stared at him for a moment and tilted her head back, directing a stream of something Eastern European behind her. Best guess, she'd figured that he wasn't Masterspy, but maybe that gave him a slight edge. The husband squeezed in beside his wife; the door didn't open any further.

"There's no one called Yorgi here — you have the wrong house."

Yeah, so the Eurospeak was a happy coincidence? He pressed his hands together and touched his lips then immediately felt foolish. He looked like his mother, back when she used to pray at home. An idea came to him. Not divine inspiration — more like desperation. He was never going to see these people again, right, so what harm was the truth?

He reached into his wallet and prised away his driving licence. Behind the ID card was a cut-down photograph, of him and Miranda. Typical adolescent photo-booth stuff; she had her arms around his neck, practically clinging to him. And he had a smile like he'd just found a fifty-pound note. The fact that she'd just grabbed his groin before the flash probably helped.

"This is Miranda. I know it's hard to protect the people we care about."

The couple studied the photograph for a long time; in the end he got so nervous they might snatch it indoors and lock him out that he asked for it back. His pulse was still racing as he tucked it carefully back into his wallet.

The door arced open. "What do you want, Mr . . . ?"

"Bladen. Thomas Bladen." Yeah, he'd thought about bullshitting them like Karl had insisted, but they just seemed like two scared people who had been dealt a crappy hand.

They sat on the sofa opposite him, their son at their feet. The man did the talking "You and Miranda have children, Tomas?"

"What? No," he shook his head to emphasise the point, hoping it would also cool his face off. "Look, I'm just here to offer assistance."

"Are you with the police?" the yummy mummy reached down, hoisting her son to her lap.

He shook his head again. "Look, any chance of a drink and can I . . ." he stood up and the sudden relief on his bladder made him exhale loudly.

She pointed him upstairs.

He heard the rattling of glasses as he closed the door behind him. Karl would probably have searched the bedroom; Karl wasn't there though. He checked the bathroom mirror. What a state! 'Are you the police?' That was a joke. Not unless CID stood for something completely different.

It seemed to be the longest piss of his life, as if his body was ridding itself of his fear. He flushed, did all the usual stuff and filched around in the wastepaper bin. Bingo — loo roll holder. He split the cardboard tube and copied out Teresa's helpline number. Then he peered at himself again in the mirror and splashed more water on his face.

Downstairs, a glass was waiting for him. He turned it around and the little boy cooed as he watched the light dancing, fascinated. Smiles all round.

"Supposing my husband and I needed help — what would you want in return?"

"Me? Nothing. I'm here as a messenger," he unfolded the piece of paper and passed it over.

The drink reminded him of the chocolate liqueurs they used to have at Christmas, in Pickering. Just the right side of sickly sweet. The couple studied Teresa's piece of paper for a long time. Or maybe they just didn't want to make eye contact, with him or each other. Yeah, they were rats in a trap all right: poor bastards.

"Look," he took pity on them, "Yorgi might be mixed up in some trouble, but you seem like good people." Okay, nought out of ten for subtlety, but it conveyed the gist.

The man cleared his throat. "Tomas, do you have brothers and sisters?"

"Yeah, a sister — Pat; she's a couple of years younger than me." What was he doing — why not draw them a bloody picture? He took another sip of alcoholic goo. The more he thought about it, they were all being used.

"Yorgi is my brother — my . . . half-brother; my name is Petrov and I am the younger in the family. When we were growing up, Yorgi was always the leader. He made the rules and I followed him. I learned very young not to challenge him."

Thomas said nothing. He noted the wall clock above the crucifix and decided to give himself five more minutes, tops. The wife stared at him as if she could pierce the façade and see into his soul. He fidgeted in the chair.

"How much trouble are we in, Mr Bladen?"

Now he felt like they were playing him. All he had to fall back on was the truth. "The authorities know about the incident." He watched their faces fall. "The victim survived though and you may have been unwilling accomplices." Unwilling? Jesus. He'd as good as accused them of complicity. What a prat. He rubbed at his forehead and closed his eyes. "I'm sorry; that came out wrong. What I meant was that so far there is no direct evidence against you."

Petrov raised a defiant hand. "He told us to face forward and to drive, said if anything happened we'd lose our son. We didn't know what he was planning."

Thomas looked from face to face. Chances were, they knew.

"Tomas, what would you have done?"

He said nothing, tried to hold their gaze.

Petrov patted his son. "I have always done what I could for Yorgi, but for many years we were apart. Then a year or so ago, he tracked me down . . ."

Thomas sat up: interesting choice of words.

". . . He leads a different life. Mixes in circles I would be afraid to. You understand?" Petrov reached for his wife's hand. Only now, as she turned towards him, did Thomas notice the reddening down one side of the face and the way Petrov shifted his weight away from one side of his ribs. "Alexandra and Lukas are my family. I must put them first. Will the people at this number understand that the way you do?"

He couldn't answer, didn't feel anything but shame. He couldn't pretend that he didn't care. And caring meant doing something. "Here," he wrote out a mobile number on the newspaper by his feet and ripped it off. "This is my number. Just in case."

His hand wavered and his stomach churned with raw emotion. "I have to go now," he stood up carefully as if his balance might be off; in a sense it was.

Alexandra lifted little Lukas aside and saw him to the door. Thomas followed her gaze to the crucifix. He blushed, caught in the act. "Bless you, Thomas Bladen," she kissed him on the cheek and then closed the door behind him.

It didn't feel cold outside, but a couple of tears gathered in his eye. He flicked them away casually, as if they were nothing. And as each step took him further from the house, he felt a growing sense of exhilaration.

He got back into the car and Karl started up the engine without a word. He ventured nothing and withstood their scrutiny; decided he'd sit this one out. Karl lasted until they'd cleared the Thames.

"How did it go?"

He took a breath and kept things simple. "They seemed pleased to have a contact number; I think they'll be in touch."

Teresa tapped Karl on the shoulder. "Anywhere around here is fine." Karl nodded and checked his mirror, pulling in along Queen Victoria Street.

Thomas watched them, saw the way Karl looked at her and how she avoided him. No goodbyes, not even a thank you. If he had to guess, there'd been words in the car while he'd been delivering a lifeline. But did that mean . . . nah, couldn't be. Surely Karl was smarter than that?

He watched with Karl as Teresa disappeared up the cut through to St Paul's. They sat for a while, the grumbling engine and indicator clicks marking off the seconds. Finally, Karl tore his gaze away from the side street. "Fancy a drink?"

"Sounds like a plan," Thomas parodied him.

Karl didn't react. He gazed out the windscreen, dull eyes watching the crowd in vain. Thomas could almost feel his longing.

"Yeah, a pub would be great," he emphasised, spurring Karl into activity. Jeez, what a pair of fuck-ups they were. Karl had fallen for Teresa, and Thomas, in his day, had all but set up house with Christine Gerrard. Women and power — it was like mixing your drinks: no good would ever come of it.

In a pub in Stratford they found a quiet table; Karl sat facing the door as usual. Thomas did the honours and got half a pint for himself and a pint of shandy for Karl, along with crisps; last of the big spenders.

Karl took a sip and smacked his lips theatrically. "Tell you what, Tommo. I'll do another little magic trick. Are you ready?"

He felt dread creeping through him.

"You gave them your own number, didn't you?"

Thomas coughed into his drink and kept his head down.

"It's okay, Tommo, I understand. It's an obvious rookie mistake — you felt sorry for them, right? I'd have done the same, at the beginning. I won't mention it to Teresa, but I need you to let me know if they ever do contact you. Deal?"

He wondered what else Karl had deduced about him.

Karl leaned back and stretched; he seemed to have cheered up no end. "You see, Tommo, we're not so different, you and I."

Chapter 20

Miranda had arrived early. Every night on the phone since Sunday, she'd been trying to talk Thomas out of this mysterious weekend job, the one he still hadn't explained. Maybe face-to-face she stood a chance of getting through to him.

She sat in the car, two streets away, flicking through a professional catering magazine that she'd already littered with notes and doodles. Thomas figured in a good few of those scribbles, not that he'd have known. She was the princess — naturally — and Thomas the face in the corner, sometimes just a pair of eyes, watching from a distance. Blimey, how accurate had that turned out to be!

More flicking, to a feature: a stylish eatery in Berkshire. She nearly drooled over the décor and the fancy name: panache. Thomas had suggested she call her club Miranda's — a talent for the obvious. But Caliban's was her private joke. At school, she'd loved The Tempest, ever since she'd caught her name in it, and had weathered the piss-taking of the other girls. The boys of course were more malleable — not for nothing did Miranda translate as 'the admired one.' Rough times, though.

She doodled some more. Whatever Thomas was mixed up in, it would be a stroll in the park compared to a gaggle of spiteful, hormone-addled bitches. Addled — she smiled at that; one of Thomas's words that had crept into her vocabulary. She fingered her neck-chain, following it round to her name, shaped in gold, and tapped it distractedly. Yeah, the only time that name had lost a little of its sheen was when her mum had told her about a chain-smoking casino croupier — the one she'd been named after.

This was bloody silly. She had emergency keys to the flat — new keys at that — just as he had to hers. But ever since the heavies had busted in while he was away, Thomas had cranked up his paranoia a notch or four and passed it on. "Sod it," she stuffed the magazine in the glove compartment; she'd take a walk past — what harm could it do?

* * *

Thomas found a parking space at the end of the street. He waited a minute, checking front and back; nothing much was happening. He reached for the sports bag on the passenger seat, containing a waterproof bodysuit, a torch so bright it could almost illuminate Karl's cryptic messages, a length of rope and a pair of walkie-talkies. He checked again — all quiet on the Western Front. Time to move.

He clocked the figure in the distance almost as soon as he closed the car door, watching as the loner crossed the street towards his flat then stopped still. He hugged the bag close and picked up the pace, moving from car to car, crouching low. Closer, and he could make out a woman in a long coat; she had her back to him and her hair was either short or tucked under a beret. She looked like she was auditioning for a French Resistance tribute act.

He used the trees for cover; good solid forest trees that some planner had approved decades before and which now bulged up tarmac and pavement in the struggle for existence. That's it, keep looking away from me; stay like that. He cantered across the road and snaked behind a delivery van; the woman still hadn't moved.

Ducking back down, he loosened his grip on the bag and tried to settle his breathing. Who? Shit. What if this was Teresa, and Miranda turned up? He went for broke and sprinted the remaining distance, dropping the sports bag and grabbing her shoulders in one fluid movement. "Right!"

Miranda gave a short yelp and turned her head. "Jesus, Thomas! You frightened the life out of me."

His heart was beating so fast that he struggled to find the words. "Don't ever stand in the street like that again."

Miranda paused, as if weighing up whether to slap him. "You arse!"

Somewhere, a bugler sounded the retreat. His head began to clear. "Sorry," he held up a hand, "I just got a bit freaked. Let's go inside."

"Well," Miranda headed on up the steps. "As long as you're not worried that people will see us."

She used her keys before he could object. He let it pass and carried on into the kitchen. Listening hard, he heard Miranda close the front door and then bolt it. So far, so salvageable.

She slumped into a chair and dumped her bag on the table. "I did bring you a present, but I'm not sure if you deserve it now."

When he returned, he was carrying two glasses of wine — his own only half-full — and the bottle tucked under one armpit; one hundred percent style.

"What's this — are you cutting back?"

He smiled sheepishly and handed her the grown-up glass. "Can't overdo it —I'm working tomorrow, remember."

She took a sip and pursed her lips, although he knew it was a good wine.

"Look, about earlier; I know I was a dick but I'm only thinking of you, okay?"

She didn't skip a beat. "Then tell me . . ."

He shook his head. "The less I tell you, the less you have to worry about."

"Is this the way we're going to live now?" She pulled a DVD case from her bag, tapping it rhythmically against her arm. "Still not sure if you deserve this . . ." The tone was playful and when he looked at her all 'puppy-dog,' she seemed to melt.

"It's not porn, is it?" Hardly likely. That one time they'd watched a porn flick together he'd sat in mute embarrassment, feeling a mix of betrayal and arousal. Getting turned on by other nubile women on the go, while your girlfriend was in the room with you, was hardly a declaration of love and devotion. And besides, those guys on screen were a lot to live up to.

"It's The Thirty-Nine Steps. And before you say anything, yes — it's the original. Seemed appropriate, what with your new life as a spy."

That lit the whole box of fireworks. "Let's get one thing straight, shall we?" he clunked his glass down hard. "I'm not a bloody spy."

She leaned back in silence, and he felt really stupid. Like the time in Leeds when he'd got drunk, taken a leak in the park and soaked his own shoes. It was time for a tactical withdrawal. "I'll go sort out the grub and then we can watch Robert Donat kick arse. Help yourself to the telly." A polite way of saying: end of round one and back to your corners.

* * *

The bolognaise was already prepared — real stuff, no crap. Made to a recipe of Pat's and freshly dug out of the freezer the night before. He kept the kitchen door open and listened as the TV erupted into life; a comedy, by the sounds of it and so sharp that a laughter track had been added. "Shouldn't be long," he called out.

There was silence from Miranda. Either the comedy was more riveting than it sounded or she still had the hump, big time. Or both. Not much else he could do, other than watch the pasta simmering, and think. Why were he and Karl going to Suffolk? He jabbed at the frothing pan with a fork, submerging the strands. How far did he want this work with Karl to go? So what if Peterson was bent? He grabbed the fork from the saucepan and held on to it until the heat reddened his fingers. No, Bob Peterson had lied to him; and Sir Peter Carroll had tried to set him up. He deserved some answers.

The TV volume rose — advert time. He smacked his lips appreciatively as the garlic and beef flirted with his nostrils. The way to a man's heart and all that — and hopefully a woman's too. "Pasta's almost done," he relayed the news. "I'll come in for a bit."

"You've Been Framed, I think," Miranda stared at the TV, deadpan.

He perched on the edge of the sofa and sipped his wine. He saw right away that she'd topped it up, but he let it pass. On TV, a child ran into a transparent patio door and bounced back two feet. The studio audience laughed and winced; Western Civilisation — coming soon.

Nothing more to be said, he nipped off, returning with a bowl of salad; quite the little Jamie Oliver. Try something new today. Yeah, like not having another argument.

The bolognaise was good when they got there; even Miranda said so. They ate and relaxed — or at least, relaxed hostilities. Onscreen, Robert Donat grappled with conspiracy, paranoia and false accusations. Thomas knew just how he felt.

Miranda nudged him, mid-film. "Bet you didn't know that in the book, there's no female lead at all."

"Maybe it needed improving."

She patted his leg: good answer.

By the end of the first bottle of wine, they'd moved past the talking stage. She sat close and ran a finger up and down his arm; he could feel the tremors in faraway places. As they watched the dying minutes of the mystery, Robert Donat finally figured out his enemies' plan and how to stop them. As the credits rolled, Thomas grabbed the remote and peered at the screen, checking through names mostly forgotten. He wasn't a film buff particularly, but sometimes, when he spotted a cameraman in a really enjoyable old film, he'd search them out on the net and see what else they'd done.

"That was champion," he sat back.

Miranda squeezed the arm she'd been teasing. "What shall we do for a second feature?" It sounded like a come-on. Then again, everything Miranda said sounded like a come-on.

"Well . . ." he stretched the word out like bait. She didn't respond; she wasn't biting. Jeez, he'd have to ask. "Are you stopping tonight? He cringed at the words — about as romantic as a six-pack of lager.

"Maybe," she smiled, and chuckled.

He turned to her and her eyes sparkled in the reflected glare of the TV. There was a heavy pause — the tipping point of desire — then his lips found hers. He was greedy for her and she seemed eager to follow his lead. He moved a hand under her buttock and tilted her towards him. He felt the shape of her mouth change and slid his left hand behind her, to the small of her back.

Her fingers burrowed beneath his shirt, ranging over his torso. An idea came to him, but he killed it dead. Since Leeds, there had been one unwritten rule. No talking — during sex or foreplay or canoodling. No declarations of love, no verbal requests.

He levered her on to one buttock and she took the hint, rolling with him in one uneven lollop. He shifted down the cushions by about a foot and she swung one leg over his, pinning him to the sofa. Now, as they kissed, they moved in rhythm, their pubic bones rising and falling against each other. He lifted her t-shirt and circle kissed her navel and stomach, enjoying the no-man's land between two leisure parks.

He could feel waves of pleasure rippling between them. She moved faster, taking control, as he'd wanted her to. He started to unbutton her jeans as she rocked, and he tried to shut out the calls of despair from his bladder: bad timing 'R' us. She bore down on him, her out-breaths reduced to faltering gasps. He gave up on her jeans, thrusting with his hips, willing her to climax before his bladder burst. He drew her closer as she came, drawing her head towards his and moving his tongue around hers as the last shudders freed themselves from her glorious body. "Now you," she said breathlessly, shifting back on to the sofa.

The relief from his bladder was like a gift from God. As he turned to her, she was undoing the last of her jeans buttons. "Hold that thought — I really need to pee." He heaved himself up with difficulty and staggered to the bathroom.

He heard her grumbling in the other room, but the call of nature would not be ignored. His body took a while to respond, as if it resented the unused hard-on. At last, everything flowed, and flowed; and flowed.

He finished up and washed his hands. His reflection looked flushed. He grinned at himself; he felt like a teenager again, copping off with Miranda on the bedsit put-you-up in Leeds. As he opened the unlocked door he repeated her words to himself — now it was his turn. By the time he'd taken half a dozen steps, he was back at full mast.

Miranda was standing in the living room. Her jeans were fully fastened and she was putting on her coat. He did a double take — twilight zone style — staring at her crotch as if he could hypnotise it back into action.

"What's going on?" His question slammed against her granite expression.

"Your boyfriend called. He'll be over in an hour. Thanks for everything."

"You don't have to go . . ." he paused, wondering if he could possibly steer the sentence towards: 'we could still have a quickie before Karl turns up.'

"What, hide in the bedroom? I don't think so, Thomas. I'm not the hiding type."

He caught sight of his mobile phone on the table. "You didn't . . ."

"Relax Thomas. I didn't speak to him and break your little code. He sent a text."

Yeah, a text that you read. "Look, I'll call you over the weekend."

"We'll see," she didn't look convinced.

He followed her to the door. "Look, Karl wasn't supposed to be coming over until tomorrow evening."

"Careful Thomas," she faced him down. "You're giving away your secrets."

As he went to kiss her, she turned her face away. "Sam'll pick me up. I'll come back for my car tomorrow sometime."

There was nothing left to be said. He settled for "I'll make it up to you," but she was already down the steps and away. She didn't look back.

Back inside, he rechecked the sports bag, tidied up and waited for the call.

"Tommo, it's Karl. Are you free to talk?"

I am now, thanks to you, you bastard. "Yeah, all packed and ready to go."

"Great — everything's gone haywire. Bring a decent sweater; they say it's gonna be a cold night."

Chapter 21

Karl had given precise instructions for the pick-up: on a corner, three streets away, in twenty minutes. His timing was exact, stopping just long enough for Thomas to get in the car and jam the bag behind him.

Karl seemed to be in a chipper mood. "We're driving to Minsmere Bird Reserve, like proper wildlife photographers. And no shag jokes," he grinned. "Now sit back, pick an album and enjoy the ride. Status Quo or Queen?"

Thomas slept for most of the journey. Karl wasn't saying a lot and there were only so many times he could hear Karl singing about 'Having a good time.' He dreamt that he and Miranda were back in the flat, arguing. Then she'd slapped him and walked out. He followed her to the street, to find Karl, Christine, Bob Peterson and Sir Peter Carroll, all slow clapping as if they'd caught him out at something.

He shuddered awake and tried to clear his head. "Are we there yet?" he tried his best child-in-car voice.

Karl glanced sideways, didn't reply.

Fair enough, he'd stick to questions. "Have you been here before, Karl?"

"Aye — once; it's a good drop off point."

Karl was true to his word; it had taken two and a half hours non-stop. The car slowed to a halt, facing a metal gate. Thomas waited; maybe this was the pick-up point and all the gear in the bag was just precautionary.

Karl got out and unlocked the gate, waving Thomas through so he could close it behind them. A more inquisitive person might have asked where Karl had got the key from, but Thomas was just about up to his limit with curiosity.

Karl reclaimed the driving seat; he sounded edgy. "Okay, here's how it works. I lead and you follow. We wait for the drop, retrieve what we came for then hightail it out of here, lickety-split."

"So if this is so easy-peasy why am I here as well?"

"Hold on there, Tommy Boy," Karl manoeuvred the car up the dirt track. "Nobody mentioned the 'e' word. And it's standard procedure to have two bodies for night-time retrievals."

Thomas checked his watch and chewed his lip. "How long are we waiting for?"

A cloud drifted across the moon, edging silver as it crowded out their only natural light source. No music now and no conversation, as Thomas watched Karl staring through the windscreen, checking the wetland for who knew what.

"You'll never get a submarine through that."

Karl smiled, but didn't respond. As he'd managed two cold pies, a large bag of crisps and taken a dump somewhere in the swamps, perhaps he was considering his next activity.

Thomas sat beside him, wearing the wetsuit. He felt like a mascot for safe sex. "I still don't see . . ."

Karl raised a finger then tapped his watch. "Sshhh. Any time soon."

Thomas released the car door on command and swung himself out. The water lapped gently, close by — water he would have to get into. Karl seemed very calm now, with a night-scope strapped to his head, like a malevolent cyborg.

The droning engine cut into the night with increasing fervour as it approached. Thomas moved to the water's edge and waited for Karl's signal. The red and green wing lights flickered through the clouds as the plane circled over and released its cargo. Soon a small, white parachute glistened silver as it spiralled down towards the water. Karl twitched like a cat, tracking the parachute's descent in jerky movements. Out on the water there was a muted splosh as the package landed.

"Now," Karl hissed.

Thomas slipped into the water, forcing through the mud and weeds that conspired to strangle every step. Soon he was in up to his thighs, half-wading half-floating in the cold gloom, gliding towards the quarry. He couldn't hear Karl anymore; it was just him, the water and each laboured gasp as he closed on the box — the parachute and cords lifeless as a dead jellyfish.

As he laid a hand on one corner, he heard a popping sound and water kicked up about a foot in front of him. By the third shot, he was rooted to the spot in panic. He did the only thing he could think of, pulling himself underwater, letting the roar of pressure in his ears drown out the screams in his head. In the murky half-light of his torch, he saw the strands of cord and dragged the box towards him.

Bad idea; the impacts in the water increased. And they were getting closer. Ice chilled his veins. Christ, he was going to die. He thought about Miranda, thought about what a shit he'd been to her. Saw his father and mother sitting in the living room in Pickering, curtains drawn; imagined his father gazing into a glass: 'I knew he'd come to no good when he went to London.'

He held on to a breath past the point of reason, heart pounding, eyes bulging, raging against the injustice of it all.

Finally, as his senses started to fade, he thrust through the surface, fighting for breath.

"Get your fucking head down!" Karl bellowed.

As he plunged below again, he heard returning gunfire. At least Karl was looking out for him — a reassuring thought that only lasted while the pressure intensified in his chest. Until the heavy heat stretched out across his collarbone, numbing his arms, choking him. Despair quickly filled his lungs as the oxygen ran out; the abject no-win terror of being shot above the water or drowning beneath it. "Argh!" he surfaced again, flailing his arms to get balance. Only now did he realise that he'd become disorientated and was a good ten feet from the package. It bobbed further away with every second, taunting him to choose between safety and failure. With a great gulp of air, he made his choice, propelling himself towards it, closing his mind to the chaos around him as he hit the water like an ironing board. He clawed blindly at the box, swearing at the strain of keeping hold.

Then he felt it, the smouldering poker against his arm; a fire even the water could not cool. White-hot light blinded him, skewering his brain awake. This was pain he'd never known before. But, then, he'd never been shot before.

His legs buckled and the mud slammed into him. He grabbed the package with his good arm as he went down, kicking wildly to make for the reed bank. Birds scattered in the commotion, but he stayed put, keeping low, clasping the package between his knees. He forced himself to breathe through his nose, gritting his teeth to try and block out the pain. He felt like his arm was hanging off — he didn't want to look, didn't want to know.

He could hear Karl, blazing away with one, no two weapons. Round after round; he lost count of the relentless rhythm — the sound seemed to fade in and out of his head. Then he heard the sound of glass shattering and the shooting stopped.

The water seemed to swirl around him. He felt his pulse go into overdrive; his hands were shaking. He wished that he were armed, so he could track those fuckers down and stick a bullet in them. But he was trapped. He couldn't let Karl know he was okay without giving away his own position; couldn't leave the cold, cloying water for fear of being shot again. As Karl might have said: he was properly fucked.

A hollow thom broke the silence then the sky high above the water lit up like magnesium. Karl's flare arced down and faded on the far side of the water.

"It's clear!" Karl called out plaintively. "Are you there?"

He turned in Karl's direction, but all he saw were blotches of light. Lesson four in how to be a spy: never look directly at the flare. He waited a few seconds, still terrified of the enemy in the dark.

"Come on, Tommo; we don't have time for this — do you have it?"

He dragged his limbs from the mud's grasp, suppressing a scream as his injured arm brushed against the reeds. Just before he clambered out, he dipped his hand into the water and washed the tears from his face.

Karl stashed the package behind the driver's seat then handed him a bath towel. "Right then, let's get a look at you."

He needed help to ease his arm out of the wet suit. Even the night air hurt. He stood flinching, eyes closed as Karl carefully touched around the wound. Karl murmured to himself and reached back into his car.

"This will hurt."

Thomas coughed back laughter. "No need to treat me with kid gloves."

Karl shrugged and poured out something that smelt like meths. Thomas braced himself, fist drawn tight to stifle any reaction. When the cloth touched his arm he thought it had caught fire. "Fuck!" he shrieked, both at the pain and the way the tears ran from his eyes.

"Hey Tommo, no points for bravery here — you did the courageous bit earlier." Karl finished dressing the wound and handed him a small bottle. "Take one of these every couple of hours while the pain is bad. Only one, mind; these are not your usual headache tablets!"

They stood grinning together, like boys who'd just completed a dare. "Are you sure you still want to play this game? Come on then, let's go finish the job." Karl opened the passenger door and helped him in, still dripping water and slime.

Thomas nodded, unable to speak, blowing huffing breaths as he edged into the car seat. His arm felt like someone had crushed it in a vice; Karl assured him it would feel worse the next day. Some comfort.

"Shouldn't we have checked their car?"

"No point, Tommo. Odds on, it's stolen. Three cheers for Robert and Lizzie, eh?"

Thomas squeezed his eyelids. Maybe delirium was setting in; Karl was making no sense whatsoever.

"In the glove compartment."

Thomas reached forward with difficulty. Inside were two handguns.

"Robert and Lizzie — the Brownings!" Karl milked his 'ta-da' moment.

Thomas laughed breathlessly and slumped back. Even with the heat on full, his legs were getting numb from the damp. He tried pushing the waders down his legs, but his left arm shrieked in protest.

"Take it easy. I'll keep the heat full blast and get us there quick as I can. But I'll not break any speed limits. Imagine trying to explain two guns in the glove box and a wet man beside me trying to get his trousers off."

Thomas smiled and rolled his head away. He felt like he was sinking into the chair. Delayed shock, come down; call it what you will, he needed to sleep.

"You get some shut-eye; we've a way to go yet."

He closed his eyes. It seemed as if Karl was talking and then the radio struck up with 'You've got a friend.' Then blackness.

* * *

Thomas felt the car rocking from side to side. Scratch that; it was Karl, applying the gentle art of persuasion.

"Time to wake up."

He opened his eyes; it looked like they were in a concrete wonderland and Karl was the tour guide.

"We're in an underground car park — I won't be long. I'll stick your bag on the backseat. You did bring a change of clothes like I told you?" Good ol' Karl — he thought of everything.

Thomas blinked in the muted neon glow; his eyes ached. First things first, he reached for Uncle Karl's all-purpose painkillers. Then he wriggled his way out of the car and squelched a few steps. His nervous cough echoed into the distance; he seemed to be alone. He did a quick scan around for CCTV then dried himself off with the bath towel one-handed and got changed with as few sudden movements as possible. There was no mobile signal and the time on the clock meant they were probably in London.

He gathered his wits and headed into the shadows for a piss. Nothing seemed real, the world rendered pleasantly numb. As he stumbled back to the car, he saw holes in the driver's door; they looked like bullet holes. He yawned, managed to clamber into the back seat and lay there in the shadows.

Memory and pain collided in his brain. At the lake, in the worst of his panic, he'd feared that Karl was actually firing at him. He giggled in the dark, overwhelmed by everything but unable to stop thinking. He mustn't forget that Karl had probably saved his life tonight. He sniffed back the emotion. Of course, Karl had put him in danger in the first place, but no one was perfect.

Next thing he knew, something squeaked — maybe a door — and somewhere in the gloom, someone started whistling 'I Shot the Sheriff.' As Thomas sat up, Karl waved, like he was just back from the shops. He held up a couple of packets and passed them through the open passenger door.

"Jesus, this car smells like a marsh! Our leader's very pleased with our performance tonight — he sent us these with his compliments."

"Hush money?" Thomas took the oblong envelopes and weighed them with his good arm.

"Danger money, more like! So how's the walking wounded?"

Thomas grimaced and waved a hand tentatively. He had so many unanswered questions he could scarcely count them. "So what did we risk life and limb for, exactly?"

Karl put a lot of irritation into one sigh. "I didn't ask; I don't need to know. Now be a good boy and open my envelope."

Thomas clamped the envelope between his knees and tore at the paper. He ran a thumb through a run of £50s and £20s. "I make it at least a couple of grand, maybe three."

"Which means, Tommo, that whatever we fished out of the wet was worth more than five grand to Sir Peter Carroll."

"And the sniper?" Thomas lifted his arm a couple of inches.

"He was probably just a hired hand, warning us off till somebody else turned up."

"He?" Thomas tilted as far as the seatbelt would allow.

"In my limited experience, Tommo, women don't miss. Come on now, enough with the philosophising. Let's go find ourselves a drink.

* * *

If the pub's name wasn't enough of a clue, then the military crests and insignia on every spare inch of wall were a dead giveaway. The landlord had greying ginger hair and a ruddy complexion. Thomas took him for a former sergeant major, still crimson from years of shouting; somehow he couldn't see a former officer working this hard after demob to earn a living.

"Mr McNeill!" the landlord all but saluted. "Always a pleasure!"

Thomas hung back; no one paid him any attention. Karl crossed to the bar, leaving him in the centre of the saloon, like a deodorant commercial.

"A shandy for me and a whisky for my associate."

Thomas felt unreasonably disappointed; not comrade or oppo, just associate. He listened with envy as Karl fell into easy conversation with Mein Host. No point standing around — might as well be comfortable. He grabbed an empty table with a view of the bar. The tabletop reeked of polish, but he couldn't see any evidence of it; even the beer-mats had formed an unhealthy attachment to the veneer.

Karl took his time coming over. Maybe it was tough leaving his army pals behind. Once or twice he looked in Thomas's direction and then carried on with his conversation. No matter — the extra time gave Thomas time to clear his head.

"Your very good and continued health, Tommo."

He managed a smile, lifting the whisky up to the light, and breathed in deeply through his nostrils. Even good whisky couldn't stop his stomach churning at the thought of cold, gushing water closing over his head.

"I know how you're feeling, Thomas," Karl lowered his voice. "There's not a man or woman here who hasn't been where you were, hasn't asked themselves at some point: Is this the end?" Karl leaned forward and produced a packet of crisps from his pocket. "The thing is, this is what we do."

There was no answer to that, but still the need to say something. "How scared were you then, when it was all kicking off?"

"Are you kidding me? I was like a brick factory on overtime. I get a sweat just thinking about it — if I hadn't brought Robert and Lizzie out for the night . . ." Karl broke off and did his customary plague-of-locusts routine on the crisps. "Look Tommo, I know it's a lot to deal with, first op and all."

"I don't know if I'm really cut out for this." It sounded so much clearer, out loud.

Karl put the crisps down and straightened his back against the chair. "Well, only you can make that choice. But meantime, the packages will still come and go, Bob Peterson will still have lied to you about being at Harwich and Sir Peter Carroll will still be playing tin soldiers with the rest of us. Come on, aren't you still the teensiest bit curious to know what the fuck is really going on?"

Thomas managed a grin and sank the remainder of his whisky. Karl had a point. But so had the bullet that had almost gone through his arm.

* * *

Thomas closed the front door and bolted it. He felt like never opening it again. He sat in the dark, hugged tight against the cushion, reliving the paddle from hell. It wasn't long before he reached for the phone.

"Ajit, you awake? It's Thomas."

"Hiya mate, 'ow's it going? Let me just take this downstairs — Geena's asleep."

Thomas pulled the phone close and lifted his feet on to the sofa. Only Ajit and Miranda could keep a meaningful conversation going for longer than twenty minutes. He knew because he'd timed it. And right now he needed to talk.

He chatted with Ajit for over an hour, about nothing in particular; the latest on Geena, the joys of Yorkshire policing and the glory days of Pickering; anything and nothing to keep his thoughts at bay. "By the way," he added as things wound to a close, "I still have your Blake's 7 annual somewhere. I saw it when I was last having a clear out." This, Ajit would know, was boys' code for 'I'm still thinking about you,' and it sufficed.

Last thing before bed, Thomas counted out his money from Sir Peter. Three grand, tax-free — nice work if you could get it. Or not.

Despite the previous day's excesses, Thomas woke early on Sunday morning; a fireworks-in-the-brain, no prisoners, wide-awake start to the day. His arm stung like a bastard and try as he might he couldn't get his body to settle. The alarm clock glowed 6.45 defiantly. He popped one of Karl's magic pills with a swig of cold tea and then got himself ready, using his left arm as little as possible. There was no pretence of putting a camera in his car; he knew exactly where he was going — across London to the well-appointed streets of Highgate. Time to start separating truth from fiction.

The traffic was non-existent so early on a Sunday. He remembered driving out to Enfield once to photograph a pair of foxes; this wasn't so different. When he got to Christine's street, he parked up, engine running. Did he really want to do this? Was it any of his business who shared Christine's bed these days? True, he reasoned with himself, but if he backed off now that would mean he had a problem with it. The words 'painted' and 'corner' formed a trio with the painkiller to cloud what little judgement remained.

He pulled out and moved into second gear, rolling down the road at a steady ten mph, scanning both sides. There were several four-by-fours on the rugged streets of Highgate, though not the one he was looking for. Instead of relief, he felt a gnawing disappointment; it was there somewhere — he was sure of it. He dug out a street atlas and rested it on his knees, tracing a grid pattern, two streets away in every direction.

And suddenly there it was, the bonnet stone cold. The same vehicle from Harwich, the one Peterson probably used for taking the wife and kids shopping. So now what? He got back in his car and stared into the distance. Too early to ring Christine and anyway, what would he say? 'Hi, I happened to be in the area and I see you're shagging your boss who's married.' Yeah, that'd be a vote winner come his next assessment.

He thumped the steering wheel, sending shockwaves up his bad arm; it concentrated the mind wonderfully. He needn't say or do anything for now — he'd leave it to Karl. Speed-dial number 4.

"Morning mate, I couldn't sleep."

Karl sounded like an advert for Grumpy Bastard magazine. "Well why don't you get a bloody paper round? Do you know what time it is — what do you want?"

"I've got some information on Bob Peterson — he spent the night at Christine's flat; just thought you should know." He rang off: mission accomplished.

An hour later he was crashed out on the sofa, lullabied by the TV. He slept deep and heavy, waking by degrees as the mobile shrieked for attention. Not now, Karl, bugger off and leave me in peace. The mobile gave up then bleeped. He yawned and looked across at the clock. Blimey, it was evening — so much for Sunday. He rolled his neck from side to side and carefully hauled himself up to sitting. Still bleary eyed, he thumbed through to voicemail.

"Tomas, it is Petrov. You must help us; come quickly. Yorgi has contacted us — I am very afraid."

Fuck. He scrambled off the sofa and grabbed the cash envelope, his mobile and his keys. On the way over, he pulled Petrov's number from the mobile and stored it for speed dialling.

He made good time into South London and called in his progress. Alexandra answered, calmer than her husband, but definitely freaked. He told her to get packed and be ready to move as soon as he got there. From the little sense she made, he gathered that Yorgi had phoned them out of the blue — pissed, high, or paranoid; possibly all three; ranting about a hospital and unfinished business with a traitor. And then he was coming for them.

South of the river and every traffic light, every fuckwit incapable of doing thirty mph on a thirty road, all piled on the minutes and the pressure. No point calling Karl now, he was practically there.

He beeped the horn three times as he pulled up. A curtain snatched back, then the family made a run for the car, dragging as many cases as was humanly possible. They didn't look as though they planned on coming back. He popped the boot and revved up to encourage them, flicking his gaze between the windscreen and his mirrors. As he pushed into the car seat, primed for the off, the clamminess of his shirt squished against his back. He shivered and smiled; he was almost enjoying this.

Petrov ushered his family in the back and climbed in beside them. He seemed to take a last remorseful look at the house then Thomas met his eyes in the mirror. Time to go. For all the fire in his blood, Thomas drove sensibly, keeping to the speed limit and watching all directions. Petrov and Alexandra said nothing; he preferred that.

As they crossed London Bridge, the enormity of his actions began to sink in. He didn't have a plan, beyond getting them away from there. He flicked on the radio for inspiration, but it was in short supply tonight. Jesus, another tailback. In a city that never sleeps, why did all the insomniacs have to drive? His passengers sat, trance-like, as he battled through the traffic. They hadn't said a word, not even to ask where he was talking them; a question he was quietly asking himself.

His first, impossible thought had been to head to Miranda's parents. Without question they'd help him, but it would mean dragging them deeper into his murky world. That was the word for it: murky. His second choice was less inventive. Pick a hotel at random; any hotel would do, but the more upmarket the better — and room service was a necessity. It had to be somewhere Yorgi couldn't trace them to. He settled on Paddington, only because he and Miranda had once spent a weekend there playing tourists. And besides, the station afforded a range of escape options if he really couldn't protect them.

The engine rumbled to a standstill. He glanced down at his mobile and thought about Karl. There was every reason to ring, and few not to. Petrov had called him though. He reckoned he could sort things out for the time being with less fuss. Behind him, Petrov's family hardly made a sound, but their expectations massed around him like the roar of a West Ham crowd. He didn't bother turning round. "I want you to stay in a hotel until I figure out the next step. You'll need to remain in your room. Order whatever you need, but stay put." He took out an even thousand and handed it to Petrov's bewildered wife.

"Why would you do this for us?"

He swallowed; he didn't really have an answer. Not without going into all the history with Ajit and . . . He stopped short. Maybe Ajit could provide police protection if he got them up to Yorkshire? The idea shattered before his eyes. Wake up; this is more than you can handle. You need help; you need Karl.

Alexandra paused from her whispered conversation and stared through the mirror. "How long must we hide there?"

"I don't know, probably just for a couple of days." He shouldered the door and breathed in the rush of air. "Remember, don't contact anyone except me."

They looked settled in the car. Tough. He emptied the boot and picked up a couple of bags, ready to start walking. "Let's get on with it."

Chapter 22

'Opportunities multiply as they are seized.'
Sun Tzu, The Art of War

Yorgi folded the book flat and closed his eyes. It was not enough merely to read wisdom; one had to imbibe and absorb it. He blinked against the harsh neon strip light and moved uneasily from the chair, holding the kitchen table to steady himself. His breath still tasted of vodka and his head bore the pitiless, unrelenting pressure of a hangover.

In the corner of the room, a black bin-liner sat and waited, serenaded by two flies. He wrinkled his nose in disgust, but did not consider moving it. He took a pub glass out of the cupboard, wiped it with his hand and ran the tap, squeezing his eyes closed to bear the whine of the pipes. Then he reached to the broken tiled ledge behind the sink and took the last of the painkillers. The box said fast acting so he sat still for three minutes. Only now was he ready to face the front room.

The table was upended — that much he did remember — but the extent of the devastation was a shock. He recalled speaking to Petrov; even the thought of his half-brother's name was like taking a candle to a fuse. His head throbbed to the rhythm: Pet-rov, Pet-rov. He picked up an armchair and turned the cushion over to sit. There was little point; it was filthy, either side. Peasants might live like this; he would not. He nodded to himself and grunted approval. It was settled; he would increase his fees, work the girls harder. He sniffed hard by his shoulder — taking in the stench of sweat and vomit. It was a disgrace, he told himself, unconsciously resurrecting his father's voice in his head — not Petrov's lineage, but his real father.

"Yes Papa," he promised aloud, "I will complete my chores and better myself." He unbuttoned his shirt, pushed the sleeve back over the grime and rubbed his watch glass; the smooth, domed surface always made him smile; transporting him back to Amsterdam. He had only been pimping back then, when opportunity had presented itself. How the American tourist had begged and pleaded. But showing mercy to your enemy disrespects him. Sun Tzu understood that. So, once he had taken the man's watch and sneered at his flabby white body, he'd brought the knife easily to flesh.

In the shower he mentally relived the scene, enjoying the steady throbbing between his legs. The way the fat American had collapsed on the floor, squealing, oozing blood across the pale carpet. It was all so vivid, so alive. The frozen horror on the girl's face, making her gleam like an angel; like a religious statue. He sucked in the shower steam, felt it hot in his lungs as his memory wound on. That sense of absolute power as he'd fucked the girl on the bed, oblivious as to whether the man lived or died beside them on the floor. At that moment he had become a god, made in his own image.

He tilted his face to let the suds run down the length of his body and squirted shampoo around his pubic hair. Water spattered off his erection as he closed his eyes, moving his hand, slowly, teasingly downwards. Images of girls — so many girls, willing and unwilling — danced around him in a kaleidoscope of pleasure. Yes, Yorgi; yes.

Now, as his hand found rhythm, the images were interspersed with the flashbacks of violence — the heavy certainty of the trigger or the knife handle. Pleasure and pain; pain and pleasure. At the point of orgasm he dug his nails hard into his penis, sending a delicious chord of agony and ecstasy through his body. When the pulses of semen had stopped, he relaxed his grip and gazed down at the savage marks on his flesh, like the bite of an animal.

He finished his shower and shaved, adding cologne to sting his face awake. A pair of trousers and shirt that had been hanging up for days gave him a respectable and inconspicuous air. He put the watch back on and checked the time: seven o'clock. Time to gather his things — the old clothes he would dump; another skin shed. A charity shop would meet his needs for the time being. He'd paid cash in advance for this hovel so no one should be visiting for at least another two weeks. By then, Mr Svenson — the name he'd given to the greedy bastard who'd made £500 out of him — would be long gone.

At Victoria station he stashed his bag and walked away with only a small carrier, stuffed in one side of his coat. He kept the silencer in the other pocket. He knew that the van driver, Dechevez, was in a private room on the third floor. But beyond that he knew nothing more than when he'd first encountered him at Harwich. Then, it had been a warning. Now, a permanent resolution was required. That it concerned politics was of no interest to him. Politics, he considered as he passed the hospital signs, was just another business — profit, loss and opportunity. Dechevez — whoever he was — was simply no longer profitable to someone.

* * *

Yorgi slipped through the open door at the side of the hospital and went straight to the basement. The stifling heat and the noise of the boiler took him back to his time at sea, stoking the engines and avoiding the attentions of the drunken louts who liked to use young boys as playthings. He remembered hiding behind the hottest pipes, risking a scalding rather than something far worse.

He went deeper into the hospital basement catacombs and pressed a hand to the boiler pipe, resting it there until it felt like the paint was searing his skin. A sharp reminder of what he had endured. His ears picked out the shuffling gait ahead of him and the squeak of the trolley. He hid in the shadows and fitted the silencer.

The cleaner shuffled past then stopped, just beyond the alcove. He let go of his trolley, paused and turned. Yorgi stepped out of the shadows like a panther, closing on his victim like the predator he was. Yorgi thought, for an instant, that the look of dread hinted at some kind of recognition. The idea amused him — that this was one of the people he'd trafficked to freedom, only to come back and claim him when the situation required. He levelled the weapon, surprised to hear a native tongue.

Sun Tzu wrote of turning every situation to one's advantage by reading the signs and acting accordingly. Yorgi believed knowledge was nothing unless it was tested in practice. He made the cleaner take off his overalls; promised him mercy as long as he didn't piss them in fear; a promise Yorgi had no intention of keeping, especially since they may have met before. The man stood before him in his underpants and vest, weight sagged forward a little, hands clasped together as if in prayer. Yorgi smiled and the man relaxed a little, smiling back. The first shot to the head — hygienic and efficient; the second, to the heart — just because he could.

He dumped the body in a laundry trolley and wheeled it out of sight. Only then did he change into the uniform; the overalls were baggy enough to fit over his clothes — a bonus, as was the ID card. When Yorgi smelt a foreign sweat against his clothes and skin, he felt a sense of transformation, as if he now inhabited the dead man's shell, claiming him. His mimicked accent might have sufficed to get to Dechevez, but this new persona offered a better disguise. Small matter that the photo bore little resemblance to him. A cleaning trolley and a hangdog expression would grant him anonymity, and people would see whatever they expected to see.

He exited the lift at the third floor. The air reeked of sickness and disinfectant; the heat smothered him like a blanket. He pushed his watch up his sleeve and wiped the tiny beads of sweat from his face. He started mopping along the corridor, head down, humming softly. The latex gloves were a little loose and he knew that later they would make his skin itch. But it was a minor inconvenience.

As the dry linoleum retreated and the room numbers counted down, he felt the thrill of anticipation and his erection pressing tightly beneath the overalls. He looked into the distance at the Asian nurse who was bent over, reading, and thought about what he'd like to do to her. He watched her for at least a minute until she looked up and gave a nonchalant wave in his direction. He responded in kind then furtively felt for the bulge through his pocket.

When she moved out of sight, he pushed the trolley closer and peered through the door-glass for the first time. Dechevez was there, sleeping like an innocent. Yorgi leered at him, his teeth reflecting in the glass like fangs. He turned towards the trolley and drew out the gun, keeping it at his blindside.

He waited, head down, watching as the pretty nurse picked up a folder and left his field of vision again. Barely breathing, he reached for the cylindrical door handle in small, precise movements. He felt the handle give way and the door ease in. Heat wafted around his face. He remembered then, as a young boy, his father coming into his room; stealthy, loving and unannounced. He always looked forward to those goodnights, but could never stay awake to catch him no matter how hard he tried. He would just open his eyes and Papa would be there, like Santa Claus, at the edge of his bed.

Dechevez sighed softly. Yorgi heard his father's voice again: 'Sleep well, Yorgi; you are my good boy.' His eyes glistened as he squeezed the trigger, his lips forming the words: 'I love you, Papa.' Dechevez's body twitched against the pillow and the blood seeped down the side of the bed, pooling on the lino.

Yorgi fired again, just to see the head jerk a second time, like one of Papa's wooden puppets. He hummed as he closed the door, carefully spraying polish over the aluminium handle and door plate and wiping it tenderly. Then he collected up his cleaning implements, pushed the trolley round to the lift and left it there. As he headed for the stairwell he heard the lift door ping behind him and a murmur of voices carried along the corridor. He removed the ID card from his jacket, looked at the name and whispered his thanks to the original owner.

Outside, he acknowledged the other cleaning staff gathered by a side door to smoke. He declined their offer to join them and muttered 'newspaper,' waving casually behind him as he reached the corner. He removed his overalls in the nearby public toilets and packed them into a carrier bag, ready for the nearest recycling bin. The ID he would keep — a souvenir of his own inventiveness. He felt for the watch underneath his overall sleeve; it was time to settle things with Petrov. And for that he'd need a vehicle.

Chapter 23

"Tommo, we got us a situation."

Thomas watched himself in the café mirror as he answered the phone, staring back in dismay; he looked rough. "I'm listening, Karl."

"I've located the hospital, but it's bad news; two dead — professional hits. One's our shooting victim from the docks — Dechevez — and the other's a cleaner. The police haven't found a connection between them yet and we're trying to keep a lid on things until they do." Karl's voice was unemotional; he could have been reading from a script. "The cleaner was Yugoslavian or . . . something Eastern European. I guess he'd be a former Yugoslavian now." Karl had probably rehearsed that line.

"What's the plan, then?"

Karl didn't respond immediately. "There's something else. I'm sorry, Tommo. There was a fire in South London, where you did the home visit."

Thomas caught his reflection, nodding needlessly.

"The house is completely gutted, apparently. I don't see how anyone could have got out of there alive," the line went quiet.

Thomas let out a gasp. "It's okay, Karl. I've got them! Petrov rang me — I put the family somewhere safe. This is down to Yorgi, isn't it?"

Karl ignored the question and let out a whoop of joy. And then it hit Thomas like a smack in the face; he'd done something amazing. He touched his neck where the crucifix chain used to rub, back when he'd worn it to please his mother.

"Are you still there, Tommo? Wherever they are, they're not safe; we need to bring them in."

Now came the familiar dilemma: to trust or not to trust.

Karl wouldn't wait. "Are you there? Listen to me. Yorgi is a Grade A psychopath. I've seen the file. If he's killed twice today, he's probably tying up all loose ends."

Thomas felt a creeping sense of doom. "But I told Petrov not to call anyone."

"Come on now — where did you take them?"

"Near Paddington — I cut through the City to save time."

"No!" Karl wailed, "Central London — the congestion charge; there are vehicle recognition cameras everywhere."

"I don't understand. If Yorgi's working alone . . ."

"That's just it, Tommo. These people are pros — they'll have connections. You better give me the details and pray Yorgi hasn't got to them first."

Thomas threw some money down on the counter — the way they do in films — and ran back to the hotel. Thank Christ he hadn't driven off anywhere. He pushed the glass door, ignored the night porter and made straight for the stairs. He took them two at a time, rounding the final flight at the Fifth Floor, and slammed through the fire door. Left hand corridor, down towards the end. He knocked politely then thought better of it, banging with his fist. "It's Thomas, open the bloody door." He stepped back and sized it up; it looked tougher than he did.

"Alright, alright; you'll wake Lukas," Petrov scolded him. The door unbolted and then the latch turned — at least they'd done something right.

Thomas pushed his way in; Alexandra lifted her head from the sofa. "We couldn't sleep so we watched television. Too much has happened; tell him, Petrov," she looked daggers at her husband.

Petrov carefully closed the door then slicked back his hair with his fingers. "I over-reacted, made a mistake. Yorgi telephoned on my mobile and apologised. He wants to make amends, to drive over and collect us, but this Alexandra does not want."

"Your house was burned down," Thomas blurted it out in one breath. No warning, no preamble; no point.

Petrov pressed a hand to his forehead and staggered to a chair. "How?"

Alexandra didn't say a word. She ran to a side room, where Thomas figured Lukas was sleeping.

He was glad she'd left the room; it made things easier. He stood over Petrov. "The fire was deliberate and Yorgi's killed two people today." And there was something about Petrov's face; a knowing look in the eyes that told Thomas this wasn't the first time. "Does Yorgi know where you are?" He felt his legs start to tremble. "We have to go, now."

Petrov leapt to his feet. "Is impossible. My wife needs to sleep. Besides, I have told him nothing. He does not know where to find us." He held up his mobile phone as if it was the evidence that would clear him.

The green light shone out to Thomas like a taunt. Oh Jesus: the mobile. As traceable as a number plate, with the right equipment. "When did he ring you?"

"About ten minutes after you left."

Thomas's mind raced through the maths. Ten minutes, plus fifteen minutes or so, equals thirty minutes max; plenty of time to be on the move. And if Yorgi could access information on the hoof . . . shit. "Get up," he snarled. "We're leaving."

Petrov's mobile rang; they both just stared at it. Thomas's senses went into overdrive; his first instinct was to grab the knife on the room service tray. Futile in itself, but a sign of how scared he was. His breath came in shallow bursts. Think Thomas, think. He grabbed Petrov's mobile and switched it off with a strangle hold. Reality kicked in: get out, go to ground and rely on Karl. He clicked his fingers at Petrov and pointed to the side room. Next, he turned the TV off and rang Karl.

"I'm organising a team, Tommo. In the meantime you'll have to improvise."

Improvise? Thomas felt the sweat trickle down his back. He gave Petrov another few seconds, mainly to avoid arguing with him. The bedroom door opened, and the family was ready to leave. They looked at him the same way they'd done at the house — as if he had all the answers. He tried to draw strength from that.

"Right," he held up a hand, as if he might grasp a passing plan, "got it. Here's how we do it. Petrov, you go alone. Alexandra, you take the boy. Yorgi is expecting three people together. Petrov — swap jackets with me; quickly."

It was bollocks, but it was a start. It gave them something to cling to; the delusion that he knew what he was doing. He and Petrov emptied out personal belongings and made the switch. Now came the tricky part.

He unlocked the door. An inch open and all he could hear was his own breathing and the television from next door. He emerged slowly, signalling for them to follow. But at the turn in the corridor, he had a flash of inspiration. "Stay in the room until the bells start."

Alexandra narrowed her eyes. "What bells?"

He blinked twice and ushered them away. "Just be ready."

He ran to the fire alarm and punched it hard, harder than needed. The sting in his knuckles felt good though; it seemed to sharpen his senses. He heard the alarm echo along the corridor; guest doors opened at random and a few simply closed again straight away. Stupid bastards.

Petrov and Alexandra wasted no time in joining the throng on the stairway. Thomas timed it and fell in close behind. He tapped Petrov's shoulder at the last landing so that he could pass him. Alexandra had already slowed up by the fire door, with the child in her arms. She looked lost.

He gently grabbed her elbow and steered her out into the street. The police were already in attendance — maybe Karl's doing, he couldn't be certain. He told Alexandra to stand by the police car. Petrov, if he'd kept to the plan, should be making himself invisible. Only Thomas — wearing Petrov's jacket — walked around slowly as if dazed by the chaos around him. He took his mobile out casually and hit the speed-dial. Now, Karl.

"I'll be on-site in ten minutes, max. I got some of the boys in blue to help out. Stay in the crowd, Tommo. Believe me, Yorgi is out there somewhere. Be safe."

Thomas didn't feel brave now, or clever; he just felt sick to his stomach. Like he was in one of those nature programmes where the gazelle stands around waiting for the lion to strike. This was insane. Easy, Thomas, just drift away from Alexandra; find a different policeman and ask some stupid questions. Anything to let Yorgi see that Petrov was smart enough to stay out of harm's way.

The police officer brushed him off and took a call on his radio, so much for Plan A. He listened without being obvious — something about sending everyone back in again. A firefighter approached, with a face like thunder.

"Some twat set off the alarm. We've scoured the ground floor upwards, just waiting on the basement. I'll give you a shout when the Incident Controller gives the okay to return."

This was where the plan unravelled. Still no Karl, and Petrov out there in the crowd — no doubt keeping an eye on Alexandra even though Thomas had told him to stay clear. They were bound to go in together, which pretty much defeated the object. He couldn't keep them out on their own, in the open; couldn't get them away, as his car was around the block. In short, screwed from all angles. He could slug the copper to create a bit of a commotion? Think again; the guy didn't look as if he took any prisoners — maybe trigger a car alarm on one of the Mercs, then? Yeah, and what good would that do?

The mobile rang; he grabbed at it as if it were a lifebelt.

Karl was breathless. "I'm at the back of the crowd; get them ready."

"Ready?" Thomas hissed. "I split them up for safety — there are over two hundred people in the street."

"Well, you better get a bloody move on. I couldn't get a pick-up in time so I'm their ride out of here."

The firefighter reappeared, had a few words with the police officer and raised a hand to sound the retreat. The residents morphed into grumbling cattle and moseyed on in.

Thomas picked out Alexandra easily. She had followed instructions and stuck by the police car. As he approached, she was in conversation with one of the cops. "Ah, here is my husband!"

He swallowed hard and hoped that the boy didn't start screaming. "This way," he all but scooped her up.

"Where is Petrov?" she whimpered.

"I'll find him in a minute. Come on," he pulled her arm roughly. They swam against the tide of returning hotel guests until Thomas caught sight of Karl's old banger in the middle of the street. His heart skipped a beat; he had to steady himself against Alexandra as he led her to the car. She stared at Karl; he stared right back.

"It's okay, really," Thomas insisted, craning the door wide and nudging her towards it. "I'll go and get Petrov."

He spotted his own jacket heading back into the hotel and elbowed his way through. Other guests had made for the complimentary drinks; Petrov was rooted to the spot, standing in the bar like the ugly one at a Valentine's disco.

Thomas zeroed in. "Alexandra and Lukas are already in the car — we'll take you somewhere safe." The way he said it, he was barely selling it to himself.

Petrov's face was as blank as the décor. Thomas eased him outside. Karl pulled up and Thomas shouldered him to the car like he was an invalid. "I'll sort your cases out later."

Petrov opened his mouth, but he didn't speak. Thomas reached for the front passenger door.

"That's okay Tommo — I'll see you back in the hotel bar for a wee chat."

As Thomas sat down in the bar, he felt the damp patch cold on his back, clinging like a dirty secret. He shifted forward and glanced around the room. For all he knew Yorgi could be any one of them — no saying he had to look like Petrov. Yeah, he argued with himself, but Yorgi was a professional. Ergo, he'd have seen Karl driving off — he'd hardly be hanging around now. Ergo? For an instant he thought of Christine, all lips and Latin. He squished against the chair again and felt a droplet trickle down his spine to rest in the crack of his arse. He grimaced and pulled his top away. Sod this for a game of soldiers, he'd nip out to his car and get the sweatshirt from the boot. On the way out, he grabbed an empty beer bottle for comfort.

After all the commotion, the streets outside seemed unnaturally quiet. There was still traffic — this was London after all — but it was reduced to glaring lights and shrouded shapes. The side street was jam-packed with parked cars. He stuck to the shadows, avoiding the sickly orange glow of street lamps where he could. He moved quickly, keeping his wits about him.

He paused three vehicles from his car, and gripped the beer bottle more tightly. It might have once held extra strong lager but it wasn't strong enough to take on a bullet. He smiled in the gloom; knowing exactly what he was doing: gallows humour. He took a breath, sucking it down like a smoker getting a fix.

Despite the bollocking awaiting him, he wished Karl were there. As if on cue, his arm throbbed through its dressing. Enough stalling. He took a final glance around then stepped smartly to the rear of his car. The boot catch gave way with a sigh; he reached in without bending his head, feeling his way around for the sweatshirt. For a split second he was going to change in the street, but he suddenly felt more vulnerable than ever. He didn't want to let go of the bottle so he did a bit of a juggling act and slammed the boot down hard. Good one Thomas; Mr Psycho might be out there but that ought to scare him off. He jogged back to the hotel, kidding himself that his panting was due to being out of condition, not blind terror.

* * *

Yorgi watched closely as the stranger fumbled about in his car then ran back towards the hotel. This was a new factor, an unknown quantity. Killing him now would achieve nothing. No, this man had chaperoned Alexandra and Lukas out of the hotel; and he would be the best way of reaching them again. He might need a little encouragement, but he would cooperate. As for Petrov, well, he could be persuaded to do anything. Yorgi leered in the darkness, remembering how he'd forced Petrov to shoot a rat on the farm. Petrov had shaken and bawled; how he had pleaded! He had done it in the end though. They always did what he wanted in the end.

He pressed his watch close. Sometimes, when he felt the glass against his ear in the night, he fancied he could still hear the American screaming. He lowered his hand

and moved the battered copy of Sun Tzu's Art of War from his lap. A phrase was underlined: 'A man who knows when he can fight and when he cannot, will be victorious.'

The traffic was a distant hum through the glass. He reached for the device and left the car, walking along the street with the transmitter nestling in his palm. The gun remained in his pocket, in case anyone was foolish enough to disturb him. He found the place, underneath the chassis near the driver's door. He pushed the apparatus up against the metal, making sure it was secure. Then he disappeared into the night to await victory.

Chapter 24

Thomas returned from the gents with his old clothes knotted together. The bar was still busy as he threaded through, holding the bundle down like a secret shame. He stuffed it under the chair, bought drinks and crisps and left them untouched on the table, feeling like a kid waiting outside the headmaster's office.

Karl arrived ten minutes later; Thomas figured he'd passed Petrov on to someone more senior — Teresa perhaps? Karl spotted him at the door, but didn't acknowledge him. This did not look good. He sat down and took his time about it, sipping at his pint of shandy before he spoke. "We're in the shit. Yorgi wasn't picked up; he's gone to ground."

Thomas opened a packet of crisps methodically. "Isn't that a good thing?"

Karl glared; wrong answer. "Grow up, Tommo; he's a fucking killer. We've no way of knowing when he's going to pop up again. Meantime his brother and that lovely wee family of his are looking at relocation and a new identity; and all because you fucked up."

Thomas jerked back as if he'd been sucker punched. "Hey, if it wasn't for me, Petrov might still have been at the house when . . ."

Karl was having none of it. "First, do you really think he'd have stayed there waiting if you hadn't agreed to pick him up? And second, what the fuck were you thinking of, not informing me? We're supposed to be a team!"

Thomas clenched his fists, under the table. "We're a team, Karl? Then who are we working for, huh? Who did you hand Petrov over to? We're a team when it suits you."

Karl closed in on him. "For two pins, I'd knock you down where you stand."

"I'm sitting down though." Not a flicker from Karl. All Thomas felt from him was a heat-haze of anger.

Karl kneaded his forehead, as if he was trying to massage the words into place. "Look, you're plainly out of your depth in all this. You're a liability."

Ouch. Thomas gulped back the shock along with the lager. There was nothing else to be said. He put his glass down — definitely half empty tonight — and started to stand.

Karl pulled at his arm. "Hey," he snarled, "we're not done yet! Petrov thinks you're some kind of saint so you'll be in on the interrogation — we're giving him a day or so to soften up. In the meantime we need to get a few things straight, once and for all." He pointed a finger dagger at Thomas's chest. "You need my help; Yorgi getting away like that looks worryingly suspicious from a certain angle."

Thomas launched himself to standing. The glasses rocked on the table, their contents swirling like miniature tempests.

"Calm yourself, Tommy Boy," Karl lifted his drink and took another sip. "This fiasco has put us both in a difficult position. I suggest you take a day off tomorrow — ring in sick — and have a serious think about your position." Karl sat back and looked away: class dismissed.

Thomas grabbed his clothes from the floor and made for the door. His arm was stinging again, but there was a kind of comfort in that. He was on the phone to Miranda before he'd reached the car.

"Thomas — it's late; what's up?" Straight to the point. He played vague. Wrong move; more questions were the last thing he wanted, and Miranda knew him too well. "Bad day at work?"

Four little words which translated neatly as 'serves you fucking right.' Before he had time to think, they were bickering down memory lane; trudging through the past in the search for survivors — his possessiveness, his secretiveness, that footballer she'd been banging — a word he knew would exocet through her defences. She told him to grow up and sort his life out. Sort it out? He didn't even know what his life was anymore.

He cut the mobile off mid-sentence. His arm was screaming now; he popped a pill and wondered how he'd ended up like this — Miranda, Christine and Karl, all blocking him like chess pieces. Shit, there was only Ajit left, and he was on the other side of the thin blue line.

The worst part of it was that he blamed himself. Oh sure, he'd make his peace with Miranda somehow and get back on side with Karl. Petrov and his family though, that was something he couldn't fix — didn't even know where to start. It was Big Boys' stuff. And there was something else too.

Yorgi was the first person he'd been afraid of since leaving Leeds. Okay, maybe Miranda's dad to a point, but Yorgi was a killer. The word made the blood slow at the back of his neck. What if . . . no, he didn't dare think that way. He'd move carefully on this now; phone in sick tomorrow, like Karl had suggested, and get his head together. He breathed a little easier and put the car radio on to drown out his thoughts.

* * *

Ask most Londoners and they'll tell you that driving is a necessary evil; a means to an end, but not a pleasure. Thomas loved it though; for him a car brought freedom. Even if he wasn't out working or taking his own photographs, sometimes it felt good to just get in the car and lose himself in the maze of London streets. A full tank of petrol and a bag of crisps, and he was a happy man. And after the day's shenanigans, what better way of winding down?

He left Paddington and turned up through Maida Vale, breezing through Kilburn. Irish Town, as Karl had christened it — and he ought to know. Kilburn High Road ran into Shoot-up Hill, worth the journey for the irony value alone. He sang to the radio, laughing at the realisation that his rendition of 'Eye of the Tiger' was as murderous as anything Karl could produce.

And okay, maybe he hadn't planned it consciously, but when the first sign for Highgate appeared, it all seemed to make sense. If he could just straighten out the whole Christine and Bob Peterson thing, it would be a start. Then maybe he could recover some credibility with Karl. At the very least he'd unsettle the happy couple and that could only be a good thing.

The closer he got to Christine's flat, the more malicious he felt. After all, hadn't Bob Peterson's appearance at Harwich been the detonator? The defining event that had bollocksed everything up? So this could be payback time.

He parked, switched off the ignition and made himself comfortable. He wouldn't bother to check for Peterson's vehicle — no point: guilty as charged. He punched in Christine's number and paused for a second on the send button. Game on. He held the phone lightly to his ear and crossed his feet. At the fourth ring he suddenly remembered the time. Oops.

"Hello?"

"Hi, it's Thomas; hope I'm not disturbing you," he winced — about as subtle as a hammer at an osteopath's.

"Thomas? Er, what can I do for you?" the curtain flicked back, silhouetting Christine against an orange glow. She looked good, even at a distance in a five second show.

"I just fancied a chat. Listen, I know it's late, but how about I come over?"

The line went silent for a moment; the kind of silence that a hand over the receiver makes. "I don't think that's a very good idea, do you?"

It was too much to ask that Bob Peterson would put in an appearance at the window. He'd settle for something less tangible, like an admission.

"Are you out there somewhere, Thomas?"

Shit. Peterson was probably right next to her, might even be listening for his reply. A large plate of 'backfire' to table four. He swallowed and stared up at the window, which showed a silhouette of Christine and Bob.

"I'm waiting, Thomas."

"I just needed to talk with you tonight. There have been developments." Jesus, what was he saying? But the idea had already formed. "I think something is going on with the department."

For an instant he thought he heard Christine gasp. Or maybe it was static.

"Look, I'm not far from your place; I could drop over — I won't stay long."

"No!" she yelped, "we've been through this before, Thomas. If you've got anything to say to me you can say it now or it'll have to keep until tomorrow."

Fuck it: in for a penny, in for a pound. "It's about Bob Peterson."

No reaction; she was good. If he knew her like he thought he did, the next words would be brief and measured.

"What about him?"

"I'd rather tell you face to face."

"Thomas, don't piss me about. I could have your mobile trigged before you got half a mile away. If you've something to say . . ."

"You do know he's married with two kids?" He winced.

"Grow up Thomas, and keep your nose out of my personal affairs."

He bit his tongue. "I'm just looking out for you, Chrissie."

"I can look after myself. And don't ring me here again, Thomas — I mean it. The next time you call me at home it goes on your report — do you understand? It's been a long day; I'm going back to bed."

"Is that alone?"

"Last warning, Thomas. Whatever you think you know, you'd best forget it. This ends here, but you are all out of favours now." The line went dead.

He hung up and exhaled deeply into his hands. Stupid bastard; what was he doing? He grabbed up the mobile again and speed-dialled number 1. "Hi Miranda, it's me again. Can I come over? It's been a lousy night."

"Do you know what time it is?"

"Late?"

She laughed. "Get some sleep, Thomas; it'll all be better in the morning."

"But your bed is so much more comfortable than mine . . ."

"Suit yourself."

He sat there for a minute, trying to think straight. Was she toying with him? She'd done that once before, and he'd arrived to find the lights out and the door locked. "Well," he told himself in the dark, "there's only one way to find out."

Chapter 25

Thomas rang the bell in shrill, insistent bursts.

"Alright!"

He squinted as light erupted, framing her blurred outline through the glass.

Miranda peered back at him, her face pressed against the frosted pane.

"Do you know what time it is?" she opened the door a degree, and instinctively he strained to see where the frayed silk dressing gown ended and her thigh began. "I wasn't sure if you were serious about coming over, when you rang."

"Well, here I am," he waited awkwardly, leaning against the door, matching her resistance. Then, as if he'd finally decided what he really wanted to happen, he pushed a little more until he felt her hand relent and the door swung in.

"Lock up, will you?" she walked off to the bedroom without looking back.

He brushed against the coat hooks; there was a man's jacket there. He slammed the door and flicked the switch. The only light now was the pink glow at the end of the hall.

"I see you've had a visitor," he called out from the shadow, tasting the venom of his thoughts.

"It's my brother's — Terry left it here. Jesus, still as paranoid as ever! Now get your arse in here; I've got stuff to do tomorrow morning."

He slipped off his shoes. "What's Terry up to these days?" His voice wavered, caught between relief and shame. She was right, still the same demons; if anything, he was worse since Christine. Something else to blame her for.

Miranda was still undressing in the bedroom. He pressed up close behind her, watched her smile and tried to fathom that look as he spread his fingers across her breasts. He touched his lips to her neck, traced a circle of kisses behind her ear. She smelt of expensive soap and perfume.

What sort of a person wears perfume on the strength of a phone call? The same kind who turns up at one-thirty in the morning, with nothing but a hard-on.

"You could've shaved."

He sighed, no arguments tonight. Besides, actions spoke louder than words. His hand travelled down between her thighs. Miranda gasped and pushed her buttocks against his groin. She leaned back, draping over him and her hair fell across his face. He studied their reflection: it looked like a still from a low-budget porn flick.

She laughed as she turned to face him and he was startled by a momentary wave of contempt. This was so easy for her. 'Sex is sex,' she'd said in the past. 'Don't confuse it with something more complicated.'

He discarded his clothes methodically, and joined her on the bed. He wondered how much activity the bed had seen since he'd last been there. Then he reached for the lamp and snapped it off, shutting out his thoughts.

He was greedy for her, eager to wrap himself in desire. But he wanted her to want him, really yearn for him; he needed that tonight. He tasted her skin, ingested the perfume's acrid undercurrent and let his tongue travel the length of her body, slowly and tentatively, as if it was a forbidden journey. Soon they moved together rhythmically as only familiar lovers can. Yet the closer they became the more he felt like an outsider.

"You're hurting my arms."

He relaxed his grip, jarred back into the moment. He was rough with her, knew that he wanted a reaction. A sudden image of Christine and Peterson, together, rose up to taunt him and he pushed hard into Miranda as if he could drive away his demons. He heard her breathing change and synchronised his body to hers, matching the frenzied thrusts to the rhythmic rocking of her hips.

"Not yet," he heard her whisper breathlessly, as she arched her back.

His mind detached itself from the scene; he became a voyeur while instinct took the lead. And then, when he felt her whole body meld around his and her low moans built to fever pitch, he tilted upwards and burst inside her.

They remained still, a tide of release and tenderness washing between them, until he slumped on top of her with a heavy sigh. She held him close and he lay there, still panting, his dry lips savouring the sweat on her breast. He felt a tear forming in his eye and lay motionless, as if he could deny its existence.

"That was epic!" she congratulated him, stroking his hair affectionately.

He knew she'd expect some salacious compliment in return, but he wasn't in the mood tonight.

"Would you rather have been somewhere else?" she read him like a book.

"Sorry," he conceded and untangled himself from her.

"Is it still about Christine — do you wanna talk about it?"

He rolled carefully on to one side and traced Miranda's face in the dark — that knowing, beautiful face. Then he kissed her; a long, tender kiss, as if to pour himself into her lips and escape his own identity. A lesser man would have called it love. But it was more than that. "I'll tell you in the morning," he promised, pulling her towards him as he closed his eyes.

Chapter 26

Thomas yawned in the gloom. He stared, bleary eyed, trying to make sense of his watch without disturbing the thick curtains. It was either five to eight or twenty to eleven. He leaned across and stroked behind her ear, certain that Miranda was awake and ignoring him.

She wriggled free from his fingers. "Listen, any chance you could drop me off at the club on your way into work? I left my car there last night and I'm picking Terry up from the airport today. I can give him his coat back too, if you like?"

"Very droll. Just take my car — I'm calling in a sickie."

"Wow. Hold the front page. Do you wanna come with me, then?"

"Nah, I'll just hang around here for a bit and meet you later at the club."

She paused, as if in mid-thought. "Well, lock up after you and no going through my underwear drawer when I'm gone."

"You know me so well."

"Indeed I do, Mr Bladen. Speaking of which, what brought you to my door last night — welcome as it was."

She slipped out from the duvet and into a dressing gown. "Something about Christine wasn't it?"

She knew bloody well it was. He sighed and tapped at the bedside table with his index finger.

"If that's Morse code, I never went to Spy School." She was still smiling.

"Christine's involved with this married bloke; and he's bad news."

"Brave Sir Knight to the rescue?" she raised an eyebrow.

"Not quite."

"Can't Karl help you out?"

He felt her studying his face. He shook his head.

"Lovers' tiff?"

"Something like that," he braced himself for some righteous piss-taking, but it never came. That was Miranda, full of surprises.

"Well, I'm here if you need an ear. And don't forget," she gazed in the general direction of his groin, "I keep all your secrets."

He waited until Miranda was in the shower before ringing in. Christine's office phone was diverted to her mobile. She sounded relieved; it was a short call. Karl had been spot-on — a little breathing space would do everyone a favour. After he'd rung off, he tried the bathroom door — locked. He felt peeved; no reason to be but there it was.

* * *

Sir Peter Carroll took the call in his limo. "I've seen the picture — it's definitely our man. Yes, indeed, very delicate. I'm certainly not aware of any affiliations. No, Yorgi, best you remain where you are — I'll handle things from here."

The call ended. Trevor, the driver, glanced up in the mirror and read his employer's mood well enough to say nothing. Another number was dialled.

"Nicholas, I have an opportunity for you to redeem yourself. I want you to supervise a collection — Thomas Bladen." Sir Peter could almost hear Nicholas salivating over the phone.

"Thank you, Sir Peter, we'll pick him up before he gets to Harwich."

"Excellent. I'm relying on you Nicholas — don't let me down again."

* * *

Miranda waited patiently at the lights, studying the pedestrians as they herded past the front of the car. Ever since Thomas had come out of the spy closet, she'd practised extra vigilance. Still, with a family background like hers, she was pretty vigilant anyway, especially where men were concerned. As a teenager, having boyfriends had been a dangerous pastime — for them. Back then, secret assignations and sneaking about were second nature. If anything, Thomas's cloak-and-dagger act had brought on a touch of nostalgia.

A young mother pushed a stroller out just as the lights started to change. Miranda sat, primed, ready to flip the finger behind her if anyone dared beep. Mother and child; it made you think. Her biological clock wasn't even building up to a tick, but that hadn't always been the way. Once . . . well, one day when she'd come to terms with what might have been, she'd give it all some thought.

The second the mother reached the kerb, Miranda put her foot down, narrowly beating the change back to amber. She stole a final glance in the mirror then powered through the traffic. Eager for distraction, she flicked on the radio and re-tuned it to something closer to the last twenty years.

The green Peugeot she'd kept tabs on had been two cars back for a good five minutes now. Probably nothing in it, but she pulled in and watched as it passed without slowing down. Better safe than sorry. Back when Dad was first under suspicion, when he was being fitted up, the Wright family had sat down together and drawn up a set of rules.

Simple stuff: mistrust everyone; say nothing; if at all concerned, go to a public place — preferably with lots of CCTV and people. Thomas had said similar things that morning, like an echo of her dad. Although he did play poker better.

* * *

Nicholas arrived promptly at Great Portland Street. He'd prepared a briefing, but it was very clear, from the moment he opened the conference room door and laid eyes on them, that he was more passenger than leader. No round of introductions here. Everyone knew their place — and their distance.

"Shall we?" he headed for the stairs, crossing his fingers that they followed him. He took the front passenger seat in the people carrier and said nothing until they were on the move. The GPS tracker showed that the car was southbound, corresponding to the map onscreen. His job, he now realised, was to relay the data and coordinate the team. So why was the blue dot travelling further and further away from Harwich?

He considered ringing Sir Peter to check. No, he could manage things. Besides, how hard could it be to pick up one SSU man? He touched lightly at his cheek and felt the last vestige of bruising from where he'd taken a beating in Thomas Bladen's flat. He blushed at the memory of waking up in the undergrowth of a roundabout, stripped to his underwear. Shameful, but he'd weathered that storm. Whereas his accomplice had never been seen again. "Get a move on; I think he's giving us the run around."

The driver obeyed him and he felt his silent companions behind him twitch to attention. "I'm Nicholas, if you didn't already know." Now he was in his stride, captain of the team.

"Alice."

He looked round at her and stared, as if to say 'really'? She didn't flinch. Alice, it was then. Jack declared himself, but the driver — a much older man — said nothing. No matter, Nicholas was used to dealing with servants. No one ventured any further information, which didn't surprise him. Scratch the surface of most departments and the protocol was the same.

They were making progress against the target vehicle and it didn't take a science degree to pinpoint the destination: Gatwick. They still had the element of surprise and the advantage of numbers, if it came to that. So what was Bladen up to? Sir Peter evidently didn't know; this could be the coup he'd been looking for.

He swapped hands with the tracker unit and felt the clamminess between his palms. "Good luck everyone; we're nearly there." He saw Jack and Alice share a glance of disdain — so much the better. He wasn't there to be liked; he had a job to do. The numbers on screen whittled down as they approached the short stay car park. He already had the number plate and gestured as he saw the vehicle parking up; gestured because he was too wired to speak.

* * *

A people carrier with blacked-out windows drew in front of Miranda's car. She heard the doors as she delved into her handbag for her mobile to ring Thomas and let him know she'd arrived. As she rifled through her things, she ran through a shortlist of opening lines and settled on: 'Are you still inside?'

Before she could dial, her driver's door opened. She turned to see a youngish man in an expensive suit. "Yeah, what do you want?"

He looked lost for an answer. She reached over to pull the handle in, but the light began to fade. Behind her, someone was blocking the passenger door. Panic time.

Posh Bloke had stepped back, allowing a woman to crank the door wider and start pulling on her arm. "Where is he?"

As Miranda felt herself being dragged out of the car, she went limp to conserve her strength. Then she grabbed the edge of her seat and pulled herself down towards the gear-stick. As soon as she was close enough, she kicked hard against the passenger window, right at the chink in the pane that Thomas had never got round to fixing, driving her boot heel into the glass with a roar. The window splintered on the third kick; a pity that light block had the sense to move in time. Now she rolled on to her stomach and let the woman pull her out, waiting until she was past the steering wheel to swing, left-handed. Not her finest work, but three years of kickboxing — and running a bar — did the job.

"Wait!" Posh Bloke held up his hand, like a teacher intervening in a playground brawl. "We're here to help you. Thomas sent us. He's in trouble."

Miranda ceased struggling and the woman let go. They ushered her into the people carrier. If this was the cavalry, they had a funny way of showing it. As everyone climbed aboard, she copped the driver sending a text. No one else seemed to have noticed.

"What about my car?"

Posh Bloke seemed subdued again. "It'll be taken care of."

Next question. "Is someone going to tell me what's going on?"

Either they were stonewalling her or something was amiss here. Eyes darted back and forth, but nobody answered. Posh Bloke seemed to be the one in charge; she'd have to work on him. She played the game of pluses and minuses in her head, as much to organise her thoughts as to try and stay calm. Pluses: they hadn't hurt her, they'd mentioned Thomas and they didn't seem like hardened criminals — and she knew what they looked like. Minuses:

Thomas must have sent them to her and she didn't know what the deal was.

Nobody spoke to her as the people carrier sped clockwise around the M25. She wasn't bothered; she had plenty to think about. How did they know how to find her, especially as she'd been driving Thomas's car? A shame about the window though — she'd better let Thomas know she was safe. "I need to make a phone call."

"Later."

Well, that was brief and to the point. She toyed with the idea of just opening her mobile, but something told her to stay submissive and bide her time. The woman beside her winced as she practiced opening and closing her eye. Yeah, as Sheryl at the club would say, in her native Brooklyneese: 'suck it up.'

Eyeball — no one had introduced themselves, bar the merest sniff of an ID card, so she had given them her name — Eyeball's face changed. She seemed more focused and detached. Miranda almost felt bad for punching her — sisterhood and all that.

"How well do you know Thomas Bladen?"

Miranda smiled inwardly. Outwardly she stayed as blank as a new canvas. All Thomas's paranoia was finally bearing fruit. "We go way back."

"And what do you know about his work?"

This was like painting by numbers. "He's a government photographer — and he delivers packages." Too much information maybe? She glanced ahead and read the A road as they turned off. Eyeball leaned over and touched her leg.

"I know this must all seem strange to you."

That was a first; good cop and bad cop all rolled together, making: average cop. Miranda nodded and bit at her fingernail. Dad had said he used to do that in police interrogations, to accompany whatever crap he was feeding them.

Eyeball continued. "It's just a precaution, you understand. Thomas's cover is at risk and he wanted you kept safe until we have things under control."

Miranda dug her nail hard into her hand, to stifle a response. They were lying, and badly. Firstly, Thomas didn't have any cover. Secondly, he was intensely private, so how would they know about her? And thirdly, if Thomas had been in any kind of trouble, he'd have contacted the family first.

But here she was, in the company of strangers, and he did have that bandage on his arm the previous night, so something didn't sit right. "Does Thomas know I'm with you?"

Eyeball swallowed and took a breath then swapped glances with Posh Bloke. "We'll contact him once you're at a secure location."

Miranda narrowed her gaze and dug her nail into her palm again: jackpot. She sat back and took stock; she was sandwiched between two of them — no chance of getting out. Best play the dumb blonde for now and try and hold it together. "Yeah, that makes sense. Do you think I could just leave him a message? Only I was supposed to feed the dog later and he might worry if he gets back and Butch . . ."

Eyeball leaned forward and Posh Bloke mumbled approval. "Alright, but keep it short — you can use my mobile." Eyeball opened her phone, punched in the digits from a piece of paper and passed the phone over.

It went straight to his office voicemail. "Hi Tom, it's Miranda. Erm, something's come up so you'll have to sort Butch out yourself today. Sorry." She returned the phone with a smile; it was up to him now.

Eyeball gave her a funny look. "I need your handbag, as a precaution."

The silent wonder on her left wriggled in his seat; no, he squirmed. Even he didn't fall for that line.

"Okay," Miranda handed her bag over.

Posh Bloke signalled to the driver and they pulled in at the next lay-by. He seemed quietly agitated. When they stopped he got out, walked a few yards ahead and got on his mobile. Whatever he was saying, he didn't look happy.

Eyeball leaned in close again. "We need to find Thomas urgently — do you know where he is, Miranda?"

"He wasn't working today so he lent me his car." Then she thought of something else. Oh bollocks, Terry would be waiting at the airport.

Eyeball seemed satisfied with the explanation, unlike the Silent Wonder. From the look on his face, he had less of a clue than she did.

After five minutes or so, Posh Bloke stormed back to the vehicle. His face was a picture — a portrait depicting 'pissed off.'

"We're to go here," he announced to the driver, passing him a note. The driver seemed unperturbed, switching on classical music as he rejoined the traffic. Posh Bloke said nothing more, but his face spoke volumes.

Chapter 27

"Anything I can get you, Thomas?"

If Sheryl leaned any further over the bar, her breasts would tumble out to greet him. "That's okay," he flustered.

Caliban's was practically empty. He felt like a teenager on a blind date, trying not to look conspicuous as he watched the minute hand inch its way round for the umpteenth time. He thought about ringing Miranda, but she'd probably be driving. He turned the mobile over and pretended he was fiddling with the casing instead.

"Wanna shoot some pool?"

"Sure," he'd never sounded less sure of anything in his life.

"Relax, Thomas. I don't bite."

No, he thought as he followed her, but you do look capable of nibbling.

"You and Miranda go way back, don't you?"

He smiled; that was the phrase they always used.

"So how come you two never quite got it together?"

He made a dumb face in the absence of a convincing explanation, and racked up the balls. The first two games went to Sheryl with ease — he barely got a look in. He turned the third game around and somehow snuck in the black, more by luck than judgement.

Sometimes when she looked at him, he wanted to ask her things — about Miranda, about herself; about why a girl from Brooklyn should wind up managing a bar in East London. But he let it go, same as always. For a while, he kidded himself that he was capable of winning, but Sheryl's soon shattered any lasting illusions.

"Did you grow up in a Pool Hall?"

"Pretty much! You're not too bad though."

He chose to take it as a compliment. As he bent down to take a shot, his mobile trilled into life — it was Karl.

"Thomas, are you free to talk? It's urgent."

"Sure," He felt the blood run cold up his neck. He shouldered the phone and moved to the main bar for better reception.

"Where have you been today?"

"Nowhere. I was out last night and I'm at Caliban's now."

"Tommo, your car's been picked up at Gatwick airport. There's damage to one of the windows, keys still in the ignition. Were you there?" It sounded like an accusation.

"No, I lent the car to . . . to a friend."

The line went silent. "Stay right where you are and I'll come get you."

The room seemed to spin; he grabbed at a chair and it shrieked. Sheryl rushed over and the shock on his face reflected on hers. He sat down before his legs buckled under him.

Sheryl quickly rejoined him with two whiskies. "Talk to me."

He shook his head.

"Is it Miranda?"

"They found my car . . . abandoned . . ."

Sheryl put a hand to her mouth. "I'll ring Diane."

"No!" he barked. "Let me take care of this. Karl's on his way." He downed most of the whisky in one go and felt the bile swirling inside him. Sheryl looked at him, as if she could see the turmoil inside. He realised that he didn't even know what to tell her.

They sat, huddled together like victims in a lifeboat, neither one speaking. When he wavered and felt he was on the verge of tears, he pressed into his wound, choosing pain over emotion. Sheryl's eyes were brimming; she just stared at him, silently, searching for something to cling on to.

* * *

Karl burst through the door. He pulled the chair back and hoisted Thomas to his feet. "Come on, we have to deal with this."

Sheryl looked up at him and Karl laid a consoling hand on her shoulder. She stared back at Thomas, wide-eyed, in disbelief.

"I'll be back later — I promise.

He shuffled to the car in a daze, Karl's hand at his back. Karl didn't speak until they were on the main road. "I'm sorry, Thomas; it doesn't look good. Your nearside window was broken — from the inside."

"Miranda had the car."

Karl didn't press him on it. "How much does she know?"

"Just the basics — and she knows about Christine." It felt easier to talk when Karl was asking the questions.

"What about her?"

"I went over to Christine's last night, to confront her about Bob Peterson. She warned me off, said it was my last chance."

"Oh Jesus, Thomas. You couldn't leave it alone, could you?"

In the silence that followed, Thomas's psyche began to regroup. "How did you find my car?"

Karl upped the speed. "That's not important now. I checked your office voicemail today — I always check it."

Thomas shot him a glance.

"Miranda left you a message about dealing with Butch."

He felt his mind shift a gear. Butch: Miranda was in some kind of trouble.

"The thing is, when I checked a little later, someone had deleted the message. I reckon someone doesn't want you to hear from her."

Thomas pushed his hands together, prayer fashion, and touched the index fingers to his lower lip. "You've got to tell me how to fix this."

"I'll do everything I can, Tommo, you know that. First, we're gonna pick your car up and get the window fixed. Tomorrow, when you go in to work, nothing has happened. Got it? If these bastards want anything, they'll be in touch."

Thomas nodded slowly as if punch drunk. "Did someone follow her?"

"They didn't need to. Somebody put a tracker on the car. I suggest we leave it there. So if you need to go anywhere private, you take a cab from now on."

Thomas covered his face with his hands, blotting away the tears.

"I don't know if I can do this, Karl. I don't think I'm strong enough."

"You have to be, Thomas; you've no choice."

He closed his eyes and tried to sleep, but Karl's supernatural silence only amplified his thoughts. Why would someone take Miranda? And what the hell was he going to do about it? He lashed out and punched the glove compartment, jolting himself into some sort of clarity. "Unless they'd been planning this . . ."

Karl still said nothing.

He looked around, aware he'd just said the unthinkable. Who the fuck were they? No, wait, he was on to something; or maybe he just wanted to believe that. He put his hands together again and rocked back and forth. "I've only done two things that would make . . ." his voice cracked. "Two things. I contacted Christine and I helped Petrov get away from Yorgi." As he said Yorgi's name, he felt sick to his stomach, as if his intuition had suddenly whispered yes. "For Christ's sake, say something, Karl."

Silence again, apart from the pounding in his head. He looked around and saw the signs for Reading. Well, bollocks to it, he'd had enough. "Stop the car, I want to get out," he already had his fingers on the handle.

"Tommo, just relax, we'll be there soon . . ."

"I said, stop the fucking car. Now!"

Karl pulled hard left and crushed the brake, screeching the car to a lopsided halt. "Listen to me; we have to do this by the numbers. I know you're scared right now, but so far there's no indication . . ."

Thomas raised a chopping hand to interrupt.

"That's enough!" Karl roared at him.

He fell back to his seat, defeated.

"Look, Tommo, I've dealt with this shit before; I grew up with this kind of coercion. When they want something, they'll be in touch. Until then, we sit tight."

He let go of the door and the car resumed its journey, snaking its way to an industrial estate on the outskirts of Reading. As they approached a set of nondescript units, Thomas recognised his car coming off a flatbed trailer to a waiting team of overalls.

"We'll give them half an hour — come on, let's take a wee walk."

Thomas looked through the glass; it felt safe in Karl's car. Somehow, if he went outside, he'd be accepting all this. Karl walked around to the passenger door and waited.

* * *

The pungent stench of rubbish and diesel couldn't disguise the chill in the air. Thomas rubbed his arm self-consciously as they walked. Karl still wasn't saying much and as for Thomas, he didn't dare open his mouth for fear of screaming.

Karl's destination soon became clear, as the white, mud-spattered caravan gradually got closer. "You need to eat something," he insisted, pointing to the bargain garden furniture.

Thomas flopped into the chair and pressed his fingers hard against the plastic's rough edges. He looked over at the counter; exactly how did his best buddy fit into all this?

Karl brought over a couple of teas and enough sugar to fell a racehorse. "Get it down yer. Burgers are on the way."

Thomas didn't protest. He hugged the polystyrene cup and tried to reason out his options. He didn't know where Miranda was or who had taken her. Okay, he had suspicions about this Yorgi, but that's all they were. The sound of nearby traffic lulled him into some kind of mental pause. She hadn't screamed, 'Come and get me,' on her phone message — according to Karl anyway. No, she'd mentioned 'Butch' instead: private code for dodgy dealing. And the car window was a smart move, but what did it mean? Had she'd been taken against her will, yet still somehow able to make the call?

Two plates clattered down on to the table. Thomas opened his eyes; bloody stupid — polystyrene cups, but proper plates. At first sight, the burgers churned his stomach, and then hunger took over as his instincts kicked in.

"Okay," Karl bit into his burger savagely; "you take the car to work tomorrow. And if anyone treats you differently, it's a fair bet they're involved."

"And then what?"

Karl chewed on a piece of burger that was putting up a fight. "Then we get a better idea of who we're up against."

Thomas tilted the bap away so that the fatty juices didn't run into his mouth.

"Come on, Thomas, think about it. Miranda left a message for you on your office phone. Nigh on two years, we've worked in the same office, and have you ever taken a personal call there? No, because neither she nor anyone else has your number; am I right?"

He nodded; he was already putting together a shortlist in his head of anyone he'd encountered since he'd joined the SSU. And while it didn't exactly give him hope, it gave him a focus.

The burger was sliding down nicely. He felt more grounded, more settled, confident enough to take a chance. "Karl, I need to ask you something," he kept his voice low and his gaze down. Here goes — "And if I don't get the truth, I'll go to the police."

It was a terrible bluff, so shit that Miranda's dad would have spotted it at a poker table. But he was desperate and it might, just might, rattle Karl a bit.

Karl took a long sip of tea. Thomas took the silence as consent to continue. "Is Miranda's disappearance connected to the missing information you're after?"

Karl inclined his head.

"Jesus, Karl!" he erupted, overbalancing the chair behind him as he stood. He was a dozen steps away when he heard Karl scrabbling behind him.

"Wait up, Tommo, please." Karl drew level and laid a hand on him, shifting his eyes about like a guilty schoolboy. "Look, I honestly don't believe Miranda is in any immediate danger. And what I'm about to tell you, well, you wouldn't have believed me before now."

"I'm listening," Thomas conceded, and carried on walking back to his car, with Karl trailing alongside.

"I don't know how well you know your European history, but the ending of World War Two was a messy one."

Thomas laughed spontaneously, surprising himself.

"Anyways, after the boys finally put their toys away and buried their copious dead, the key players decided that steps had to be taken to avoid making it a hat-trick of stupidity."

Thomas stopped in his tracks.

"Now, whatever you think of the European Union's track record, the wars have at least been kept regional. It doesn't take a rocket scientist to see that a few years down the line, a United States of Europe is a real possibility."

"And the point of this bollocks?" Thomas felt his fist tightening again.

"Some people aren't willing to wait a few years; important and influential people with something to gain, throughout Europe and beyond. That's the kind of information I've been looking for."

Chapter 28

The technician greeted Thomas and showed off her handiwork on the side window. "Good as new," she joked, as if she'd just done him a favour. He let it slide and collected his keys.

Karl tailed him back to a service station off the M25. When Thomas came out from the gents, Karl was kneeling by his car at the driver's side. He didn't seem at all embarrassed to be caught in the act.

"I was just checking the tracker on your car — it's still active. Remember, anywhere you don't want people to know about, use alternative transport."

Thomas joined him by the wheel, determined not to comment on the gizmo Karl had in his hand.

"I need you to trust me, Tommo," Karl whispered, close enough that Thomas could see the fret lines in his face. "Don't go off doing anything stupid. And don't forget, we're talking to Petrov after work tomorrow, so get a good night's sleep."

Yeah, that was Karl: the wellspring of compassion. Thomas opened the driver's door, nudging Karl out of the way. "And what do I tell Miranda's family? Her brother's already messaged me asking why she wasn't at the airport."

Karl shoved his hands in his pockets. "I'd, er, appreciate it if you stalled them for a while. A missing person report will only complicate things."

"Yeah, but for who?"

"For all of us, Tommo. We all want the same thing," he faced him. "Miranda safely home and the people who did this held accountable."

He paled at the thought of lying to Miranda's family. That was a complete no-no. But the alternative was equally unthinkable. So he made a pact with the devil. "Three days, Karl — tops. And understand this: I may not have your connections, but if word hasn't reached me that Miranda's safe . . ." he couldn't finish the sentence because that sickening feeling rushed up to gnaw at his guts again.

Thomas sat in the lay-by and stared at his mobile. The car rocked as another juggernaut thundered past. As he switched the phone on with one hand, he was wiping away tears with the other. The most precious thing he had with the Wrights was trust and now he was destroying that. For a greater good perhaps, but it was still a betrayal. As the phone dialled out, he wondered, if he could do this, then what else was he capable of?

Judas time. "Terry? Hi, yeah, sorry mate, I've been really busy at work. Ah, mate, total balls-up. Miranda had to go out of town, short notice . . ." the monologue went on, each line more forced and implausible than the last. Maybe Terry would just assume they'd had a huge fight, and Miranda had swanned off to the coast, like she'd done before. All he could do was act vague and leave Terry to join the dots for himself.

Terry seemed to accept everything he said; it was like taking a sick dog to the vet's on that long, final walk. When the deed was done, he needed a drink. And where better than Caliban's, where he could pimp the remainder of his soul by persuading Sheryl to back up his story.

He'd barely stepped through the door before Sheryl called him over. "Let's go through," she raided the scotch optic with two glasses on her way up to the office. The barmaid smiled at him; nothing seemed out of place as he passed. But he still felt like a condemned man.

Sheryl closed the door. "Have you found her?" she thrust a drink into his hand as if it was some kind of truth serum.

He shook his head.

"So what the fuck have you been doing since you left here?"

He let her anger run its course. She had a right; and yes, Miranda deserved better — far better than him. And something told him that when it came down to it, when Karl and all the monsters had finished playing their games, it would be left to him to pick up the pieces. So he cut the crap and told her straight; about Terry, about how he'd lied to buy Karl and him a little more time. And he pleaded with her to just let things lie for three more days.

Sheryl took a last gulp of scotch and set her glass down. Her hand trembled a little, but she raised her head to look him in the eyes, slowly and deliberately. "If anything happens to Miranda, you're a dead man."

He chose to take that as agreement to his request and started to reach out to her hand, then thought better of it.

"Is this to do with that Irish guy — the one you had a showdown with?"

There it was again, that uncharted territory: to trust or not to trust. "Sheryl, don't take this the wrong way, but I can't talk about it with you."

She swooped for his glass. "Hey, the only reason I'm even listening to you now is because I know that's what Miranda would want. If it was down to me I'd make a couple of phone calls and . . ." she blinked twice slowly, ". . . well, I'm sure you can figure it out."

On the drive home, he added Sheryl to his mental list of people to keep at a distance; hard to do when he'd promised to ring her mobile, twice a day — without fail.

* * *

Back at the flat, there were no messages — too much to hope for. He took the Leeds photograph of Miranda off the wall and propped it on the table. Just sitting there, he could hear her laughter merging with the sound of traffic, the scene ablaze with sunlight and the promise of happy ever after.

The oven pinged and he returned to the present with a thud. Only now did he remember that he'd put a cottage pie on. He took another shot of Southern Comfort to dry his tears.

He fired up his laptop and ate beside it, going through his usual anonymity server for untraceable web surfing. It wasn't hard to get lucky on the conspiracy sites; everything and everyone had an opinion, and by Christ they were going to share it with you. After twenty minutes of being distracted by 9/11 theories he set about his search in earnest, following trails that led to the Bilderberg Group and the New Holy Roman Empire.

After that jaunt to La-La Land he narrowed his quest to historical documents relating to Europe from 1945 onwards. What he wanted were facts, and they seemed thin on the ground. Finally, he located a 1946 speech given by Winston Churchill, in Zurich. There, in black and white, was the phrase 'United States of Europe,' along with the proposal to first set up a Council of Europe. Maybe Karl was on to something after all.

Chapter 29

The mobile went off at 6.30 am. Thomas spasmed awake from a nightmare and made a wild grab for the phone.

It was Karl, with nothing to report. He repeated the need for a veil of normality and reminded him about seeing Petrov after work: he was business-like, and, in a way, Thomas drew strength from that. If Karl was used to dealing with situations like this, then maybe everything would turn out okay.

Now wide awake, he showered and dressed, stared at Miranda's photo for longer than was healthy, and then was out the door. The seven-fifteen traffic offered little resistance — so much the better for the two-hour slog to Harwich. Perhaps someday they'd get a surveillance gig in Chingford. He noticed that the radio had been retuned — it was obvious who'd done it — and he couldn't bring himself to change it back.

Desperation was a strange thing; he'd learned that from his mum when his gran was dying. When you're trying to negotiate with the Man in the Sky, you'll offer up just about anything. So, by the time the first sign to Harwich had appeared, he'd resolved to cherish Miranda on her safe return, the way he'd always meant to. In the last chance saloon of life, he was still asking for one for the road.

* * *

Miranda liked to sleep in; that whole 'up before the dawn' insanity was Thomas's thing. Unless it was for bedroom athletics, she'd always opt for easing herself into the morning. Today was different though. It wasn't every day you found yourself the honoured guest at a bona fide cloak-and-dagger convention.

She'd turned in early the night before and now it was some God-awful time, and here she was, sat up in bed wide awake and thinking about Thomas. Okay, so they'd bullshitted her about being sent by him, but that didn't mean he wasn't in trouble. She went back over the previous day's events again, to fix them clearly in her mind. The same things stood out — the driver stashing his mobile as they got in the car and Posh Bloke losing his rag in the lay-by. And repetitive questions about not much in particular. Conclusion: either something was wrong or they were really shit at this. Or both.

The night before, she'd asked how long her stay was likely to be and all she'd got back was a few nervous glances. She smirked now as she pressed her back against the pillows — maybe the answer was classified. She'd get some sense out of them today. The woman, Eyeball, seemed like the best candidate for new friend.

She slithered out of bed and threw on an oversized dressing gown — blue towelling, not very chic. No harm in having an early morning wander, maybe watch a little satellite TV. She turned the door handle with infinite care — no sense in disturbing anyone else. As soon as the door clicked she heard scuffling in the corridor and caught the last moment of Eyeball launching from a chair.

"Good morning," Miranda opted for friendliness first. Eyeball — and that eye certainly shone today — nodded blearily; she looked as if she had spent the entire night on the chair. That was a worry. Miranda ambled over, smiling like she was back on a Bermuda fashion shoot, and made a mental note to check if the windows were locked.

"Would you like some breakfast?" Eyeball said it like she meant it.

"That'd be great," Miranda retraced her way to the kitchen.

Eyeball tagged along like the less attractive one on a double date. Miranda filled the kettle and tried the thing that usually worked on men — Thomas being a rare exception: keep them focused on one topic then switch channel suddenly to get a straight answer.

"If I'm staying tonight I'll need more clothes . . ." she stopped there, hoping Eyeball would suggest that she pop home to fill up a suitcase or an overnight bag. No dice.

Instead, Eyeball asked for her sizes and promised fresh clothes, later that morning. They sat together at the breakfast bar, drinking tea and eating toast, like the new girls at boarding school. Eyeball must have been bottom of the pile, she reasoned. Because, let's face it, you don't get the top brass strapping their arse to a chair for the night.

A till receipt was still on the work surface — Miranda clocked yesterday's date before Eyeball tidied it away. Okay then, back to Project Best Friend. "Look, I feel really bad about your eye, er . . ."

Eyeball glanced at the open door and replied, "It's Alice."

Alice Eyeball, it was then. "Alice, I don't suppose there's a gym around here? I could do with working off last night's curry."

A bloody takeaway — hardly James Bond. Useful though, Miranda recalled, as Alice rinsed the cups. The round-trip for the pick-up was about forty-five minutes so they couldn't be that far from civilisation. The trouble with country lanes was that they all looked the same. With all the excitement the previous day, after leaving the M25 the rest was a bit of a blur. Unless they'd dropped something in her curry.

She told Alice that she ran a pub, which seemed to rattle her a bit. Probably because it meant another closely supervised phone call. She smiled again, remembering the one from last night. Ringing home was a tricky one. A calculated risk as Mum could have blown it, but she was brilliant.

'Okay Miranda, thanks for phoning. Did you want Butch taken care of while you're away, or is Thomas looking after him?' Even the way she had told Miranda: 'Take care and I'll see you soon.' It still sent a shiver of delight up and down her spine. Mum was on the case.

* * *

Thomas looked out across Harwich and tried to concentrate. Just him and the gulls, not so different from the day Bob Peterson appeared. What if he'd been less attentive that day? What if the shooting and Peterson had been all someone else's problem — Karl's, for instance? What if . . . and then a flashbulb went off in his brain, illuminating what was already there.

The door opened downstairs, shortly followed by the strains of 'When Irish Eyes Are Smiling.' Karl huffed and puffed up the stairs, depositing his cases on a table with his usual lack of care. "Grab hold of these sandwiches while I do a sweep of the premises."

Thomas watched as Karl went to work, checking for other people's devices: surveillance on the surveillers. Karl worked quickly and methodically around Thomas, as he stood in the centre of the room, sandwiches in hand. Finally, Karl pronounced, "Clear!" with a dramatic flourish.

The morning soon filled up, with tracking shots of Her Majesty's Customs and Excise at work in a busy British port. Thomas even fitted in a couple of brooding skylines.

But whenever he stole a glance at his companion, Karl was looking right at him.

"It's alright, I'm not about to crumble into pieces." Not in front of you, anyway.

"I know that, Tommo. No news, I take it?"

"Shouldn't that be my line?"

Karl shrugged with just his face. "Investigations are continuing. And just so you know, as soon as we get what we want from Petrov, we're shipping the family far away."

Like that was supposed to make him feel any better? Before Thomas could respond, the walkie-talkie crackled.

Karl made a face approximating 'intrigued' and nodded to whatever was being said. "Thanks Ann, out."

Thomas furrowed his brow and Karl was immediately on the defensive. "What? Can't I extend a little professional courtesy to my esteemed colleague?"

Thomas shook his head in mock disgust. Clearly, somewhere along the line, they'd had words and put their childish spat to rest.

"Anyways, she was letting us know that Christine will be on-site shortly." Karl sat bolt upright, like he'd been stung in the arse. "Hey, shift; get your lens on the staff compound. Let's see if she so much as twitches at your car."

Brilliant. He and Karl took up position, two cats after the same canary. Christine Gerrard's Mercedes glided up to the compound gate. She flashed her ID at the attendant — who looked like he couldn't give a shit — and veered left where there were still spaces. Thomas's heart was racing; unless she was planning to vault the fence she'd have to walk back past his car. If she even coughed beside his replacement window he'd have his first genuine lead.

Come on, come on; out you get. Any second now . . . nearing the front of the car . . . He held his breath and pushed hard against the viewfinder, swallowing Christine's face. She had a faraway look about her, as if she'd rather be somewhere else. Closer . . . and . . . nothing. The moment passed. She crossed the bonnet and walked beyond Karl's shit-heap of a car without blinking an eyelid.

"What do you think?" Karl was still tracking her.

"I don't think she faked that."

"Well," Karl looked up with a wry grin on his face; "You'd know more about that than me. Okay, she's eliminated herself from our inquiries — for now."

Thomas smiled back, a small crumb for Karl's ingenuity. He liked the sound of 'our inquiries'; it made him feel less alone.

Christine headed straight for their block. Karl made a half-hearted attempt to tidy away the remnants of breakfast and his newspaper, but as soon as he heard the door downstairs he busied himself with his camera.

She clip-clopped up the steps, clearing her throat by the doorway. Thomas turned, catching Karl out the corner of his eye following suit.

"Gentlemen, we're downscaling our presence here — by two."

Thomas looked over at Karl. Was downscaling even a real word?

Christine crossed the threshold. "Karl, why don't you take a break — I'd like a private word with Thomas."

Karl nodded gladly, as if he'd had the same idea himself. "I'll go over to see Ann Crossley — call me there when you're done," he rattled a walkie-talkie.

* * *

Christine waited until they were alone. "After our last conversation, I thought we'd better have the next one face-to-face."

Uh-oh. Suddenly she reminded him of her mother doing the 'And what are your intentions towards our daughter?' routine.

"I don't know why you're so fixated with Bob, and not that it's any of your business, but yes, we are seeing each other on a casual basis."

Seeing to each other, more like. But he wasn't going to rise to the bait this time. Instead, he separated his Bermuda key ring methodically, detached the cover and applied it to his laptop's USB port. Christine stood beside him while the software whirled and opened the folder.

"Bob Peterson was here on the day of the shooting," he clicked on a series of folders and opened the one named Uncle Bob. As if to emphasise the obvious, he'd superimposed a black frame over Peterson's four-by-four.

Christine stared at the screen for maybe a minute. Thomas handed her the gift of silence. She looked shaken. And if he were honest, he was savouring every second.

"Has Bob seen this?"

Thomas opened up the file marked Uncle Bob V2.0. "No, I filed this version with my report. But he probably realises I saw him there," he paused, hoping that if he gave her enough space, she'd say something about Miranda or his car; a forlorn hope.

"Where is this going, Thomas? I mean, what's brought this on?"

He stood up; they were almost toe-to-toe. "I have a friend who's in trouble." He stopped and looked into her eyes. "I think it's connected with Bob."

Her demeanour changed; she came over all Florence Nightingale and pressed his hand tenderly. "Bob's okay, really."

"Come on, Christine, he lied about being at the docks — in front of all of us."

"Well . . ." she seemed to struggle for logic, "he stayed with me that week."

"Yeah, but you're not in the pictures. And the only day Bob turns up on site — unannounced — happens to be the same day someone is shot."

"You're surely not suggesting Bob was behind that?"

He pushed his hand up a little and felt hers firm against it. "No, Bob wasn't behind it. I think I know who's involved. But I don't believe in coincidences."

Christine stalled; it was as if a cloud of doubt had settled on her face. He imagined her asking herself the same question he had: was Bob the witness or the lookout?

"What kind of trouble — it's not Karl is it?"

"No, it's not Karl. But I can't say any more — I don't know who I can trust."

"Hey," Christine squeezed his fingers, "you know you can trust me!" She seemed to gaze at him in a way that she hadn't done for a long time. "It's a woman, isn't it?"

Bollocks. "Chrissie, can you just leave it please?" He felt tears welling up and withdrew to the window, coughing to stop his voice from cracking.

She took the hint. "Alright, I'd better be going, Thomas. If you want to talk, you know where to find me. I promise I won't say anything to Bob."

He kept his back towards her, staying that way until he heard the door close. As soon as he composed himself, he rang Sheryl. "Hi," he kept the tone sombre; "no, nothing yet, but I'm a little closer to figuring out what's going on. I'll call you this evening. And Sheryl, thanks — you know."

Karl sauntered back within minutes of the call. Anyone would think he'd been watching Thomas through binoculars. "So, we're leaving Harwich soon," Karl was trying his best to be subtle. "What did Christine drop by for?"

Thomas parked himself on a stool. "I called her at home."

Karl's face was blanker than usual.

"I was pissed off with you and myself, after our discussion in the hotel bar. So I took it out on Christine. I rang up and slated Bob Peterson, reminded her that he was married. Less than bright; I think he was in the flat at the time."

"You don't think Peterson is anything to do with . . ."

"Miranda? No, and I'm pretty sure Christine's clean. She came here to smooth the waters. And if I really thought Bob was responsible, I wouldn't be standing here now."

Karl stated the obvious. "Not Christine or Uncle Bob — the list grows shorter."

"Maybe Petrov will have some suggestions when we speak to him."

Karl feigned disinterest, but his body language screamed 'fuck off.'

* * *

At four o'clock on the dot, Karl was packing his equipment away, having got Ann Crossley to cover for them. "Here's how we play this," Karl sounded masterful. "First we drive back to your gaff because that's where you're supposed to be. Then you transfer to my car and we go talk to Petrov."

Thomas brightened a little. He was in the game, though God knows what they expected him to get from Petrov. Still, anything was better than sitting in that flat alone.

He parked down by Lloyd Park, on the opposite side of the road, to avoid scraping bird shit off the roof later on. He moved his stuff into Karl's car — quicker than taking it into the flat.

Karl welcomed him into the dry passenger seat, inviting him to check out the glove compartment. No guns this time but there was a choice of albums. Thomas opted for something reflective — ACDC's 'Let There Be Rock,' which Karl seemed to appreciate.

Karl swung out to the North Circular, picking up the A10 north.

"What do you want me to say to Petrov?" Cut to the chase; always the best way of dealing with Karl. Even if it meant shouting over 'Whole Lotta Rosie' as it fried the speakers.

"There's no subterfuge here," Karl notched the volume down. "We need to know everything about Yorgi; where the red car was before Harwich, past haunts, anything."

Thomas nodded and twisted the volume back up. What he really wanted to know was whether Yorgi was capable of kidnapping Miranda. That question made him shudder.

Chapter 30

Thomas zoned out for the rest of the journey; Karl left him to it. Somewhere, between drifting off and Karl nudging him awake, he remembered Sir Peter Carroll's very first pep talk about loyalty and confidentiality.

"We're here," Karl sounded apologetic.

Thomas soon saw why. It was one of the ugliest buildings he'd ever laid eyes on. The sign at the front — next to 'cars parked illegally will be clamped' — read 'Conference Facilities.' It all looked like a very bad joke.

"It's a converted telephone exchange."

"Shame they never converted the outside — it looks like a prison."

Karl nodded. "Or a fortress."

"And Petrov's family have been living here?"

Karl waved a scolding finger. "Uh-uh. More than you need to know."

Thomas tried not to stare at the CCTV cameras. They reminded him too much of being at Caliban's.

Teresa met them at the front steps. Thomas took it as read that she already knew all about Miranda; he wasn't about to confide in her in any case. They threaded past a series of doors to one with a sign that read 'occupied.' She gestured to Thomas to go in first.

Petrov leapt up from his chair, with a look of rapture. Alexandra was there at his side and Lukas was in the corner, playing with some toys on a rug. It looked like a Social Services training film. "Tomas! It is so good to see you!"

They shook hands enthusiastically; Alexandra kissed him on the cheek. All hail the conquering hero. Teresa and the quiet one on her side of the desk seemed to relax.

"You are well, yes?"

There was a question. He swallowed and let out a breath. Then replied, "Yes, I am well," with all the enthusiasm he could conjure.

They all sat down and the silent wonder — Thomas labelled him the Handler — took orders for drinks and left the room. Teresa started recording, assuring Petrov and Alexandra that they were assisting of their own free will and were not obliged to answer. Nonetheless, it was clear where this was going; they may as well have had a tick list.

How did Yorgi contact them? Why did he contact them? What were they doing in Europe? Where did they meet him? Where was he likely to be now? Teresa's formidable line of questioning didn't take long to put Petrov on edge. Several times he shot glances at Thomas, a searching look as if to say, 'Why are you allowing this?'

By the time they reached a comfort break — Teresa did a neat line in irony — Thomas had just about reached the end of his tether. Petrov was in danger of clamming up and that didn't suit his needs at all.

The tape was switched off; he had nothing to lose. He put his mug down and leaned across the table. "How dangerous is Yorgi?"

Teresa made a mad scramble for the 'on' button and glared at him. Tough shit.

"Very dangerous. Tomas, I tell you the truth; Yorgi fears nothing." Petrov sat back a little, as if to consider his

247

own words. "Well, except snakes. One time I saw him scream at the sight of a snake on the farm and when I laughed, he nearly broke my arm."

Thomas wasn't sure how you could nearly break an arm, but then he recalled that he'd nearly been shot. Karl nudged him to carry on.

"Have you ever met anyone with Yorgi? Or maybe you spoke to them on the phone?" He almost said 'at the house' then he remembered that they didn't have a house any more

Petrov nodded. "On the phone; maybe twice. An older man — British, not foreign."

"What kind of British?" Karl pitched in. "Like me?" He sounded like he was trying to prove his own innocence.

Alexandra searched the ceiling for recall. "He was English, well-spoken; and he called from a mobile."

Thomas smiled at her. Less use than nothing, but it was a step in the right direction. "Why would Yorgi still want you — want to see you, I mean? You told me before, that you sometimes didn't hear from him for months."

Petrov and Alexandra shared a none-too-subtle glance and neither responded.

Thomas took a sip of tea, felt the warm liquid swirl around his mouth yet still leave it parched. He knew he would have to be quick and concise before they bundled him out of the room. He felt a cold numbness at the base of his skull, spreading down his body. There was only one question he was interested in now.

He turned his head away slightly, certain that if Karl saw his face clearly he'd spot something was amiss. He cleared his throat and took in a great gulp of air. "I think Yorgi may be holding a hostage, someone important to me . . ."

Alexandra covered her face. Petrov gaped at him, and Thomas remembered showing them Miranda's photo at the house.

"No!" Alexandra called aloud and little Lukas stopped to look up at her.

Karl leaned his arm across Thomas's chest, as if that would somehow stop him speaking. Petrov and Alexandra launched into an argument, in a language Thomas didn't understand. Now Alexandra was crying, shrieking at Petrov who kept waving his arms to shush her. Thomas flitted from Petrov to Alexandra, waiting for them to revert to English. When they did, he wished they hadn't.

Petrov made a last comment in his native tongue and wiped a tear from his face with a handkerchief. His face was red and sweaty. "Yorgi would not take hostages. I am sorry — if Yorgi took your friend, she is dead."

Thomas felt his whole body convulsing; there were voices around him, but they all blended into one chaotic chorus. His breathing went into overdrive. He pushed against the table and propelled himself up, lunging for the door. His stomach congealed as he ran along the corridor, snaking back to the main door. He only just made it outside when the wave of nausea and abject terror hit him, like a force ten gale; he retched and retched, until his stomach seared, until the tears were dripping off his face.

When he was done, he staggered away from the pool of vomit and sank to his knees, closing his eyes against the world. He'd never felt so alone, his life so utterly devoid of meaning. He'd fucked up the one beautiful thing in his life, and he'd lost her.

It was futile, but the next thing he decided to do, as he choked back the despair, was to send a text to Miranda's mobile. Maybe her killer would read it, maybe no one ever would; but his last act to her would be one of contrition.

He fumbled the security code on his mobile first time and had to try again. As the screen lit up the text icon appeared. He gulped again and wiped the blur from his eyes. Was this the final text they'd let her send, made her send? Oh God, anything but that. His hand trembled as he thumbed the button — he had a voicemail.

His first instinct was to switch the phone off, shield himself from any more pain. But that was just cowardice. He owed her more than that, so much more. He input the code with a cold resolve and braced himself for the worst.

"Thomas, it's Diane. Miranda called me earlier about Butch."

He dropped the mobile. Miranda had phoned today — she was still alive! It couldn't have been Yorgi. He started laughing — at himself, at the absurdity of a second chance, at all the stuff his mother used to tell him as a child about God's mercy. He fingered his neck where the crucifix used to be and felt the sweat, sodden against his armpit. She was alive; Lord have mercy, Christ have mercy.

He texted Diane straight back, in no fit state to speak to her: I can't talk now — I'll come straight over. It was weak, but it was honest. He glanced at the mud and puke and snot all down himself — Diane would understand.

His mind was racing as he walked back. Whoever had taken Miranda was the enemy — and enemies had to be dealt with. It may not have been Yorgi who did this, but it had to be connected with him.

Karl opened the door; Thomas pushed past him. He felt like a man redeemed — a man on a mission. He returned to the interview room and shoved the door. Everyone turned; Petrov stared up at him as if he'd never expected to see him again.

Thomas stood over the table and faced them down, slamming his palms against the wood. "I'm only going to ask you this once — what does Yorgi still want with you?"

Petrov shrank back. "He gave me a package to look after; I should have left it for him at the house."

Chairs scraped behind him, but Thomas didn't react. He glared at Petrov as if he could incinerate him by force of will. And Petrov evaporated. "It is in my case. I never meant to keep it. I thought it would be something to bargain with, if we needed such a thing."

Thomas gazed around the room with a look of contempt. It seemed like everyone was holding out on him. As he made for the door, Karl stood aside.

"Tommo, I'm so sorry; I didn't know . . ."

"I need your car — now."

As he pulled into the Wrights' drive, the first thing Thomas noticed was the lack of cars. The doorbell only managed three chords before Diane was standing there.

"Jesus, Thomas, you look like shit."

"Where is everyone?" he was starting to feel mildly freaked.

"I sent them out for a while; said I wanted time to myself. By my reckoning, you've got a couple of hours to get your story straight, right after you tell me what's really going on."

She walked off, letting the door swing in; he followed her inside. "Let's cut the bullshit, Thomas," Diane was already pouring herself something strong. "I know all about Butch and your little code — Miranda told me what happened a long time ago."

He turned a shade of scarlet.

"Something's up — I get that. So where's my daughter and what's going on?" Diane pushed a drink across the table to him.

The sudden heat in his stomach brought him to his senses. He told her what he knew, which wasn't much. It was work related — his work — 100% personal. And he was going to sort it. He'd made another decision on the way over. Fuck Karl and his cloak-and-dagger antics; he would go and see Sir Peter Carroll, do things properly through official channels.

She took it surprisingly well, listened attentively until he'd finished then got up to go to the kitchen. He heard a kettle switch and followed her in.

"Look Diane, I never meant for this to happen . . ."

She span round and slapped him hard across the face, sending him flying. "Don't you dare make excuses to me;

you should have come to us at the beginning. We're your family, Thomas — don't you ever forget that. Now, you better take care of this and deliver Miranda back to me, or we will deal with them and you."

He got up from the floor and tried to regain some dignity; he didn't know whether to stay or go. Diane had frozen him out; the way she looked at him, he was nothing to her. That was even worse than the shame. "You know where the door is."

He wanted to apologise again, to extract an ounce of forgiveness from her. But who was he kidding, he couldn't forgive himself so why should she? He got to the front door and went to open it, but she blocked him with her arm.

"If anyone has threatened her or hurt her, they're never going to hurt anyone again. I want your word — swear it."

He felt his jaw harden. "You have my word." As the door slammed behind him he thought, just for a second, that he heard her sobbing.

Chapter 31

Thomas drove back to the flat and tried to pacify himself in front of the TV. Any relief about Miranda was tempered with an aching sense of loss, of still not knowing where she was. Added to that, Petrov had lied to him — a man he'd put himself on the line for. And for all Karl's efforts, if Yorgi was holding Miranda, well, Karl was just as powerless and clueless as he was. It all added up to a very poor starting point. He couldn't settle, roaming the channels, wondering whether Karl would bring any more super-duper painkillers when he collected his car. And speaking of killers, was that his destiny now?

Karl turned up an hour or so later. They sat in Thomas's flat, the TV turned low in the background, not achieving a great deal. He put Karl straight about Diane's phone message, early on — no point torturing the poor guy. But Karl had little to share in return.

"Honest to God, Tommo, we're doing our utmost." Which was like saying: 'A' for effort, 'F' for achievement.

Thomas sat back in the armchair. Karl was sitting pretty much where Miranda had been, last time at the flat. "Did you get the package from Petrov?"

Karl shifted on the cushion. "Yeah, it's a sealed DSB — can you believe that? Teresa's speaking to her people tomorrow about what we do with it."

That hurt. Yeah, no rush or anything. He decided to leap the ravine. "Only you and Christine knew I wasn't working when Miranda was taken — from my car."

Karl banged his cup on the table. "Now wait a minute . . ."

Thomas held up a hand. "So they can't have been after Miranda. I mean, why then, the day after we spirit Petrov and his family away? And if they'd had the tracker on my car beforehand, they could have picked me up with Petrov at his home."

Karl calmed down. "I see your logic. Then the tracker must have been put on your car at the hotel or later on. But who else, other than Yorgi, would be interested enough in Petrov to want to get hold of you?"

"Dunno. Someone who's interested in Yorgi? Or working with him? It's the same thing from our perspective. Maybe *our* was stretching things a bit, but he was softening Karl up for the biggie. "Miranda's missing and she's still at risk. It seems to me that Petrov and the DSB are our best leads. I want the DSB."

Karl's eyes widened. "And just what are you intending to do with it?"

"I'll take it to Sir Peter Carroll. He has connections — MI5, Army Intelligence; I don't care who. I just want Miranda back. There could be something in that DSB that leads to Yorgi." The thoughts came thick and fast now; "Perhaps it's Yorgi they want and they think I can give him to them."

Karl scratched his teeth on a knuckle. "What you're asking — the DSB . . . it's not something . . . it's not my decision. I can speak to Teresa later, but even then . . ."

Thomas looked at Karl, really looked at him. Did he already know what was in the DSB? Had Karl been playing him for a fool?" "Well, I'm going to see Sir Peter tomorrow, with or without the DSB."

"Look, I understand where you're coming from, Tommo. You do what you need to," Karl held up his hands. "I just wouldn't want you to be disappointed if your 'special relationship' with our glorious leader isn't as special as you think it is." He checked his watch. "Look, you've had a hell of a day so I'm going to piss off and give you some breathing space."

Thomas tossed Karl his car keys.

"All I'm saying is: don't be too hasty. I'll talk to Teresa and get back to you."

* * *

"Hi Sheryl," Thomas kept his tone measured, leaving little space for her to interject. He focused on the things that he wanted her to know, starting with the biggest and the best. "Miranda called home today; no, Diane told me. Yeah, it's great news. I'm seeing someone official tomorrow . . . yeah, straight after, I promise." It was gone one when he finally mustered the energy to go to bed.

He put the call in to Sir Peter's office at seven thirty next morning; he'd been thinking about it since six. In the intervening time, he'd come up with nothing by way of a story, so he'd stuck with the need to see him urgently. He'd still head over to Harwich and play the waiting game.

When he got on site, Karl wasn't there. Ann Crossley was none the wiser on his movements. At ten thirty, Thomas rang him on his mobile, but it was out of use. Christine was the next logical choice; she had mixed news.

"Karl has been assigned elsewhere and is subject to a lockdown. Sir Peter Carroll has asked me to pass on an open invitation to Whitehall." She sounded bemused.

Thomas had once been subject to a lockdown. Standard procedure on some assignments — all contact with the rest of the team or anyone else expressly forbidden. It was the closest they ever came to secret squirreling.

He weighed up the situation. An open invitation was a definite plus; unusual too, given Sir Peter's fondness for protocol. What about Karl? True, Christine had warned them that the job was coming to an end — bloody suspicious timing though. His own lockdown had been a three-day stint with the Serious Fraud Office, but lockdowns of just a day had been known; all the more reason to follow things up with Sir Peter in the meantime.

* * *

The sun glanced off Main Building, illuminating it against a photogenic blue sky. In other circumstances, he might have stopped to admire it. Not today though.

After reporting at reception, he gave his details and took a seat. He tried playing it out in his head, sifting the facts to choose what he wanted to share. Someone was missing and somehow he'd got mixed up in helping the brother of . . . He backtracked; how could he explain knowing that Yorgi was a gunman? He was still juggling the facts when he noticed someone standing over him.

"I'll take you up now."

No hello, no introductions; this was evidently the kind of person who smiled on the inside, if at all. There was no eye contact in the lift; just the definite sense that this guy thought Thomas was the shit on his shiny boots. Another warm welcome extended to Floater colleagues in the Surveillance Support Unit.

As the lift door opened, he felt a rush of excitement. This was the big step that would bring Miranda home. He should have done this when it first all kicked off. And besides, he'd already passed Sir Peter's loyalty test; this was like repaying his trust.

The escort left him at the door. He knocked confidently. Sir Peter opened the door and welcomed him in. "Thomas, your message sounded important. I've cleared my appointments for the next hour or so."

Brilliant. Just what the doctor ordered.

"It's a little early for a drink — I thought perhaps a coffee?"

Thomas smiled as he sat down. Now for the tricky part, keeping Karl and Teresa out of it. Bob Peterson was the logical fall guy, by process of elimination. That and the fact that Thomas thought he was a snake.

Anyhow, big breath and straight in at the deep end. "I'm in trouble, sir. A friend of mine has disappeared and I think it's connected with something I saw." He'd barely got two sentences out when there was a rap on the door. He almost jumped out of his chair.

"It's just the coffees. Come in!" Sir Peter boomed.

Once he had a cup in his hand, Thomas resumed his story — the edited version. Harwich — Bob Peterson — the red car — Petrov — Yorgi — his missing friend. There were gaps wide enough to park a bus in. He didn't explain how he'd tracked Petrov down or why he'd kept it all to himself. But the old man was still listening, which was a good sign.

Sir Peter had stopped making notes, right at the point where Miranda went missing. He put a spoon in his cup and stirred it slowly, rhythmically tapping the cup three times. Then he put the spoon down in a precise fashion and laced his fingers together, like some mafia don. He seemed to grow in stature. "Now then, Thomas, why don't you tell me all about it?" A self-satisfied leer lit up his face like a Halloween pumpkin.

Oh fuck. Thomas tried to quell the trembling in his hand as he put his cup down. He understood now, and felt sick at his own stupidity. Behind the desk, even Winston Churchill seemed to be smirking at him: checkmate. Then the penny really dropped — the Churchill speech, off the net, the 'United States of Europe' speech from 1946. Jesus, short of taking an ad out in the papers, the clue had been in the painting all the time.

Sir Peter puffed up his chest and cleared his throat. "Let me be frank, Thomas. I'm extremely impressed by your resourcefulness and I regret the recent turn of events. But I believe I can bring about a mutually satisfactory conclusion. Will you let me help you?"

Thomas's first instinct was to hurl the bastard through the window and watch him crash to the concrete below. But this was the real world and he was all out of options. "What do you want?"

"Supposing Petrov had something that didn't belong to him; something we could exchange for Miranda."

Thomas froze. He hadn't mentioned Miranda by name.

"Can you get it, Thomas?" the voice was insistent.

He closed his eyes and drew breath. "I'll talk with Petrov."

"I'm sure you'll be very persuasive. Shall we say twenty-four hours? And Thomas, it would be better for everyone if the package remained unopened," Sir Peter slid out a desk drawer and retrieved an A4 Civil Service envelope. He passed it across, but before Thomas could break the seal, Sir Peter brought the meeting to a close. "I think that's all we have to say to each other at this juncture. Goodbye Thomas — twenty-four hours. It's best if we resolve this without Yorgi's involvement."

He had to use the chair to stand. He felt Sir Peter watching him as he staggered for the door. A guard was waiting in the corridor. Thomas shuffled along behind him in a daze, brown envelope in hand like hospital bad news. At the lifts, he felt his insides shatter. "I need the gents."

The guard stood outside the main door, like a bouncer. What did the guy think he was going to do, swim down the u-bend to freedom? He leaned against the sink and ran the tap to try and drown out the hissing in his head. A spasm brought up a clump of brown-stained sick. It reeked of coffee and fear. He let it slide down the plughole then splashed some cold water over this face. He left the tap running and dried his hands.

And now for the envelope. It was sealed tight; not last minute, and still wet with spit, but something planned in advance. Inside were photographs. The top one was a herd of people, slightly blurred, moving away from the camera. A sign on the wall settled the mystery: Walthamstow Central. He looked more carefully at the centre of the picture; and there he was, merging into the crowd.

He flicked through the other photographs frantically, half expecting the worst. He wasn't disappointed; there was Pickering — his parents' house, Pat and the kids. Those bastards had everything on film. The last shot was the final dagger through the heart. A telephoto lens of him and Ajit, sat in a car by the police station. It had been a rat trap from start to finish.

He sneered at his reflection and shook his head. His eyes were red from lack of sleep and the tears he was holding back. He slipped the photos back into the envelope, turned off the tap and opened the door.

* * *

Back on the street, everything seemed larger than life; everything except him. As he looked over his shoulder, Main Building soared above him, all-powerful, impregnable. On impulse, he opened his mobile to try Karl again. Did he dare? It would be a disciplinary offence if he got through — both for him and Karl. He was completely screwed.

He walked over to the park and sat down on a bench, the open phone still in his hand like a weapon. They might be watching him, even now. He hunched forward, pretended to play with the buttons and glanced around. The only people nearby were a woman with a baby in a stroller and two college kids playing with a Frisbee. The stroller could be a disguise for a directional microphone and a camera, with the students waiting for him to move. Yeah, right. And maybe the Frisbee was a hover camera.

He cradled his head and leaned forward, tasting bile. Through the chink of light between his fingers, he watched people ignoring him. He needed coffee; he had a lot of thinking to do.

The espresso he bought from the coffee stand in the park didn't taste so great, but its effects were undiminished; such were the restorative powers of premium caffeine. He needed a plan, fast. He sipped rhythmically and went through a list in his head.

Point 1: Sir Peter Carroll had said they'd prefer that the package wasn't opened. So who had the package now? Answer: Teresa. But he could hardly ring up every Intelligence office and ask if a Teresa worked there. But . . . he did know where she'd been — he could go back to the building where they'd interrogated Petrov. Someone there must be able to get hold of her. He took a bite of the muffin as a reward and held the sugary stodge in his mouth until it melted.

Point 2: Get some time off work. He couldn't be in two places at once. Christine would sign it off, and if she took issue with it he could always refer her to Sir Peter. He texted her to say he was coming in for a chat when he picked up his car. She responded immediately that she'd wait in for him.

By the time he got to the park gate he breathed a little easier. At least he knew what his next steps were. One glance back told him that Buggy Woman and the Frisbee Kids were either holding position fantastically well or they were just innocent civilians. If there was such a thing anymore.

Chapter 32

Thomas felt safe among the crowds — buoyant amid a sea of tourists, shift-workers and pickpockets. True, the mass of CCTV cameras threw him a little if he thought about it too much, but he'd already reached his paranoia limit for the day.

The next train was three minutes away so he grabbed a bench and tried to lose himself in the giant poster opposite. A suspiciously attractive couple beamed down on him, extolling the virtues of some European bank he'd never heard of. 'Small savings and big decisions,' they smiled. He mused on that; it was the big decisions that everyone was afraid of.

The open plan office at Liverpool Street was deserted; no surprise, as it was the middle of the day. He'd harboured the tiniest of hopes that Karl would be around, but a lockdown meant restrictions on contact, movement and behaviour.

Christine's light was on and the door open, so he didn't think twice about approaching. Inside, she and Bob were reading through files. They seemed to be looking for something.

Thomas quickly stuffed the envelope of photographs inside his jacket and zipped it tight. He rapped on the door. Bob looked up, gave him a half nod of recognition and returned to his reading. Christine did the talking. "Hello Thomas, please come in. Bob and I are just finishing up."

Of course you are, he thought. He said nothing, watching from the door as they continued their synchronised folder stacking. Then he grabbed a seat in one corner, a good vantage point to see who was the most unsettled.

Eventually, they took the hint and gave up on their search. Bob Peterson didn't look happy about it though, which pleased Thomas no end.

"Back in a mo," Christine explained with a grin, "call of nature."

It was a little informal for Thomas's liking. And judging by the look on Peterson's face, he felt the same way. Thomas looked him over, trying not to appear like the aggrieved ex.

"So," Bob glanced at the top folder on the pile, "how's Harwich?"

That was all it took. The red mist that Karl used to joke about became a sunburst. Thomas leapt the distance between them, grabbed Peterson by the lapels and slammed him up against the door. A mountain of folders seemed to scurry for cover.

"Fuck Harwich!" Thomas snarled, through a haze of rage. "When all this is over, I'm coming back for you."

"What the hell is wrong with you?" it took Peterson a moment to take it in. He started thrashing about, but Thomas had him pinned.

It had been pure instinct, nothing more, and already he was wondering what was wrong with him. Peterson struggled a second time then, before Thomas even realised it was coming, his fist blasted through his arms with an upper cut. Thomas took it on the jaw and reeled backwards, dragging Peterson with him to the floor, only twisting at the last moment to try and cushion his fall.

Peterson wasn't going down without a fight. And there was a score to be settled. Juvenile? Definitely, but Thomas felt that Uncle Bob had it coming on two counts: one, playing away with Christine — no doubt in his mind at all now — and two, Peterson was somehow the starting point of all his troubles.

* * *

Christine opened the door to find the two of them locked in combat. The main punches had already been traded and now it was about who could rough who up the most. At first, she didn't speak. Thomas was glad of that. It might have distracted him from his main intention of hammering the shit out of Peterson.

"That's enough!" she slammed the door. Then she pointed to two chairs in either corner of the room and they both complied.

Thomas looked first at Peterson and then at the mess. And he couldn't help smiling. He'd finally fulfilled a personal ambition and landed some punches on Peterson, even if he had taken a few knocks himself. His only regret was that he hadn't drawn blood; maybe next time he'd staple Bob's ear.

For a while there was silence. Christine bent down to retrieve some of the paperwork. She looked pained, which pained Thomas. Just because Peterson was an arsehole, it was no reason for her to suffer.

He stood up; in all the excitement he'd almost forgotten what he came there for. "I need some compassionate leave — I'll be on the mobile." He spoke directly to Christine, ignoring Peterson altogether.

Christine looked down at the floor and waved him away like he was too much to bear. He straightened his jacket as he walked out, patting the envelope as he closed the door behind him. He called Diane on his way out of the building.

"It's Thomas. I'm off work now . . . indefinitely, until this is sorted out. Nah, I'll tell you face to face when I have more info."

"That's good news, Thomas, because you're going to be busy."

* * *

He drove out beyond the North Circular, ditching the car at Hatch End. Best to assume the tracker was still working, like Karl said. He jumped a cab at the station — finding the old Telephone Exchange wasn't difficult; there couldn't be too many buildings that ugly.

"Wait here," he waved a £20 note under the cabbie's nose.

The car park was empty; gates locked. Nothing fancy, no barbed wire or anything to excite the interest of your average industrial burglar. He looked back at the cab, figured the driver was engrossed in his horses — or the £20 — and launched himself over.

The place seemed deserted; even the conference centre sign was gone. A quick scout around the perimeter confirmed that the good guys — if that's who they'd been — had left without a trace. Bollocks.

The cabbie didn't seem surprised to see him back so quickly. He folded his paper away and unlocked the passenger doors. Thomas was still catching his breath as he tumbled back on to the seat. "Any idea who owns this place?"

"No, guvnor, it's been shut for ages. We used to get quite a bit of trade there; you know, corporate knobs with their laptops and that. You, er, interested in buying it or something?"

A chink of light in an otherwise shit day. "Well, not me," Thomas went into bullshit mode. "A mate of mine is looking for office space round here. He's small time with big ideas." He raised his eyes in mock disdain.

"As you'll likely be a big tipper, I'll tell you who the estate agent is when we get to the station."

Cheeky bastard. He checked his watch; still time to ring them. As soon as the driver had sodded off at the station to spend his big tip, Thomas dialled from a super-duper phone box. Funny how things changed; he almost missed the smell of piss and sweat. He leaned against the metal back-plate and sighed. He and Miranda had once shared a knee trembler in a phone box, after missing the night bus, one stormy night in Balham. No chance of anyone repeating that here unless they enjoyed the open air.

"Yes, hello, I wonder if you can help me. An associate of mine recently rented a property in Larchall Road — the converted exchange building. I was supposed to meet them, but my flight was delayed and I was wondering . . ."

Wow, stonewalled straight away. Karl had made this stuff look so easy. "You haven't? Well no, what about . . . no, right . . . I see." If only West Ham had as good a defence.

The senior partner had handled all the arrangements and she was now on holiday in Canada. Hence: no names, no contacts and no yellow brick road.

He got in the car and headed south, with only the radio for company. It was all going pear-shaped again. He had Diane and Sheryl pulling his strings from one side and Sir Peter the Bastard on the other side. Ping: small savings and big decisions. He'd seen that ad before, at Holloway Road tube. He'd even had a discussion about finances, in which Karl had revealed his own astute investment strategy: saving is for pussies.

Thomas allowed himself the luxury of a smile. Now he had a way forward again, sort of. He could find his way to the Gun Club but would they let him in? He pulled over and stared at the A to Z intently, like an ugly man checking out the foreign bride catalogue. Nope, it wasn't coming together at all. The only thing for it was to drive down to the tube station and retrace his steps.

* * *

The industrial estate was half full with cars. He remembered that Teresa had been driving a silver coupé the day Karl had bought Petrov's red estate, but it could have been a hire car. And of course, he hadn't made a habit of carrying his driving licence and passport around, so getting in might be a tad tricky. Three men got out of a BMW; for a second he thought he'd seen one of them before. But he could hardly wave and explain. They glanced in his direction and didn't glance again. This was getting him nowhere.

He walked up to the thick metal door with as much confidence as he could fake. The camera stared at him implacably. He pushed the intercom and said that he'd been there before and was looking for a member named Teresa. He let go of the button and waited. Nothing happened.

He tried again, a different pitch — same basic facts and that he needed to speak to her urgently. He held up his SSU ID card, for good measure. Finally, he got a response: "You must have the wrong place." Now he was getting seriously pissed off, and desperate. He hit the button again. "Look, I don't have a lot of time. If she's there, I need to see her; she'll know what it's about. Be a good girl and stop fucking me around."

He did elicit an immediate response, but 'if you don't go away I'll call the police' wasn't the one he hoped for. He took a breath. "Look, I'm sorry for behaving like a twat. But it's really important and I have been here before, more than once — you can check your records against my ID and name. And I've got nowhere else to go so I'm just going to sit out here in my car and wait until she turns up - today, tomorrow, whenever. I'm not going to cause any trouble, and if you want to call the police, then you go right ahead."

He took a step back, raised a hand as if he was being sworn in on a jury, and backed away slowly to his car. Then he drove around the car park, clocking the security cameras on poles, and managed to find a space facing the door.

Sunset came and went; evening crept upon him, a staring contest with a steel door that was only interrupted by the occasional visitor and an emergency piss in an old lemonade bottle. He tried the radio for a while, but it took the edge off his concentration. Even his survival ration granola bar — the only food he'd had all day — couldn't lift his spirits.

He figured he'd fucked his job now; he couldn't see how Christine and Peterson would keep him on the team. In the unlikely event that Christine took his side, he'd given Peterson the ideal excuse to prise him out. Stupid, Thomas; really stupid. He closed his eyes for a few seconds, and fantasised that he and Miranda were running over the North Yorkshire Moors.

Tap, tap, tap; tap, tap, tap. Jesus! They must have called the police after all. He turned to the window, ready to surrender. Teresa was standing outside. He pushed the sealed piss bottle under the passenger seat before he lowered the window.

"You shouldn't have come here."

Okay, not the welcome he'd hoped for but he still felt like hugging her. "I was desperate. It's become . . ." he searched for the right word. ". . . complicated." Yeah, if complicated was another word for meltdown.

"What's the problem?" Teresa stopped short. "Have you been in a fight?"

"Yeah, with Bob Peterson." He figured she knew who Peterson was. Heck, maybe she'd always known. He passed over the photos in the envelope and waited for comment. Then he got tired of waiting and told her about

Sir Peter Carroll. After all, what did he have to lose now? He was all out of friends on this.

"You drive," Teresa insisted. "We'll go back to yours."

"What about the bug in my car?"

She held up two fingers, like a victory salute. "Bugs, plural. That's how I'm here. Karl's been keeping an eye on you."

He couldn't help, but smile. Karl: the wily little Celt.

* * *

It wasn't difficult to understand what Karl might see in Teresa, apart from an air of mystery. She was very capable and clearly didn't take any shit. Once inside the flat, she assumed control, drawing the curtains before she did a sweep of the living room using a hand-held detector. He left her to it, put the kettle on and dug something resurrectable out of the freezer — two portions.

"Karl thinks very highly of you," she carried on talking with her back to him. "But he's worried you'll do something rash about Miranda."

No mistake there. He'd already decided he would sort out whoever was involved — every last one of them. "So how did Karl send you to find me, exactly?"

She snapped the portable shut and turned round. "Simple," she tilted her head to one side. "He knows the OS ref of the indoor firing range and he tracked your car."

"What about the lockdown?"

Her face was calm, as if she could say much but was choosing not to. "It only takes one text to me, on a throwaway mobile — T at CLUB." She paused and folded her hands together. "Then smash the mobile and it's like it never happened. You just have to make sure you don't get caught."

He felt his mouth form into a wow. Karl had been covering his back after all. The kettle clicked, breaking the spell.

"I'll just sweep the other rooms, starting with the bathroom."

"Sure," he nodded, waving a hand behind him. "It's just off..."

"I know where it is, Thomas; I remember from the last time I was here."

The wow expanded into a cavern. Of course, Karl had saved his bacon before, at the flat, when he'd had the good sense not to be there. Teresa must have been involved.

He made the tea. "So what's the deal with you and Karl?" his voice seemed to echo through the flat. There was no answer, but he felt sure that she'd heard him.

* * *

It was strange, eating dinner with another woman. Having another woman in the flat at all, come to that. Christine Gerrard, in her time, had never been a fan. She always seemed to treat the east of London like some sort of infection.

The food settled him, helped his thoughts to fall into place. "Has the DSB been opened?" he hovered, mid-fork, waiting for her answer.

"No, not yet. It's sealed and there's no tag inside — we X-rayed it."

He swallowed. "Have you made a decision — do I get it?"

She made a smacking sound with her lips; he doubted it was the quality of the food. "It may contain vital information about the cartel..."

He nearly countered that but he could see, by the way her eyes flickered, that she was still thinking it over.

"...And can you afford to trust Sir Peter Carroll?"

The room went very cold. Any optimism he'd been nurturing, including the comforting notion that a simple trade-off could be made, was dangling by a thread. Teresa was right of course. How could he trust these bastards, when he knew what they were capable of — two corpses at the hospital, Petrov's house torched, and counting.

"I'm sorry, Thomas; it could be too valuable to lose," she sounded like a bank manager, turning him down for a loan.

Desperation wrote its own scripts. "What if we copied it first? You'd keep a copy and I return the original." Okay, it was feeble, but at least it was a plan. It wasn't as if they'd come up with a better option.

"We know it's a document box," she backtracked, softening her voice. "The paper may be heat and light sensitive. Photocopying or scanning is just too risky."

"What about photography?"

"I don't know Thomas," she flicked the hair from her face. "I don't know. And besides, once we open the DSB, the seal is broken."

He tapped his chin. "I might be able to solve your problem." Your problem, good one: reverse psychology for beginners.

Teresa listened as he told her about the DSB he'd kept from Leeds. Maybe it wouldn't be an identical match, but if it meant having something to exchange for Miranda and not, he'd take that gamble.

"Now," he gathered up the plates; "I've also got a couple of ideas about special paper." No sense losing momentum while she was still malleable. "How about doing the photography in a darkroom?" He gestured out towards the hallway. "Or I can try one of my Internet buddies, see if they know anyone with a Starlight camera."

Buddies — that was stretching it a bit — a bunch of ultra-competitive snappers and geeks, who would tell you where to find equipment, as long as you knew what you wanted in the first place.

He dumped the plates in the sink and fired up his laptop, waiting until he'd cleared the minefield of password and security protection before he brought Teresa screen-side.

"Great for night shots," he pulled up a couple of images from a folder. She didn't respond, but that was fine — he was impressed enough for both of them. "Someone hired one for me once; back when I thought I'd be the next Andy Rouse."

She stared at him blankly and he sighed, appalled.

"I'm supposed to contact Sir Peter tomorrow so I need an answer."

She was quiet for so long that he thought he'd finally met his match in the silence game. He studied her as she stared off into space. The way her hair fell, just above the collar-line; the slightly muscular legs and that cluster ring on her right hand. If she noticed him watching her, she didn't seem at all perturbed. He wasn't perving or anything, he told himself. He just wanted to weigh up what sort of person he was investing with his last few ounces of faith.

Teresa turned suddenly, catching him off guard. He felt a pang in his heart — Miranda used to do the same thing. Whoa, used to? He swallowed hard, deciding at the last minute not to punch himself.

"I'll tell you what," Teresa narrowed her eyes, "Why don't you give me a few minutes and I'll make a couple of calls?"

He headed for the kitchen, pausing along the way to lock his laptop. He turned the radio on and did his domestic thing to the soothing sounds of Seventies Soul, courtesy of Dobie Gray and others. Except, tonight, they weren't so soothing. Suddenly, for no reason at all, he recalled the first time he saw Miranda naked. How she'd made him close his eyes. And then, for the only time in his life, all the clichés had been true. So beautiful; the sort of enchantment that made him want to cry, then and now. He looked skyward and closed his eyes.

* * *

Teresa returned after a handful of songs; long enough for him to pull it together again. "My people have agreed to let you take the DSB to Sir Peter Carroll, once the document is copied to our satisfaction. After that we'll monitor the situation closely."

Very generous of them. With Sir Peter firmly in the frame and copies of the papers safely tucked away, they had very little to lose. Whereas . . .

He thanked her and tried to warm it up. Things were improving. He had allies now, although the odds were still stacked against them. He stopped mid-thought. "I need a car tonight."

"I'll arrange something, and I'll be back tomorrow with the package."

Chapter 33

Teresa had given her assurance that the car wouldn't be tracked. He wasn't sure if he believed her, but he was in no position to be fussy. The Wrights knew to expect him. On the drive over, he ran through different versions of what he wanted to say, but in the end he decided to let them take the lead.

When he arrived, the driveway was full of cars — a packed house tonight. He stood outside for a moment, trying to get a grip on his fear and his bowels. He took another breath as he held his hand over the bell. This was going to be rough. He pressed the button lightly, reminding himself that they were the ones really suffering here.

"It's open," Diane's voice wavered from behind the door.

He gave it a tiny shove and it released inwards, drawing the light from the kitchen through the open inner door.

"We're in here."

It took all his courage to step across the threshold, knowing as he did that he was turning his back on everything he had selfishly tried to preserve.

Well, best not keep the family waiting. He pushed the living room door and went in. Sam and Terry looked up from their armchairs; neither spoke or acknowledged him. Diane was sat on the settee with Sheryl next to her, holding hands as if it was the only thing keeping each of them together. Miranda's dad, John, was nowhere to be seen.

"Come sit down," there was kindness in Diane's voice and he felt wretched at that; it was something he hadn't earned and didn't deserve. Sheryl wouldn't look at him, but if he was honest with himself it was one less face to deal with.

There was no point beating around the bush so he told them what he planned to do. To get a package which someone else — he stressed that — had kept secret from him and deliver it in exchange for Miranda.

It was less an interrogation than a series of silences, speckled with short exchanges. Mostly, they wanted answers he couldn't give. What was it all about? Why Miranda, or him? Why couldn't he let the family deal with it? Someone — Sam or Terry, it all got lost in the stillness and the unspoken fears — passed him a drink. As if he'd won it on merit by his responses. He gripped the glass so tight he thought it might break, wanted it to break and pierce his skin so he could feel something as acute as the pain on their faces.

"I'm so sorry," he hung his head and waited for the room to swallow him. The tension wrapped around him like a physical pressure. It was harder to breathe now. He felt tears forming. Not now, Jesus; they'd think it was staged. He took a gulp from the glass and pinched the tears back, rubbing his eyes clear. He kept his head down, not wanting to read their expectations.

"Thomas," Diane spoke his name and she sounded like a stranger. "John wants to see you in his office." She didn't say now but that's what she meant.

He finished his glass and set it on the floor; last drink for a condemned man. His limbs dragged like dead weight as he walked through to the other side of the house. It was quieter there, and devoid of comfort. There was a line of light under the closed door. He knocked twice and went in.

* * *

John Wright was hunched over his desk, hands crushed together. Thomas felt his shoulders sink, almost smelt those Saturday dinners again when his dad had come home, spoiling for a fight.

The main light was off and the desk lamp shone away from John, casting him in shards of shadow. The hands on the desk didn't move at all. Thomas stood in no man's land, waiting for sentence to be passed.

"Close the door," John managed to convey resolve without menace. The room shrank around him.

Thomas waited for John to speak again — he had little to say, himself, other than repeat what he'd said to the others. In the semi-darkness, he could still make out the photographs on the wall — small comfort.

John's hands moved to his face and he blew his next breath through his fingers; the breath was long and laboured. "You found Miranda in Leeds, kept her safe and brought her back to us." He nodded for Thomas to sit opposite him. "Diane tells me that Miranda is in trouble because of you." It wasn't a question because they both already knew the answer. "When you came to London and we set you up in a home together, you made us a promise. Do you remember?"

Of course he remembered. One simple sentence: he'd never let her down. No matter what happened between them in the future — and God, how prophetic that clause had turned out to be — he'd never let her down. "I know."

John took a sharp intake of breath. "You've always been a man of your word, Thomas, and I look upon you as one of us." John was struggling with the words, raw emotion choking every syllable.

Any moment now, Thomas thought, that fist would come flying across the small space between them.

"Diane says this has to be handled a certain way — and it has to be done by you." He took another long breath. "Miranda is our little girl, Thomas; she's precious. So I expect you to do what's necessary."

Thomas tensed up, half closing his eyes against the light and whatever was to come. He heard a drawer being opened and then a thud on the desk. He looked down to see a pistol, light gleaming along its edge. John nudged the gun over to him with the heel of his hand.

Holy shit. John was stone-cold serious. Thomas reached forward and touched the barrel, felt the metallic chill seeping into his skin.

"Do you know how to use it?"

Thomas took the gun, slipped out the magazine and checked the chamber was clear. He also noticed that the mag was empty. As he looked up, there was a thin smile on John's lips. He swallowed and let the gun rest in his hand; he had just crossed the line, on a one-way ticket.

John leaned down and lifted a carrier bag onto the desk. Inside was a shoulder holster and ammunition. Thomas weighed the gun in his hand and, as if demonstrating his side of the pact, loaded the weapon. This was a moment that would live with him forever, like scar tissue that appears healed. But it's always there, beneath the surface.

Chapter 34

Not long after Thomas returned home, Teresa was at his door. He checked through the curtain first — she was alone, though logically she must have come with someone to take back the Audi.

She watched him as he gazed forlornly out of the window at her, as he looked past her in the vain hope that Karl was around. Nothing doing. He opened the front door, car keys in hand. She edged forward and he stood aside.

"I won't stay long," she seemed almost cheery. "I've got good news."

Yeah, Thomas thought; maybe she'd found some affordable body armour to go with his new gun. He put the kettle on and joined her in the lounge. She perched on the edge of the sofa arm, hands together.

"I'll bring the DSB over to you tomorrow evening." There was a 'but' coming. ". . . But we'll need some extra time before you give it back to them."

He felt his jaw dragging down. The kettle clicked; he ignored it. "You want me to put Miranda at further risk?" He felt his shoulders hardening.

"If the information is useful, we'll have to act before the cartel gets it back."

He made a break to the kitchen. Teresa followed him.

"Look Thomas, I know this is all—"

Thomas rounded on her. "You don't know shit. This is business as usual to you people, but for me, it's personal."

Her next move was textbook — the reassuring hand on the arm. "If you tell Sir Peter you can get the DSB in a couple of days, and that it's still unopened, he'll accept that. Why wouldn't he? He'll still get exactly what he wants."

She negotiated the cups and spoons through trial and error as he sat and watched her. Maybe she could tell he wasn't convinced, still not a card-carrying member of their gang. "Let me put this another way," her voice moulded into concrete. "We need two more days, with or without your cooperation."

He blinked a couple of times, waited for the heat across his face to subside before he spoke. She beat him to it.

"This isn't a game, Thomas; this is life and death to our operatives. The contents of that DSB could save lives."

He nodded without saying a word.

"I'll be back here tomorrow, around six."

All he could do was sit there like a statue and listen to the door closing behind her.

* * *

The dream returned that night — the arguing downstairs, him and Pat cowering under the covers together and that terrible silence when their mother capitulated. As if the world had ended. Pat, crying and shaking under the sheets, as the heavy thud thud grew closer on the stairs. He was holding her tightly again, so that she couldn't feel his own trembling.

The hollow catch as Dad gripped the door handle. And even though it hadn't moved, you knew he was there because his legs stole the light from underneath the door.

The handle turning, the light switch driving out the comfort of shadows, and then the footfalls to the side of the bed. Pat's nails, digging into his skin so hard that he wanted to cry out, only Dad would just call him soft and take a swipe at him. He could smell the hand on the sheets, stinking of shame and self-loathing

But when the covers were snatched away, it was Miranda at his side, warm and sensuous. And Dad wasn't there in the room this time: it was Sir Peter Carroll. He was speaking, whispering as his hand stretched towards Miranda.

And Thomas couldn't move; he was paralysed until somehow he remembered the gun. The sweet, silver pistol with the magic star on the handle; the one that meant he was the sheriff. He reached under the pillow and as soon as he felt it, he drew out the gun and thrust it into Sir Peter's face.

Sir Peter took a step back in the dream, standing there, daring Thomas to 'be a man.' His eyes blurred, but he wiped them one-handed, the gun still at arm's length to ward off evil. Then his fingers slowly closed together and pow, the gun went off.

* * *

Thomas shocked awake, rigid against the bed with tears spread across his face. Slowly, he regained movement in his limbs, felt the muscles in his shoulders and back release. It was a little after five in the morning; he flipped the mobile on, in case there'd been word from either Miranda or Karl. Then he ran for a shower to avoid the disappointment.

After toasting the last of the bread, he took John Wright's pistol from where he'd hidden it in the kitchen and re-examined it — no serial numbers or distinguishing marks. It might never have been used before, but he doubted that. He tried on the shoulder holster, adjusted it a couple of times and nested the gun. He must have stood in the middle of the kitchen for a minute or more, no quick draw bullshit or confronting the mirror. No, the only thought going through his brain was whether John had started like this himself; whether one unfortunate situation had turned an honest man into . . . into someone like him.

He ditched the holster in a drawer and stowed the gun away carefully. The mobile phone had nothing for him. Only six o'clock now; way too early for Whitehall.

So many times in the past he'd worked his way through London, cursing the traffic as he inched ahead, bumper to bumper. But today, when he wanted the drive to take forever, nothing doing. He parked at the work compound, just to keep his car handy, and went walkabout. He'd brought along a Pentax Optio to kill some time.

London, before the rush, was a different place altogether. The city breathed softly before the hordes invaded; the haze lifted off the Thames in the first light of morning. Walking beside the Embankment, lulled by the lapping water, it was easy to forget just how much shit he was in and how deep.

The police launch prowled along the Thames as he watched, lens poised; the sun burst through the mesh of steel and brick and glass behind it to light up the skyline. He drank it all in — better than espresso. When did he last do this? When did he last feel such a connection to London? He couldn't remember. It was Miranda's city, but it was also his.

By the time he'd had his fill and grabbed a coffee at St James's Park, it was just after eight. He felt limbered up after all the walking and, thanks to the coffee, as sharp as a blade. Grateful too, that he hadn't followed his gut and brought the gun along.

A few miles on foot had given him time to reflect a little. No one had suggested that Thomas was anything more than an innocent in all this; and basically that's what he was. As long as he played it that way and didn't come across too cocky or clever, why wouldn't they give him a couple of extra days?

At first glance, Main Building looked closed for business, but the door gave way and the security staff squared up to him from across the polished marble flooring. He moved to the glass screen, stated his name and flipped them his ID.

A receptionist directed him to the hand-scanner and checked a list of names. Yep, there he was, all present and correct. Sir Peter wasn't in his office yet, so he waited in the foyer, with an early morning broadsheet for company.

Coming from Yorkshire, Thomas was no stranger to the class struggle, but never was the divide more clearly defined than in the newspapers — insightful information for the movers and shakers, and tits and celebrities for the plebs. Oh, he liked a tabloid as much as the next man, but it didn't equip you for understanding the bigger picture. Take today — a Benelux corporation was holding strategic talks with a French business partner, ahead of a meeting with representatives from the EU Commission. Jesus. The more he read, the more it seemed like Karl's mythical Superstate was already in place.

After fifteen minutes of isolation therapy, a guard came over: Sir Peter would be ready for him shortly. Okay, final run through of what he was going to say. The DSB was unopened; no, he hadn't seen it and yes, he would bring it to them in a day or so. As to anything else, he knew nothing: if in doubt, say nowt.

He stood and stretched. Sir Peter might have him on CCTV that very minute, just watching him sweat. Not a very comforting thought. He heard boots on marble and turned to face them; it was show time.

The journey to the lift took place in customary silence. He thought maybe he'd seen this guard before. As they exited the lift, he realised where — at the gun club. He nodded and smiled as they entered the last leg of the corridor. The guard paused and looked him up and down, as if trying to place him. "Are you ex-mob?"

Fortunately, Thomas had had the benefit of Karl's education: mob, for military. He tilted his hand noncommittally: could be.

Three raps and away, leaving Thomas standing there like the last virgin in a nightclub. Sir Peter took his time about answering; he probably thought he was piling on the pressure. This was Pickering all over again, but now the bullies were grown up and infinitely more savage. It would be harder to get away with it this time; a shove into the pavement wouldn't quite cover it.

Thomas knew the score. For the terrorised, it went one of three ways. You resigned yourself to it, withdrew as much as you could and survived, day to day. Or else you crumbled, lost hope; gave up on yourself. But if there was still some part of you that they hadn't got to, hadn't chewed up and spat out, you bided your time and then you struck back, hard.

He heard Sir Peter's voice and meekly entered the office. Meek: that was the watchword. And no need to fake the unease; he already had that in spades.

Sir Peter offered him a chair, all very civilised. It was bloody obvious that he didn't have the DSB with him, but they went through the master and servant formalities. He delivered the agreed message and then asked if there was news about Miranda.

It seemed to throw the old man. Even though he'd been listening attentively before, that one small question upset the apple cart. "I'll see what I can find out for you, Thomas." He looked at him differently after that, like Thomas was a simpleton.

Thomas thanked him, said how grateful he was and shook his hand. It sealed the deal. Two days' grace and the promise of a telephone call later that day — quite a result. At this rate, he decided, he might even let him live, when it was all over.

* * *

Two days to put together a plan; afterwards, there would be no going back. That was fine — it meant he had nothing to lose. He made straight for the Victoria line and waited on the platform, fantasising about earning a crust as a freelance photographer — every snapper's fantasy. Maybe he and Miranda . . . The soundtrack in his head stopped abruptly. She'd probably never want to lay eyes on him again. Like he said . . . nothing to lose.

He made it to the office just after nine. Hopefully, Christine would be in and he could set the record straight, come clean about Miranda and everything. There was even an outside chance that Christine could help him, somehow. Because, now that he thought about it, there was something he needed. First though, he had to fetch something from the car, something he'd bottled out of at Whitehall.

Christine's office light was a lone beacon. He glanced around at the empty desks, shrouded in shadow; he'd miss this place, even the crap coffee from the machine. He thrust his hand into his jacket pocket and opened the box one-handed, positioning the bug ready for attachment. Christine's door was closed; he knocked, tentatively. But the voice that answered was Bob Peterson's.

Always have a Plan B, and preferably a Plan C as well. Karl called it The Dorman Rule, after a bloke he'd met in a pub once. Plan B was to proceed as planned. There was no Plan C, short of walking away.

He opened the door with his left hand and tried to play nicely.

"You're the last person I expected to see, Thomas. What do you want?"

Count to ten. This was too important to screw up for the sake of scoring a few points. "Bob, can I sit down, please? I need to discuss something."

Bob Peterson gestured to a chair opposite, ever the genial host. Thomas drew close and slipped out the bug under the table, leaning forward earnestly as he applied it to the underside of the desk.

"Christine isn't here!" Peterson sounded triumphant.

"When's she back?"

"I don't know."

"Look, it's really important that I speak with her."

Peterson laced his fingers back behind his head and breathed in deeply. "Anything you've got to say, you can say it to me. I run this team, remember? Christine's been temporarily transferred."

Thomas gave the bug one last touch for safety's sake and brought his hands to his face, like a poor impression of The Scream. "Bob, I need your help . . ." Now he was totally winging it, leaping from word to word at twenty thousand feet. "They've got Miranda and they want the documents from Harwich."

Pure bloody guesswork, but Peterson twitched at the 'H' word. Shit or bust. "On the day you were there, Bob, the day I photographed you." Now, just rest a minute and see what happens.

Peterson's face turned a sickly shade; he folded like a bad poker player. "If you've got something they want, just give it to them — for all our sakes."

"I need to know Miranda's okay — can you get a message to her?" Subtext: are you involved, you bastard?

Peterson wiped the sweat from his lips and stared at the desk; he looked like he wanted out, in a bad way. "Why did you have to get involved? I mean, you're not with SIS or anything. You're a bloody civilian!"

"Hey, I was doing my job. And then you turn up at this office . . ." And pause again to let Peterson fill in the blanks.

"I was sent here, Thomas," Bob Peterson raised his hands like a beggar. "You think I wanted to be at Harwich, or here? I've a wife and family, for God's sake — you're not the only one with something to lose."

Thomas's immediate reaction was 'tell that to Christine.' But he kept his mouth shut. Peterson was just a pawn in someone else's game. "Do you know where Christine is?"

He shook his head; he looked like he wanted to cry. "She took a call early this morning, at the flat. They came and collected her — she looked pleased . . ."

Well at least they were past the pretence; he almost warmed to Peterson for that.

". . . In a people carrier. I was told not to contact her — executive orders, you know where from."

And he did know, now. All roads seemed to lead back to Whitehall.

"Thomas, you can't fight these people. Do what they want and maybe they'll leave us all alone."

He considered that for maybe half a second. "Yeah, and maybe they won't." It was time. "There's something else; I want you to sign out a vest for me."

Peterson's eyes widened. "Body armour?" He gulped. "I can't issue you with a weapon — there's no way . . ."

Thomas shook his head slowly, crediting him with enough intelligence to figure it out. "I only need the vest."

Peterson made the call and signed the chit for Stores. It was a shame that Bob's voice was so off-key, for the recording. Still, Thomas could always edit it afterwards; he was good at that.

"What . . . what are you going to do?" Peterson handed over the chit, like a signed confession.

"I don't know. It depends on Yorgi . . ."

The face before him drained; it was like someone had slit Peterson's throat. So, Bob was in deeper than he'd imagined. He knew that if he stayed any longer, he'd end up asking questions about Yorgi; things that would only weaken his resolve, the way that Petrov had crumbled every time his maniac brother had got in touch.

"One more thing," he stopped at the door. "If you can get a message to Miranda," he paused, trying to think of something more meaningful than 'I love her.' "Her dog's very ill; tell her that Butch will have to be put down."

Chapter 35

"So," Thomas said to himself in the car, "that went well, all things considered." On the seat beside him was the latest, lightweight, standard-issue body armour. It had pinched a bit under the arm when he'd tried it on, but he could live with that. If things went badly — and he had a nasty feeling that things could get very bad indeed — it might make the difference between living and not living.

All reason told him to go back to the flat and stay put, but he was past the point of reason. As the car escaped from the gridlock of Liverpool Street, instead of heading east for Walthamstow he turned north, ploughing through trendy Islington, dodging scooters and Smart cars, through to the Angel where he picked up the A1.

One thing was nagging him, something Peterson had said about Christine. She'd looked pleased. Not coerced, not under duress: pleased. A pound to a penny then that she had to be involved. Stupid of him to have trusted her; she'd always been a career woman. Bob was probably just her stepping-shag to something better.

He drove on to the Welcome Break and re-stocked the car with snacks and petrol. On the way out he powered up the mobile, ever the optimist. And on to Plan C. If

Christine was involved, there was one person sure to know. A person so close to Christine that she even discussed her sex life with her. As he'd found out before, to his cost.

* * *

There are some journeys in life that a person never looks forward to — the dentist, funeral directors, and the STD clinic. Thomas had added Gerrard Hall a couple of years back, when he and Christine had been involved. In what her mother apparently still referred to as 'the social experiment.' Okay, so the imposing house wasn't actually called Gerrard Hall — except by him — but it might as well have been. The class divide again, large as life.

On the drive over, he worked through his pitch. Christine was missing and no one was talking. But if she'd gone willingly, surely she must have been expecting it? Another of Sir Peter Bastard's little exercises, perhaps?

The sign for the village of Ampthill triggered all kinds of memories. Meeting her parents for the first time; the great sweeping drive, Christine beside him — poised but nervous; the house staff looking at him with disdain, like she'd found Heathcliff in a ditch. He laughed at himself as he drove along, remembering his dire attempts at fitting in — the diamond-patterned sweater and the new jacket: priceless. All he'd needed was a pair of plus-fours and a silk cravat.

The sight of the gates sobered him. He pulled over and stared through the bars. The CCTV cameras were an innovation; they must really be serious about keeping the oiks out. This would not be easy; any inquiries would not be well received coming from him, oik that he was. He checked for voicemail and came back empty-handed.

A Land Rover towing a horsebox passed him and the passenger swivelled round to get a good look. The sticker on the back said: 'I slow down for horses.' Big deal. 'I give blood for horses,' now that would be a sacrifice.

He started up the car and fell in behind at a respectful distance. He breathed in the great expanse of greenery and tried to prepare himself for the inevitable welcoming committee. The horse saviours peeled right, towards the stables; he waved them off.

The car made that wonderful sound on gravel, the one that reminded him of horse drawn carriages, and Pride and Prejudice. In the Gerrards' case, class and prejudice. He couldn't even cut Christine some slack on that score.

One of the staff was on him before he'd opened the door. "Excuse me, sir, but this is a private residence — can I help you?"

"I'm here to see Mrs Gerrard — Francesca."

The underling scuttled away. A curtain flickered ever so slightly behind one of the drawing-room windows. He waited outside and listened for whinnying from the stables. There was the faint whiff of horseshit, which he'd always found appropriate on those few occasions in the past when he'd been allowed to cross the threshold.

The butler, or whatever he was, returned, his back bent forward slightly as if in permanent deference. Most likely his family had come over with the Gerrards when the Normans arrived on their expansion tour of Britain. "If you'd like to come this way, sir." The last word sounded a little like cur.

* * *

Francesca Gerrard was waiting for him in the doorway. Everything about her was tailored; tailored skirt, tailored cardigan, tailored smile. A string of pearls circled her neck, knotted and extended to her waist like a pendulum. "It's been a long time, Thomas."

It was a cool reception, bordering on frosty. Not like when she'd come on to him, that one time, when the champers had flowed on Christine's birthday. A polite, but firm hand extended in his general vicinity. "Why don't you come through?" she walked off, leaving him little choice other than to stand there, gathering dust. The manservant nodded to her and retreated to the shadows.

The room that Thomas found his way to was like an American vision of liddle-biddy ol' England. Mahogany furniture fought for floor space with oak and ash. Displayed in one corner of the room was a suit of armour. He wanted to go over and lift up the visor, do the classic joke: anything to calm his nerves. She seemed in no rush to hear what he had to say; which made him even more nervous.

A servant arrived, with an extra cup, placed it on the tray and glided out.

"Please make yourself comfortable."

As if that would ever be possible here. He caught the look on his face in a mirror, and blushed. He was behaving like a lout and with no good reason. He was, in truth, a snob. Christine had seen that from the off. Maybe that had been part of the attraction.

"I take it you're here on business?"

"Ah, yes. Mrs Gerrard — Francesca, I really need to see Christine."

"I'm afraid that's not possible."

He squinted: interesting choice of words. "Is she here?" he glanced in the direction of the stables.

She looked worried for a moment then recovered her stone façade. "Christine is very discreet about her career, but one gets a sense of these things."

He sipped his Earl Grey and tried to keep a lid on his temper. "Do you know where Christine is? I have to talk to her." The words came out like a threat.

"After the damage you've done, I hardly think she'll want to speak with you." Francesca snorted, like one of her precious horses.

He tried her words on for size. What damage had he done? "Look, Francesca, I don't have time for this."

He launched out of the chair, and through the open French doors, round to the courtyard at the side of the house. All the while, yelling for Christine. One of the stablehands rushed up to see what the commotion was.

"It's alright, Stewart," Mrs Gerrard appeared by the arch.

The stablehand took a long hard look at Thomas, who shook his head slowly and flexed a fist. Today, he was not in the mood.

Horse-boy retreated and Francesca sauntered towards him. "Christine isn't here; satisfied? She's working on something clandestine," she paused, "but you of all people should know that." Her hand lifted to catch her jaw.

He couldn't help yielding a tiny smile at her discomfort.

"What's going on, Thomas?"

His mobile rang and they both jumped. "Thomas, it's Ann Crossley. Karl asked me to look out for you. You need to get out of there now."

He left Francesca standing and sprinted around the side of the house, back to the car. The manservant was bending down close to one of the tyres. "Touch it and I'll break your face!" he hollered, rising a fist to show he wasn't pissing about.

It bought him the precious seconds he needed, better for everyone. Given the choice he would have run him over, no question about it. The car roared into life and wheel-span, showering the hapless butler with gravel.

He saw the blue sedan approaching at speed; it wasn't budging for anyone. At the last moment he swerved wide, churning up the carefully tended lawn like a protest vote. He heard the car screech to a stop behind him, but he'd already veered around it, gunning towards the open gates to rejoin the road, his heart thumping in his chest like wardrums.

* * *

Thomas opened the driver's window; he needed some air. What the hell was going on? Nothing made any sense. If this was Sir Peter's people, they'd already know he'd agreed to get the DSB so why the intercept? If it was Yorgi — he took a deep breath — how would he know where Thomas was? Maybe Francesca Gerrard had arranged some secret signal to bring in the heavy mob? He tried to stick to facts. How many had he seen in the car? Two, he thought. But you don't stop to do a headcount when someone's trying to run you off the road.

Back on the A1, with no sign of the blue sedan following him, he turned his deductive powers to the phone call. Karl had said he was on better terms with Ann Crossley so that made sense, sort of. And Karl might have told her about the legit tracker on the car, same as Teresa. So why were all his allies keeping their distance?

When he got back to the flat, there was a message waiting on the machine, blinking insistently. The voice was measured, under control. "It's John; ring me with an update." He cleared it off, poured himself a Southern Comfort and stood for a while, gazing at Miranda's photograph. "I won't let you down," he whispered.

It was early in the day for a drink, but he figured he'd earned it. The need to ring John back pressed hard upon his temples, but the sweet, sharp taste on his lips won on points. He moved the chair round to face the door; too much thinking — that was the problem.

And what about Teresa? If Karl was an enigma, then Teresa was a sphinx under witness protection. Maybe that was the draw for Karl — a mystery deeper than himself.

He dug out a notepad and pen and wrote down all the names, hoping it would help: Karl, Teresa, Ann Crossley, Sir Peter Carroll, Bob 'scumbag' Peterson and Christine Gerrard. Then he scrawled lines between them, linking some and excluding others. He stared at the page until his eyes ached, as if he could solve it like a logic puzzle. But all he noticed was that he'd extended the double 'r' in Gerrard, making them look like a pair of legs. His arm throbbed and his head hurt, and he was all out of ideas.

Chapter 36

Eighteen . . . nineteen . . . twenty . . . done. Miranda eased back on the exercise bike and glanced over at the wall-length mirror; a good workout. The sweat dripped from her headband and had stained her top like heavy raindrops. She was alone, save for 'Pumping Classics 3 — music to shape and tone to.' They left her alone in the exercise room because there were no windows, hence no way out. At this rate she'd be super-fit again; she visited three or four times a day, for short bursts, just for something to do.

She'd surprised herself by how quickly she'd adjusted to the regime; and maybe disappointed herself too. Three days? Four days? It all blended into one. Everywhere she went was supervised, except the bathroom, the bedroom and the gym. Though no doubt someone was always close by. This was like the worst health club in the world; talk about killing with kindness. No one had threatened or mistreated her; they just kept her under watch and interspersed the boredom with twenty questions; the same twenty questions.

Mainly they asked about Thomas; otherwise it was the Irish bloke, national security and random stuff that made no sense whatsoever. And always there was the suggestion that Thomas was in real danger and that her information could be vital. No one seemed to know how long she would be there, or the specifics of why Thomas was in trouble. Or else they weren't saying.

And what did she know? Well, there was one tarmac lane to the front of the house and high fencing around the estate. A walled garden extended to the back of the house with a single arch at the far end and some trees beyond it. Not that she'd ever got close. Whenever she was outdoors, someone always stood back there, supposedly to check it was safe for her. At first, the mixture of bullshit and bureaucracy had been amusing — for a day or so. The thick glass on the sealed bedroom windows was the first wake-up call.

The exercise bike bleeped as the last of the dials powered down, so she relaxed her grip. Alice Eyeball had promised to try and find out more about Thomas today, but that was hours ago. Face it, Miranda, she told herself, until they find whatever they're looking for, you're stuck here.

She checked her no-run make-up and pressed her palms against the glass. Maybe this was one of those two-way mirrors like the police were supposed to use. Like Elvis. She put a finger on her sweatband, traced it down the side of her face and diagonally across her top. If there was a perv watching, he was very quiet about it. Then she sniffed at her shoulder and wrinkled her nose. Funny really, the way her own sweat reminded her of Thomas, the scent of their bodies after their favourite exercise routine.

Time to hit the showers. She wiped the bicycle seat then grabbed the door handle. Alice was standing in front of her like an apparition.

"Jesus!" Miranda flinched.

Alice jumped back about a foot. "Sorry, didn't mean to startle you," she blushed. "Somebody's on their way here to see you."

"How long have I got?"
"She'll be here in about twenty minutes."
It would have to be a quick shower then.

* * *

After making herself presentable, she sat down on the bed and picked up her notepad. The one they gave her to write down anything important she remembered. The one she was certain they checked whenever she left the room.

How many former couples still bother to recall where they met and what they know about their ex's job? Play twenty questions at least twice a day and it soon comes back to you. This was the sanitised version, of course. No Bladen family back-story — nothing about the blazing row with Thomas's parents when they first met her or their jaw-dropping opening line: 'Are you pregnant?' No, this was the family-friendly set. Met in Leeds, moved back to London, Civil Service, break-up, SSU: neat and tidy as a stashed roll of £50s.

Alice was at the bedroom door again, so she picked up the notepad and brought it out with her. Alice led the way to the interview room. "In here please," she said, standing back a couple of feet. She didn't stick around either.

Sod it, Miranda thought; I'm not knocking. The catch turned quietly and the first thing she saw was a dark-haired woman looking out the window, talking on a mobile. Her lips formed the words 'fucking 'ell.' Her mouth ran dry. The world of strange had just acquired a new territory. She reached back and pushed the door until it clicked.

The woman at the window looked round and abruptly finished her call. Miranda couldn't be certain, but the last words sounded like, 'Thanks Bob.'

"Hello, you must be Miranda!" All smiles. Miranda played Simple Simon and mirrored her. "I'm . . ."

Yes, Miranda beamed; I know who you are.

". . . Christine. I work with Thomas. I've come for a little chat."

Miranda sat on the sofa and wondered how long she could keep a straight face. She'd only seen Christine twice before — and one of those was at a distance. But you never forget your ex's new girlfriend — you don't need a notepad for that. The first time was when Thomas had arranged back-to-back pub meets. And even though she'd teased him about staying in the bar, in the end she'd scarpered out the side door, just in time to peer in through the window.

Seeing Christine brought it all back — how jealous she'd been at the way Thomas had got on with his life while she was in Bermuda; had got on Christine, that was. Horses, that had been it; she smiled at the recollection. Christine was into horses. She'd pranced into that pub like an Arabian, all high-headed and flighty, trotting round the bar as if she owned it. Not a way to win friends in Whitechapel. And Miranda herself? Well, a thoroughbred of course. Yeah, ancient history now, but all the same she had to catch her breath when Christine leaned forward to speak.

"I can only imagine how difficult this must be for you, Miranda."

Miranda opened her notebook, as if she was rehearsing a play. Christine flattened her hand over the page. "Thomas hasn't been himself at work lately — you've probably noticed that, too?"

Miranda tilted her head back and nearly laughed. "We're not a couple."

"I'm sorry, I thought . . ." Christine seemed to give the sentence up as a bad idea.

Miranda turned the spotlight round. "Have you talked to Thomas?"

Christine did the 'eyes to one corner' thing. Sheryl at Caliban's reckoned it meant whatever came out next was either a memory or a lie.

Miranda got in there first. "I know you and Thomas were involved."

Christine nodded. "I thought as much; the way you reacted just now..."

"Then let's cut the crap," Miranda chucked the notepad in her direction. "That's as much as I know. Now, have you spoken to him; is he okay?"

Christine surveyed the pages and without looking up, whispered, "He saw one of my colleagues today." She put a finger to her lips and glanced at the door.

Miranda watched as she carefully tiptoed over. A second's pause then she wrenched the door open; no one was behind it. "Good," Christine turned and smiled; "now we can talk a little more freely."

It was stupid and clever at the same time, but Miranda knew this was the first person she'd seen who definitely knew Thomas. And maybe cared about him too, in her high-handed, flighty way. "Would that be Karl or Bob Peterson?"

Christine blanched; Miranda fought hard not to gloat. That ought to burst the balloon. "So now we understand each other, why don't you stop fucking me around and tell me why they're keeping me here?"

"He said you were confrontational," Christine managed a sliver of a smile.

"Look, let's get on with this — we both want the same thing, for Thomas to be safe."

"Thomas?" Christine went a funny shade again.

* * *

Christine ordered coffee and Posh Bloke acted as a waiter. When he'd gone, she scanned through Miranda's notepad again and went down a different line of inquiry. How did Thomas get on with his family? That one drew a wry smile, from both of them. Next it was: how often did Miranda see Thomas? That was a weird one. And then the topper: why was Miranda driving his car that day?

Miranda gulped at her coffee wearily. "What're you actually after?"

"Alright," Christine closed the pad and passed it back to her gently. "What if I were to say to you that Thomas is suspected of corruption or espionage?"

"Bollocks," Miranda erupted, "I don't believe it."

"Good — neither do I." That sounded like a confession.

"So why am I stuck here, then?"

Christine rolled her shoulders back, as if she was trying to shrug off a great weight. "It appears that Thomas helped someone steal a package."

"The ones he delivers for work?"

"Hmm." Christine stopped short of confirmation. "Only this one was being carried by someone else."

"Can't help you there," Miranda pulled down the shutters. "But I do know he was worried about you — because of this Peterson bloke. He's the bent one, by the sound of things."

"Listen to me very carefully," Christine brought a hand under her mug. "It would not be in your interests to repeat that to anyone."

Miranda tilted her head to one side and stuck out her jaw. "You don't scare me; you're just a posh bitch in a suit. What are you supposed to be — the heavy?"

"No," Christine looked down at the floor, "not me," her voice wavered.

For a moment, Miranda felt something for her other than contempt — only for a moment though. "I think we've both said enough, don't you?"

Christine conceded the point. "Yes, why don't we draw a line there; we can always speak again later. I brought some DVDs over."

"Great," Miranda bubbled with mock enthusiasm. "Let's go watch a film together," she searched her brain for something apt; Thomas would have been brilliant at this. Got it. "How about On Her Majesty's Secret Service?"

Judging by her face, Christine was not impressed. "Look, Miranda, we're on the same side — let me prove it to you. I was given a message today, relayed from Thomas." She paused and lowered her voice. "It's bad news I'm afraid; your dog's very ill."

"My what?" Miranda flinched back against the cushion.

"Thomas said that Butch would have to be put down." The room went deathly still. Christine moved back to the window.

Putting Butch down? How? Was Thomas mounting some sort of rescue — did he know where she was being held? Shit. They were all armed here; they made no secret about that. Even Alice Eyeball was packing a piece.

"I'm very sorry about your dog; was he old?"

Miranda closed her eyes and tried to focus. "Er . . . yeah. I . . . I need to lie down for a while."

Chapter 37

The shrill ringtone on Thomas's mobile sliced into his brain like a steak knife. He woke, all arms and legs, sending his notes across the floor. He stabbed at the green button, working his lips to try and dispel the gummy, stale taste in his mouth. "Hello?"

"It's Teresa; open your door."

He checked the curtain; she was alone. In her hand was a small holdall.

"What kept you?"

"Sorry," his head felt muzzy, "I was asleep."

"Have you been drinking?" she pushed straight past him like she owned the place.

"Only a couple. Listen, Christine Gerrard has done a disappearing act." He'd expected some kind of reaction. But no, Teresa was too good for that.

She opened the holdall and carefully removed the Document Security Bag. "Over to you, then," she put it down and folded her gloved hands together.

"I won't be long. Try not to search the place." Not even a glimmer; not a flicker of warmth. Karl must really suffer on cold nights.

His initial trepidation faded the moment he closed the darkroom door and latched it. No surprises there. Whatever crap the world was throwing at him, all he needed was a camera or a darkroom and he was transformed. Christ, even his dad became a better person when cameras were introduced into the equation.

He snapped on a pair of latex gloves and broke the seal on the yellow DSB. Under the red light it looked a murky orange brown. The box inside was untagged, just as Teresa had promised. He slid the lid off and immediately turned the pages upside down. Stupid as it sounded — even to himself — he wanted to be able to say he hadn't read any of it. Not deliberately, anyway.

That was easy for the first four pages — two in French and two in German. After that he focused on the top left and top right letters, now inverted, to get the focus. He checked after every photograph that the camera's infrared dot was still off in case it marked the paper. He kept his movements controlled and precise; his teacher from school Camera Club would have been proud.

Once he'd reset the box and sealed it in the new DSB — the one from Leeds — he felt the sweat nestling between his shoulder blades. The photos were fine, but he was a wreck. He unlatched the door and went out, still wearing the surgical gloves. "It's done."

"You've been in there for thirty minutes — what took you so long?"

Jesus; talk about ungrateful. "You wanted this done right, didn't you? I'll set up the printer for you."

She followed him to the laptop. "I'll need your camera data-card as well."

Of course you will. God forbid you should start trusting me now. He connected everything up, set it to print and walked off to the kitchen. "Call me when you're done. Do you want any tea?"

"No thanks; I had some while I was waiting."

He took his tea and loitered near the doorway until she called him back. All done and dusted, pages printed and enveloped; data-card removed. As if it had never happened.

"Thank you, Thomas." She looked relieved, already putting her coat on. "Remember what we agreed. At least two days."

Well, agreed was putting it a bit strongly. He walked her to the door. "So what do I do, then? Ring up Whitehall in a couple of days' time and tell them Special Delivery?"

"You'll need to figure that out for yourself. Whatever it takes, we need those two days. Ideally we'd have preferred more time, but under the circumstances, we're willing to compromise."

He felt like punching her face in — that, or crying. She opened the front door and pulled her holdall close. He pondered its cargo, and tried to forget that the pages included names, addresses, account-like number strings and some sort of contract.

"And this is where I return to the shadows; goodnight, Mr Bladen, and good luck." She'd only taken a few steps outside when a car started up, flicked on the headlights and pulled up parallel to her. In the blink of an eye, she was gone.

* * *

He bolted the door and stood in the centre of the living room. After all the tension, the silence in the flat seemed forced and unnatural. He waited for a moment, until his breathing had subsided. Then he reached into his back pocket and pulled out a second data-card, twin to the one he'd handed over to Teresa. Clever boy.

At that point he didn't really care what was on it; it was collateral. He had recognised one upside word though, in French: état — state, in English. United States of Europe, maybe? He checked the clock — time to make that call.

"John, hiya mate. I got your message. Tonight? Sure. I've got a couple of things to do before . . . right . . . I understand. I'll be in a cab in ten minutes." A minicab to Dagenham then; no expense spared.

Camera, secret data-card, gun and ammo, clothes, DSB, toothbrush and shaver, laptop and Sherlock Holmes book — everything for the modern spy about town. Thanks to traffic, it took almost an hour to get to Dagenham so he opted for the station. £45 all told, but the cabbie did throw in a series of free lectures on the way.

About the class divide, the racial divide, about what a pain in the arse lazy good-for-nothing sons were and how all the bloody immigrants coming over here were ruining everything. And all to a musical backdrop of what he now knew to be Bengali Asian Fusion. And every second or third sentence from the driver rounded off with 'Do you get me?' which he quickly learned didn't require an answer, as it made no bloody difference.

* * *

It was a surprise that Diane was the pick-up. The only time Thomas saw her at the wheel was when they were going out for the evening and John had decided to make a serious assault on his own liver.

She didn't have much to say, which was fair enough. He was probably the last person she wanted to see so he didn't push it. She seemed to thaw a little by the time they reached the house, but it was hard to tell; at least she was prepared to look him in the face now.

Sam and Terry's car spaces were empty; it looked like dinner for three, unless Sheryl — the other member of his fan club — was putting in an appearance. As they went inside, Diane told him, "Dinner will be ready in fifteen minutes." Which played in his head as: you have fifteen minutes to give us some good news.

He cut straight to the chase and dug out the sealed DSB, reminded them how he'd acquired it and why it would secure Miranda's safe release. It all sounded foolproof until he noticed the gun, amongst his things in the bag. If Diane had seen it, she didn't react; it might have been business as usual for her, given the nature of their business.

After the DSB, he handed over the data-card. "It's an unauthorised copy of whatever's in the pouch."

John held the little case carefully at its edges. "We'll keep it safe for you."

Over dinner, Diane pressed him on how the transfer would be made; an answer he still didn't have. John Wright had ideas of his own. "Take the boys with you, as back-up."

Diane slammed her cutlery down.

Thomas read her face and winced. "It's fine, John, honestly."

"No." John looked first at him then at Diane. "You misunderstand. I insist."

In all the years Thomas had known him, John had never done menacing, until now. Not even when Thomas had turned up on their doorstep as a stranger, with Miranda on his arm. Forthright and unequivocal, maybe, but never this.

"The boys will be waiting at the scrapyard, first thing tomorrow."

Thomas had to force down the rest of his meal; hungry as he was, he couldn't dislodge a bitter aftertaste. He skipped the post-dinner drink and followed them to the comfy chairs, for more questions.

He offered up Bob Peterson's promise of getting a message to Miranda. Then Diane had to spend ten minutes talking John out of making a personal visit to Uncle Bob. Which reminded him . . . "Can I use your internet?"

John and Diane pulled up chairs behind him; he didn't comment. First, he picked up an anonymous server, then he took a slip of paper out of his wallet and set it on the keyboard; no point being coy now. He touch-typed a URL and went through the appropriate security, clicking on 'telephony,' and upped the volume. "This is a recording of all Bob Peterson's calls from Christine's office, today."

There were seven calls in all. The kick-off, provoking a chorus of obscenity from everyone, was Bob Peterson ringing Sir Peter Carroll's office to warn him that Thomas had requested a protective vest. The reply was dismissive; Thomas was being cautious, nothing more. He was just an amateur.

For some reason Thomas couldn't fathom, that still cut deep. Two calls later and it was Christine ringing in on Peterson's mobile. The sound wasn't brilliant, but Miranda was mentioned, with Peterson relaying the message about Miranda's dog Butch.

"Huh?" John said. Diane reached forward without a word, pressing Thomas's shoulder: the boy done good.

Thomas went through the calls sequentially. Peterson kept trying to extricate himself. "I've got a wife and child!" he pleaded, the signal swooping and dipping as the mobile moved about.

"Well then," the line on the recording suddenly cleared; "You'd better think about them very carefully."

Poor sod. The caller was male, well-spoken, midtwenties. The sound quality dipped again, as if a moment's grace had passed. Then the voices went metallic and Thomas started to lose the thread. But one word pierced the cacophony: Yorgi.

He felt sick to his stomach; it as good as proved that he'd been on the right track since Petrov. He blinked back a tear and stayed schtum because he couldn't deal with their fear as well as his own. Because if it was Yorgi, then Miranda was in more danger than they could imagine.

Now what? He opted for distraction. "I'll leave the login details here, for tomorrow," and listened to the sound of his heart pounding against his chest. What would Karl do? He stared at the screen, catching sight of John's inbox, scrunched up onscreen and half-filled with porn and spam. Karl would improvise, that's what he'd do.

"Could you give me a few minutes please?"

John and Diane took the hint, left him to it and moved over to the sofa.

* * *

He worked quickly, without an audience.

Step 1: Set up a webmail account with a slew of random numbers and letters.

Step 2: Get the six-digit Ordinance Survey reference for the Wapping scrapyard.

Step 3: And here was the bit so clever that Thomas grinned as he was doing it — translate key words into something that would pique Karl's curiosity.

Irish Gaelic was a bit too obvious so what about . . . Kosovan Albanian. A quick internet search and he plumped for two words, cutting straight to the point: betejë and shpëtim — battle and rescue. He figured Karl would have picked up at least one of those words out there during his army days; he was counting on it.

In the body of the email from his seemingly random email address, he put in a message: 'Are you looking for gud time, big love? Order now.' Then he added '0800' followed by the OS reference. He kept the title as informative as he dared: 'Sexi Kosovo Girls betejë and shpëtim . . . spurm.' An easy to find reference to tomorrow, a few more keystrokes and away the email went, hopefully winging its way to Karl's spam email folder, where only Karl would see it. Job done.

John or Diane had put the telly on; though neither of them seemed to be watching.

"I'll get her back." Now seemed a good time to make outlandish promises. It was one he'd made himself. He had a Plan B. If the worst happened — and he'd confronted that nightmare frequently since Miranda had been abducted — he would track down and kill everyone responsible. No question; no messing; no macho bollocks — no exceptions. He gasped for air and swam to the surface of his thoughts. "I'll need more ammunition."

Diane actually smiled at him.

Jesus. He felt like he'd just shared dinner with the Grissom Gang. "I just want to say that I really appreciate you letting me deal with this."

John crossed his legs. "For now," he looked away at the clock. "Right," he decided aloud, "you better turn in for the night; early start tomorrow. You're in Miranda's room."

Thomas dragged himself out of the chair, said his goodnights and took his bag off with him. The door still had Miranda's nameplate on it. He almost knocked; he felt like an intruder.

Closing her door behind him, he stared at the bed, bag still in hand as if he wasn't sure whether he would be staying. Now and again, they'd shared that bed — in their crazy on-again, off-again merry-go-round. He approached the duvet and ran a hand along one edge reverently.

Either Miranda had stayed there recently or Diane had left a trace of her favourite perfume to really twist the knife. He closed his eyes and inhaled deeply, imagining her in front of him.

He checked the en suite — for no reason other than to be away from the bed. The figure in the mirror looked haggard and drawn; he barely recognised himself. He closed his eyes again and tried to feel Miranda close behind him, the soft pressure and heat of her breasts against his back; her laughter at his 'oh so serious' face and the sparkle in her eyes under the starry ceiling spotlights.

He wanted to pray, the whole shebang. To kneel down right now on the bath mat, asking for intercession and atonement for his sins. But the thing that stopped him cold wasn't a lack of faith — patchy as that could be. No, he still didn't know what he'd done wrong in the first place, not where Miranda was concerned.

He brushed his teeth, did the necessary and confronted the bed. He chose Miranda's side of the duvet. And okay, he wasn't proud of it or anything, but the bedside cabinet was just too tempting. And it wasn't like he was going to search through the whole room or anything. But he was restless and it was still early . . .

The top drawer was a mass of little yellow post-its, built up over time. He flicked through, tracing Miranda's neat, round handwriting with his fingertips. Underneath that little memory sculpture, he found some old lunch menus from Caliban's and even one from its former incarnation. Was chicken and chips ever really that cheap? This was stupid, he told himself, and carried on anyway. Just the top drawer, he promised himself, digging deeper past the tampons and some paperback called Perfumed Garden. Below all that was a 'confidential counselling' leaflet with a date and time scribbled on it. He blushed and lifted it out, along with a couple of postcards — both from Bermuda, from Miranda. One, to Mum and Dad, read: Everything will be alright. Miranda x. The other, to the whole family, said: Looking forward to coming home again. I love you. Miranda x. He put everything back in order and shut the drawer.

Chapter 38

Miranda, Christine and Alice sat on the sofa together. In any other setting, this could have been a mid-week girls' night in — complete with chick flick, pizza and red wine. Posh Bloke, now identified as Nicholas, had been a right misery about the choice of film; he'd claimed his share of the deep-pan and left them to it. Jack had stopped for a while then announced he was going to patrol the perimeter. Silently, Miranda presumed, like he did everything else.

It was an okay film — they'd let Miranda choose it. When Jack had fetched it back with the food, it was missing a label, a receipt and a bag. Maybe they'd shoplifted it to order. Still, she'd resolved to make the best of it.

Everyone laughed or held their breath at the right places; they just didn't speak to each other, except to move the goodies around. Just at the point in the film where the sassy-yet-caring girl-next-door realised that her best friend was a better match than the scuzzball of a boyfriend, a small green light in the wall flickered into life.

Christine jumped up, barked a code word to Alice and shouted for Nicholas and Jack. It didn't take Brain of

Britain to work out that all was not well. "Jack — comms room, now!"

Miranda sat and watched the mayhem play out. She wondered if Christine had spoken like that to Thomas; maybe she still did during office hours. Then the penny dropped: they had a comms room — probably hidden cameras outside. What if Thomas was out there?

She stood up — on the pretence of stretching — and hugged herself like an orphan, in the centre of the room. Alice had her gun drawn and looked very, very scared. "You'd better go to your room."

The door sprang wide open, almost as wide as the look on Alice's face.

"Oh, for heaven's sake, stand down," In a single sentence, Christine turned Alice into a child.

Miranda looked at Christine through narrowed eyes; what was really going on here? Christine twitched and broke eye contact. Nicholas strode into the room like a lion. He did everything but spray the place, and by the look on his face, he was thinking about it.

"May I have your attention everyone; my colleague will be staying with us for a couple of days."

The stranger waited at the doorway until he had everyone's attention. "Ah, my dear," he crossed the floor to Miranda and extended a well-manicured hand. "Such a pleasure. You may call me Yorgi."

She accepted graciously — no sense getting off on the wrong foot. Nice watch, if you were into retro.

"And you," Yorgi clicked his fingers at Nicholas, "you will join us in the interview. The rest of you are not required." Then he laughed; the kind of laugh that makes you check where your children are.

Miranda found herself complying, meekly following them to the interview room. No one else had moved. Earlier, she'd thought that she and Christine had made some kind of connection. Well, maybe that was just a mind game to soften her up for the big one.

* * *

Yorgi didn't take prisoners. Initially he was all charm and sophistication but, Jeez, the cruelty in that man's eyes. He looked at her with the cold gaze of a predator; a woman gets to know the type, if she's unlucky.

At first Miranda figured she'd ride out the storm and basically wear them out. But this guy was good; he asked the same question ten different ways. No drinks, no comfort breaks and no one to help her. Nicholas seemed to relish every minute, watching the master at work. And even though she knew she had nothing more to tell them, after an hour in their company, she wished she had.

"You must think!" Yorgi banged the desk again. Nicholas jumped too. Yeah, for all that alpha male act, he was as frightened of this bloke as the rest of them.

"Did Thomas mention a package — a delicate matter of security?"

She shook her head again then remembered his insistence on verbal responses. He made Nicholas write everything down, questions and answers. "I need the loo," she was shocked by how small her voice was. She waited while Yorgi considered her request, didn't leave the chair until he pointed to the door.

"Four minutes. No more."

Nicholas marched her to the toilet; he looked smug, repeating the time span as if he'd thought it up himself.

She remained on the toilet seat afterwards, watching as her legs twitched. The tears came without warning; she pulled at the loo roll and dabbed her eyes furiously. Not now, not when that fucking savage was trying to break her down. She pinched at her arm — an old trick to displace her weakness in front of her brothers. God, she wished they were here now. She checked her watch — it was going to be a long night.

Chapter 39

Thomas jolted to attention as John rapped on the door and called out 'six o'clock.' He yawned and rubbed his eyes; he'd been awake for ages. He recalled being a boy, woken up on Saturdays for his paper round. Looking back, it always seemed to be raining — or snowing — everyone else still warm in bed. His dad would make him a mug of hot, sweet tea to see him on his way. 'Mustn't let 'em down, Thomas, mustn't let 'em down.' Those words seemed to have followed him around his whole life.

He showered, using Miranda's gel, even though he'd brought his own along. Then he dressed and sorted through the bag for the fifth time. Shit — no protective vest; he'd left it at the flat. Well, he weighed the pistol in his hand; if push came to shove he'd just have to get the shots in first.

Diane was milling about in the kitchen; she looked like she hadn't slept a great deal either. She kissed him on the cheek, same as she did all her children, and he felt his stomach twitch. Breakfast was a welcome escape from the possibility of conversation, and Diane had done him and John proud. She sat down with them, nibbling at the world's smallest piece of toast.

John ran through the itinerary. "This early, I reckon an hour will be plenty."

Thomas kept his thoughts to himself. An hour? Just to go ten miles up the A13. What was John planning to do, make him walk there?

Diane saw them to the door. The way that she and John held each other took Thomas's breath away; he thought that kind of certainty only existed on television. It brought him up short — didn't he and Miranda used to have that kind of relationship? He turned away, but not before he heard John promise Diane that it would all be okay.

"Bring them all back safe, Thomas," she sounded like she was sending him off to war — and maybe she was.

* * *

John didn't say much until they were on the A13, joining the other poor bastards travelling into work.

"I put extra clips in your bag while you were in the bog."

Thomas smiled. He would have made a joke about firepower if his guts weren't churning. He wondered about the gun again — about where it had come from, and its history. His stomach flipped another somersault; better off not knowing.

"Can I ask you something, Thomas?" John didn't wait for permission. "Where'd you learn to use a gun? At the house, you seemed to know what you were doing."

"Indoor firing range."

John looked disappointed. Thomas thought about showing off his flesh wound, as credentials; bloodied in battle, as Karl would say. Yes . . . Karl. Would he have read the email by now? Would he even be able to act on it if he had? Great — something else to stress about.

"Listen . . ." John kept his eyes on the road. "What are you going to do when all this is over? I can't see you keeping your job if you pull a gun on 'em!"

Yeah, that's right, John; lap it up.

The lights hit red; John turned to face him. "Only, me and Diane were talking last night. And, if you needed a job, we could take you on, part-time, like — with the family. 'Cos sometimes people come to me with the sort of problems that someone like you can handle."

Wow. Thomas locked eyes with John for a second or two. He felt the heat rise up his face and choke him. After all the shit he'd brought on Miranda and the family, they were still willing to chuck him a lifeline.

"No, er, need to commit yourself right now, Thomas."

The lights turned green and his guts did more gymnastics. Back in Pickering, Ajit's dad used to take them out on the moors. Often, on the way back, he'd wish that the car would break down, just to delay getting home. Or he'd count down every ten trees or street lights, surrendering territory in batches of ten. He was doing it now; he didn't realise it at first, but he was still wishing for something he couldn't have.

* * *

"We're here," John kept the car running. "I'll check that website for any more phone conversations from that Peterson bloke and ring you if anything turns up."

The breezeblock walls of the scrapyard were covered in graffiti, making it look like a techno-fortress. Thomas figured Sam and Terry weren't fussed; he remembered Sam's fondness for the spray can in his teens. What goes around, and all that.

Above the wall was a layer of corrugated steel. Some of that had been colonised by Street Artists Anonymous too. The E1 posse might be feerlezz, but he didn't rate their chances if they ever went over the fence into the yard.

The door set within the main gate was open and waiting. He banged on the panelling and announced himself.

"Hey Thomas, how's it going?" Sam could always be relied upon for a warm welcome. Terry though, looked like he was sizing him up. Sam elbowed him sharply.

"Alright, Terry?"

Terry sniffed aloud, like a Rottweiler gauging the scent of a rival. "Are you sure you're up to this?"

Up to this? He took a few steps forward, into their domain. No question, because when it all came down to it, he'd have to be. He dropped his bag by the door. "I am, if you two back me all the way."

Good answer. And true, as it goes. John Wright was a shrewd man. Now there were three chances of getting Miranda out, and if it all went pear-shaped he had people he could trust implicitly.

He closed the door behind him and drew the bolt across the gate. Terry led the way, through the scrapyard, deep among the junk-filled skips and piled up cars. In one derelict cul-de-sac, a series of crude targets had already been set up, ready for practice.

It took less than half a clip to realise that drawing from a shoulder holster was too slow. It was Terry who nailed it — too clumsy, too telegraphed; the way Thomas moved one arm across and the other instinctively backwards to give better access to the weapon. Plus, he'd hopefully be wearing a vest and that might slow him further.

He reverted to the basics and once he'd cleared a row of targets, both brothers seemed to lose their scepticism. Okay, they weren't slapping him on the back or anything, but they listened now when he gave instructions for repositioning new targets. He shot from standing, kneeling, lying down; a crash course in 'aim and fire' — not 'think then aim then think and fire.' Think too much, on this occasion, and it could be the last thing he did. He yawned; fatigue and the constant spectre of fear were taking their toll.

Sam came to the rescue. "Don't worry, Thomas, I'll make us all a brew."

Yeah, nothing like a nice cuppa after a hard day's shooting. They sat on planks raised up by milk crates, staring down at the makeshift targets — two shop dummies and beer bottles on poles.

"When are you ringing the geezer to make the switch?" Sam sounded so much like a cinema gangster that it was painful.

Thomas turned it over in his brain. Teresa wanted two days' grace so was that the day after today? And how was he supposed to stall everyone? He scuffed at the ground with his boot. "I'll contact him later today." Sam and Terry nodded in unison and the three of them sought refuge in their mugs of tea.

* * *

All Thomas heard was a click, far behind him. It was the only warning before a shot rang out, shattering one of the beer bottles. The boys dived for cover; Thomas threw himself on the ground and scrabbled for the handgun, which he'd zipped up in the bag. He was still fiddling with the handle — jammed, naturally — when he heard the boots crunch against the ground towards him.

"See here, Tommo, is this a private party or can anyone join?"

Thomas saw Sam and Terry standing on the periphery, gripping metal bars: futile but admirable.

"Karl McNeill, at your service," he took a bow and holstered his weapon, which looked like one of his beloved Brownings.

Sam and Terry gave each other a strange look, dropped their weapons and approached him.

"Terry and Sam, I presume? Is there anything left in the pot; I'm gasping!" Karl released a rucksack from his back and cricked his neck in several directions. He was dressed head to foot in black.

"What are you supposed to be?" Thomas thought it best to get in early.

"That's a fine welcome for a man who's driven half the night to be here. Seriously, how are you, Tommy?"

After tea, Sam and Terry did the decent thing and buggered off to the nearest café for supplies. Thomas set up new targets — under Karl's instruction — and Karl unveiled the contents of his rucksack — a veritable armoury.

"So you obviously got my clever message. How did you get away?"

Karl laughed, rat-a-tat-tat style. "Well, my mammy wasn't willing to write me a note so I did what any decent pal would do — I walked off the job."

"Really? Shit." Thomas floundered for words. "So what's going to happen?"

"Hey, don't sweat it, Tommo. We have other things to sweat about. Bottom line is, Miranda's caught up in someone else's fight — that's unacceptable. You let me worry about my blistering career. Some things are more important."

Thomas gulped some tea down to soften the lump in his throat. "So where have you come from then, if you've driven half the night?"

"Hey, hey, Mr Bladen," Karl weighed the two Brownings in his hands, squinting one eye. "That's confidential information. I'll have you know that I've signed the Official Secrets Act."

"Twat."

Karl answered with a volley of two-handed gunfire, blasting bottles in all directions. "So how are you gonna tell Frank and Jesse James about the two-day hiatus?"

Thomas curled a lip. So, Karl had been speaking to Teresa as well. "Dunno — any ideas?"

"As a matter of fact, I have," Karl exchanged weapons with Thomas for a try-out, "but I'm not sure you're gonna like it."

Thomas followed Karl's drill to the letter, first kneeling then crouching, coming belly down to the ground, walking straight ahead, and all the while shooting. Karl was a natural; no, scratch that, he was an un-natural. His hit rate was mesmerising, against an assortment of bottles, headlights and shop dummies.

"You're really serious about taking down these bastards?" There wasn't a trace of mockery in Karl's voice.

Thomas laid the weapon on the ground — safety on — and brushed dust off his jeans. "Yorgi's definitely involved and he's not the negotiating type." He relayed the fruits of his intelligence gathering.

Karl poked his tongue out and licked his upper lip. "Hear me out now," he made the pistol safe and passed it over. Thomas put it on the ground. "If we're getting Miranda in exchange for the papers, and taking care of Yorgi — assuming he's there . . ."

"Oh, he'll be there," Thomas felt a shiver run down his spine.

"You need to be somewhere safe; a place you know well. Your life could depend on it. And hers."

Yeah, thanks for that. Thomas opened his hands to catch some more pearls of wisdom from Guru Karl.

Karl got the message after a few seconds. "Oh, right. If it was me, I'd make the exchange somewhere secure — only one road in and out."

Thomas wiped the sweat from his neck. "Yeah, but it's not that simple, is it? They've got Miranda — I can't take any chances; if anything . . ."

Karl brought his hand down hard on Thomas's shoulder, as if anchoring him. "Do you trust me, Tommo? I mean, really trust me? I see a way through this, but you'll need to do things my way."

Thomas looked around him; everything was still. There was that feeling again; a sense that Karl knew this was coming and had always known. Still, weigh that up against any other options — precisely none — and what else did he have? Nowt. "I'm listening."

"You have to dictate the terms. Name the place — and state your price. If you give them a price, they'll have you down as a rank amateur — which you are not. This gives us a certain, minimal advantage."

Thomas picked up the empty mug and stared inside. He felt like crying, and he could have filled it to overflowing. "I don't know. I can't afford to fuck this up," he heard the panic in his own voice.

Karl play-punched him on his good arm and shook his head dismissively. "It's like automatic doors. You keep right on walking at a steady pace and they just open — because it's what they're supposed to do." He did an exaggerated slow march on the spot.

"No guarantees though," Thomas wasn't smiling.

And neither was Karl. "No, Tommo, no guarantees."

He dropped the tin mug, the hollow clatter echoing in his brain. And shielded his eyes with his palms. He asked for guidance in the darkness, a solitary waiting, throbbing in his chest. But all he felt was the breeze stirring against the backs of his hands and all he heard was the hiss of his own breath. He lowered his hands and sighed. "Okay, how's this going to work, then?"

By the time Terry and Sam returned, the guns were stowed away and Karl was making stick drawings in the dirt.

"Who wanted the runny egg?" Rely on Sam to break the tension.

* * *

Thomas sat down with Sam and Terry, as Karl repeated the plan for their benefit. As it was the second time he'd heard it, his mind began to wander. With hindsight, it was easy to see the choices he had made as inevitable. The mind played tricks, picking out key pieces of information and stringing them together like second-hand pearls. Wrap the parts in meanings they never had before and hey presto, it's destiny. But mostly it was just making the best of a difficult situation at the time, and wanting to feel good about it.

Karl did some keypadding on his new state-of-the-art mobile and the Internet flashed up the bunker, not too far from Fylingdale; the one that Thomas and Ajit had rediscovered as kids. It was closed, Saturdays and Sundays. One road in and the same road out; surrounded by open moorland. Even Thomas had to admit that the location was damn near perfect.

Terry raised a few objections while Sam wanted to be convinced. Thomas watched as Karl sold it to them; how the setting, time and place would work in their favour. Except he referred to it as 'securing the objectives.' It was a new side to Karl, decisive and with a certain, clinical eye. If the army was missing him, Thomas figured, it wasn't missing a mere squaddie.

Once the boys were on board, Thomas made the call to Dagenham. Diane and John didn't take the change so well — not at first, anyway. And bringing Karl's background into the picture seemed like the desperate act of a desperate man. Thomas was past caring; he just wanted it all sorted.

It still sounded a bit sketchy in his head. Karl and the boys would dig in on the moors. Then Thomas would make his call to Whitehall, giving details of the exchange and adding a £40k fee to the mix. He could follow Karl's logic that Sir Peter would deduce he was a greedy bastard, and that Thomas had probably sent the document up country, ahead of time. But what if they just sent the police — or worse — round to his mum and dad's, or Pat's? Karl's logic to the rescue again; so what, they wouldn't find anything. No, but they might take a few doors off in the process. Anyway, the plan was set and there was no going back now.

* * *

Thomas was alone again, but not abandoned. He loitered for an hour in Wapping Gardens, near the scrapyard, and then at the Turk's Head Café, cradling a coffee he didn't need. He figured it was a better option than waiting around Wapping Underground, trying not to look suspicious. The last thing he wanted was an overzealous copper doing a bag search.

When it was time, he took the tube to Victoria and wandered the station complex, psyching himself up for action. If he didn't commit soon, the spare-any-change brigade would bankrupt him. He chose a phone stand to use and waited for it to be free. Which phone made no difference at all, but every little firm decision was a toehold on reality. He slid in his card and dialled the number from memory, in slow, steady movements.

As the number connected he checked the time — Karl's team should be well on their way now. The phone picked up on the third ring — no switchboard interrupt or invitation to leave a message. He stalled for a second, led with his name — always a strong opening — and took the plunge.

"So, Thomas, what do you have for me?"

He closed his eyes. "I can get the DSB to you in a couple of days' time."

"I see," the voice was non-committal. "How do you propose to do that?"

Half-truth time. "I'm to await a phone call at home and then I'll be texted a time and place." In his mind's eye, he saw Sir Peter scribbling notes down in red ink. "I go there alone and collect the package then we do the exchange and I leave with Miranda." He tried not to sound too authoritative, but hey, he wasn't asking permission either.

Sir Peter Carroll rasped down the phone. "That's settled then — I'll await your next call." The line went silent.

Thomas fought the panic and followed the plan. "There's one more thing." Steady now, not too eager.

"What's that?" It sounded like the old man had tapped a spoon against a cup, like he was waiting for a punchline to a joke he'd already heard before.

"I'll need £40,000, for services rendered."

"I see."

Can two words be made to sound smug? Those did. He hoped Karl was right — better they had him down as a chancer, than as honest and predictable. The line cut off while he was waiting for a reply.

Chapter 40

Miranda woke up with a migraine. Not a drink hangover, but a stress, dehydration, unable-to-sleep headache from hell. She hadn't had one of those in years. Last time? Probably the break-up with Thomas; the final break — a funny memory to dredge up. Doors: that was it. Those bloody doors slamming in the night and someone messing with a portable TV or radio in the corridor outside her room. And all that shouting — some bloke yelling at the top of his voice. Who was she kidding: it had been Yorgi.

She stumbled to the en suite and ran the tap, scooping the cool, stinging water to her face. It was the crying that did it; always gave her a bloody headache. The bathroom cabinet had been thoughtfully stocked with the female guest in mind — tampons, painkillers and cotton-buds. She snatched a couple of tablets and sank her head below the tap, pushing past the nausea by focusing on the craving for water.

A quick shower, then she changed into her gym wear — well done, Alice. It was a masochistic never-fail cure: exercise. True, you felt like shit for three quarters of the time, but afterwards, if your head hadn't exploded, you were in a better shape to face the world. She stuck a body spray in her waistband, ditched the lid — funny how they all looked so phallic — and opened the bedroom door.

The corridor was empty — hardly surprising after last night's aggravation. Even so, she tiptoed past every door to make it to the exercise room on the far side of the house.

The strip lights flickered with an angry buzz, gleaming off the shiny surfaces in a riot of light. She gave her eyes a moment to adjust, then began with a few warm-up stretches, progressing to practice falls and rolls on the mat. Back when she'd spent time in Bermuda, she had started kobudo defence classes. Her commitment had more to do with a guy she'd been dating, but now and again she still went through the kata at home.

Soon she was getting into her stride and the painkillers were kicking in. She flicked the CD player on, turned the sound down slightly and cycled like a maniac. The blood started pumping, and she turned her thoughts to the previous night. That Yorgi bloke was really unhinged. If Christine hadn't finally intervened, he'd have probably kept her there all night. But . . . Christine had left her there in the first place. So much for her promise of friendship. Jesus, this bloody CD — she must know every beat of every track by now. Maybe it was time to send Alice shopping again.

The shift of air, as the door opened inwards, broke her train of thought. She turned behind her — stupid really as she was facing the mirror — and there was Yorgi, looking like he'd had an argument with his suit, and lost.

He didn't speak, just stood with his back against the door. Miranda lifted her feet off the bike, swung over it and jumped down; the bike whirred on. "What do you want?"

Yorgi seemed to look beyond her, as if it wasn't really her he was seeing. In two words: coked up. She edged back and felt the sweat running between her shoulder blades. He was whispering to himself now; maybe it was deliberate, to freak her out. If so, he was succeeding. "I asked what you're doing here."

He snapped out of his torpor and glared at her, opening his mouth to a sneer. Miranda narrowed her gaze; flicking her eyes over him, fixing the vulnerable points in her brain the way that her sensei had showed her, long ago. She moved out into the middle of the room, facing him. Then it happened.

In a second, he had leapt the distance between them and had his hands on her shoulders, pressing down with such force that her arms felt weighted. He leaned in close to her face. "I have had a hundred dogs like you," he hissed, the words spattering against her skin. "Now, I ask you for the last time — where is my package? Does Tomas have it?"

She felt her face flush at Thomas's name and looked away, trying not to react. But Yorgi swung his face round to fill her gaze. He reeked of sweat and rage. Yeah, that was it: rage. And he was barely keeping a lid on it.

His hand drove into her collarbone and at first she resisted, pushing back as if to pretend it wasn't crushing into her. Then she relaxed and the weight of him toppled her off balance. Now he looked at her differently, as if she'd awoken something in him that was even more dangerous. Every woman knows that look, and what it means. Dread and anger mixed inside her like the elements of a Molotov cocktail. And the flame was coming.

He moved his hand down to her breast and flattened against it. She smacked it away, full force, and a malevolent leer rose up on his face. "I will enjoy teaching you . . ." he squeezed with his fingertips, digging into her flesh.

She kept her gaze on him, implacably hidden behind mental defences she hadn't had to use in a long time. A slight shift to one side and her leg was primed. At the first movement, his hand came down hard to block in front of his groin, but she crosskicked and slammed into his knee with the top of her foot.

Yorgi let out a roar of pain and fell to the floor, dragging her down with him. He was bigger and heavier. Despite his pain, he used his descent to his advantage, pinning her down and straddling her. Red fury burned in her eyes as she rocked him from side to side with little effect. "Now I give Tomas a message you will both remember for a long time."

Miranda pushed her arm forward, across and below her abdomen. He cackled with laughter, as if he relished the struggle. With a grunt of determination, she stretched her fingers, slipped into the waistband and palmed the bodyspray. The adrenalin was in full flow now; she wanted this fucker dead.

He bore down on her and she felt the obscenity of his bulge against her clothes. He pushed again, burrowing his nails under the elastic of her leggings.

She bent her neck back, drew down a snort of phlegm and spat in his face with all her might. He withdrew his hand to wipe it, and she took full advantage, emptying as much spray as she could into his eyes. He screamed and clawed at his face.

She swung a punch at his throat, but hit wide of the mark, catching a glancing blow against his chin. At the same time, she wrenched one side of her body up, screaming at the effort. He fell to the right and she dragged her legs out from under him.

"You bitch!" he choked through his hands, launching at her blindly from the floor — half grabbing, half flailing, crashing the two of them into the full-length mirror. They rolled together, mid-trajectory, and he hit the glass first, bearing the brunt as shards blasted from the wall.

She felt for her balance, sensing him crumple. But Yorgi had only folded momentarily to arm himself. She saw the blade glint against the ceiling lights as his hand swung towards her face. She dug her elbow in hard, twice in succession, against whatever flesh she could contact and swerved to one side as his hand arced in.

As she rolled on the glass-strewn floor she heard the crackle of fragments and curled in tight to protect her face. As soon as she came out of the roll, she leapt for the door and wrenched it open. Outside, she pulled the door to and stood behind the frame, frantically bracing herself for the tug-of-war.

"I kill you, you whore!"

She leaned back to counter jam the handle and bellowed for help. What the fuck was wrong with everyone — were they all deaf?

"Tomas and Petrov — they are dead men!"

She shuddered at every syllable. Then a shot rang out, dead centre of the door, blasting a hole through like a tiny explosion. She screamed and pulled her arm rigid until the bicep burned. The only way this bastard was coming out was if he shot a hole big enough to climb through. The stench of scorched wood and hot metal stained the air. A second shot burst out the door, splintering against the opposite wall.

At last, she heard people galloping towards her. Christine got there first. "Quick, come with me," she pulled Miranda away and threw an arm around her.

Only now did Miranda feel the flecks of glass in her hand and the sting as she brushed them aside.

"Nicholas, keep him here. You'd better sort this out — now!" Christine demanded, half-carrying Miranda away. Yorgi was still yelling as Nicholas attempted to placate him from the other side of the door.

Miranda made it as far as the kitchen and retched in the sink. Christine stood back, but she could feel her staring. "You've got to get away from here."

"You think?" That was all Miranda could manage before another bout of vomit erupted against the stainless steel. Not so stainless now. She felt her legs buckling and gripped the side of the sink unit.

"Come on," Christine insisted, "we don't have much time."

Miranda turned, and for a moment she thought of striking out. But by the time she had chambered her knuckles, Christine had moved out of range.

"Miranda, hurry, please!"

She followed the voice through to the lounge. Christine was unlocking the patio doors.

"Right," Christine's voice sounded shaky. "Take my phone . . ." she fumbled about in a small shoulder bag. "Give me your hand — quickly," she scrawled four numbers on Miranda's arm. "My cashcard — and there's twenty pounds." She thrust plastic and paper into Miranda bloodied hand. "And you better take this."

Miranda looked on in amazement as she passed her the gun. "Why are you doing this?"

Christine hyperventilated a little as she searched for the words. "Just go and don't stop — I'll say you overpowered me . . . get out while you still can."

And that was all Miranda needed. Adrenalin flooded her muscles and the survival instinct drove her past the pain, past the terror and through Christine. Afterwards she'd try to rationalise it as giving Christine an alibi, but right that second Christine had simply become another obstacle to be dealt with. She struck with a well-aimed heel of her hand, contacting under Christine's chin with a satisfying thwack. Christine went down like the proverbial sack of shit, but Miranda didn't wait around to watch the finale. She launched through the doors, straight across the grass, barrelling towards the arch at the far end of the garden. She flew like a Valkyrie, gun primed. Like Mum used to say, when they'd really misbehaved as kids: all bets were off now.

Chapter 41

06.30.

"Yes, this is Sir Peter — do you know what time this is? What? No, you did the right thing calling me, Nicholas. I can be in Whitehall . . . let's say eight o'clock. Take command up there under my authority and keep Yorgi under control — whatever it takes. Medicate him if you have to. Who was the senior officer? Christine Gerrard. Right, here's what I want you to do. Widen the search and put a surveillance team on the girl's parents' home."

Sir Peter glanced over at his wife trying to get back to sleep. He turned his back to her, and whispered. "Monitor Bladen's phone — I'm sure you don't need me to tell you of the difficulties the organisation faces if she makes it home before we get the package back. Do we understand one another, Nicholas?" He placed the receiver down and sat up in bed.

"What is it, Peter?" his wife fumbled for her bedside lamp.

"It's nothing, dear, just work. I need to go to Whitehall urgently." He didn't wait for an objection; too many years had passed for one to be raised. He picked up the telephone again. "Phillip, how soon can you have the car here? Forty-five minutes will be fine."

Chapter 42

Thomas span the plastic token in the air, pleased that he'd stored the DSB in a locker at Victoria. Just in case someone came knocking on his door before he left for Yorkshire. Everything was in play now and all he could do was wait at the flat. Teresa had dropped off the radar altogether; Karl, Terry and Sam were en route to somewhere Karl had promised 'would be close enough to the bunker to see Miranda's smile.'

He wandered, room to room, staring at the pictures as if they were an exhibition of someone else's life. And hadn't it been that, really? Leeds was a world away; the Miranda he knew — carefree laughter, sardonic wit and a lithe body with visiting rights — that was all gone now, surely? Somehow he'd overstayed at the theatre of life and seen the magician packing the tricks away; he'd never be so enthralled again, nor fooled so easily.

In the kitchen there were more photographs: a couple of panoramic views of the moors, at dawn and dusk. He remembered spending a whole day on that. For reasons he still couldn't fathom, it had to be dawn and dusk on the same day. The entire photography club had been there, all sandwiches and flasks, and a sneaky lager for him and Ajit that he'd found at the back of the Christmas cupboard. The photos were amateurish, but there had been potential in them; the composition of the shot, two trees together silhouetted against the orange glow; the way he'd waited and only taken two frames of each. Just two frames a piece in a crazy shit-or-bust challenge to his own abilities.

Looking at the pictures now opened a narrow window to the past. He could just about glimpse what it was to be a teenager again, to be outdoors and not be afraid or isolated or . . .

He coughed, as if to attract his own attention. Another photograph, lower down, cradled his reflection and he stared at the tears without reproach. Well, almost without reproach. "Finished?" he asked himself aloud.

* * *

Later that morning a text came in from a mobile he didn't recognise. 'Get new mobile, text us here with our names. Kosovo Girls.' At last, something to do. He grabbed the bag and took the car; might as well give them some activity to track.

The salesman looked all of seventeen, but that didn't stop him trying to sell mobile-phone insurance and a host of accessories that only served two purposes — to delay Thomas and to really piss him off. Once he'd escaped his clutches, he found a camping shop and bought a compass. Not quite a Silva, but a decent enough copy.

Back at the flat he dug out the old maps — the ones that only saw daylight once a year at most, ready for the joyful family reunion. It was a deal he'd hatched with himself, many years ago — every time you spend a little time with the Bladen clan, I'll let you out on the moors.

The new mobile fired up with a little fanfare, which was the first thing he changed. He followed Karl's instructions and programmed in the Kosovo Girls number; he was in Karl's hands now.

The landline call came soon after. "Thomas? John." This was minimalism played to Olympic standards. "How's it going? The boys are in Scotland for a few days, on a fishing trip . . ."

He winced: way too clever.

". . . And did I tell you that Uncle Robert's been unwell — last I heard. I might pop round there, just to see if he needs anything."

He gulped. Did John Wright have enough information to track Bob Peterson down? Well, Bob would have to fend for himself.

"Anyway, have a good weekend and remember, Monday night is poker night. Everyone's expected."

The call ended. Thomas put the phone down and unclenched his teeth — a stupid, unnecessary risk. That settled it; he'd ring Sir Peter Carroll now and then get his arse up to Yorkshire.

"Hello Sir Peter, it's Thomas. I've just received a call — I've been told to head up to Yorkshire tonight. I'll pick up the DSB, then hand it over to you tomorrow. Hmm yes, I'll drive up. And Sir Peter, I really appreciate what you're doing for Miranda and me." The line nearly choked him. "Now, let me give you a handover site for tomorrow morning — I'll be there nine-thirty." He rattled off the OS reference, matching the red circle on his old map.

* * *

By the time he got to Victoria to retrieve the DSB, everything he needed had been transferred to a large rucksack, including the vest. Uniforms were funny things; hill-walker or vigilante — it all depended on what you kept beside your Kendal's mint cake.

Back in the car he hung an old St Christopher over the rear-view mirror. He didn't have the balls to string JC up there yet, but he was willing to take any help he could get.

Three hours into the drive to Yorkshire, the mobile flashed so he pulled over. It was Karl, in his own inimitable style: 'Dug in. drive safe, no speeding!'

Mum and Dad had been thrilled to hear he was going to be in the area for a couple of days. Well, not thrilled; pleasantly suspicious was closer to the mark. Understandable though, considering he'd generally rather walk through nuclear waste than spend time with the Bladens. And he wasn't very subtle about it.

As much as he'd wanted to, he knew it would be wrong to drag Ajit into everything. Ajit would want to help through 'official channels.' But that was the kind of thinking that had dropped Thomas in the shit in the first place. Although, now that he came to think about it, a copper like Ajit could be useful under certain circumstances. Thomas weighed it all up as he exited the last services, before leaving the M1.

Chapter 43

Be it ever so claustrophobic, there's no place like home. And, if Thomas were honest, Pickering was no place like home either. If it weren't for the fact that he was bloody tired he'd have driven out, anywhere, rather than do the reunion bit now. But, as things stood, he was all done in. Not just the driving, tortuous as that had been, but the endless mental coin flipping; the absolute conviction that this would all be okay, followed by an all-consuming dread that it was all beyond his grasp, no matter what he did. It put a whole new sheen on: 'Are we there yet?'

The homestead curtains twitched as he was parking up; Mum had probably been waiting there for the last half hour, watching cars. He took a long breath and swung the rucksack over to the driver's side, checking that the box of chocolates had survived the journey intact.

His mother was at the door while he was still three feet away. He switched the rucksack to one hand, opened his other arm and engulfed her.

"It's good to see you, lad."

He used to scoff at the way she could produce tears — once he accused her, harshly, of manufacturing them to order. Today, he had to stay focused to stave off his own.

His father smiled from the armchair and they did their usual strong father-and-son handshake act. Bladen senior waited until Thomas's mother had skipped off to the kitchen to re-boil the kettle.

"It's grand to see you, Thomas. Is everything all right?"

"Not exactly," he replied, then suggested they talk later, in private.

"Are you, er, stopping long?" His father stared at the rucksack, which Thomas had pressed tightly to his leg.

He pulled out the chocolates and placed them on the floor.

"Helen, come look at what Thomas has brought us."

Blimey, who is this impostor and what's happened to my real dad?

Pat put in an appearance later, with the kids. Gordon even managed to travel four streets to pop his head round the door when he came to take them home. It was like Thomas had slipped into a parallel world, where no one was using the next person in line for emotional target practice.

Karl was there at the back of his mind, but all he could do was wait for an update. So basically, he was Johnny No-mates for the night. He'd fed the family a vague story about being in the area for work — another half-truth that Karl would have been proud of.

His mother said she was going round to keep Pat company, while Gordon nipped out for a few jars. It sounded staged, but Thomas didn't care. He sat, statue-like until the door closed behind her.

"So," James carefully shut the hall door behind him, "what's to do, Thomas?"

He'd played it out so many different ways in his head, but however he began there was no easy opening. He unclipped the top of the rucksack and looked inside. "Why don't you sit down, Dad; this is complicated."

"Look, if there's summat troublin' you lad, just spit it out."

Easy words. He made two false starts, opening his mouth without speaking.

"Come on, Thomas, why are you really here? I don't buy all that rot about being here for work."

He nodded and pulled the drawstring closed. "It's Miranda, Dad. She's being held by someone — because of me."

"Is it drugs?"

Thomas erupted. "Of course it's not bloody drugs — what do you take me for?" Right, bollocks, he'd let him have it all, chapter and verse. First, the photograph at the Harwich, then Petrov's car, and then Yorgi. It was all loosening up inside his brain and oozing out like molten wax. He didn't know if his father was really listening — it almost didn't matter because now he was talking he didn't want to stop. Karl, Bob Peterson, Sir Peter Carroll, Christine — he knew they'd just be names to his dad, and quickly forgotten. But he wanted to get it all out now and lay it bare before him.

It took nearly half an hour to get to the present day, how Karl and the boys were already out on the moors, risking life and limb to help him bring Miranda home. And how he was really in Yorkshire to make the exchange.

His father had said very little. He seemed to wait until Thomas had run out of commentary. "And you've not thought of going t' police?"

Thomas raised his hands, clawing at the air in sheer frustration. "What did the police ever do for you, Dad?"

"Aye, I know; I'm only saying, like. But . . ."

Thomas reached into his rucksack — it was time.

"But won't it be dangerous?"

Thomas smiled; his dad was a master of understatement. He pulled out the bulletproof vest and passed it across.

"Blimey, there's nowt to it; doesn't look as if it'd stop a cough!"

They both laughed; it cut through the tension like a cleaver.

"And that's why," Thomas lowered his voice even though there was no one else in the house, "I wanted to talk to you in private, because I need your help."

His father leaned in and the flickering fire reflected in his eyes. "I'll do anything I can."

Hold that thought. "I need the gun," the words plummeted to the floor.

"Now, look . . . Thomas; I can see how you're fixed . . ."

He stood up and his father looked ever so small. "Don't fuck me around — is the gun here or not?" He could hear the desperation in his own voice and he felt ashamed. He hated feeling like that, hated being there, asking for help from the one person who'd never been any help to him, ever.

His father hadn't spoken for maybe a minute.

"Look," he reached into the rucksack again and drew out the .38 automatic. "These people don't mess around. I need the gun you kept in the shed."

His dad looked up at him one last time, and sighed. "Wait here."

Thomas called after him, making sure they understood each other, once and for all. "Make sure it's loaded."

He put the vest and pistol away, and stared into the flames, close enough for the heat to sting his eyes. At least, that's what he told himself.

His father took a good five minutes. Thomas was in no rush though, as long as he got what he came for. A second weapon could make all the difference.

"Here," his father put a rolled up cloth on the table with a soft thud.

Thomas picked it up, trying the weight for size. When he looked up, his father's face was frozen. "Did I do summat to make you like this?"

"No, Dad," he spoke through his hands, just like he used to as a boy when he'd been caught out at something. "You've always told me about the Miners' Strike, about the struggle against Thatcher and the government. It's my turn now, Dad; I'm the one fighting and these bastards," he felt the tears falling but he didn't care anymore; "these bastards have got Miranda and she . . ." Fuck, he couldn't even say the words. He choked on a breath and looked up. His father was wiping his face with a hankie.

"Now, I need you to do summat else for me, tomorrow — have you got some notepaper and an envelope?"

His father watched as he wrote out a letter to Ajit, detailing where he was going and when and what was going on. If it all went to shit — and he pretty much expected that, one way or another — at least the police could clear up the aftermath.

"I'll tell thee something, Thomas, and I've never told a living soul. That little gun there has only been fired twice. I took it down to the allotments one time and fair scared myself to death with a single bullet. And of course the other time . . ."

Thomas sniffed and stared at him blankly.

"Bloody 'ell son, don't you remember?"

He shook his head, as if he could deny the truth.

"It was you, yer daft bugger. I caught you in the house messing around with it and, well, we'd had words the day before. You only went and pointed the bloody thing at me and it was loaded. You couldn't have known that of course."

Thomas felt the heat roasting his cheeks. He had known; he was sure of it.

"Aye, bloody thing went off and shot a plate from the wall. It were like something out of Spanish City Amusements at Whitley Bay! Anyhow, you were so scared, you peed yourself and to tell the truth I think I might'a done as well!" His father folded the hankie and dabbed his forehead. "Look, I hope you know what you're doing."

A cog rotated in his brain; there was something else to take care of tonight. "I'm going out for a couple of hours." He picked up the Makarov pistol in case his father changed his mind and added it to the rucksack. It felt good to have it, as if he were reclaiming it from the nightmare.

"Are you out seeing Ajit, to drop off your letter, then?"

"No," Thomas raised a stop hand, "he doesn't know I'm here — he mustn't get the note until tomorrow morning. Tell Mam I'll not be back late."

He drove to York, for no other reason than that it was a good distance from Pickering. Far enough away for a DSB pick up, if there'd actually been one.

He wandered among the crowds — there were always crowds in York, no matter what time of year. Always a group of twats in Viking helmets and club sweatshirts, who thought they were able to hold their drink.

Despite his own prejudices, he opted for a busy pub — something with sport splashed across a widescreen TV. He squeezed through the throng and made straight for the gents, emerging a few minutes later with the vest on, under his sweatshirt, for practice. He settled for a pint of shandy and found an abandoned table at the far end of the pub. Nearby was an old man with a Border Collie at his feet. They were like two refugees from the twentieth century — the old man clinging to his pint of bitter and Thomas pawing over a hiking map of Fylingdales Moor.

A woman arrived with a buggy and commenced her double experiment, trying to poison her kid with cigarette smoke and mobile phone radiation. "Come on, Crystal, say hello to Daddy."

Thomas watched and swapped raised eyebrows with the old feller. The poor little mite in the buggy didn't stand a chance. Daddy was probably on the other side of the pub somewhere, stuck in the crowd. Or in a young offenders' centre.

He sighed into his shandy and puzzled over the map, a map so old that the bunker tourist attraction wasn't even printed and had been added in by felt-tip pen. One road, in and out. He looked at the surrounding terrain and access roads; it would entail at least a two-mile walk, maybe more; something else to factor into his non-existent plan. He put his glass down on RAF Fylingdales.

How was this supposed to work, exactly? Just walk up and say, 'I'd like my girlfriend back please?' And what about Yorgi — Yorgi was bound to be there and he was, by any reckoning, a nasty piece of work. No wonder Petrov had wanted to keep hold of the DSB. And where were Petrov and his family now? All safe for the night, no doubt, and with no idea what was going on all because of them

He took another gulp of shandy. How do you solve a problem like Yorgi? The more he thought about it, the more he felt his stomach shake. A man who feared nothing — Petrov had said so. Well, almost nothing. Maybe the Yorkshire Police Air Support could drop a crate of snakes on him . . .

The pub crowd cheered at a goal or a try or a foul; they were leaping up and down like a troupe of morons so Thomas couldn't tell what the payoff was. He raised a glass to them anyway, for living for the moment — lucky bastards.

Time for home; he'd been there long enough for an imaginary pick-up. He folded the map carefully and re-tied the rucksack. The barman received his glass, and exchanged it for a sneery look. Yeah, do come again.

* * *

Out in the car, he had another attack of the dreads and slipped the .38 between his legs. Unlikely anyone would try to lift the DSB from him, but better to be prepared. He checked his reflection. Is that what he'd become — a walking worst-case scenario?

Nothing happened on the drive back to Pickering. If the Eurostate Cartel had planned to storm the car, they'd obviously thought better of it. Karl probably had it right. All they wanted was the package back; Peterson had fallen meekly into line so why wouldn't he naturally do the same, especially as he'd asked for a forty grand disturbance allowance? And if they did stop him tonight, what was he gonna do — start a shootout on the A64? Good point. He stuffed the .38 back in the rucksack and pushed it out of reach.

Ma and Pa Bladen were watching TV when he got back. James glanced up and tried to wink reassuringly. But try that when you're terrified, and a tenner says it will look like a facial tic. "I was telling your mam, I'm thinking o' getting a dog."

"Thomas," his mum made his name sound like an alarm call, "your dad says you're off early morning — are you coming home tomorrow, then?"

He had to walk to the kitchen so they couldn't see his face.

"Kettle's not long boiled, if you're making," his mother called out.

He brought back a tray and noticed his dad had forsaken the armchair to squeeze in beside her on the settee. Wonders would never cease.

Thomas set the tray down. "Yeah," he started, smiling as his mother mock-frowned at the word, "I'll be back tomorrow."

Dad reached for his cup. "I were thinking, Thomas, 'appen I might drive out with you, tomorrow morning, and get a bit of fresh air. I've already rung work and taken tomorrow off, especially."

"Ooh, that's nice, Thomas; you turn up out of the blue and your father's already taking holidays. You should come up more often."

Thomas blew on his tea.

"That's settled then, lad," his dad sat back.

* * *

He lay in bed, letting pixel thoughts scatter and reform of their own accord. It wasn't long after ten — he'd turned in early, on account of the long drive. He tried to picture Karl and the boys — sleeping underground. But all he could see when he closed his eyes was Miranda.

Some time after eleven he picked up a text: Bunker road now closed for repairs. Don't take chances tomorrow. Kosovo Girls Brigade.

Chapter 44

The wall clock read six thirty.

"Do you want some breakfast, Thomas — a bit o' toast maybe?" Thomas's dad stood by the kitchen doorway. It could have been a father and son day trip but for the ominous rucksack on the table. "All set then?"

They moved to the front door. "Don't forget the letter, Dad..."

"It's in safe hands, Thomas."

There was no small talk in the car until they reached the great outdoors. His dad was the one to break the silence. "You don't have to answer, but is this what you do for a living, like?"

He felt for his dad, trying to fathom all this out and come up with a new picture of the way things were. He shook his head, offered up as much explanation as he thought would help and directed them along the map. There were no police roadblocks to contend with, no suspicious vehicles with blacked out windows. In fact, the roads were so clear it was as if no one else existed.

For a few minutes he lulled himself into memories of the two of them out on the moors, photographing the sun as it struck the heather at dawn. He still had a print of that one somewhere, back at the flat.

"Here's good — don't stop until I tell you. And don't hang about afterwards; straight to Ajit at the police station."

"I could come with yer, Thomas; the two of us, together, like." There was an edge to the voice, like ice cracking on a pond.

"No, this is something I have to sort out. You taking my car away will really help though, honest." Hopefully it would buy him a little extra time when they tracked it to the police station.

"If they . . . if they harm a hair of your head, I'll not rest . . ." his father was crying now.

"I know," Thomas shook his hand; he didn't know what else to do.

The car rounded a hill and disappeared. He cleared the road and swung his binoculars wide. If he was really lucky, he could still pull this off. He had Karl and the Dagenham Duo on his side — so why were his guts still churning up like Robin Hood Bay in a spring tide?

It took an hour or so of scouring the moorland before Thomas found the habitat he was looking for: a pond. What was it the teacher used to say in Photography Club, at school? Take every advantage.

'It's possible, sometimes, to be so still that you almost merge into the landscape. Photographers and birdwatchers, the good ones anyway, they know how to do it. It takes patience and planning, but if you're really lucky all that hard work pays off.'

Thomas remembered his teacher's speech and tried to take comfort. His muscles were past numbness, beyond cramp; he'd been crouching in the same position for a good ten minutes now, glancing sideways on, as the grass snake wove through the grass. He fixed it with his gaze, as if he could magnetise it to the spot while he inched the canvas bag forward by degrees. He felt a bead of sweat slide down the side of his nose, trickling over skin cells, gathering pace. But he didn't dare flinch in case it broke the charm. The grass snake licked ahead of it, unaware of the converging bag. A little closer... and... bingo!

He flicked the forked stick, lifting the wriggling snake high into the air, twisting and contorting it to keep control. With his other hand he moved the bag underneath — the one with the DSB in it — and brought the two together, pulling the drawstring of the bag with the snake safely inside. Then he allowed himself the luxury of a smile and touched the crucifix at his neck.

As he stood up and stretched, he felt the .38 pulling a little in its shoulder holster. Not to worry; it wouldn't be for much longer. He took a celebratory sip of water, apologised to the snake and checked his compass bearing. Time to get walking again.

* * *

The entrance to the bunker beckoned, like a doorway to the Underworld. He surveyed the site through binoculars and tried to imagine Miranda down there, counting the minutes to freedom.

He squeezed the fear down into the pit of his stomach, telling himself silently, over and over, that they were all on the same side. That Sir Peter had entrusted him with the recovery of the sealed DSB. Entrusted, coerced — what was a word between friends? Their only interest was in recovering the DSB; his sole concern was Miranda.

Only one thing for it now: to set things in motion. "Hello, it's Thomas Bladen." There wasn't an echo on the moorland, but the words seemed to magnify. He announced himself again just to make sure he wasn't startling anyone. And hopefully Karl would now know he was on site.

As he walked forward into view, someone surfaced from the bunker — a suit. Thomas raised a hand in greeting and forced a smile upon his face. The suit half-turned and Sir Peter Carroll emerged, shadowed by another man.

Thomas advanced a few more paces until Sir Peter raised a hand. "That's quite far enough, Thomas. I must say, you've picked a fine spot — reassuringly secure." There was bravado in the voice yet somehow Sir Peter didn't have his usual unassailable confidence.

He watched the old man and kept his smile high, forcing it until his mouth ached. "I've got the package here. When can I see Miranda?" He lifted the canvas bag high and held it out to one side.

The other man beside Sir Peter shifted his feet, the bodily equivalent of licking his lips. This must be Yorgi; he wasn't massive, although he looked formidable. And even at that distance, Thomas could read him: a face unencumbered by conscience.

Thomas took another pace forward. Sir Peter stalled him again. "First things first. I think we'll have your weapon on the ground; we don't want any accidents."

Hook, line and sinker. Thomas reached under his arm slowly and tossed the .38 to the ground with his thumb and forefinger. A pity, nonetheless.

Yorgi seemed much amused, but he already had his gun drawn so he could afford to be jolly. "And now the bag, if you please," he affected a bow.

Thomas felt the tension in his throat, squeezing the words out in single file. "I need to see Miranda." But the next face he saw was Christine's, rising from the depths of the bunker. His legs turned to lead.

Yorgi was laughing now, waggling the gun towards him like a taunt. "Now, smart boy, give me the fucking package or I kill you."

And they say manners are a thing of the past. Not now, he told himself: no distractions. This was it then. He backed his arm up for a half-decent throw.

"Quickly," Yorgi sneered, or you'll never see your whore again."

He felt his breath turn to fire. Chances of making the distance without being shot — very low indeed. Willingness to try anyway — almost absolute. Almost. He fed on the rage and helplessness that swarmed inside him and drew them down, until he felt a strange sense of stillness, as if the world was narrowing in. Yorgi, prick that he was, had done him a favour; he had brought Thomas into what Karl called 'the kill zone.'

The bag sailed through the air and landed near Yorgi's feet. He grinned like a ravine, lowered his gun and retrieved the bag.

Thomas inched his hand up the side of his jacket to the pocket: shit or bust.

"What? You think you are smarter than Yorgi; you and that piece of shit, Petrov? No, Tomas, you are a fucking moron. Your precious Mi-ran-dah isn't even here! But I made sure I fixed her for you."

Yorgi opened the bag and shoved his hand in. Any . . . second . . . now . . . "Argh!" he screamed and snatched back his hand.

Thomas took his cue, drew the Makarov from his pocket and fired. No hesitation, no deliberation; aim, shoot to kill.

Yorgi jerked backwards, dragged into a spin by a shoulder wound. But that didn't stop him returning fire.

Thomas was momentarily stunned by his own incompetence. Then he heard the blast as the bullet slammed into his chest, smashing him down. He felt the ground punch him in the head and a clamour of voices swirl around him as the blood oozed down his face.

He must have been dreaming; Miranda was calling his name. He dragged himself to sitting, gasping for air, just in time to see Miranda materialise from the sidelines like some glorious angel. Then it all got very frightening indeed.

"You bastard!" Miranda roared at Yorgi and shot him, square in the chest.

Yorgi went down, but Thomas knew a pro like him would have a vest on as well.

Thomas heaved himself to standing, screaming with the pain; waving Miranda frantically aside, out of the line of fire. She didn't get it and started running towards him.

Yorgi jerked back up mechanically, wide-eyed and bloodied, like a homicidal marionette. Suddenly there was gunfire overhead, seemingly from all directions.

In the confusion, Karl barrelled through the scrub, slamming into Miranda side-on as he carried her to the ground. Yorgi's second shot went wide of the mark and whizzed past Thomas's head.

Karl rolled away from Miranda and recovered to face Yorgi with one of his Brownings drawn. Thomas dropped to one knee and kept his gun hand level.

Yorgi remained absolutely still, blocked by two weapons. His face twitched, like a trapped animal; Thomas figured Yorgi wasn't ready to call it quits yet. Yorgi turned to Sir Peter, pushing the barrel into the old man's face. "I take my package and I walk away."

Thomas was still wondering if Karl could make the shot when Karl abruptly lowered his Browning. Yorgi emptied out the bag and then he looked directly at Thomas. His gun wavered for an instant. "This isn't over, Tomas."

"Yes it is," Sir Peter's voice was as clinical as his marksmanship.

The bullet slammed into Yorgi's skull in a flash of red, propelling him to the ground as blood and brain matter pumped free. Sir Peter Carroll stood rigid, flecks of Yorgi's blood glistening against his face and clothes.

Karl holstered his gun and helped Miranda to her feet. She took his hand reluctantly and looked across at Thomas. He ran to her, clutching his chest on the way — it hurt like a bastard. Then, as Karl stood aside, Thomas gritted his teeth and squeezed Miranda hard against his jacket. She felt cold, in every sense. He breathed her in, pressing her face against his neck, and watched Karl surveying the scene.

Karl turned to face him. "Well, turned out nice again." He threw his one-liner away and advanced on Nicholas, who was already by the package. "Hey, hey," Karl called out, "don't make me shoot you. Leave it be." Then he looked over at Christine, who nodded to him.

The air crackled; Christine lifted a walkie-talkie from her back pocket. "It seems a local man drove through the road barricade; Jack and Alice have been detained by a policeman on the scene. Police Air Support is on its way."

Sir Peter Carroll lowered his head. Thomas pointed at him, the Makarov still in his hand. "He goes down for this, Karl."

"Hold on there, Tommo . . . that's not the way these things work. If this goes public, we all crash and burn — that'll be the end of the SSU and all those Euro bastards vanish into the night."

Thomas had already started walking. Miranda was at his side, her hand in his. He'd seen enough, heard enough and had enough. Karl shouted after him. "I'll sort it, Tommo; I promise. No loose ends. Leave it to me — I know how these things are done."

Miranda nudged Thomas as they crossed Christine's line of sight. He watched as the two women eyed each other silently. Miranda dropped a cash card, a gun and a mobile phone at Christine's feet, and then pulled Thomas away.

Chapter 45

It had been seven days. A whirlwind of events that, as Thomas lay listening to the birds outside, almost seemed like they'd happened to someone else. As he rolled over on one side, the bruise in his chest reassured him that it definitely had happened to him. He caught the alarm clock on the first bleep — he'd been awake for ages anyway. It was his second morning back at the flat.

Sam and Terry had taken Miranda back to London after a hotel overnight. He'd wanted to drive her home, but she made it very clear she didn't want him around. So he'd stayed on in Yorkshire for a few days, just until the official story unfolded: Eastern European drug trafficker apprehended, following combined operation between police and security services. He left after that — he couldn't stomach any more lies.

He'd been ringing John and Diane's twice a day, to check on Miranda. There had been a suggestion she might go abroad again but, thankfully, Diane had talked her out of it. Said that what she needed was the family around her.

Give her time, they told him — and that was about all they told him. Did they blame him? Not as much as he blamed himself; that wasn't possible. John reassured him that he'd be welcome at the house, in time.

And Karl? Well, Karl was another huge disappointment; he'd showed his true colours in the end, and tidied everything up. John Wright even got his gun back, apparently. Last Thomas had heard, Karl was back at work, resetting the clocks once more.

As he lurched out of bed, the previous night's phone call with Karl stung his ears. 'Trust me, Tommo, I've got your back covered.' Yeah, right.

He showered and then stared at himself in the mirror. The bruise on his chest had come up a fine shade of purple. Right about where the heart was; Yorgi was a true professional to the end.

Today was the big day — off to Whitehall to face Sir Peter Carroll. As he grabbed his coat off the peg, he noticed two brown envelopes on the mat — minus addresses or stamps. The A4 photographs were a mixture — some colour, some monochrome. There was a woman going about her daily life — at the shops, with her children, and a family photo in a park. As to the black-and-whites — well, not quite porn, but the couple weren't holding a raffle. Not unless they'd found a novel way to pick the winners. Sir Peter Carroll was evidently more athletic than his physique suggested. It looked like some sort of downbeat hotel or a motel, and it definitely wasn't the woman from the colour shots. The very last photo was different to all the others — an outdoor scene, long lens — Sir Peter's gun up against Yorgi's head.

A small card fell out of the envelope. He bent down to read it and a lump came to his throat. 'I never break a promise — K. See you back at work soon.'

He ditched the card, checked the other envelope — a copy of everything — grabbed Exhibit A and headed out the door. At Walthamstow Central he filed through the gate with the masses and enjoyed the rich travelling experience that was the Victoria line.

He walked past the lockers at Victoria and shuddered. He needed coffee, a double espresso. As he savoured its umber goodness, a text message came in: Dinner tonight? Caliban's — 8 pm. Don't be late! Give Karl my regards. Mx. Wow. He texted back a glib comment and marched right into Whitehall, holding up his ID like a badge of honour: Floaters Anonymous.

"Are you delivering that?"

He glanced at the resealed flap. "Yes, it's for Sir Peter Carroll's eyes only."

A guard escorted him towards the lift, same as ever. The door pinged open and a half-familiar face greeted him. It took a second to place him — Sir Peter's chauffeur. They exchanged the briefest of smiles and Trevor — that was the name that had eluded him — subtly tapped his own chest as he passed, mirroring where Thomas held the envelope over his bruise. By the time he'd turned around, Trevor had gone.

* * *

Three raps and there he was, back in the spider's lair.

"Please take a seat, Thomas."

He leaned forward and passed the envelope. If Sir Peter had looked pale before, by the time he'd viewed the contents he was positively anaemic. "What . . . is it that you want?"

Thomas smiled, a little smile to let the old man know that things were about to change. "These are my terms. You'll sign an executive order today, prohibiting Karl and me from being moved to separate teams without your express consent — which, of course, will be up to Karl and me. Bob Peterson's to be transferred immediately — I don't care where — and Christine Gerrard promoted in his place."

Sir Peter shrank back in his chair, like a slug at a salt-fest. As Thomas looked up, even Churchill's portrait seemed shocked at such audacity. Well, bollocks to them both.

"Are we finished, then?"

The cheeky bastard. "No, there's the small matter of forty thousand pounds outstanding — for Miranda." He put his hands on the hallowed desk. "And let's be clear: if you or your representatives ever take an interest in the private lives of anyone associated with me again, you'll wish they hadn't. You can keep the photos — they're copies." He stared at Sir Peter, waiting until the old man broke eye contact; it took about thirty seconds. A voice in his head muttered 'overdramatic,' but he shushed it silently.

"So now what, Thomas? I presume you know about my new working relationship — with Mr McNeill's associates?"

It wasn't a surprise, but it still left a bitter aftertaste. Karl had explained the rationale: run Sir Peter Carroll as a double agent; preserve the SSU, blah blah blah. It stank, however you pitched it, even if Karl was right and it suited the greater good.

"What happens is that I collect the money and then I'm out of here."

The bundles of notes were lifted from a safe behind the desk, all ready and waiting; he didn't bother to count them. Sir Peter handed them over solemnly, like a school prize; Thomas stashed them in a carrier bag.

"I hope you're not thinking of leaving the Surveillance Support Unit. You're a resourceful man, Thomas. I can always use a good man like you."

Thomas picked up the bag. He was halfway out the door when he turned and looked back. "Not any more."

THE END

My thanks to the following people:
Christine Butterworth, David Brown, Elizabeth Sparrow, Helen Rathore, Jane Pollard, Jeremy Faulkner-Court, Kath Morgan, Martin Wood, Michael Wise, Richard Coralie, Sarah Campbell, Sue Louineau, Susie Nott-Bower, Villayat Sunkmanitu and Warren Stevenson.

Thank you for reading this book. If you enjoyed it please leave feedback on Amazon, and if there is anything we missed or you have a question about then please get in touch. The author and publishing team appreciate your feedback and time reading this book.

Our email is jasper@joffebooks.com

http://joffebooks.com

You can follow the author on his blog or twitter account
www.alongthewritelines.blogspot.co.uk

@DerekWriteLines

Look out for the sequel to STANDPOINT, coming soon in 2015!

You might also enjoy:

HABIT

A young woman, Rebecca Heilshorn, lies stabbed to death in her bed in a remote farmhouse. Rookie detective Brendan Healy is called in to investigate. All hell breaks loose when her brother bursts onto the scene. Rebecca turns out to have many secrets and connections to a sordid network mixing power, wealth, and sex. Detective Brendan Healy, trying to put a tragic past behind him, pursues a dangerous investigation that will risk both his life and his sanity. Habit is a compelling thriller which will appeal to all fans of crime fiction. T.J. Brearton amps up the tension at every step, until the shocking and gripping conclusion.

ABOUT THE AUTHOR

Derek Thompson grew up in London and started writing fiction in his teens. After spending a year in the US, he returned to London and subsequently moved to the West Country.

He wrote a commissioned piece for The Guardian in 2008 and entered the world of freelance writing in 2009. His short fiction has featured in both British and American anthologies, and can be found online. He has also written comedy material for live performance and radio.

His love of film noir and thrillers began with The Big Sleep, and has never left him. Much of his fiction involves death, loss or secrets. As the saying goes: write about what you know.

Printed in Great Britain
by Amazon